Cambridge, Massachusetts
The Home of Julia and Paul Garrett

The doorbell rang. Julia Garrett opened the door to two men.

"Mrs. Garrett? We'd like to talk to you for a few minutes," one of them announced.

"Who are you? What's this all about?" she challenged.

They stepped away from the door and into the living room.

"We work for the government. I've got to ask you some important questions, if you don't mind."

"What's this for? Do you have some identification?"

"This won't take long. Please cooperate with us."

"Either you tell me exactly who you are or I'm calling the police."

"Just a few questions," he said. . . .

He extracted a small picture from his coat pocket. It was of Julia walking across Harvard Yard with a man. "Who is this man?" he demanded.

"It's none of your business," she retorted.

"I'm afraid it is," he said.

She glanced quickly from one to the other. Her eyes were wide with terror. Then she bolted for the bedroom door.

The second man pulled two pairs of rubber surgical gloves from his pocket and approached the bedroom.

EINSTEIN'S BRAIN

MARK OLSHAKER

PUBLISHED BY POCKET BOOKS NEW YORK

POCKET BOOKS, a Simon & Schuster division of
GULF & WESTERN CORPORATION
1230 Avenue of the Americas, New York, N.Y. 10020

Published by arrangement with M. Evans & Company, Inc.
Library of Congress Catalog Card Number: 80-28662

ISBN: 0-671-43210-9

First Pocket Books printing September, 1982

10 9 8 7 6 5 4 3 2 1

POCKET and colophon are trademarks of Simon & Schuster.

Printed in the U.S.A.

For Carolyn

AUTHOR'S NOTE

This is a work of fiction, and while certain actual historical individuals are mentioned from time to time in the narrative, all characters appearing in the book and all situations are fabrications of my own imagination.

My deepest thanks go to a number of people who gave me support, comfort and substantive help during the conception and writing of this book:

To my mother, Thelma Olshaker; Ray Hubbard; and my editor, Herb Katz, for their constant ideas, encouragement, criticism, and understanding ears. To Marty Bell and Jay Acton for their enthusiasm, advice, friendship, and shepherding of my career. To A. E. Claeyssens, for making me want to be a writer and then showing me how to do it.

For help with numerous and complex medical details my thanks go to the following physicians: Orville Donnelly, Ronald Kurstin, Sanford Leiken, James Winston Watts, and especially Harvey Ammerman and Harold Stevens. I received substantial guidance in science from my brother, Robert, and from Dr. Dror Sadeh of Tel Aviv University and Dr. Herman H. Hobbs of George Washington University. They can be credited with enlightening me as to the incredible realities and possibilities of physics, but not faulted for the excesses and liberties I have taken on my own in the interests of my story. In scientific detail as well as in plotting, this remains a work of imagination rather than fact.

For their various and sizable contributions, I also want to thank Irwin Altschuler, Linda Cabasin, Larry Klein, Bob Levey, my father, Bennett Olshaker, and my other brother, Jonathan.

And finally, of course, my wife Carolyn. For all the general reasons, and all of my specific reasons, this book is dedicated to her.

Mark Olshaker, Washington, D.C.

"None but those who have experienced them can conceive of the enticements of science."
Mary W. Shelley,
Frankenstein

"Perfection of means and confusion of goals seem—in my opinion—to characterize our age."
Albert Einstein,
Out of My Later Years

Part One

Chapter One

An image stuck in his mind. It obsessed him and it plagued him, as much now as ever. It was the only thing of value that had lasted out of that clouded year. First, there was the list—neatly typed on the back of a single sheet of gray stationery and pinned precisely—like a specimen—on the cluttered bulletin board outside the anatomy lab. He still knew every word of it by heart:

1. You are here for a serious purpose.
2. No foolishness or horseplay will be tolerated in the anatomy lab.
3. You will wear a clean white coat in the lab at all times as a sign of respect toward your study.
4. Any student misusing an anatomical specimen, treating it with disrespect, or removing it from the lab for purposes of levity or humor will be dismissed from the course.
5. You know your responsibility and obligation. There will be no exceptions or warnings.

And there was Professor Hardy himself, the author of the list. He was slight and white-haired and always wore a striped shirt and a bow tie. And at the end of the term—before the final exam—he led his class in a moment of silent devotion for the memory and immortal souls of those who had come to lay as cadavers on the rows of grimly gleaming steel dissecting tables.

Most of the students laughed off the exercise as soon as they left the lab. But not Paul Garrett. To him, it was

3

the only genuine article of faith he had seen in a year in medical school.

The image played powerfully and violently around the edges of Paul Garrett's consciousness. It had been twenty-one years since he'd left the school, but the image had only grown stronger with time. Until now, no matter with what unit of time he chose to measure his life—weeks, days, hours—the image would come back to him during every interval.

It was as if he had come to feel a degree of kinship with those bodies mutilated for science.

London

There were vestiges of the Past Age about the room— from the crenelated plaster cornice edging the high ceiling, to the gas-lit crystal chandelier that hung down almost to the top of a tall man's head, to the vaulted leaded glass window that now only looked out onto a blank brick wall. But whatever its Victorian designer had intended for the salon in the way of ageless opulence and contemporary social grace, its current occupants were of a purely functional mind.

Six men sat around the battered oak conference table. It was not worn in the typically English sense that venerates continuous use; but merely battered, the stock of a second-hand office furniture supplier. A gray-haired man of medium height, with pointed features, was talking. And even if he hadn't been sitting at the head of the table, it would have been obvious that he was in charge. As he spoke, the other five did not take notes. They merely followed along in the dossiers they'd each been handed upon entering the room. The gray-haired man slowly and continuously scanned the gathering, knowing it was foolish to proceed before the previous statement had registered on the other five faces and in the other five brains.

When he had assured himself that everything he'd said up to that point had been assimilated—and in the proper sequence—he motioned to the khaki-clad guard by the door to switch off the lights. The guard raised one hand from his Uzi submachine gun just long enough to flick the light switch, then returned his hand to the weapon. In actuality, the gun was more symbolic —a tonesetter, really—than a genuine precaution. Because on the other side of the door, a second khaki-clad guard stood with a second Uzi, and he wasn't expected to divert his attention with such additional tasks as turning lights on and off.

The fluorescent lights that competed visually with the chandelier darkened, and until the projector came on, the only illumination in the room came from the small reading lamps provided at each place along the conference table.

The gray-haired man stood up but did not leave his place. He faced the screen at the far end of the room as it lit up with a carefully drawn mathematical equation.

"This represents the current limit of our knowledge," he stated. "Everything up to this point has been a linear progression of logic and empirical verification. The next step . . ." He paused and clasped his hands behind his back, ". . . if there is to be a next step, is going to require something more, something we can't explain or even predict. Some incredible kind of inspiration. From who or where, we can't be sure. So we've got to be prepared on all fronts."

He pressed the button that advanced the projector. What looked like a blown-up driver's license photograph came on the screen.

"Gentlemen, this is Paul Garrett."

Chicago

The corner office looked out over Lake Michigan, ninety-two floors below. The rosewood paneling blended serenely with the cream-colored carpeting so thick and deep that most visitors had the momentary urge to remove their shoes and wriggle their toes around in the plushness. But no one did, as the gesture would not have been found amusing. In this room, personal whims were controlled, and personal opinions —unsupported by hard factual evidence—were contained.

The Vice-President was talking to four associates who had arrived precisely at the appointed time for the conference and would leave just as precisely upon the termination of business. They gathered in the corner of the room, where two glass walls joined at an almost imperceptible miter seam. As always, he let his guests sit on the sofa and enjoy the spectacular view of the lake while he faced them in a swivel chair more noted for its appearance than the comfort it afforded. A more comfortable chair, or greater concentration on the view, would have provided distractions.

"What's the next item?" he asked, appearing to look directly at the speaker but actually turned somewhere within his own thought processes.

One of the visitors read from the typed agenda on his lap. "Abner Rutherford," he announced. He waited for some sign of recognition.

"Who's he?" the boss said crossly, annoyed at the waste of these several seconds.

"Methanol. The new conversion process. The one-man laboratory in Arizona."

"Oh yes," he finally acknowledged.

"There was a fire there Tuesday night."

6

"How unfortunate," he said without emotion. "Was anyone hurt?"

"Second- and third-degree burns. Just Rutherford. He'll be out of action for a while, but it looks like he'll live."

"Very good. Was it a clean job?"

"Very clean. They're not even putting an insurance investigator on the case."

"Excellent. Next?"

"Langford Industries of Dallas. Their loan was called in at a time when they didn't have the resources to pay it off and they couldn't come up with any alternative financing. We offered them new money through one of our banks—all indirectly, of course. . . ."

"Of course."

"With the stipulation that the interest in their solar patents be turned over to the bank as collateral."

"We're going to have to stay closely on top of that one. It all comes down to a matter of careful timing."

"It will. We should take over the patents—that is to say, Langford should go bankrupt—just about the time they start on the final phase of research."

"And do we have someone who can take it from there?"

"We don't, but we will."

The man looked at his watch—a gold Patek Philippe. "I'm going to have to cut this short. I'm meeting with one of the Partners for Progress. Tell me about 'Basic Research.' That's what they're most interested in right now anyway."

The visitor withdrew a file from the briefcase on his lap. "First, there's Paul Garrett."

Cambridge, Massachusetts

Paul Garrett looked up from packing his suitcase and suddenly noticed that Julia wasn't packing hers. She sat in the lounge chair near the corner of the bedroom, hands folded in her lap and legs crossed comfortably. She gazed at him placidly, as if she intended to sit like that forever.

"What's the matter?" he asked. "We'll just barely make the plane as it is."

"I'm not going," she announced, and watched him as he dropped the shirt he was holding.

"Do you feel all right?" He started over toward her.

"I'm not sick, if that's what you mean," she responded.

"Look, Julie. Stop playing games with me. What's this all about?"

"I'm just not going to Washington with you, that's all. You don't need me there." She paused, rubbed the back of her neck and sighed. "Matter of fact, you don't really need me anywhere."

So this is what she was getting at, he realized. How many times had he had to go through this lately? But what a hell of a time to put him through it. He looked at his watch reflexively. He hated having to rush for planes.

"Julie, why don't we talk about this when we get to the hotel? Better yet, we'll talk about it on the plane. But we don't have time to fool around right now. I mean, look what time it is."

"You call this fooling around?"

God. He'd said the wrong thing.

"Like it's some quirk in me you've got to put up with? Some cross you've got to bear to keep things functioning at home? No, Paul, I'm not fooling around. I'm not going to Washington."

8

He continued over to her. She didn't budge from her position. "Do you want me to stay home? You want me to forget about the trip? Is that it?"

"No. That's not it. I want you to go and do what you have to do and just leave me be."

"But it isn't just business this time. Besides the Academy meetings there's that Hollister party at the Maryland Eastern Shore. I'm not sure why we were invited, but there'll be a lot of people who control heavy funding. I think it's important for both of us to be there."

"I'm sure you'll enjoy it just as much without me. Now you'd better hurry up or you'll miss the plane."

He was torn whether to continue packing while he talked or demonstrate his full commitment to the conversation by dropping everything. Maybe the fact that he hardly ever dropped everything was one of the problems. But God, now wasn't the time to deal with it. She had to know that.

"What can I do to make you come with me?"

"Twist my arm behind my back and threaten to break it off." A slight smile finally crossed her lips.

He frowned in disapproval. "Short of that."

"Nothing."

He sat down on the edge of the bed and held his head in his hands. "Julia," he said after a moment. "Why are you doing this to me?"

"I'm not doing anything to you," she countered. "If anything, I'm saving you."

"From what?"

"From us."

"I don't want to be saved from us."

"You don't even know that."

"I know I want to be with you."

"As you said, Paul, now is not the time to discuss that. Maybe we can talk about it when you get back."

His throat constricted and he dropped his arms onto his knees and looked up. "Will you be here when I get back?"

She turned away from him toward the window. "I

don't know. I'm not sure what I'm going to do. My last final is Tuesday. After I grade it, I might go away by myself for a while."

He stood up, crossed to where she was sitting and took both her hands in his. "Julia, you at least owe it to me to be here when I get back so we can talk about it. All right, maybe you do need a chance to be alone and think things out. But now you'll have the whole weekend."

"You think that's enough time?"

"I think it's enough time to be ready to talk to me when I get back." He looked again at his watch, then looked around for anything remaining to be packed. "Will you do that for me?"

He stared straight into her eyes, still holding both her hands in his. She tried to look away, but he jerked her arms forward to make her face him. The firmness of her facade seemed to melt with his intensity.

"I'll be here when you get back," she assured him. "But at this stage of the game, I don't know what good it's going to do either one of us. We've each got our own lives, Paul. You've got more than I do. But it's not too late for me, either, if I don't waste any more time."

He stared at her another second or two, then released his grasp and went back to the suitcase. He stuffed in the rest of his clothing in silence.

He walked across the room, leaving the suitcase where it lay.

"Are you going?" she asked.

"I've got to make a phone call first."

"To who?"

"Harry." She already knew, and he resented her for asking.

"You already talk to him more than you talk to me."

"This is about work."

"Of course it's about work. It always is. And we can't get along without Harry, can we?"

"I don't intend to discuss this any further," he said tersely. "I know you don't like Harry. You've made that quite clear. But he happens to be my closest associate, and the only one who I can always discuss my work with."

"You seem to forget I'm a physicist, too," she called after him.

A few minutes later he came back into the room, picked up the suitcase, and looked at her.

"Take care of yourself," she said to him as he was walking out the door. She stood by the window and watched as he came out onto Memorial Drive and raised his arm for a taxi.

She shouldn't feel guilty about doing this to him, she told herself. After all, how many times had he done similar things to her? Anything, it seemed, was more important to him than their life together. Especially those endless discussions with Harry Gillette. At least, that was the message he kept giving her.

She should have known better than to marry a physicist, even if she was one herself. But you just don't know when you're young, when the future seems like a bright adventure intertwined with the two brilliant scientific careers predicted for the outstanding man of the Yale Physics Department and the outstanding woman at Radcliffe.

She couldn't mark a specific time when it had gone wrong. She supposed it had always been like this to a certain extent with Paul. There had been the occasional co-eds for a while. But they both knew that hadn't been the real issue. If she'd wanted to have a fling with one of her more attractive grad students, she doubted he would have objected. At least he wasn't hypocritical about that sort of thing; not that that made it any easier, really. The main problem was the detachment; the gulf that never seemed to widen, but never narrowed, either.

Had he always been like that? Ever since school, at any rate, though she hadn't known him when he was a medical student. He should have gone back to medical school. If he could have been as involved with each of his patients as he turned out to be with each of his physics problems, he would have made a hell of a doctor.

But she guessed he had reason enough for not wanting to go back. God knows what an experience like he'd had can do to a person. They'd come through all that, so there still had to be hope for everything else. When he got back from Washington, they'd both have to be more understanding.

Chapter Two

Easton, Maryland

The last house had been five miles back and the unpaved road now twisted through the tall, dense trees. Despite the printed directions, which he thought he'd followed to the letter, Paul Garrett was convinced he'd taken a wrong turn somewhere. Penetrating deeper and deeper into the forest, he was nearing that agonizing point of not knowing whether to press on in the hope he was headed in the right direction, or turn back toward the last turnoff he was sure of before getting hopelessly out of reach. He wished Julia was with him. She had the confidence he lacked to be a good navigator.

He slowed the rented Ford at an intersection to see if he could at least identify the road he was on, but there weren't any signs. Anybody who's gotten this far either knows the way or deserves to be lost, he figured. The worst of it was the feeling of helplessness, of knowing all his intellectual powers were worth nothing in finding his way through the damn trees. How did other people find their way all the time?

He stopped the car, held the directions directly in front of his face and matched up each line with the visualization of the turns he had made. When he was absolutely sure that each one corresponded, he started up again and headed straight down the road with a "to hell with it" determination.

Four minutes later he saw the stone gate bearing the name, "Shorecliffe."

He came up the gravel drive a quarter of a mile before he saw the house—a large, picturesque colonial manor that must have been expanded by each succeeding generation. Now it stretched along an entire side of the land pressing out into the Wye River.

The place looked like a summer camp. Thirty or forty people were scattered about the grounds, playing, chatting, sitting with glasses in hand. A doubles tennis match was underway on the court next to the swimming pool. In the pool itself a dozen splashing bathers cavorted around a woman on a floating lounge chair trying vainly to avoid the turbulence. A croquet game was taking place on the lawn between the house and the water. One of the horseback riders ambling across the field of play drew loud shrieks as the animal mashed the red ball into the turf.

Charles Hollister was standing on the front porch, a drink in one hand and the other ready to receive the still arriving guests. Paul could only remember meeting him once, but Hollister's eyebrows raised in delighted recognition as soon as he was halfway up the front walk.

"Paul Garrett, isn't it? Good to see you. So pleased you could make it." The sentences all ran together into a continuous standard greeting. "But where's your lovely wife? Julia, isn't it?"

"She had to take care of some business back in Cambridge. Sorry she couldn't make it."

"Well, so are we, so are we. You know my wife, Sandy."

"No, I don't think we've ever . . ."

"Darling, come over here for a moment, won't you?" he called to the midst of the croquet tournament.

"Just a minute, dear. I'm about to 'send' someone!"

"Look, well don't send them too far, right?"

Alexandra Hollister strolled over to the porch and took her place beside her husband. She was tall and graceful but slightly rugged looking, obviously from the numerous outdoor activities Shorecliffe had to offer.

"Darling, this is Dr. Paul Garrett, the physicist from MIT. His wife's a physicist too, you know."

"At MIT also?"

"No. Harvard," Paul said.

"My, my. So nice of you to join us, Dr. Garrett. And I'm so looking forward to meeting . . . ah . . . Mrs. Dr. Garrett." She smiled demurely and retracted her hand and was off again to croquet before Paul could explain. Hollister just shrugged and put his arm across Paul's back while he guided him down across the lawn.

"We've got plenty to do here, as you can see. Where's your overnight stuff? In the car? Fine. Just leave it all there for the time being. Roberts will take it up to your room."

Hollister was taking him across the front lawn toward the river. He was moving aimlessly, as closely as Paul could figure, but with that proprietary sense of purpose of a squire surveying his lands.

"If you continue down that path, you get to the dock," Hollister explained. "There's a sailboat tied up there, and we also have a rowboat fitted with fishing gear, if that's your pleasure. I can't promise you the lobsters you're used to up in New England, but our Maryland blue crabs are the best in the world!" He gave Paul a slap of camaraderie between the shoulder blades.

Paul couldn't figure out why Charles was showing him this much personal attention when he obviously had other guests still arriving. In truth, Paul wasn't sure why he'd even been invited to the weekend party at all. The only time he could remember meeting Hollister was last year when the lawyer had prepared him for some Congressional testimony he was giving for the Scientific League. Hollister was what the papers always called a "prominent Washington attorney," meaning a power broker. He was the Scientific League's general counsel.

Maybe it was Hollister's wife who invited him, Paul thought. In addition to her reputation as a horse breeder on the Eastern Shore, Sandy was a socialite of some repute whose parties in their Georgetown house were frequently written up in the *Post* and *Town and Country*. She had a penchant for collecting interesting people, Paul had heard. But she hadn't seemed the least bit interested in *him* when Charles had pulled her away from croquet. Well, he supposed it really didn't matter. Who the hell ever knew with rich people anyway? He was glad he'd been invited. It was a chance to mix with potentially influential people, even if most of them would be insufferably boring. When your work survives on grants and bequests, you learn to put up with boring people. And the idea of getting out of Washington for the spring weekend, when the city crawled with tourists, was an attractive prospect in itself. It still annoyed him about Julia not coming, but let that ruin her weekend, not his.

"Quite a place you have," Paul commented when they had completed their circuit of the grounds. It was the only thing he could come up with.

"There's kind of an interesting history," Charles replied. "The house was built right after the Revolution by Colonel James Otis Beaumont of the Maryland Rifles. He made quite a bit of money in the North Atlantic wine and spice trade, and his wife, Martha, was one of the earliest horse breeders on the Eastern Shore. Beaumont left the estate to his oldest son, Augustus, who shot his wife one night after dinner, probably in that upstairs bedroom."

He indicated the side of the house closest to the water. Just my luck, that's the room I'll get tonight, Paul thought.

"I'll tell you more about the house later," Hollister promised.

They were on the back porch when Charles stopped and turned to a dark-haired man in a checked sport coat. "David, we were talking right up your alley, just now. Dr. Paul Garrett, meet Dr. David Sherman."

"What's my alley?" Sherman demanded.

"Insanity, of course!" Charles retorted. "David's a psychiatrist over at St. Elizabeth's in Washington. You want to talk craziness, David's your man."

"I just might," Paul said. But no. This was neither

the time nor the place. He had to forget about all that for a while.

They exchanged the appropriate small talk and drifted inside the parlor together after Hollister darted off, leaving them to their own social devices.

The spacious room overlooked an expansive terraced lawn that ran all the way down to the Wye River. From where Paul and David sat, they could see clear across to the far shore, where evergreen trees so thick that no light shone through them seemed to grow right out of the waterline.

"Has Charles been giving you the official history of Shorecliffe?" David asked.

"About how Augustus Beaumont plugged his wife in an upstairs bedroom," Paul confirmed.

"Did he tell you how Augustus was later judged insane and shut up in an asylum? I think that began the long tradition of family insanity Charles was referring to. You get a lot of that sort of thing on the Eastern Shore. Then the house went to his only daughter, Philippa, who married an English duke who beat her regularly, and in front of the servants, no less."

"Are you a friend of the Hollisters?" Paul asked.

"I guess everyone needs a token shrink," he replied. His eyes darted, taking in the gathering, inside the house and out. "Especially this close to Washington."

As he spoke, a green Frisbee sailed magically through the open door, ending its graceful flight at Paul's kneecap. A kid with a stringy blond beard and an open shirt came in after it.

"Hey, sorry, man. The thing's like got a mind of its own, you know? No one controls the super brain. Not even me." He retrieved the projectile and headed back outside.

"See what I mean? Oh . . . and there's another reason I'm here," David continued. "I'm Sandy Hollister's brother. But don't tell anyone. I like people to think I've made it on my own."

"Your secret's safe with me," Paul assured him.

"And how do you fit into all this chaos?"

"I guess everyone needs a token scientist, too."

Sandy Hollister poked her head into the parlor. "David, dear. You're needed!"

He stood up. "I hope she doesn't expect me to give anyone first aid," he said to Paul. "See you later."

"Good enough."

Paul sat by himself for a few minutes. When no one came over to talk to him and he began feeling awkward, he got up and headed for the hallway that ran the length of the house. A spirited discussion, punctuated by frequent raised voices, was emanating from the porch. One of the voices sounded familiar, and when he reached the doorway he saw that it belonged to Andrew Beckwith, the public relations director of the American Academy of Science, Paul's Washington employer.

Paul took a seat on the bench swing that hung on chains from the floor of the pillared balcony above. Andrew was trying to hold his own in a debate over the merits of genetic engineering, a subject Paul knew would be over his head. Since the Academy had taken no official position on the issue, Andrew had no personal position, either. Instead, he bobbed along the surface of the conversation the way a cork bobs along in the water. He would make a statement that sounded intelligent and reasonable to him, and then when another conversant made a conflicting statement, he would agree as if he'd said nothing to the contrary all afternoon. Paul knew he was successful and good at what he did, because floating with the tide had become second nature to him. It had become his essence.

Andrew had apparently recognized Paul out of the corner of his eye, and when the debate broke up for lack of opposition, he came over and sat beside him on the swing.

"Quite a grilling they put me through. Why didn't you rise to my defense and take my side?"

"I was afraid I'd drown in your wake as you scrambled back for the other shore," Paul answered.

"Cute. So what were you doing out here? Casing the joint?"

"I was, actually. I didn't expect to find you here."

"In this nest of Scientific Leaguers, you mean? I know. We staid Academy members rather fade into the woodwork next to our more flamboyant brethren from the rival organization."

"I'm a member of the Scientific League, too," Paul pointed out.

"I keep forgetting you play both sides of the street," Andrew commented. "But I like to think your heart lies with us—with pure, nonpolitical science."

"One thing you can tell me, though. Do you have any idea why I was invited?"

"You said yourself you're a member of the League. And you know all the work Charlie Hollister does for them."

"There're thousands of members."

"You're more prominent than you accept, Paul."

"Come on."

"Seriously. You should pay more attention to what the outside world says about you. It wasn't a bad write-up last year in *Time*."

"It has no bearing on my work."

"Have it your way." He shrugged.

Paul grabbed onto the swing's chain and pulled himself up. Andrew followed and they found themselves walking down the slope from the porch in the direction of the tennis court. When they neared the chain-link fence, Andrew asked, "You play tennis?"

"No. Never bothered."

"You should. It would be good for your image."

"I don't have an image. I don't want one."

"You should." He pointed at the four players who were just finishing up their set. A man with straight black hair and a beard was putting the yellow balls back into the can while his partner dabbed at her brow with a hand towel. "Now what does that image convey to you?" Andrew pressed.

"That tennis is a sweaty game?"

"Look again."

Paul focused on the figure with the towel, which had now been put down in favor of a bottle of Gatorade. Everything else seemed to fade before his eyes. She was in a trim little tennis dress, balancing her racket gracefully on one shoulder, sipping the drink between beguiling smiles. There was a wonderful fluidity to all her motions, even just walking across the court, and Paul was sorry he'd missed her actual play.

Her dark blonde hair, still glistening with perspiration, fell in loose, wavy wisps between her shoulder blades. She had a pale oval face with high cheekbones, a straight, pointed nose and large round blue-gray eyes. Deep and inquisitive eyes. And medium, faintly pursed lips. Her tennis dress was pale yellow, almost the color of her hair—a tightly fitting costume that accentuated her stunning form down to her gently curving hips. Following the line down from her matching yellow panties trimmed with a thin border of white lace, Paul gazed at her long, trim, athletic-looking legs. Maybe thirty years old, he figured, not more than thirty-two, of glittering charm and unmistakable confidence. Even from this far away, he could tell she knew who she was . . . and liked it.

"Who's the blonde?" he asked without taking his eyes off her.

"Her name's Amanda West," Andrew said. "Quite a cupcake, isn't she?"

"Where have you been living, Andrew?" he chided. "You should know we don't talk about women that way anymore."

"I can never tell when you're being serious."

"I'm always being serious." Paul grinned. "What do you know about her?"

"She's from New York. She's the editor of *Aurora*, the Scientific League's magazine. They say she's as smart as she is attractive. An enviable combination, I'd say."

"Certainly is," Paul agreed absently. But he felt a clutch of uneasiness. He was put off as much as he was captivated. He always felt strangely uncomfortable in the presence of people he referred to as "total beings" —those in whom all the right pieces fit together and everything works out just right.

As Amanda West came off the court with her bearded companion, a man she called Carl, Paul turned hurriedly in the other direction, taking Andrew with him back toward the house.

"Don't you want to meet her?" Andrew asked slyly.

"Later, maybe."

"Has the interest faded that quickly?"

"This doesn't seem to be the right time."

"Don't tell me the great and accomplished Paul Garrett is intimidated by such an imposing and delicious package."

"Come off it, Andrew. Act your age."

"If I was any more mature, I'd be acting *your* age."

"Very funny."

On the far side of the barn, the open field had been set up as a skeet range. Paul stood along the baseline, rifle in hand, watching the other shooters trying to knock the small clay pigeons out of the air. Most of them were obviously participating for the novelty effect, and the vast majority of the ceramic birds reached the turf in one piece. He couldn't remember the last time he'd shot at moving targets, but the precision of the two lines of force intersecting at a specific point in time and space pleased his scientific sensibility.

The woman next to him was clearly more interested in him than the contest. After every shot—which she missed—she made some allusion to his plans for the evening after dinner. Finally, when none of her entreaties had the desired effect, she asked him to hold her rifle while she rummaged through her pocketbook.

He stood there impatiently with the gun, but she was in no hurry, occasionally looking up and smiling at him in feigned helplessness.

"Are you offering me your room key?" he finally asked.

She tried her best at a sultry wink. "My door won't be locked," she said.

Just what I need, he thought to himself.

"Your turn, Dr. Garrett," he heard from the end of the line. It came as a deliverance. He lifted the rifle to his shoulder, pressed his cheek against the stock, sighted down the barrel and yelled:

"Pull."

He followed the missile in its ascending arc over the field, pulled the trigger at the zenith of flight, and blew it to bits with satisfaction.

"Is that who I think it is?" Amanda West asked Sandy Hollister. They were sitting with Carl Grover on a deck that had been built out from the renovated hayloft of the barn.

"I don't know, dear. Who do you think it is?" Sandy replied.

"Paul Garrett. The physicist." She set her vodka down on the deck, stood up and leaned on the railing for a better look.

"That's right. Charles did say he was a physicist. From MIT. Do you know him?"

"We've never met," Amanda said. "But I recognize him from his picture."

"Is he someone *we* should recognize?" Sandy asked.

"You might someday," Carl said to her. "If his hunches are correct and he can prove them with his research, he's practically assured of a Nobel Prize in Physics."

"My, my. And how do you, an advertising executive, know this, my sweet Carl?"

"I read Amanda's magazine." He winked conspiratorially at her.

"Sandy, you have to introduce us," she insisted.

"It's the first thing on my agenda."

"Not now," Carl broke in. "He's in the middle of his shooting."

"He looks like an interesting guy," Amanda said, her

elbows supporting her on the railing. "Too bad he goes in for that disgusting activity."

"Come now, Amanda," Carl retorted. "Your pacifism is well known, but does that bleeding-heart radical sentimentality actually extend so far as to include clay pigeons?"

"Stop picking on me."

Paul was sitting again with David Sherman in the parlor when Sandy charged into the room clapping her hands twice like the King of Siam and rousing the listless gathering into activity. "Dinner is being served on the front lawn. Let's move now, everybody. The crabs are getting cold!"

Everyone rose and began filing dutifully through the hall and out the front door. Charles was on the telephone in an alcove off the hall, nodding his smile to everyone as they passed by. Paul thought he overheard him murmur, "Yes, he's here. Alone," but he couldn't be sure. Charles immediately cupped his hand over the receiver—ever smiling—when he saw him.

The lawn had been set up with rows of long folding tables covered with butcher paper, and at every place setting was a nutcracker and a wooden mallet—the ageless symbols of the Maryland crab-feasting ritual. Under a stand of massive oak trees the serving table had been piled with corn on the cob, potato salad and cole slaw, fried chicken, and bean salad and muffins. And next to the table, a barrel loaded with icy beer and a huge cauldron of dark red steaming crabs.

Paul stood off to the side, between the gravel path and the tennis court, letting the bulk of the crowd funnel through the serving line before bothering to queue up himself. He wasn't that hungry anyway, for some reason, and all the effort necessary to pry the meat from those sharp, pointy shells without lacerating your own fingers in the process didn't really thrill him at the moment. New Englanders consider lobsters to be eminently more practical shellfish.

By this time Charles Hollister had come up beside him. "What's wrong, Paul? Not hungry?"

"No, really, I'm fine." At first he'd felt complimented, but now Charles' solicitousness was starting to get to him.

"We have other food we can make for you if you don't find this menu appealing."

"Believe me, Charles, it's fine. I'm just waiting for the line to clear out a bit."

Sandy Hollister came charging across the lawn, pulling the woman from the tennis court along with her.

"Well, look who's here!" Charles declared.

"Dr. Garrett . . . Paul, dear, you must meet Amanda West. You two have so much in common, you know."

"We do?" Paul stood his ground.

"I'm the editor of *Aurora* magazine," Amanda explained. He could tell she was slightly embarrassed by Sandy's forwardness.

He glanced up and down, from her boots to her head and back again. She was wearing a tight white blouse and tan slacks, and a very tailored tweed riding jacket, all of which looked just as terrific on her as the tennis outfit had. "*Aurora* must be trying to change its image," he said.

"Do you read the magazine?"

"I look at the pictures."

"Very clever." She gave him an aloof smile.

"Too bad there aren't any of Amanda in there," Carl Grover added. "That's what I'd have if I were running the show."

"We're a science magazine, Carl."

"Yes, of course. Oh, I'd keep it intellectual . . . on a high tone and all. Maybe pose you in a mortarboard and big round glasses."

"And nothing else?" She looked askance at him and grimaced playfully. Then she turned back to Paul. "Would you consider a male scientist shallow if you met him for the first time in a social situation like this?"

His eyes fixed on her firm, upright chest, then moved

down to the shapely backside peeking out from under the hem of the jacket. "I doubt I'd meet him in an outfit like that," he commented. "And if I did, I doubt he'd want to meet me. Actually, I saw you earlier on the tennis court."

"Ah. Perhaps you'd take me more seriously if you saw less of my legs."

"Perhaps. But it'd be my loss, I'm sure."

"Thank you for that, I suppose. Is it me or *Aurora* you don't approve of? From the conversation so far, I'm not sure you know enough about either of us for what I'd call an informed judgment."

"I don't mean to give either impression, Miss West. Let's just say we each approach science from a different perspective. You can't advocate the banning of advanced research with the same hysterical stridency that you advocate the banning of sugar-saturated cereals. I don't personally feel there's much room in the field for advocacy. It can't coexist with professionalism. And advocacy, if I'm not mistaken, is *Aurora*'s stock-in-trade."

"But aren't you a member of the Scientific League, our parent organization?"

"That doesn't mean I agree with everything they do. I'm a scientist, not a social critic."

"Still, I think we're on the same team."

"I'm comforted by that knowledge," he said.

She extended her hand. "Nice meeting you, Dr. Garrett," she stated with finality, turned and walked away.

What'd I do to him? Amanda wondered while she waited in the food line. Can he find me that threatening? And why did I react to him that way? She had known she'd be fighting a lot of battles when she took the job with *Aurora*. But this particular one was growing tiresome.

And why was she so concerned with earning Paul Garrett's respect right away? At this stage, wasn't she beyond that need? What was so special about him?

Well . . . right off the top he's one of the leading theoretical physicists in the country; a little too theoretical for her taste, but no denying his stature. And she had to be honest. She was attracted to him beyond his reputation.

She stared at him from across the lawn. He was tall, with sharp, intelligent features and black hair just starting to gray on the sides. He looked like he probably ran or played some sport regularly. Not tennis; that was too chic. More likely handball, or maybe squash. His jaw was square but his chin was pointed, giving him almost a chiseled look. He had the kind of body that would take clothes well if he cared at all about the way he dressed, which he clearly didn't. And she wondered how good he'd be in bed.

But there was something more than just physical attraction operating here, and she wasn't sure what it was. Men didn't normally interest her the way he had when she first spotted him, and certainly not after the crap he'd handed her. What was his special appeal? And why did it make her uncomfortable?

She would make one more stab at getting close to him. It was worth that. After all, he hadn't said he hated her. She'd give it another go. And anyway, there had to be a story in it somewhere.

Sandy Hollister was up in front of the parlor with a list of names in her hand. She should have been a camp counselor, Amanda decided.

"All right, time for bridge assignments," she announced. "Jane Blakemore, you'll be with Albert Walsh. Ruth Hamilton, I want you with Dan Cooper. Jerry Simonson, you're with Herbert Putnam. Amanda West, you have Paul Garrett."

Sandy came through, Amanda thought.

She's probably as great at bridge as she is at everything else, Paul thought.

As the cards were being dealt, he could already feel the collective ego—dormant during the lazy cocktail hour and even during the various sporting events of the afternoon—gearing up for the contest. He knew that bridge was the one activity that nearly all its devotees, regardless of their positions or occupations in "real life," considered to be the truest test of self.

Paul had played extensively in college, but lost interest after he left medical school. Years later, a colleague in the MIT physics department who happened to be a bridge fanatic, made the observation that one's regard for the game corresponded to whether one sided with Bohr or Einstein on quantum theory. Bohr said that the best we could hope for on a subatomic level was to predict general or statistical behavior of particles rather than what individual electrons would do at any given moment. His camp, the man asserted, relished the intellectual exercise of having to impose order and method on randomly dealt cards. Einstein found it unacceptable that the theory only showed the behavior of the group and could not predict what a single particle would do, issuing his celebrated "God does not play dice with the universe" statement. His supporters were supposed to feel uncomfortable with the fact that they were expected to deal with a hand they could not predict or prepare for in advance.

Paul and Amanda started off in the North-South position until Sandy Hollister walked by and screeched, "Amanda West sitting at South? No, my dear. This will never do!" They were content to just turn the score pad around, but their tablemates, clearly purists, insisted on a physical switch. So North-South ended up being occupied by Melanie French and Duncan Lindley. She was an incredibly thin, elegant-looking woman who made a habit of tilting her head back so she could look down her nose on everything and everyone. She explained that she owned the even larger estate next to Shorecliffe, which didn't surprise Paul in the least. Duncan Lindley was an equally thin man who seemed chronically nervous and had a tic. He also had a propensity for shuffling the deck, which gave his hands something to do. From the way they were looking at each other across the table—Melanie through her slitted eyes and Duncan from behind thick tortoise-rim glasses—Paul could tell they were frequent partners. Apparently, he and Amanda were the only new pair— an added disadvantage.

On the first deal Paul came out with nearly everything: all the aces, every king but hearts, and the queens of hearts and diamonds. He bid two clubs, to convey to Amanda how impressive his hand was. He hoped she wouldn't think he was grandstanding or trying to dominate her. Women like Amanda were always sensitive to that kind of thing in his experience. His fears were eased somewhat when Duncan passed and she bid two diamonds, indicating to him she had a nothing hand. At least that's what he hoped she was telling him. Since they'd never played together, he couldn't be sure.

On each round of the bidding, Melanie and Duncan continued passing, making it a dialogue between Paul and Amanda. "Two hearts," he bid next, thinking, "I'm long in hearts."

"Three diamonds," she replied, telling him the same in her suit.

"Four no trump," he declared, mentally asking her, "How many aces do you have?" He had them all, but wanted to "test" his mastery of the Blackwood bidding system.

"Five clubs," she said. None.

"Five no trump," he pressed on. Do you have a king?

"Six clubs." No.

Melanie passed again and Paul thought for a moment, rubbing his chin and staring straight at Amanda. The odds were wrong, he knew, but there was something about his rapport with her through the bidding that gave him confidence. They were "communicating" with each other, a technique regular partnerships spend years perfecting. Melanie and Duncan both glared at him for hesitating; they obviously took their game seriously. Well, he decided, let's see if the girl is all she's cracked up to be.

"Do you intend to bid?" Melanie muttered coldly.

"Yes, yes," Paul said. "Seven diamonds," thinking to Amanda, "I hope Melanie's holding the king of hearts and I hope she doesn't have anything guarding it."

Amanda looked at him with raised eyebrows.

Melanie's expression grew even more smug as she led with the jack of spades. Amanda reached for Paul's king of spades to play the dummy hand but Melanie grabbed her wrist. "Only the dummy can touch the dummy's hand," she chastised.

Paul and Amanda smiled at each other and Amanda instructed, "Play the king, please." She and Duncan threw in low spades.

As Amanda was about to play the dummy hand again, Paul had a thought. If Duncan holds a singleton king in hearts, we could smother it and establish the rest of my hearts. And if it works . . . Lead my ace of hearts, sweetie, he concentrated his mind to tell her. Let's go for the glory and show up these stiffs.

A wry grin came over Amanda's face, almost as if she'd heard him. "Play the ace of hearts, please," she requested, as they both saw Duncan's mouth drop open. He then contributed—and lost—his king.

I knew you could do it! Paul thought to Amanda. At this point the hand is over; everyone follows suit and on our first try together we pick up a grand slam and 1,510 points!

Melanie broke out into a hoarse, choking cough and repeatedly rapped herself on the breastbone. Duncan turned to the side, trying to avoid her germs.

On the next hand Duncan played a three no-trump contract. Paul took the first heart trick with a king and Amanda took the second with the ace, cleaning Paul out of the suit. He held only the ace of clubs with the six, five, and four showing in Melanie's dummy hand.

But on the next lead, Amanda played her four of hearts, surprising everyone. Paul was starting to pick up some vibrations. The dummy played the jack of hearts. Paul was out of hearts and knew his opponents would be trying for a long-suit run. It also seemed clear that Duncan needed to keep the lead to accomplish it. What's going through my mind, Paul wondered. She's got two playable hearts if she can get the lead back eventually, he found himself thinking, but it was an imposed thought, not one he could consciously trace on his own. She's setting up a high club, he realized— though again he didn't know how—and I've got to get out of her way.

Melanie was just about to protest his delay again when he played his ace of clubs. He heard an audible gasp coming from her general direction, and when he glanced up he noticed a small coterie of onlookers right over her shoulder. Duncan played the queen of hearts and took the trick.

But the strategy worked. Unlikely as it was, it eventually forced the lead away from Duncan and Melanie when Amanda broke in on Duncan's strong club run with her jack. And having cleared the way for retaking the lead by getting Paul to discard his ace, she was able to set up two heart tricks and defeat the contract!

On the faces of both their opponents was a combination of awe and disgust.

She'd done it. Somehow she'd engineered the only possible way of holding them to less than nine tricks and gotten him to make the one crazy play that allowed it to happen. Or had she gotten him to do it? How could she have? They hadn't exchanged a word or a gesture between them. But something *was* happening. He looked up and saw Amanda's face registering smug satisfaction, as if saying, "I *am* everything I'm cracked up to be." But he supposed she'd earned that.

Several more hands went by and the game was going like magic. They were in perfect harmony with each other. There was no other way to describe it; no logical explanation. And it was just as confounding to Paul as it obviously was to the dour Melanie and Duncan. During the bidding, he always seemed to guess right about Amanda's strengths, and on two occasions he jumped from two to four spades with foolhardy confidence. But they made both contracts and racked up the sensational scores that reward successful boldness in bridge.

On defense, when they'd both passed throughout the entire bidding and so had no clues as to each other's holdings, he still felt a certain intuition every time he had to make a choice between two seemingly equal cards as an opening lead. And in nearly every case, her subsequent play proved he had made the right decision. Whenever he concentrated on what he had in his hand, it was as if she picked up on it and set up the proper combination. Actually, the only time it failed to work was when Paul felt his mind wandering.

Melanie sat there fanning her cards annoyingly, eyeing the two of them warily as she tried to size up their system. "Are you sure you've never played together before?" she finally demanded.

"We've never even met each other before today," Amanda retorted mischievously.

"Deal the next hand," Melanie instructed Duncan with a withering tone. But it only got worse for them when she answered his one spade bid with one no trump. He raised to two spades and she went to two no trump, and when he gritted through his teeth, "Three spades," she almost spat back at him:

"Three no trump!"

"I think they're coming unglued and losing it," Paul said to himself, and Amanda instantly looked up at him and suppressed a snicker. He hadn't articulated a word, but he was sure she knew what he was thinking.

Paul had to make the opening lead but had no compelling logic to choose between leading a heart or a club. Keeping in mind the cardinal rule about leading through strength and up to weakness, he focused his thoughts into, "Are you strong in clubs or hearts?" Amanda continued looking down at her cards, and no specific word or instruction came into his head, but he decided to play a club and the decision felt comfortable. Sure enough, she was long and strong in clubs and they easily broke the contract.

"Are you paying attention?" Melanie snapped at Duncan.

Uh oh, Paul thought. Now it's really starting to get ugly. Bridge players have as much sense of humor as bankers writing off bad loans.

"Sure I'm paying attention!" Duncan snapped back. "But what the hell difference does it make when they're both practically playing each other's hands?" He whipped off his thick glasses and wiped them with an overly dainty monogrammed handkerchief. He replaced them on his head and in the same motion crossed his legs so tightly it made Paul uncomfortable to watch. "If this were a more formal situation, I'd demand an inquiry. Their play has been highly unusual, to say the least."

They just gave him a pair of innocent shrugs.

Sitting across the table from Amanda, Paul had to admit he was captivated by her. If anything, the contest had only confirmed his initial evaluation of her as a "total being." But she was so completely, refreshingly natural, so obviously accomplished and self-confident while possessing not an ounce of pretentiousness or false cool, that he already regretted his repartee with her when Sandy had introduced them.

By the time they got to the last hand of the evening, they were so far ahead in points that Melanie and Duncan were not only out of it, but humiliated as well. They'd stopped talking to Paul and Amanda shortly after the ace of clubs play and to each other not long after that.

Paul picked up a strong hand but decided to pass. Melanie passed and Amanda bid a club. Duncan also passed and Paul came back with one spade. Duncan and Melanie continued passing.

When Amanda then bid four no trump, Paul knew she was now using the Blackwood convention and asking him, "How many aces do you have?"

What the hell? he thought. It's the last hand and I'm

not going to rub their faces in the mud. He had two aces but replied, "Five diamonds," indicating one.

Amanda looked perplexed. Could she possibly . . . ? "Seven no trump!" she said firmly.

Paul felt his heart skip a beat and he coughed once in reaction. She knew he had two aces! Duncan led the eight of diamonds and Amanda immediately claimed all thirteen tricks! An incredible ending to an incredible game.

Before he could even rake in the cards to put them back in their box, Melanie and Duncan had excused themselves from the table and disappeared from the noisy room.

"I don't know when I've had such a satisfying evening," Amanda said as she rose.

"I know what you mean. A victory like that brings satisfaction out of all proportion to its significance." They both laughed.

"Quite a tour de force!" Andrew Beckwith came over to congratulate them. "I always say, when it comes to permutations of numbers, you physicists can't be beat."

"I assure you, I'm as stunned as you are," Paul said.

Andrew sidled up closer and cupped his hand near his mouth. "Tell me the truth, what kind of signals did you use? I thought Melanie was going to get the vapors right on the spot."

"I'm telling you, Andrew, we didn't cheat. We just happen to be very well suited to each other." He finally felt right putting his arm around her.

They drifted out into the garden together, not quite hand in hand, but close enough so that their arms grazed against each other as they walked, and neither took a step away. The garden was on the side of the house closest to the river, and, surrounded by a stone fence and shade trees, which had been there long before the house, it afforded a degree of seclusion in the midst of the summer-camp atmosphere.

A flagstone path wound through the area, eventually reaching a pond and continuing across it. Large goldfish swam between the stones and under the dense bushes that overhung the water. A single wooden bench rested on the far side of the pond.

It was long past dark, but the combination of light spilling out from the parlor and the full moon gave the garden a comfortable, shadowy glow.

"Are you cold?" Paul asked.

"No," she said. "I'm fine." There was a quality of contentment in her voice that made him relax more. They followed the path across the pond where the flagstones left off at the base of the grassy bank. "It looks so soft and inviting," she commented. "Do you mind if I take my shoes off?"

"No, not at all."

She steadied herself on his arm while she slipped off her sandals. "Thanks," she said when she let go.

He motioned her over to the bench. She sat down and pulled one knee up to her chest and clasped her hands around it. He sat down next to her, extending his arm along the back of the seat, not yet moving it any closer to her shoulder. He sensed that she wouldn't have resisted the gesture; would have welcomed it, actually. But he couldn't bring himself to increase their level of intimacy. What was it about this woman that was so different?

"It's beautiful out here, isn't it?" she said.

He nodded, wanting to add that it was nothing compared to her own beauty.

"I'm basically an urban creature," she went on. "Living in the middle of Manhattan I'm not really used to this big an expanse of nature . . . except Central Park, and that doesn't count."

He found her statement curious. She seemed to fit in and belong in any situation he could imagine her in. Maybe she was just trying to be disarming. And when he looked at her she once again flashed him that alluring smile.

Then they were silent again. There were so many things he wanted to say to her, so much he wanted to establish. Why couldn't he articulate it?

But even without talking much, just sitting there next to her in the darkened garden, he sensed something like . . . an aura. Was that the right word? It was just like the bridge game. A kind of communion with her. His mind was flooded with her image. He gazed into her shining blue-gray eyes. She was staring out across the pond, searching for a pattern in the endless rippling circles. She might as well have been staring across the Wye River beyond the sloping hill. Tiny shapes darted across the surface of the pond, intersecting the circles, like elementary particles moving about the nucleus of an atom; moving about the center of physical existence. There it was, represented before him—the basic relationship, the components of the atom. How they fit together determined every relationship in that outer universe.

That was what he'd been thinking about all along, he realized. Relationships. Relationships and connections. His connection and attraction to Amanda, whatever it was, was all part of the same enigma he thought about all the time. The elemental relationships. Gravity. Electromagnetism. The weak and strong nuclear forces. The terms that gave his life meaning, that dominated most of his working—and most of his waking—hours.

They were becoming steadily clearer. Relationships and connections he'd grappled with for months. Each force links two entities. It stands to reason that the forces themselves must somehow be linked. Square One. First Premise.

Then he felt a sensation coming over him, or rather a sensation he'd been subconsciously aware of all evening crossed over into the realm of conscious cognizance. It wasn't a fulfillment. It was a beginning. The beginning, as a fellow scientist in Cambridge would later put it, of the cessation of ignorance. He was fitting pieces together in his mind. Connections and relationships. Not an overview yet; not a grand visualization. Just pieces. But incredible pieces! Pieces in the form of equations which suddenly took on the pristine clarity of light rays, as simple, correct equations always do when perceived by the gifted mathematician or physicist.

Now he understood the energy level that had been building and coursing throughout his nerve endings all evening. It was the body preparing itself for the exertions of the brain. The thrill was electrifying, physical, sexual. It was the thrill of discovery and pursuit, and next to it, every other experience in life paled. And he knew that like every other scientific breakthrough, it was the result of the convergence of many lines of influence in one spot . . . within his being at this particular time and place. And had it not happened here as it did, it might never have occurred at all. What those lines were, he could not begin to fathom, of course. But that the convergence had taken place, he had no doubt.

He looked again at Amanda, and was surprised that she was staring straight at him; for how long, or for how long he had been in this ecstatic trance, he didn't know.

"You're trying to solve a problem," she stated. "Something that's very important to you."

"How did you know?"

"I can just tell."

He was flooded with desire for her. Right now, he wanted to have her, to possess her, more than anything else in the world. Anything except . . .

"I've got to get back to the house," he said.

"Is anything wrong?"

"No. Nothing at all. I've just got to write something down before I forget it."

"I hope I haven't disturbed you."

"On the contrary. You've been a source of great inspiration."

"Just by sitting here?"

"Evidently."

He got up and raced back through the garden, only approximating the slabs that led across the pond, struggling to keep the ideas level in his head, still aching for her.

* * *

Within ten minutes, the time it took to get back to the house, rummage through the library desk for paper and pencil, and write down his ideas while he still held them all in mental balance, Paul was on the telephone. It rang for a long time, and when he glanced up at the formidable cherrywood grandfather clock and realized it was after midnight, he thought momentarily about hanging up.

But the impulse was brief. Who could possibly mind being awakened for such thunderous news!

Finally, a haggard voice answered the phone.

"Harry, is that you?"

"What? Who the hell is this?"

"It's Paul. You've got to listen to me, Harry."

"Paul? Are you all right?"

"Yes, I'm fine. I'm fine."

"Then why the hell are you calling me? This connection doesn't even sound like you're back in town."

"I'm not. Listen, I've had an inspiration. I had to talk to someone . . . to you; run it by you while it was still fresh in my mind and make sure it makes sense, make sure I'm not misinterpreting my own logical jumps."

"Paul, are you crazy? Where are you?"

"What's the difference? I'm in Maryland. Somewhere out in God's country, I could hardly find my way. Now listen. Better yet, get a pencil and write everything down as I give it to you."

"I'll never get back to sleep now. You know how I am. Didn't you know we always go to bed early? We're not partyers like you and Julia."

"Harry, forget about sleeping for a minute. Now another thing: don't say anything to anyone. All right?"

"Sure, sure. I don't know what you're talking about. Can't this wait until morning?"

"No!"

"Okay," Harry sighed wearily. "What is it you're giving me?"

"Remember, just between you and me. No one else."

"All right already. Are you going to tell me why you called or aren't you? Now what is this?"

"Step One of the Unified Field," Paul slowly articulated.

There was dead silence on the other end, lasting so long that Paul thought the connection had been broken. When Harry Gillette's voice came back on the line, it had taken on a tone of reverence. "Are you serious?" he asked.

"You listen and then tell me."

Cambridge, Massachusetts

Harry Gillette put down the receiver and stood at the telephone stand in the upstairs hallway, waiting for his hand to stop shaking. His wife must still be asleep, he reasoned. Otherwise, she would have called out to him by now. But she was bound to wake up when he came back to bed and ask him what was going on. So he'd have to have a story ready.

An old friend had just gotten into Boston, was lost and had called from a phone booth in Roxbury. No. That was too strange and elaborate. It led to more questions. It would have to be something ordinary, even banal. An obscene call—a bunch of kids on the line. And then he'd called the police and the phone company to report it. That was much better.

When he was sure he was steady enough to manage the stairs, he went down to his study, turned on the reading lamp, and spread out the notes of the conversation with Paul across the desk. From left to right in linear fashion; he wanted to be able to see everything at once.

The equations were too arcane, the mathematical reasoning too complex to make a definitive judgment on the basis of one quick pass-through. And this was material Paul Garrett had been working on for years, so he would have sensed nuances and shadings Harry wouldn't even have picked up on. But the way Paul had taken him through it on the phone had seemed to make good sense. And studying it now under the glaring light of the reading lamp, he could detect no obvious flaws. He would go over the equations again tomorrow in his office, when he was fresh and could be more objective. But if they held up, Paul had indeed hit a grand slam. Or as he said, reached Step One. How many steps there were altogether was anybody's guess.

He'd promised Paul he wouldn't say anything. Paul had trusted him and made him his scientific confidant, as Harry knew he would should anything like this come up. And he would have done the same for Paul, though he certainly didn't consider himself in Paul's league.

He pulled the telephone closer on the desk and thought about his promise to Paul as he dialed the international access code. But he had no choice. There were larger issues involved.

Langley, Virginia

Five somberly dressed men, none of them a standout, were seated in a perfect semicircle facing George Henderson's desk. Each had a green government-issue writing pad on his lap and a black looseleaf briefing book on the floor beside his chair. On either end of the semicircle, a heavy canvas-covered burn bag awaited the written discards of the meeting.

Henderson had arranged the men in alphabetical order. It was easier to remember them that way and he could keep his own shorthand notes of the meeting simply with letters. Bass, Cooper, Horton, Martin, Steiner. If pressed, he could even come up with their first names. But for his needs, there was really no point.

He recalled the early years, during the war, before there even was an Agency, when the field operatives all referred to each other by code names. His had been "Expedience."

"Is everybody clear on our thinking up to this point?" Henderson asked. He sat hunched forward with his forearms on the desk.

Since the group was silent, he continued, "Now, on the matter of the Garrett case, please add the name of West, Amanda Jane. White female, thirty-two years of age, resident of New York, Manhattan."

Five pencils went instantly to green pads with identical notations.

"I'd like a Level Two profile developed as soon as possible," the chief stated. "No significance has yet been assigned to the encounter with the principal subject, but we'll want to be able to follow up all relevant possibilities. And of course the situation in Boston . . . it could be very sensitive. Martin, your people are going to have to be ready to react."

"They already are, George," Martin assured him.

"I know that." Henderson stood up and began pacing behind his desk, signifying to those familiar with his personal traits that the meeting was nearly over.

"I don't want any action taken as long as this business remains manageable. It would be better for all of us to just let it lay. But if it does show potential for getting out of hand, I want to be ready to make sure it doesn't."

Cambridge, Massachusetts

When the doorbell rang, Julia Garrett assumed it was a salesman of some sort, perhaps peddling magazines. No one else was likely to come calling on a Sunday afternoon. She had just gotten back herself and certainly wasn't expecting anybody. Unless it was that grad student, Frank. He was a pain, but she guessed she should be flattered by his interest. Would he know Paul was out of town?

When she opened the door, the two men standing there seemed a little too old and dignified to be magazine salesmen.

"Mrs. Garrett? We'd like to talk to you for a few minutes," one of them announced.

"Who are you? What's this all about?" she challenged.

By this point they had stepped away from the door and into the living room.

"We work for the government. I've got to ask you some important questions, if you don't mind."

"What's this for? Do you have some identification?"

"This won't take long. Please cooperate with us."

"Either you tell me exactly who you are or I'm calling the police," she warned. She picked up the telephone receiver, but the second man snatched it from her hand.

"Just a few questions," he said.

"Get out of here!" she yelled. "My husband is coming back any minute and . . ."

"That's sort of what we want to talk to you about, Mrs. Garrett. But it concerns you, too." He extracted a small picture from his coat pocket. It was of Julia walking across Harvard Yard with a man. "Who is this man?" he demanded.

"It's none of your business," she retorted.

"I'm afraid it is," he said.

She glanced quickly from one to the other. Her eyes were wide with terror. Then she bolted for the bedroom door.

The second man pulled two pairs of rubber surgical gloves from his pocket and approached the bedroom.

Chapter Three

Washington, D.C.

Paul Garrett let the telephone ring nineteen times before putting down the receiver for the sixth time that hour. He'd been calling home ever since he returned from the Eastern Shore—two days now—but Julia had yet to be in. He'd called the phone company to see if the line was out of order. He'd called neighbors, friends, and faculty colleagues of hers at Harvard. Several people had seen her, but only in passing. And she hadn't shown up to give her last exam.

He sat in one of the offices set aside for visiting scholars at the American Academy of Science headquarters on 17th and M Streets. From his window he could see the strong, regular vertical shafts of the glass and marble National Geographic building across the street. The policy meetings that brought him to Washington as an Academy consultant at least once a month were over for this trip, and now he was preparing the final paperwork for his study project. It was a grant that would finance his research into the advanced interrelationships of gravity and electromagnetism. He'd been working toward it, vying for it for years. The grant would let him go wherever he wanted, use whatever academic or scientific resources he chose to further knowledge on a subject of which he was one of the acknowledged masters.

And yet every time he turned back to the typewriter and saw the "Scope and Methods" heading staring back at him, he thought of Julia, and the clarity of scientific thought drained from his brain. Not even Harry Gillette, who followed his thinking as well as anyone, would be able to make any sense of it. It should have been easy cranking out this homogenized layman's version, especially after that stupendous breakthrough of logic Saturday night. But he just couldn't concentrate.

Maybe she wasn't coming back at all. Maybe what she was telling him that night when he was packing was that as far as she was concerned, their life together—such as it was—was over. He knew it had been shaky from the start. That fact was never far from his consciousness. But with all the things wrong . . . or more to the point, with the lack of things right, it was a way of life. He felt he belonged with Julia. Well, he'd be going back home at the end of the week, and there would have to be some resolution.

He folded his arms across the top of the typewriter, rested his chin on them, facing the possible end of the relationship, thinking back to the beginning. She was so sensitive, so understanding, trying to shield him as best she could from his ordeal, trying to put that all behind both of them and helping him face the future with serenity and optimism. And everything had been better for a while; mostly because of her. The dreams, the vague and not so vague fears let up, and it was almost as it had been. For a while.

But the odds against them had been too strong, he supposed, and neither one, in the long run, could give as much as was required.

He picked up the phone and dialed one more time. He let it ring for what seemed like minutes. Then he hung up, stared once again at the page in the typewriter, and the image of Amanda West intruded into his mind.

Tel Aviv

As Rabbi Nathaniel Kagan left the El Al Boeing 747 at Ben-Gurion International Airport and stepped down the metal stairs onto the tarmac, he spotted the airport's traditional greeting committee: two young Israeli soldiers with Uzi submachine guns hanging loosely from their shoulders. The first time he'd seen them, Kagan had wondered out loud to his Israeli host if the soldiers could react quickly enough from such a seemingly relaxed position. His host, who was in a position to know, assured him they could.

That same host greeted Kagan at the other side of Passport Control inside the spartan, hangarlike terminal building.

"Shalom," Moshe Baruch said as he extended his thick hand.

"Shalom," Kagan replied, taking it.

"And how was your flight?"

"The usual. El Al doesn't believe in frills."

"That's what you get from a country of pioneers." Baruch was a short, barrel-chested man with thinning hair and no neck. He pulled both suitcases from Kagan's hands and continued walking toward the curb without breaking stride.

Though he knew he shouldn't be, Nat Kagan always felt intimidated by Israelis of Baruch's—which is to say, his own—generation. They were the front lines, living every day the pioneering life Kagan only raised money to support. He defined that life as a kind of virility, which he didn't see much in his own congregation on Long Island or in his professional contacts in the States.

And there was another factor accounting for his discomfiture. Israelis as a population were markedly unreligious. Here they were, the pioneers of modern

44

Judaism, and the last thing they seemed to need was a rabbi.

Baruch's car was standing in the middle of the "No Parking" zone. It was a maroon Mercedes Diesel, one of the few luxury items commonly seen in Israel. Baruch had obtained his in the same fashion as most of his fellow Israeli Mercedes owners—as a war reparation. A "partial compensation," as the bureaucrats called it, for members of his family butchered by the Nazis.

On the way to Tel Aviv Baruch asked, "So what have you been doing since you were the last time here?" He spoke English with near perfect fluency, but with that occasional awkwardness of sentence construction that marks the assimilation of foreign grammar from a textbook.

"Oh . . ." Kagan answered him, "preaching to my congregation, mostly about things they don't pay any attention to. Then there's weddings, bar mitzvahs, funerals. The usual."

"Everything with you is 'the usual.' "

"I've also spent a lot of time raising money," he added defensively.

Baruch noted his reaction. "Hey, I'm not accusing you of anything."

"Nothing but not living here."

"You're too sensitive."

Kagan watched the endless concrete apartment blocks pass by on either side. From their precast construction and unyielding gray facades, it was difficult to tell which ones were completed. There was always building going on everywhere you looked in Israel. Kagan's only real clue to habitation was the brightly colored curtains trying to dress up the windows of the lived-in apartments.

"Whenever I'm here, I feel as if I should stay," he said. "Just send for Eleanor and set up shop."

"Actually, you can do more good for us right where you are," Baruch commented. "That's one of the things we have to talk about." He turned briefly to his right to see if Kagan was returning his glance, but the rabbi was staring straight ahead. And swallowing hard, if Baruch was not mistaken. He turned his full attention back to the road and said nothing more for several minutes.

"Look, I know this makes you uncomfortable," he said at last. "But it's something we have to talk about."

A car tried to cut in right in front of Baruch, who reacted by jamming the accelerator to the floor and swerving ahead of the offender onto the other side of the street. He pulled back to his own lane inches before a cement mixer lurched around the blind curve and just barely grazed the left-side door handles. Kagan felt his heart stop momentarily in his chest.

"For God sakes, Moshe! All the Israelis drive like maniacs!" he screeched as he found himself flattened against the front seat.

"I couldn't let him get away with that," Baruch said angrily, then softened. "Anyway, we have to take out our frustrations somewhere. Now, let's get to the main point."

"Yes," Kagan agreed. "But I find it difficult to say 'no' to you."

"Then don't!" Baruch laughed. That was the trouble with Israelis. They had a simple solution to everything.

"Look, Moshe. The Committee for Jewish Unity has an established purpose. I can't change that."

"I'm not asking you to change it," Baruch countered. "I'm only saying you could expand it a little."

"We can talk about it. But I think it's too dangerous."

"Look, Nathan. Everything around here is dangerous. Getting up in the morning and going out on the street is dangerous. We accept that. As we say in Yiddish, *Azay geht es*. But the question is, is it too dangerous?" He glanced back at Kagan. "And I think it's an acceptable risk."

Washington, D.C.

Amanda West returned to the apartment the Scientific League kept at the Watergate West and her eyes were caught by the two tickets she had stuck into the frame of the foyer mirror. As it had turned out, she would only be needing one of them.

Dan Snyder, the high-priced lawyer she had been seeing on her last several trips to Washington, made no pretense regarding his distaste for chamber music, but had reluctantly agreed to go along when he realized it was the only way he'd get to see her this visit. And now that she faced the prospect of attending the concert alone on her last night here before going back to New York, a pang of disappointment gripped her.

She was as lonely now as usual after breaking off with a man, and knew the feeling would only be intensified by an evening out alone, especially in a city away from home. But she accepted this as her punishment for leading him on long past the point of reasonableness, and she didn't want to miss the concert in any event.

As usual, she was running behind schedule. She wouldn't have time for dinner if she was going to make the opening number on the program, so she'd have to grab something to eat afterward. Fortunately, the Kennedy Center was only a five-minute walk. She stepped out of her skirt and slip. On the way to the closet she wriggled out of her T-shirt. She snatched the dark green silk shirtwaist off the rack and put it on en route to the bathroom.

She could have done her makeup at the vanity. But the Scientific League had been talked into furnishing the apartment in high-tech style, which the tasteless decorator thought would be a perfect projection of their scientific image. And the vanity mirror, surrounded by glaring marquee-style bulbs, was the most oppressive piece in the whole dreary place. Of course the reflective foil wallpaper was pretty disarming. And the bed looked like something from a giant Erector Set. She liked the pun better than the design. Actually, the only thing she loved about the apartment was the wall of glass doors and the balcony that faced the Potomac.

Standing in front of the mirror, Amanda applied the base cream to her face, massaging an extra layer onto the scar along her left temple, near the hairline. She squinted to study the deepening creases at the corners of her eyes. The lines had been there a long time, almost as long as the scar, but she had always figured they contributed to an intellectual look. A young, pretty girl just out of college had trouble being taken seriously. But now that she was past thirty with a reputation as a first-rate science writer and editor, all that had changed. She self-consciously pulled the dress tight, examining her body along the line from breast to hip to make sure nothing else had.

On the walk over to the Kennedy Center—the curving sidewalk around the Watergate complex— Amanda thought again about Dan. Why had these relationships become so tiringly predictable? Did she just have a talent for picking men who quickly came to mean nothing to her, or was there something fundamentally within her that wouldn't permit her to share a lasting and meaningful relationship? Would she even recognize a healthy relationship at this point, or know how to handle it and keep it that way? The questions turned over and over in her mind, but there were no answers.

Each time she visited the Kennedy Center, Amanda was struck anew by the sweeping sterility of its massive blank marble front, and when she entered the building and walked down the flag-festooned Hall of Nations, she felt, for an instant, totally insignificant, out of scale in the vast hall.

This was her first visit to the Terrace Theater, though. It was a medium-sized auditorium on the upper level, and she found it, surprisingly, quite warm and subtle, and executed on a scale to which a human being could relate.

The concert wasn't a sellout—she didn't expect it would be—but there was a respectable turnout; proof perhaps that the nation's capital was finally acquiring some of the cultural sophistication it had been claiming for years. The New England Chamber Music Ensemble was performing a program that included Mozart's G Minor Piano Quartet, the C Major Quartet, and Bach's Suites No. 1 in A Major and No. 6 in D Minor.

Amanda had always liked chamber music, ever since her early teens. It was both soothing and intellectually stimulating, and at such times as this she regretted not playing an instrument.

As the music in the hall enveloped her, one of her most enchanting fantasies returned. She closed her eyes and pictured herself in some small but stately drawing room, probably in Vienna or Zurich, violinist for a trio playing Bach or Vivaldi sonatas. For some reason the other two musicians were always men. The appreciative audience of ladies in evening gowns and gentlemen in cutaway coats sat in gilded ballroom chairs under the gently flickering candles in a delicate chandelier. Amanda, in a lacy white dress with flowing train, grasped the instrument firmly under her chin, her right hand held out high, gracefully drawing the bow across the strings. At the conclusion of the piece, she would bow her head demurely to the sound of applause politely muffled by white kid gloves. The image gave her a feeling of serenity, like sitting in a secluded knoll in Central Park on a warm afternoon.

By intermission, the cooler night breezes had removed some of the smothering humidity from the tropic-like air, and Amanda strolled out onto the terrace, where the panoramic view of Washington was one of the most breathtaking in the city. On one side, the top half of the Washington Monument rose beyond the horizontal plane of the State Department, the Reflecting Pool, and the one public building in the city with authentic emotional impact—the Lincoln Memorial. On the other side, the rugged naturalness of Roosevelt Island interrupted the graceful width of the Potomac and lent an eerie contrast to the crass commercial development on the Virginia shore.

She could see the lobby lights blinking through the glass. She eased her way back through the jostling crowd near the terrace entrance, avoiding thoughtlessly held cigarettes and sloshing plastic wineglasses. She had almost made her way to the plate-glass door when she felt a hand clutch at her so quickly there was no time to think or consider. A cry for help welled up in her chest. She turned suddenly.

It was a smiling Paul Garrett.

"Hey, I didn't mean to startle you. I'm really sorry," he spluttered.

She felt the looseness of relief throughout her body. Her hand went over her breastbone and she caught her breath. "I'm all right. It was just . . . kind of . . . unexpected."

"I'm sorry."

"Don't be."

He waited for her to continue.

"You like chamber music?" she asked. It was the only thing she could think of.

"Passionately," he replied. He paused, then added, "I'm really glad to see you."

It was an ordinary enough greeting, but she found it strangely affecting.

She drifted toward the door as the crowd funneled through. Paul caught her arm.

"You know something?" he said. "Meeting like this . . . I don't think we were meant to go back inside."

"You mean the roof is going to fall in after the intermission or something? I heard the Kennedy Center had construction problems, but . . ."

"No. Just that I've been thinking about you a lot since Saturday night."

"Me too," she admitted.

"Would it be very forward of me to ask you to go have a drink with me?"

"Right now?"

"Right now."

"But I paid for the ticket," she protested. "In fact, I paid for *two* tickets."

"I'll pay you back."

"If you'll buy me dinner you've got yourself a deal."

When they came down the steps into the main dining room of Dominique's Restaurant on Pennsylvania Avenue, Diana, the vivacious, yellow-haired hostess, brightened.

"Good to see you again, Dr. Garrett. You've been away a long time," she said, planting a friendly kiss on his cheek. She led them over to a table next to the fireplace, where they could take in the entire atmosphere—the jarring, bustling, boisterous friendliness, the plant baskets hanging from the two-story ceiling, the backlit stained-glass windows and other neo-Victorian clutter and—since this was Washington—the wall of celebrity-autographed pictures.

When Diana had scurried back to the door to greet the leaders of the already growing line waiting to get in, Amanda commented, "You've cut a rather wide swath in this town."

"Not really," Paul said. "But when you're down here by yourself as much as I am, the most basic survival instinct dictates that you find the good restaurants." He scanned the physical madness swirling around them. "It reminds me a lot of MIT, but the food's better."

The waiter came around for the drink order. "Extra dry vodka gibson," Amanda stated.

"I'll have the same," Paul said.

She raised her eyebrows and nodded, noting the coincidence. "So do you get to Washington very often?" she asked.

"At least once a month, I'd say. There isn't a tremendous amount of important physics research going on here. But it's a fact of modern life that the seat of Big Government is also the seat of Big Science. What about you? Spend much time here?"

"Enough to know some good contacts. Not enough to know some good restaurants."

"I didn't know you could separate the two."

She smiled. "You can't always. In my business you usually have to feed people before they'll tell you anything."

"Then I'll withhold my most probing questions until after we order."

The waiter delivered the drinks. Amanda took a sip and said, "One swallow on an empty stomach and I'll probably tell you more than you could ever want to know."

"I doubt that," he replied, looking directly into her luminous eyes, which showed gray in the restaurant's subdued lighting. "How did you get to be the journalistic crusader you are today?"

She raised her eyebrows again and shrugged. "I wish there was an exciting story to go with it, but there really isn't. It just sort of happened naturally. Ever since I can remember I wanted to write. And from about the age of eleven or twelve I've been interested in science. When I got out of college the most obvious way to make a living as a writer was in journalism. I worked for *Time* for a while, eventually working my way into an anonymous slot on the science staff, and when the job at *Aurora* opened up, I enthusiastically went for it. I got lucky."

"Are you happy at *Aurora?*"

She twisted her glass by its stem, hesitating a moment. "Yes, I'm very happy there," she replied at last. "I believe in what *Aurora* stands for—the responsibility of science and scientists. I think we run interesting stories, and I like running my own show." She took another sip. "And if it doesn't sound too childish or immature in light of everything else I've said, I like being a woman in a man's business . . . especially since there's no reason it should be overwhelmingly a man's business."

"I think I read a column you wrote on the subject," he said. "Something about making enough progress in science so that women don't have to invoke the memory of Madame Curie any more than the blacks still have to invoke George Washington Carver."

"That's right. So you really do read *Aurora* after all."

The waiter came back with the red, leather-covered menus. Amanda opened one of them and scanned the page-after-page list of entrees. "This thing has to weigh four pounds," she said. "You can work up an appetite just lifting it."

"According to my informal survey, it's the heaviest menu in town. I'm told it's the thickest document some of the congressmen who eat here ever read." He gave her a few minutes to orient herself among the exotic offerings, such as rattlesnake and hippopotamus, then suggested, "I'm going to have Trout Bretonne, but there's a trout stuffed with crabmeat and mushrooms that's excellent. I think you'd like it. Over here on the second page."

"That's exactly what I was looking at. Your powers of inductive logic are beyond me."

"How long will you be in town?" he asked her.

"I'm leaving tomorrow morning. My assistant claims the office is caving in in my absence, but she's probably just trying to make me feel needed. How about you?"

"Some time this week. I wasn't going to be here even this long, but as it turned out, there was no compelling need for me to get back."

Her lips parted as she began to follow up on his answer, but she stopped herself before she'd spoken. Don't push it, she told herself firmly.

When the coffee arrived after dinner, Amanda opened two packets of sugar, emptying the first into her cup along with half of the second, and handing the remainder to Paul along with another full packet.

"Why did you do that?" he asked.

"I don't know." She looked up. "For some reason I just assumed you took one and a half sugars, like me."

He poured them into his cup and stirred the spoon around longer than necessary.

"You're married, aren't you?" she said.

"Do I look married?"

"You look separated . . . and confused."

"Very astute. At least I think it's astute. My wife hasn't had the good form to tell me yet." His faint smile faded.

Well, is this what I want? Amanda asked herself. To get involved with a married man? That was generally a no-win proposition. At least it always had been for her. But she couldn't mistake that feeling of terrific attraction; that was real enough, and along with it at least the momentary banishment of anxiety and self-doubt.

"Where are you staying?" she asked him as they were leaving the restaurant.

"The Jefferson. I always stay there. What about you?"

"Watergate West."

"*Aurora* must be selling well."

"The Scientific League keeps an apartment there. It's kind of amusing, really. They spend most of their time and energy raising money, and then look what they spend it on."

"I'm going to withhold my dues in protest."

"Instead of that, would you like to come back with me and get some of your money's worth yourself?"

"I'd like nothing better." He put his arm around her waist, pulled her close to him and kissed her affectionately on the cheek.

They walked down 19th Street to H, and then cut across George Washington University's concrete-shell campus. Their pace gradually quickened as they walked, almost imperceptibly at first, noticeably by the time they reached Virginia Avenue. Their movements began to take on the tense, decisive quality characteristic of physical anticipation. They turned frequently to look straight at each other, and did not look away in embarrassment when their eyes met.

At that moment, one thing was dominant in Paul's mind. He wanted her, more than anything else. He felt his heart racing, pounding against his rib cage as he thought about her. And as they kissed again just outside the Watergate West's lobby entrance, this time full and exquisitely on the lips, it took little insight to sense that she felt the same aching for him. He could see it in her eyes.

Once inside the metallic apartment, they wasted no time. They fumbled at each other's clothing on the way to the bedroom, not willing to stand still long enough to complete the task. She reached the bed first and pulled him down onto her, both of them laughing at their own enthusiasm. Within moments, they were moving in unison, as if performing to the same inner rhythm, their bodies in perfect harmony.

Their lovemaking was protracted and breathless, and when they finally finished, they lay next to each other, exhausted, watching the flickering lights of Georgetown in the distance. Occasionally he would reach out and pull her over to him for a quiet kiss. Then she would lie back again, staring up, looking for some pattern in the tiled ceiling.

A few minutes later she sat up with her legs crossed under her and said, "So tell me something about your research."

"Do you really want to hear about it?"

"I do. I'm here to pick up on scientific trends; not just to pick up scientists."

He laughed. "Okay. I'll give you the short form. I'm working on the relationship between gravity and electromagnetism, which I then hope to be able to relate to the weak and strong nuclear forces and any other natural forces that make themselves known along the way. If all this works out somewhere down the road—and the chances that it will are exceedingly remote according to most of the people who claim to know—we'll have what's known as a Unified Field Theory. A fundamental statement of all the forces in the universe in relation to each other."

"Isn't that what Einstein was involved with?"

"That's right. But he died before he could come up with one. A lot of the conventional wisdom says that if he'd lived to be two hundred, he still wouldn't have been able to come up with one because there isn't any."

"So why are you wasting *your* time?"

"Scientific breakthroughs always fly in the face of conventional wisdom. Everybody thought Einstein was crazy on relativity until he proved he made sense. The same with Newton on gravity and the components of light."

"Do you enjoy looking for this theory that might not be there to be found?"

"I love it. It's the ultimate quest. The ultimate cause."

She turned her body slightly and stretched one leg out to its full length. She had a sensational body, Paul thought. "Now I don't want to start another conflict like the one when we first met," she stated, "but you already know my scientific orientation, and . . ."

"I know what you're going to say, Amanda."

"I know we each have our own axes to grind, but isn't it possible that someone as gifted as you could better spend his time on something more . . . productive . . . than a Unified Field Theory?"

"Ah, the old Scientific League utilitarianism rearing its ugly head."

"It's a valid question," she protested.

"Queen Victoria once asked Michael Faraday, 'What good is a magnetic field?' "

"And he answered?"

" 'Madame, what good are babies?' "

The cab taking Amanda to Union Station let Paul off at the American Academy of Science. Once out of the car, he kissed her through the open window and held onto her fingertips until the movement of the vehicle pulling out from the curb physically pulled her away.

And as he stood watching from the sidewalk, he felt as if a secure and comfortable part of himself—a vestige of the distant past, suppressed but not entirely forgotten—was pulling away with her.

He could still see the back of her blonde head through the rear window as the taxi merged with the line of traffic waiting to turn left onto L Street, but the hours he had spent with her already seemed remote. They were a carefree and lighthearted interlude, which now contrasted sharply in his mind with the business that lay ahead. That portion having to do with his work would be intense and probably frustrating. That portion having to do with his wife and marriage would be frustrating and probably worse.

When the cab was completely out of sight, Paul turned mechanically toward the building lobby, colliding as he did with a man in a medium brown suit. The man stumbled and Paul reached out to steady him, but the man seemed to regain his balance on his own.

"I'm terribly sorry," Paul said. "I guess I wasn't paying attention."

"Quite all right," the brown-suited man reassured him. "No harm done."

As Paul and the other man were about to part and go their opposite ways, a third man came up, asking, "Are you all right?"

"Yes, I think we're both fine. It was nothing," Paul said. "Thank you for stopping, though."

Paul was sure he had seen both of them before, but couldn't place them. Had it been at the Hollisters' party? There were so many people there he couldn't be sure.

The third man nodded and followed Paul into the lobby, joining him in the elevator and remaining there when Paul got off on the Academy's floor.

He tried to stop daydreaming and keep his mind on where he was walking as he stopped by the receptionist's desk and asked if there were any messages.

"You just got a telegram," the girl announced, handing him the sealed yellow envelope.

"Hmm," Paul uttered, momentarily impressed with himself. "I wonder who cared enough to write." He continued down the hall to his office.

As he sat down at his desk and fished through the top drawer for a letter opener, the possible contents of the message finally dawned on him. Either Julia was formally demanding a divorce . . . or the Academy was withdrawing his grant at the last minute. But how could they—either one of those parties—be so cowardly as to inform him through the cold detachment of a telegram?

Paul slit open the envelope and felt as if a hammer had punched through his chest and then been ripped out again as he read:

```
TDMT CAMBRIDGE MA  14 05-12  0643P EST
PMS DR PAUL GARRETT, DLR
C/O AM ACAD SCIENCE
1150 17TH ST NW
WASHINGTON DC 20036

HARRY GILLETTE DIED THIS AM  HEART ATTACK
PLEASE CALL SOON AS POSSIBLE  SORRY TO
HAVE TO SEND THIS NEWS  WAITING TO HEAR
FROM YOU

LEWIS PENSLER
PHYSICS DEPT  MIT
```

Chapter Four

New York

Amanda sat in her office, hoping for an interruption. She hunched over her typewriter, periodically brushing aside the strand of dark blonde hair that kept falling to block her view of the page. And every time she saw the page clearly, there was still nothing written on it. The whole idea of an article on telepathy and psychokinesis seemed silly to her.

She stared intently at the pencil sharpener sitting near the corner of her desk and concentrated as hard as she could on moving it. And to be sure the experiment was strictly controlled, she lifted herself slightly off the chair and sat on her hands.

She concentrated on the object with her full will for nearly four minutes, until the muscles in the back of her neck ached from the tension. But nothing. Not even a millimeter budge from the metal lump.

The hell with it, she decided. Bertrand Russell had said it was a basic law of something or other that when you have to accomplish some difficult mental task, the most efficient course is to back off, not think about it, and it'll eventually just come to you. She'd met Lord Russell once, in Sweden, and had instantly felt a tremendous rapport, as if he was an old friend. Maybe he was right. But if the inspiration did come, she just hoped it came before this issue's deadline.

She pushed herself away from the typewriter, grabbed her floppy suede bag from the visitor's chair, and went out to her assistant, Nancy Flanagan.

"I'm going out for a walk to try to get the cotton out of my head," she said. "Hold down the fort while I'm gone."

"If anything comes up, I'll contact you by ESP," Nancy replied.

"If you can do that, you've solved my problem with the story."

"Don't count on it!"

She left the flat-fronted, unimposing five-story building and headed across 49th Street to Lexington. There was a strong southerly wind at her back which seemed to have blown all the gray city pollution straight up to Westchester.

The deep breathing and brisk pace made her pull back her shoulders, thrust out her chest and revel in her own physical self-awareness. She reveled, too, in the discretionary freedom of her fiercely fought-for executive status, which let her set the pace of her own professional life; including, if she wanted to, taking the afternoon off for a walk. On a day like this, New York could be thrilling. Not simply the soaring shafts and planes of the audacious architecture, but also the kinetic energy and the unabashed power lust. To have arrived, to be a success in the eyes of fellow successful New Yorkers, that was the ultimate kick.

And in the face of such a positive mental atmosphere, the unwritten telepathy piece had already been relegated to somewhere at the far end of her consciousness, back with those formless but enduring fears which were on some occasions more easily suppressed than on others.

What came into her mind was another sort of image. As she crossed 59th Street and saw the Bloomingdale's entrance looming dead ahead, she suddenly visualized the silver plastic charge card tucked discreetly into her wallet. She had an overwhelming impulse to put it to use. As she walked into the commanding entrance foyer on the Lexington Avenue side, she was again a seven-year-old, hearing her mother's oft-repeated admonition, "Now don't go buying something just for the sake of buying it." But at the moment, that was as easy to banish as all the other negative thoughts. She'd worked hard on the Washington trip, and it had gone well in many ways. She'd even written and filed her extensive memo on her findings, including Paul's research. So she deserved a present.

Just to the right of the doors was a handbag counter. Examining the leather items that were on sale to make way for the straw summer bags, she glanced around furtively, guiltily expecting to run into someone from the office and have her whereabouts revealed. But then she reasoned that anyone seeing her here would be skipping too, of course, so they wouldn't blow her cover.

But as she moved to the adjacent counter, she was sure someone *was* watching her. He stood at the far end of the entry hall, at least forty feet away, next to a platform display of a mannequin in a long, offensive purple T-shirt dress, pulling on an equally offensive stuffed poodle. He had one hand jammed into his pocket and the other held a cigarette that he jerkily moved up to and then away from his lips. Did Bloomingdale's allow smoking in the store? Maybe he was finishing out here before he went in. He was tall and looked like the cover of a "Frank Merriwell at Yale" story. His athletic body looked as if it were straining to get out of the carefully bland clothes he was wearing—brown plaid sport coat with coordinated charcoal brown pants. Brown tie, medium width; brown shoes, brown socks. Everything about him seemed bland and medium, except the Frank Merriwell build. When she glanced at him, the man busied himself with lighting another cigarette.

A pickup who hasn't got the balls to come over and say anything witty. She was glad she didn't have to involve herself with the Upper East Side pickup game.

She climbed the stairs to the concourse level, with its brass-trimmed ebony walls and black and white dazzle. The place was so "done" that it taxed the eyes to look in any one direction very long. And it was equally difficult to move in any specific direction without bumping into someone. Nobody in this part of Manhattan must work, Amanda reasoned, because they're all here at Bloomingdale's.

She made her way over to the store directory and scanned down the listing of departments, trying to decide what to shop for. She could use a new dress for work. And the way she was feeling about herself the past couple of days, she decided she might visit the lingerie department on the lower level before she left the store. But she also wanted to buy something just to buy it—she couldn't get away from that.

What she really wanted at that particular moment, she impulsively concluded, was a Braun coffee maker. She'd had coffee brewed from one for the first time only the week before at a friend's apartment, and just now remembered that it came from Bloomingdale's housewares department. She casually wondered if Paul was a coffee connoisseur.

She was near the top of the escalator when she saw him again. That same man—the Frank Merriwell character. He had just stepped on from the floor below, and when he looked up, she thought she caught him winking at her. She pushed a few steps ahead and quickly stepped onto the next escalator, and by the time she was halfway up to the next floor, he was still not in sight. Maybe he found someone else to amuse him in Sportswear, she thought.

Housewares was up on the sixth floor—a long, imitation-marble arcade lined with mirrors. On the left, a series of alcoves displayed the gadgets and culinary utensils the chic, Upper East Side cuisine could not be without. Half the department seemed to be taken up with floor displays—tableaus, actually—showing well-dressed mannequins employing everything from CO_2 wine-bottle openers to electric lettuce washers. It made the housewares section look almost like a boutique. Even if her secret admirer followed her up here, it should be fairly easy to lose him, she assured herself.

As she surveyed the scene, the department was full of young, attractive men who, in fine Manhattan tradition, thought that the way they acquitted themselves in the kitchen was second only to their performance in the bedroom, and a dazzling preliminary to it, in any event. A tall, athletically built specimen was sweeping an Alfred Zanger ten-inch chef's knife back and forth in front of him to get the feeling in his wrists, the same way he would test a new set of golf clubs.

The corridor was so crowded that it was literally hard to move around, which made Amanda a little bit nervous since she was in one of the two alcoves displaying knives. Everybody wanted to try one or two out, and if someone got carried away, there was a potential for serious harm. Sales people scurried around trying to discourage those making the most florid gestures.

Amanda herself couldn't resist a collection of Ed Wusthof Trident blades that caught her eye in one of the more prosaic displays—a square butcher-block table with the entire set of knives encircling an artificial crown roast.

She wandered over toward a display area, above which a larger banner suspended from the ceiling read, "Sabatier—THE Name to Remember in Cutlery." Nearby, a man in a white tunic and chef's hat was giving a demonstration. She glanced at her watch and decided that as soon as the demonstration was over, she had to buy her coffee maker and get going.

She caught the chef saying in a delicate French accent that blunted his *t*'s: "Dese Sabatiers are de finest knives you can buy, *mesdames et messieurs*. Dey are chosen by professionals for dere balance, quickness and precision. Dey can be sharpened to a perfect edge almost instantly, and in the madhouse of a restaurant kitchen, time is more precious dan truffles, *n'est-ce pas?*"

A few knowing titters arose from the crowd. "Just one ting I must remind you," he continued. "Dese are fine, untreated carbon steel blades, and dey *must* be wiped off *immediately* after use. You understand *me?* Yes. Wipe dem off right away or dey are—how you say?—'guaranteed to rust.'" More knowing titters.

There was some kind of commotion at the next display in the alcove, but the crowd was so thick Amanda couldn't see what was happening. She tried to get through so she could get over to the coffee counter, but it was just as easy to move in the direction that everyone else was going. When she finally did get close enough to see between the first row of onlookers, it struck her that Bloomingdale's was being particularly tasteless with some of its displays. Chic was one thing. Crude and vulgar was something else.

"I've never seen anything like it," she heard one woman casually proclaim.

Directly under another large banner, a mannequin had been splayed across an oak butcher block, its head hanging backward over one end and its arms dangling oddly into midair. But when Amanda took her second look, she realized that the absurdly contorted figure was not a mannequin, but Frank Merriwell—the one who'd followed her into the building, through Handbags and right up the elevator. A Sabatier carbon steel boning knife stood impaled in his chest, just to the left of his breastbone, and his open plaid jacket revealed a still-widening pattern of blood reaching all the way over to an empty shoulder holster. His wide brown eyes stared lifelessly up at the ceiling. And since no one had bothered to wipe the knife clean immediately after use, it was already beginning to rust.

Cambridge, Massachusetts

"It was apparently a heart attack. It must have been very sudden, while he was driving," Lewis Pensler told Paul. "It happened on Commonwealth Avenue right past Exeter. He hit a parked car. Thank God no one else was hurt."

They were in the Center for Theoretical Physics office on the third floor of Building 6. The department chairman sat in one of the venerable brown overstuffed leather chairs. Paul, who had tried sitting for a while in its companion piece, found it less agitating to stand and pace back and forth in front of the window. Final exams were just about over, and the emptiness of the grassy court he could see from the office gave the MIT campus a ghostly feeling, as if he had returned to a place that did not exist as he had left it. And with Harry gone, it really wouldn't ever be the same for him.

"I'm sorry to have dragged you up from Washington," Pensler said. "But I knew you'd want to be here. And I know how much it would have meant to Harry to have you at the memorial service."

It sounded strange to hear Harry Gillette talked about that way, especially by a fellow physicist. In all the years Paul had known him, the only time he'd heard Harry speak of God was as a term for what he called "First Cause," the original moving force of the universe. And as far as any concept of afterlife, he dismissed the discussion with, "It's nothing we can prove or disprove so there's no use fretting about it. As a scientist I have to assume that this life is it. If it turns out I'm wrong, so much the better." Unless he had changed radically in death, Paul couldn't imagine him sanctioning Pensler's attribution of living emotions and sentiments to the deceased.

Even so, his own living grief was staggering. That was a good word for it. As the reality of the loss gradually sank in, Paul began to sense an unnerving void, both in his friendship and his professional life. Harry had been his confidant, the one he bounced his ideas and theories off of before he trotted them out in public. And Harry—plodding, picky, methodical Harry —had saved him from more than one embarrassment by taking Paul's own concepts and pointing out the direction he really ought to have been heading in. And now all that was gone. For good.

"He never said anything about having a bad heart," Paul said.

"All I can tell you is what the Suffolk County coroner

said. And Harry's own doctor confirmed it. Maybe he didn't know."

"Seems crazy, somehow."

"I know what this means to you, Paul. And it's difficult to accept something as impersonal as this . . . even for a scientist."

"I guess that's it," Paul agreed.

"How's Julia?"

Paul could actually feel his depression deepening. It was like the bottom had dropped out of his stomach to be replaced by a solid lead mass. He could only shrug.

"I'm sorry. When I didn't hear anything for a while, I was hoping things had sort of smoothed out."

Paul shook his head slowly. "I've been trying to get in touch with her since I got to Washington. But she must have moved out. I thought it was getting better, but then . . ." He frowned and swallowed hard. "I hope she at least has the decency to show up at the memorial service . . . if she's heard about it. Maybe we can talk afterward."

"I hope so. Sounds like you've really been through the wringer lately. I'm glad you've got the grant project this summer. It won't do you any harm to get away and not have to think about any of this for a few months."

Paul tried to smile at this genuine gesture of friendship from an autocratic man who had obvious trouble with personal warmth. "Who knows?" he said. "I might even discover something."

He crossed back to the door. "I'm going back to my apartment. I came right here from the airport. I'll see you at the service tomorrow."

"Right, Paul."

On the walk back to his apartment, Paul could think of nothing but Harry; not just the sadness of his loss, but also the joy of his companionship, which made Paul realize he would miss him all the more. They both knew that Harry had never possessed Paul's scientific vision, but he had been the consummate physicist, allowing for all possible theories and explanations, but accepting as fact only what could be proven or empirically inferred. He thought of where Harry must be today . . . if he could be thought of as being anywhere at all. And that response of Bertrand Russell's came back to him, when the famous atheist was asked what he would say to the God he didn't believe in if he died and *did* go to heaven. "You gave us insufficient evidence!" Lord Russell replied. In spite of himself, Paul had to smile.

But thinking of Harry naturally led him to think of Julia. It usually did. They were opposite sides of the same coin, representing the two key forces in his life, tearing him in opposing directions. He resented the time and energy he took from his work to devote to Julia. He felt guilty about the time and energy he took from her to devote to his work. And he never felt free of the struggle.

He didn't expect her to be there when he got back to the apartment, but he wondered if she'd left him a note. Just speculating about this made him feel his loneliness more acutely and made his sense of loss even greater. Why should he feel such loss when he couldn't honestly say he valued possessing her that highly? Why did he feel the pain of her absence more than the comfort of her presence? And why did these four days away seem like so much longer? Why did it feel like weeks had gone by? He steeled himself for what he would face when he got home.

At least if she'd left him a note he'd know where they stood. He doubted that she had, though. It would be typical of her—of their relationship, really—to let him sweat it out, not knowing what was happening. Not that he figured he deserved any better, really. He could think of numerous occasions when he'd left her hanging, so he couldn't condemn her for it. Maybe she was right. Maybe they should just forget about the whole thing. They either didn't mean enough to each other, or they hadn't been able to figure out how to deal with how much they did mean. The marriage had certainly lost whatever resilience it once had. Maybe he wasn't capable of that kind of commitment to anyone, and she should be free to find someone who was. That was probably all it would take to make her happy—something God knew he was incapable of doing. Then, although he tried to put her out of his mind, he thought of Amanda; he sighed, and his chest ached.

There was no one in the lobby or halls of his apartment building, which extended the sensation of emptiness he'd experienced looking out the window onto the court. It was a perfect visual symbol for the way he was feeling. A profound sort of emptiness. With Harry dead, with Julia gone, with his classes over for the summer, all of the anchors in his life—the things that kept him, if not *happily* going, at least going—had crumbled.

The corridor was so quiet that he was aware of the dull metal clank as his key hit the tumbler inside the dead-bolt lock. But when he turned the key, he did not feel the familiar resistance. It turned quickly, smoothly. He tried the doorknob with his hand. It didn't turn. She'd obviously left without bothering with the dead bolt. He tried to suppress the anger he felt welling up inside him. He couldn't let himself get upset over minor things like this if they had any hope of reshaping their life together. But how could she be so careless? Without the dead bolt locked, any petty thief could slip the lock on the doorknob. If anything's been stolen . . . Oh, the hell with it. He couldn't think of any material possession he prized that highly, especially now.

He opened the door and called to her. "Julia?" But there was no answer. He put down his suitcase in the front hall, draped his trenchcoat over the side chair and walked into the kitchen. Whenever Julia left notes for him, they were always on the kitchen counter by the telephone. There was a chance she had left him something. But when he got to the kitchen, the only evidence of her having been there was a pot, two plates, and some silverware soaking in the sink. And judging from the residue that had built up on the surface of the grimy water, they'd been there for several days. It was rather thoughtless of her to take off with dirty dishes still in the sink, he thought. And then he realized that this, too, was a statement—about how he mindlessly expected her to take care of all the details of his personal maintenance without doing anything in return. Maybe he needed this jolt, though he didn't know at this point if he was capable of changing.

At this point, all he felt was tired, exhausted, not from physical exertion, but emotional fatigue. He was no longer agitated or nervous. He had entered into the "come what may" phase of stress. He went into the living room and sat down on the sofa, not knowing what he wanted to do next and not wanting to move.

Then suddenly he felt a twinge in his stomach; an unsettling feeling was the only way he could describe it. Not pain so much as . . . He jumped to his feet and darted for the bedroom. The door was closed. As soon as he opened it he could see the dresser and a corner of the unmade bed, but no more.

One more step and he could see it all. His whole being froze.

She was lying motionless on the bed, face up, wearing only a nightgown that fell open to either side.

"Julia!" he shouted as he hurried to her side. He grabbed the hand that was resting on her stomach and shook it vigorously, trying to force her awake. He grabbed both shoulders and jerked her upward, but her head thudded heavily backward onto the pillow. "Julia!" he shouted again. "Wake up! Listen to me!" He slapped her once across the face, and when he got no response, slapped her again and again, harder each time. But still nothing.

Then his eyes darted over to the night table. An empty white plastic bottle of Nembutal lay on its side. Next to it were bottles of Imipramine and Doriden. And on the floor, its remaining contents having emptied onto the beige carpet, was a bottle of gin. He seized the Nembutal container and brought it up to his face. Julia's name was typed on the prescription label.

He pulled the nightgown further away from her naked chest and pressed his ear flat against her sternum. But he heard nothing. He pushed up both eyelids with his thumb. The pupils were fully dilated. He dug his index finger as far as he could into the underside of her wrist, but couldn't detect the faintest pulse.

He sat up and looked again at Julia lying there, and this time the actuality sank in. Her skin was bluish and her whole body—particularly her face—was puffy and bloated. She almost looked waterlogged. That meant she couldn't have just died. Her limbs were limp, so it must have happened long enough ago for the rigor mortis to dissipate.

A cry of anguish welled up and exploded within him. He couldn't cry out. He couldn't talk. He couldn't move and yet he couldn't stand still. What . . . why . . . when did it happen? Oh Jesus! The whole time he'd been trying to call her, maybe, she'd been right here, lying on the bed with her nightgown falling off her body. He couldn't bear it. All the horrifying possibilities careened through his mind.

He was shaking again. He couldn't stop shaking. He wanted to do something—just a gesture. Something for the belated dignity of the dead. He would cover her up. She shouldn't be exposed like that . . . her nakedness and her suffering. He stumbled to the linen closet to see if he could find a blanket.

But no. He'd better not. Nothing should be moved before the police come. That's the way it has to be.

So he stood there, as long as his legs remained stable, trying to remember the prayer he'd offered up for the cadavers in the anatomy lab. But nothing came— nothing but that horrifying flood of memory.

Again it plagued him. When had it happened? How could she want to kill herself? What made her decide? Had she been planning it for a long time . . . for as soon as he left for Washington? Or had it been an impulse, a momentary surrender to grief that he could have prevented if only he'd been there? Oh God! How to live with something like that? Whatever it was, he knew one thing instinctively: if it weren't for him, she'd still be alive.

If it weren't for him, she'd still be alive.

He staggered back into the living room, over to the dining area, to a dining-room chair. He gripped the bottom for stability. He was suddenly very dizzy. He couldn't get rid of those cadaver images. He saw himself cutting and slicing, casually removing organs and setting them on the drainboard beside him. He couldn't stand it. He pressed in on the sides of his head as hard as he could. He would have crushed his own skull if he could have. He had to get rid of the image while that hideous body that had been his wife lay in the other room.

He didn't know how long he sat there, clinging for stability and sanity to the bottom of the chair. But finally, he felt a certain fragile equilibrium. He didn't have to think anymore for a while. Thinking would come later and that would be the hard part. Now, all he had to do was react; go through the prescribed motions.

He stood up, walked slowly into the kitchen, picked up the telephone receiver and dialed 911.

"I need the police," he told the emergency operator, revealing not a trace of emotion in his voice. "I need them right away."

The police arrived quickly, made a cursory search of the scene, took several flash pictures and covered up the body. Lieutenant Bert Kennedy asked Paul if Julia had been despondent, whether they had been fighting recently, and where he had been for the past few days.

Did she take sleeping pills regularly? Had she ever threatened or attempted suicide before? Did she have any known allergies or medical problems? The questions kept coming; routine, tactfully presented questions, but each one like a kick to Paul's gut. All the things he should have done, should have been aware of kept coming back to haunt him.

Lieutenant Kennedy asked him finally if he'd be all right by himself for the evening, or would he like them to take him to a friend or relative's house. Paul assured him that he'd be fine. Kennedy gave him his card and said to call any time during the night if he changed his mind or needed anything. Paul watched the coroner's deputy wheel the body out of the apartment and then saw Kennedy and the rest of the police team to the door.

As soon as he saw them out, he collapsed on the sofa again. The numbness that had blissfully tranquilized his mind just after he discovered Julia in the bedroom had now worn off, to be replaced by the searing reality, the consuming horror of the situation. The agony of that discovery, of seeing that twisted and tormented face for the first time would, he knew, remain with him always. One more paralyzing image to plague him and gnaw at his psyche. But equally as horrible, if relative values could be given to such things, was the incompleteness—now the eternal incompleteness—of their relationship. She'd died without their being able to resolve their differences. She'd taken her own life with an emotional agenda still pending. If they'd had a chance to make up, or had even talked the whole thing out and agreed to a separation, that would have been some consolation. But this way, he would forever feel that a major aspect of both their lives had been left hanging. Maybe later on, after the shock had worn away and some perspective had set in, it wouldn't seem important. A trifling footnote, perhaps, to an appallingly tragic episode. Right now, however, as he faced back-to-back funerals, it seemed to rank among the most important things in the world.

And he knew she'd done it because of him.

New York

The tears had long since stopped. In fact, they had stopped shortly after the detective told her she had every reason to react the way she had, and he just wished that everyone who had some proximity to a violent crime was as observant as Amanda. With that, she wiped her nose with the edge of her index finger and managed a faint smile as she noted that a reporter wasn't good for much if she couldn't at least pay attention and remember what she'd seen.

She sat in the interviewing room of the 19th Precinct station house on East 67th Street with Detective Lieutenant Lawrence Klein, who passed the statement across the table to her for a final reading before she signed it. Klein was just under six feet tall, with that indeterminate age of most bald men who lost their hair in their twenties. He was both patient and sympathetic, Amanda thought, for a man who must face worse than this every day. But from the heavy, downward-turning brow and the muscular build, she could just as easily picture him in a nighttime alley, feet braced apart in the standard police firing position, as sitting in the fluorescent glare of the station house tenderly calming a slightly hysterical witness.

He told her she could use the room or the lounge as long as she liked, but she'd have to excuse him because he still had all the other statements to take. And with Bloomingdale's as crowded as it had been that afternoon, and knowing how those women liked to talk and talk—if she'd please excuse his disrespect—he might still be taking statements on the Fourth of July. Amanda thanked him for his kindnesses and said she was sure she was all right now. All she needed now was a telephone.

"You can use the one on my desk, right over there," Klein offered.

"It's a long-distance call," she explained.

"That's okay. One more call won't break the city. At least I don't think it will," he declared.

She called Washington information, then dialed the number.

"Jefferson Hotel," the voice on the other end announced.

"Dr. Paul Garrett's room, please."

There was a slight pause, then, "I'm sorry, Dr. Garrett checked out this morning."

Amanda put the phone down without answering and began crying again.

Langley, Virginia

As usual, George Henderson had his agents arranged in a semicircle. And as usual, once they had taken their alphabetically assigned chairs, there was no small talk.

"I will summarize item one," Henderson announced. "Agent Sullivan was killed by a carefully aimed stab wound to the heart. So far as we know, he had no contact with, nor was he aware of his assailant. Since this was a routine surveillance detail he was operating solo and there were no backup personnel on the scene. And according to our brothers at the N.Y.P.D., despite the fact that there were at least a hundred and fifty shoppers in the general vicinity, no one actually saw the murder. Okay. Steiner, Sullivan was your man. What are the possibilities the girl picked up the tail and tipped someone off, who then came out of the woodwork and did the deed?"

"Highly unlikely," Steiner responded. He flipped three pages back in his green writing pad. "Although there's no way of knowing what happened once they both entered the store. Since it was a routine tail, there was no depth on the coverage."

"And the weapon was definitely from one of the floor displays?"

"Correct."

Henderson squeezed one hand around the other fist and rubbed vigorously. "It doesn't fit the S.O.P. of any organization I can think of. Using a weapon you find at the spur of the moment. It's just not professional. And yet, the guy . . . or woman, was obviously a professional of some sort. Or else pretty fucking lucky."

"Sometimes it's better to be lucky than smart," Cooper offered.

"Is it possible the assailant didn't just pick up the knife; that he had it with him before to look like it was just a casual thing?"

"Almost impossible," Henderson said. "How did the assailant know Sullivan was going to end up in the housewares department?" The double meaning dawned on him after he'd said it, and he quickly shifted pace.

"What if the guy was actually following Sullivan, not the girl?" Martin asked.

"We'll have to follow it up," Henderson acknowledged, although he hated the idea. It meant there might be some unknown threat to the Agency that hadn't surfaced in any other form. Or else the possibility that Sullivan had been working more than one side of the street. Reluctantly, he told Bass, "Check all of Sullivan's contacts for the last year. I want to know everything about him."

Bass nodded obediently.

"Okay, item two," Henderson continued. "The name is Harry Gillette, late Professor of Physics, Massachusetts Institute of Technology. The profile is in today's briefing book. At the time stated, he was pronounced D.O.A. at Massachusetts General Hospital, apparently due to acute myocardial infarction. At present, there is no medical evidence to the contrary.

But on the Paul Garrett satellite chart, Gillette was a Level Two. He was in a position to know everything Garrett was doing and understand its scientific implications. It is also possible that if Garrett sensed any doubts about his own status, he conveyed them to Gillette. So if this is more than just coincidence, I want to know about it. Horton, this is yours."

"Okay."

"Now, item three, which I find personally most distressing. This being the death of Mrs. Julia Garrett."

Martin recoiled slightly in his chair. The movement was almost imperceptible to an outsider, but for those trained in the traditions of Agency stoicism, he might as well have jumped up and beat his breast.

"I take it that the action was unavoidable?" Henderson asked, but his question carried the tone of an accusation.

"Of course it was!" Martin fairly shouted. "I'm no psycho. I don't get my kicks from stunts like that."

"Why didn't it come back to this office for a policy decision first?"

"George, we were all agreed that if any one of Garrett's satellites threatened to spill or defect, termination was the only course. This was a matter of national security, for Christ's sake. You read the report. We had zero setup time and we had to act immediately or not at all. It was either this or the Rape-Robbery Scenario. We were lucky to pull this one off under the circumstances."

Henderson sighed. "I'm sure I would have done the same thing." Martin eased back into his chair with a quiet look of triumph on his face. "I trust you made it clean."

"Very clean," he said. "Not a mark on the body."

"Good. Because we have to assume there's a chance the Cambridge City Police and the Suffolk County Sheriff's Office could crawl all over this." He waved his hand. "I realize it probably won't happen, but we have to be ready for it. And for God's sake I don't want to have to head off our opposite numbers at the Bureau."

"From what we understand of Dr. Garrett's marital life, the suicide should fit in perfectly," Martin explained.

"That's fine, except for one thing," Henderson pointed out. "This was a potential jeopardy to us, but it was the man's wife to him. If Garrett cracks from the shock and grief, where does that leave us?"

London

The gray-haired man sat behind his desk and followed with patient eyes as the young khaki-clad courier entered the room.

"Mr. Dunninger, this is the communication you were waiting for." He handed him the lock-seal pouch.

"Thank you very much." He handed the young man an envelope addressed to Mrs. Harry Gillette in Cambridge, Massachusetts, U.S.A.

"A terrible shame about Harry," he said to his assistant, Walter Oppermann. "His heart," he muttered, and shook his head.

Oppermann was sitting on the ageless linen sofa. It had originally been white, but no one currently at work in the building could remember it in any color other than gray. "This could be promising," he said to Walter. "I have a feeling we're about to see progress."

With that, he tore open the pouch and extracted several typewritten pages. He scanned the documents silently, gently nodding his head in recognition every couple of lines.

"What is it?" Walter asked.

"A copy of the memo Amanda West wrote for the *Aurora* story file after she talked to Paul Garrett in Washington. Take a look." Dunninger handed him the papers.

"Was it hard to get?" Walter asked him.

"Not terribly. After all, we do have access to the

office." He gave Walter a few moments, then asked, "What do you think?"

"I think it's very exciting. Miss West is no physicist, but for a layman her descriptions and understanding are remarkably acute. I'm sure our people can infer quite a lot."

"That's what I'm hoping. But I think you'll agree, our efforts here are starting to pay off."

"No question." He put the papers down next to him on the sofa. "But tell me one thing, Nigel. Why have you been so sure lately that Garrett's work, or somebody else's work in the same field, was about to break through?"

Dunninger leaned back in his chair and smiled. "Kind of a visceral feeling, I guess. But you have to remember, science is a historical progression. Nothing happens in a vacuum. Everything indicates we're ready for the next step. And for something like this, I had no trouble convincing the rest of the Foundation that we should take on the project, whatever it cost."

"It's interesting that a magazine would offer the first real indication of progress," Walter commented.

"I was thinking that myself," Dunninger retorted. "If Miss West knew the extent of her service to us, or even that we were paying her salary, we'd have to give her a raise."

They both smiled.

"For the time being, let's just concentrate on keeping her out of trouble."

Chapter Five

Jerusalem

It was 7 PM when Moshe Baruch swung his stocky legs across the sweat-stained bed, planted them on the floor and finally forced himself into an upright position. He stretched his arms almost up to the ceiling and let out a long, creaking groan. He walked over to the window and parted the blind enough to view the street below filling up with the typical early-evening activity. And as he watched the life of the street, Ariel Herzen watched him.

"What's wrong?" she asked.

"Nothing," he said. "I've got to get dressed and get back is all. I said I'd be home by dinner and I'm already late as it is."

"So why not wait till morning now?" She spread her legs enticingly under the sheet, as if he needed further convincing.

He came back to the bed and stood over her. "I'm flying to the States tomorrow for some baby-sitting."

"But that's tomorrow."

"Why do you always make it so difficult for me?" There was irritation in his voice. She did make it difficult for him to leave, he knew, but it wasn't through anything she said. It was her long straight black hair, smooth tan skin, memorable face and even more memorable body lying there ready to receive him again that dissuaded him from leaving. He watched her full breasts rising and falling lightly under the sheet that just covered her nipples.

She had high cheekbones and a square jaw line, which gave the sides of her face an almost hollowed-out look. This tended to accentuate her already dominating brown eyes and long lashes. Ariel was one of the most beautiful women he had ever known, and Israel was a land full of beautiful women. But what ate at Baruch was the feeling that despite her entreaties, she didn't really care whether he stayed or not. She meant much more to him than he did to her, he was sure. And it was completely against his nature to stay for long in such an emotionally dependent and fragile relationship.

Moshe Baruch only felt secure when he was in control.

The only sane way to carry on this affair was to always take the initiative himself, he realized. He had decided it was time to leave, and that would be that. He grabbed his pants from the nearby chair and then the rest of his clothing. Ariel was still lying in bed, casually watching.

"What will you say about why you're late?"

"To who?"

"To your wife, of course."

"I don't know. I'll think of something." Actually, that was one item Baruch had given little consideration. He had become extremely adept at lying to important people over the years, so coming up with one more story for his wife was at most a minor challenge. And, thank God, Dora was a trusting woman.

"Is it still Rabbi Kagan you're working on?" Ariel asked.

"You're not supposed to know anything about that," Baruch stated.

Ariel smiled slyly. "You don't have to have any secrets from me."

"That's not for you to say."

"What makes him so important?" she persisted.

"That's not for *me* to say."

"Well I've heard some people at the Weizmann Institute are interested in him."

"Maybe, but it's not part of my responsibility. So what'll you do tonight?" he asked, trying to divert the subject. "Are you staying in?"

"I don't know. Maybe I'll go out for dinner; find some friends or something. It doesn't matter."

Nothing really seemed to matter to her. But maybe that was the best type of woman to have an affair with, especially in his work, with all the traveling. She made no demands on him, didn't want to be with him on holidays, and didn't mind when he picked up and left.

He bent down to kiss her. "Have a good trip," she said. "And bring me back something nice from America."

"Remember what happened last time when the Customs people caught me?"

"Just be cleverer this time. That's your job, isn't it? Oh, and don't forget to turn the lock before you shut the door behind you."

"Don't worry. Certain things I'm not likely to forget."

"But you can't be too careful these days, can you?" she stated, growing more animated as the discussion turned to routine matters.

Baruch checked his pants pocket for his wallet and conducted a brief self-frisking. He kissed her once again, then crossed over to the door—turning the lock on his way out—and headed for the Mercedes parked under an alcove off the back alley.

When she heard his footsteps beginning on the stairs, Ariel got out of bed and walked naked across the room to the door. She slipped the chain into place and fastened the dead bolt above the knob lock. Then she padded over to the window, pulled the blind slightly to the side and peered out until she saw Moshe emerge onto the street and turn back toward the alley. She watched him walk out of sight, then went into the bathroom, brushed her teeth and examined her face in the mirror. As always, she was quietly satisfied by what she saw.

Her own clothes had been lying under Moshe's on the chair. It took her no more than three minutes to dress. After zipping up her skirt and buttoning her blouse, she reached for the rather large handbag hanging on the back of the chair. She walked over to the night table by the bed, opened the second drawer and felt way in the back for her .22 caliber Beretta. She placed it in her handbag with some delicacy, since the trigger mechanism had been filed down for easier firing and the spring-loading magazine had been altered to accommodate the lighter than normal powder charge in each bullet. She opened the closet door, gave herself one more critical glance in the mirror, and decided she was ready to face the world.

Washington, D.C.

Of all the things that bothered him about working at St. Elizabeth's Hospital, what bothered Dr. David Sherman the most was the lack of a decent place to eat lunch within a twenty-minute drive. Other psychiatrists at the public mental facility complained about how small their income was compared to what they could be making in private practice. But David figured that, unlike some of the patients, no one forced the doctors to be there, so you lived with your choices. And besides, the way the nation's capital was saturated with shrinks, filling up forty hours of private practice a week was far from a sure thing.

The lunch situation, on the other hand, was something he hadn't considered when he signed on as a medical officer for the hospital's Alfred Noyes Division. He didn't equate acceptance at a good restaurant with the womb like so many of Washington's socialites did—his sister included—but it did help break up the day. On days when he didn't feel up to facing the marginal offerings of the cafeteria, there were only two realistic choices within walking distance of the institution's front gate on Martin Luther King Avenue, S.E. And if he didn't care to eat at either McDonald's or Holly Farms, he had to get in his car and drive who knew where to find a halfway decent restaurant. Once a week David got together with several other doctors to sample likely places, and they all felt this diffused their own depression about the conditions at St. E's. It was what in psychiatric terminology they called "recreational therapy."

David was at the desk in his small ground-floor office sorting mail when Margie Ferenbach, the assistant administrator of Noyes Division, popped her head in.

"Want to go to lunch?" she asked.

"McDonald's or Holly Farms?" he replied without enthusiasm.

"Take your pick. I'm adventurous. Anything but the cafeteria." Margie's large eyes and shining face were among the few things that brightened the place up; small, cute, sandy-haired and only two years out of social-work school. Though he considered it a weakness in himself, David didn't want to be around St. E's long enough to watch her become cynical. To him, the inevitable transformation of this bright young girl whom he liked more than he admitted would represent the ultimate futility of a system he already knew was ultimately futile.

"Can you wait awhile?" he asked. "I've got to release a patient first."

"Which one?"

"The Ambassador of Jupiter."

"I noticed on the charts that His Excellency was leaving us," Margie commented. "Where's he going?"

"After the Secretary of State turned down an audience with him and Blair House 'misplaced' his room reservation, he thought it best to repair to the nearest YMCA to await further instructions from his home planet." David leaned back in his chair. He stretched his arms out behind him for balance and rested his feet on the desk. "He'll be back. Cops brought him in two weeks ago for directing traffic in the middle of Connecticut and K. During rush hour."

"Cops didn't want anyone taking their job, huh?"

"The cops don't do it stark naked."

"Maybe it's an old custom on Jupiter."

"Maybe so. But it tends to disrupt traffic here on Earth." He pushed himself off from the desk and rolled his chair until it hit the gray metal bookcase against the wall. He looked upward, as if for guidance. Margie sat herself on the desk and dangled her feet back and forth over the side.

"Hey, David," she said, her tone at least half serious. "Do you ever think about the possibility that maybe the guy *is* the Ambassador of Jupiter?"

"Yeah, I considered the possibility. But then I dismissed it."

"But think about it . . ." She was getting enthusiastic now. David could sense her imagination racing. "If someone did come here from another planet, no one would believe him, everybody'd think he was crazy, and he'd end up in a place like this. Right?"

"Right."

"So how do you know he's not for real?"

"Just my vague impression. Psychiatry's not an exact science, you know. Plus the fact that we admitted the same guy three months ago and last time he was the Ambassador from Mars."

"The guy gets around."

"Let's eat."

He locked his desk, grabbed his jacket from the matching gray metal coat rack, closed his office door and walked with Margie down the hall. The Ambassador from Jupiter could wait until after lunch without causing any major interplanetary scene.

In the corridor was the usual collection of half-dressed, half-shaven, half-awake men, wandering about as if they didn't know where they were; or just as frequently, as if they were sure they were somewhere else. The conditions and the attitude had improved in the last hundred years, David knew, but other than that, a public mental hospital had not changed its function substantially in a century's time. Dorothea Dix's dream was still largely just that. The hospital remained what it had always been—an asylum, a refuge, a repository for people who had no place else to be. With this volume of patients, treatment in the sense of making someone better was just about out of the question. The best a psychiatrist could do was fulfill his legal, court-articulated function: determine whether the individual in question was a danger to himself or others. And as far as David could determine, the Ambassador's overt behavior, while bizarre, was relatively harmless. Words such as "relatively" continually surfaced in this business. Nothing, of course, was absolute.

As they were walking past the front office on their way out the door, one of the secretaries called out, "Dr. Sherman, there's somebody here to see you."

David stopped and turned back in the direction of the voice. A rather tall man with graying hair and sharp, distinctive features was standing next to the office door. His gray suit indicated he must be a lawyer. Doctors and reporters didn't dress that conservatively, and no one else bothered coming out. On second glance, the man looked familiar. Where had he seen him?

"Dr. Sherman?" the man said. "I don't know if you remember me. I'm Paul Garrett. Can we talk?"

New York

The knoll is insulated from the rest of Central Park by a high stand of oak and evergreen trees, and from many angles it is even difficult to see the Upper West Side apartment buildings. At the top of the knoll where the grass is the thickest, a large, almond-shaped rock juts out defiantly to form a promontory on which one can sit and gaze and contemplate the miniature valley it overlooks. Only one path leads into the area, it isn't near the pond or playing fields, and so most of the time the area isn't inhabited. In the spring, when the red and orange wildflowers come out, it is one of the most serene and lovely places in New York, a haven for those few who know about it.

Amanda looked forward to being there by herself. But as she came up the path through the trees, some-one was sitting on the rock, and it was too late to stop and turn around without seeming awkward or fright-ened. He was a large, bearded man who must have been in his late forties. His tie was pulled loose and his sport jacket was folded on the rock next to him.

He looked up as soon as Amanda entered the knoll and sensed her surprise.

"Oh, I'm sorry," she said. "I didn't mean to disturb you."

"Not at all," he replied. "It's a public park. Please join me." He spoke with a strong Brooklyn accent, but not lower class; not the cliché type. Instead, it was the deep, even, and very pronounced voice she associated with people who'd gone to City College during its intellectual heyday.

"My name is Nathaniel Kagan," he introduced him-self. He indicated a place for her on the rock. When she hesitated he said, "Don't worry. I'm perfectly safe. I'm a rabbi."

All she could think of to say was, "Really?"

He looked up to the sky and raised his right hand, palm forward. "As God—such as He may be—is my witness."

She sat down.

He looked around, as if taking in the beauty of the place for the first time, and asked, "Do you come here often?"

"All the time. I find it very peaceful. What about you?"

"This is the first time, though I've lived in New York my whole life. I don't know why I'm here, to tell you the truth. I decided to take a break from my office, and I ended up here by instinct. I just followed my nose, I guess. Or maybe I followed your nose; I don't know." She smiled. "I'm getting a real sense of déjà vu here, though. I feel like I've had a mental picture of this place all along."

"That's funny," Amanda said. "When I first came here I felt the same way."

"Life is full of mysteries." He was staring at her breasts, she thought, and she felt a tremor of nervousness. Then she realized she was wearing her "Aurora Illuminates!" T-shirt and relaxed.

"What's an Aurora and what does it illuminate?" he asked.

"Oh, it's a magazine. A science magazine I edit. Oh, I guess I should introduce . . . my name is Amanda West." She extended her hand.

"I'm rather interested in science myself," Kagan said. "At least certain aspects of science. I'll be speaking downtown at the anti-nuclear rally."

"I was thinking of covering it," Amanda admitted. "I think it represents a real trend."

"Let's hope so."

"It's kind of surprising to see a rabbi involved with scientific issues."

"Not really, although my congregants would rather I stayed out of all of it. We men of the cloth are supposed to be concerned with questions of morality and existence. At least that's what they told us in the seminary. And what could be more concerned with those two subjects than the possibility that we'll all blow ourselves off the face of the earth in our mad pursuit of scientific adventurism?"

"You should come write editorials for us, Rabbi. You sound just like the *Aurora* party line!"

"It's just the line of reason, my dear. And more and more people are accepting it every day."

"As you just said, let's hope so."

They sat silently for a long time, and Amanda realized that she felt very comfortable with him, as if they'd known each other for years. Perhaps he just reminded her of someone else she couldn't place at the moment.

"I'm just curious, Rabbi," she said after a while,

"how you resolve your interest in science with religion? I ask because we've got an article coming up, and I know it's going to be a can of worms."

"The orthodoxy of organized science is as strong as the orthodoxy of organized religion, eh?"

"Exactly."

"My wife's father, may he rest in peace, was an orthodox rabbi. Everything he believed in, everything he taught his students and his followers, he didn't have to think about or figure out. He knew where he stood—with God, with the religion, with everything."

"A very secure position to be in."

"Now I live in King's Point, not Brooklyn, and my congregants are a lot more affluent than his were. But that's the least of the things that separate us. I find myself questioning almost everything. Maybe my interest in science is just a manifestation of that."

He looked as if he were surprised he was confiding this much in her.

"Are you saying I've just met an agnostic rabbi?" she asked.

"I'm not sure. I know there's something out there; no question about it. You'd have to be a fool to believe we were all just here the way we are by chance. But you see, one of our traditions in Judaism is intellectual honesty. And for me to say to you here and now that I have faith in an old man with a long white beard dispensing justice from on high . . . that I can't say."

"It's very interesting. I guess I feel just about the same way. Though I'm not Jewish. I guess I'm not anything religious, really. I think I believe in some sort of God."

"I'm afraid I feel more comfortable with the God of Spinoza than the God of Moses. Sort of a unifying force of nature. But then I'm telling you things I don't get to say in public very often."

"Has anything ever happened to you that tangibly made you think, maybe there is a God?"

He looked perplexed. "Why do you ask?"

"I'm sorry. I didn't mean to pry."

"No, that's quite all right. Really. It's just surprising. I did have one experience, actually. About twenty years ago. I was in the hospital. I recovered when I was supposed to die. And I thought to myself, did I just recover by chance, or was it God's will? But then, why was it His will that so many others all around me didn't recover? What made me so special in His eyes? Or does God just play dice with the universe?"

The question riveted her and she didn't know why. It was like it was echoing through her brain and Kagan was merely playing back one of the echoes. "That's incredible," she whispered.

"What is?" he asked.

She bit her lower lip before speaking. "If you don't want to tell me, I understand perfectly, but I have to ask you: what were you in the hospital for?"

"A brain tumor," he answered. "Why?"

Amanda trembled slightly and fingered the scar along her temple but couldn't bring herself to speak.

About two hundred and fifty feet from the knoll, on a direct line with the one pathway through the trees, two men sat on a bank behind a row of waist-high hedges on a hillside. One man stood up and made a large fuss about taking pictures of the birds that darted in and out of the trees above him. He had a heavy Nikon 35mm camera around his neck and every time he moved he scared the birds into flight, so he seldom got any clear photographs. But he was not particularly concerned about wasting film on poor shots, since he was actually there as a lookout and decoy for the other man, who sat patiently behind another Nikon. This camera was mounted on a rigid tripod, was loaded with Kodak 2475 Recording Film and had a 1200mm telephoto lens attached.

"Are you getting good stuff?" the standing photographer asked.

The sitting photographer looked through the horizontal plane viewfinder affixed to the top of the camera, framed the blonde woman and the large, bearded man together on the screen and pressed the button on the motor drive, snapping off twelve pictures in rapid succession.

"Very nice," he said without looking up. "Very nice stuff."

Washington, D.C.

"Tell me, Dr. Garrett, why exactly are you here?"

David Sherman leaned back in his gray swivel chair, supporting his head with one hand.

Paul Garrett sat straight up in the rather uncomfortable molded plastic visitor's chair. He'd said he was forty-one. Except for the prematurely gray hair and the deeply etched lines around the eyes, he could have passed for a good deal younger. He was handsome and athletic-looking—probably a runner—and David imagined he must have been the subject of romantic fantasy for numerous college girls.

Paul slowly breathed out, a long, drawn-out sigh. "I guess I should have come to see someone like you years ago. My wife told me I should often enough. But I guess I always felt that my problems were manageable and as long as I concentrated most of my attention on my work, I could hold myself in some kind of reasonable emotional equilibrium." He paused briefly as David sat upright. His chair creaked. "I guess in light of what's happened recently, I don't feel that way anymore."

In no particular order, he told David everything he could think of that might relate to his psychic state. He told of the recurring image of the anatomy lab that had remained vivid and indelible ever since that year in medical school. He told of the vague, formless fears and gnawing anxieties that related to nothing more concrete than his own sense of himself and who he was.

"That," David commented, "might have been called

classic 'existential anxiety' by the previous generation of psychiatrists, but we don't pay much attention to that explanation anymore. We like to think we're somewhat more sensitive and enlightened." He smiled and raised his hands in a pacifying gesture. "Of course, what the *next* generation will say about us is anybody's guess."

Paul told of the ongoing marital problems with Julia, the woman who, up until the end, he thought he loved, in spite of everything. And he told about the circumstances surrounding her death, immediately following the loss of his closest professional friend and colleague, and how he was now haunted by the visualization of her suffering—the suffering he had caused—and how he had been too blind to alleviate it, or even recognize it. How he had obviously made her life so unbearable that she saw for herself only one way out. By the time he finished his eyes were moist and red.

"And in the face of what I've just told you, at the same time that I mourn for a wife who, if she were still alive, I'd probably be separated from right now . . . at the same time I find myself obsessed with thoughts of a woman I met the week before the . . . the tragedy." He shook his head in confusion. "It's the most powerful, consuming feeling I've ever had toward a woman. So to net it all out for you, Doctor, I'm confused, unnerved, and sufficiently racked with well-deserved guilt to know I need some kind of help."

David picked up a pencil and began lightly drumming it against the edge of the desk. "I can say that it's perfectly understandable that you'd be confused after all you've obviously been through. And what you said about the other woman—it's not at all unusual under the circumstances. If nothing else, perhaps I can help alleviate your guilty feelings about her. But one thing still confuses *me*, Dr. Garrett . . . may I call you Paul?"

"Please."

"Just why did you come to me? There are plenty of good psychiatrists up in Boston."

"It's no big mystery, really. I'm fairly well known in

what you might call the intellectual and social circles of Boston, and I thought it would be best to stay as far removed from that as I could if I was going to seek treatment. I didn't want anyone talking about me at parties and I thought I would probably be more candid with the doctor if he was someone totally removed from my own element. I'm a consultant to the American Academy of Science and I'm down in Washington at least once a month anyway, so I figured this would be the logical city to look in."

"But why not a private psychiatrist? I don't have any private patients."

"I didn't want to go to a private-practice doctor for the same reasons. They're too much of a cohesive group and I know too many of them socially and professionally. But after meeting you at the Hollisters' party—which is, by the way, where I met the woman I mentioned—you struck me as being pretty sensible and down-to-earth, and I figured you could probably help me as much as anyone."

"I'm moved by your faith. I don't know if I can live up to it."

"I'm not expecting miracles, Dr. Sherman. Just someone to talk to."

"David, please."

"You'll take me on, then?"

"You're already my most interesting case. When would you like to start?"

"How about today?"

"All right. Give me a little bit to think about before we meet for real. These feelings of internal conflict you say have been getting worse lately, how long would you say you've had them? Or, another question we use in psychiatry these days is, how long have you not been feeling completely like yourself?"

"If I had to take a guess, I'd say off and on for twenty years. But I can't really give you specifics on how I feel. All I can do is talk around it."

"In my line of work we often get where we're going by roundabout ways, just as you do in yours," David said. "But can you think of what might have happened twenty years ago that could have started you feeling the way you do now?"

"I know one thing," Paul stated with assurance.

David blinked, not expecting such a sudden break in the rhythm of the interview.

"I was in a hospital in New York with a brain tumor," Paul went on calmly, "and I knew I was going to die."

After seeing Paul out the front door of the building, David returned to his office and found both Margie Ferenbach and a serving of cold, limp chicken sitting on his desk.

"I was afraid you were unreachable for the day," she said, her large brown eyes betraying obvious pleasure at seeing him. "I was about to give Chicken Little here a decent burial." She indicated the Holly Farms package sharing the desk top with her. David unwrapped it and picked at it with instantly greasy, disgusting fingers.

"How's our friend in the suit?" she asked.

"Fascinating. A really brilliant guy. Confidentially, I understand he may be in line for the Nobel Prize in physics. He had a supposedly terminal brain tumor about twenty years ago and recovered."

"You think he has organic brain syndrome?"

"That's always something to consider in a patient presenting with known brain history. But I did a complete mental status exam and just for the hell of it, I did a Rorschach, too."

"Schizophrenic?"

"I seriously doubt it."

"You sound like you're really into this case."

"I guess I am." David felt almost embarrassed, sensing there was something wrong in becoming so instantly involved with a single patient. But there was an undeniable charge in being able to deal with someone who wasn't just the general run-of-the-mill uneducated, alcoholic indigent psychotic who frequented St. Elizabeth's; the type who didn't get any better or any worse as a result of treatment. The type who, while certainly deserving care, made a psychiatrist feel his medical education had been a waste.

But here perhaps was someone David could have an impact on. He didn't place such great faith in medicine as to suppose that there was a solution to every problem, or an answer to every question. But if there was a rationale to the way Paul Garrett felt, or a key to his unhappiness, he would try to find it.

Once again he felt excited about psychiatry. Once again, he had an actual mind to work with, rather than the absence of one.

Chapter Six

The emotional symbolism of that year in medical school, and specifically the anatomy class, was a key to Paul Garrett's psyche; of that much David was convinced. It came up almost right away in their first full session together, vivid and haunting, without any prodding on David's part.

The image didn't end with the professor's list or the moment of silence at the end of the term. It took in almost everything.

In the lobby outside the anatomy lab there were four tall, room-length glass cases with five or six glass shelves in each one, Paul recalled. All the cases were filled with preserved human specimens. A permanent exhibit of medical gore and related subjects. The best of what had come across those gleaming steel tables.

Everything was there and Paul remembered all of it. A yellowed, wrinkled, disembodied foot and lower leg sewn shut at the knee . . . just standing there by itself against its metal support. A knee joint in flexed position, just as sallow, just as unrelated to an entire body. A thigh-pelvis insertion. Pieces. Chunks of people.

Then there were the babies . . . dead babies, pitched slightly forward from the head and shoulders, floating mystically in clouded jars of formalin. Next to them were smaller babies . . . creatures that never made it as far as birth, that never had the opportunity to develop a personality, that never—so far as could be divined from the current state of the medical art—entertained a thought or willed an action. Day and night they floated naked in their jars, behind their glass walls. Silently.

But there was one specimen in the center case that made him jump every time he turned the corner and came upon it, even though he tried to prepare himself each time for the confrontation. It was a head, a part of a head, the sagittal section of a Negro male. A slice two inches thick from fuzzy black scalp to Adam's apple right down the middle. It was all there and perfectly preserved—hair, skin, cranium, brain, sinus cavities, eyeball. And it was just like in the anatomy books. But there was more to it, and that was devastating.

There was an expression on the partial face. Closed eyes, closed mouth, absolute serenity. And whether the man died and was sliced down the middle with that expression or whether it was put there on him afterward to try to say that he didn't mind being like this for the rest of forever, Paul could not tell. And either way it did not matter. Either way, what it looked like to him, was frozen terror.

"But if you went through a year of medical school, you had plenty of experience with cadavers," David pointed out.

Paul shook his head emphatically. They were sitting in the living room of David's undersized, overpriced Foggy Bottom townhouse, opposite each other in diagonal corners, which David felt made the room seem a marginally tolerable size.

"This was different," Paul explained. "All the cadavers were the same. No expression, no personality. We cut them apart according to instructions and then they took them away, and that was that. But this one was so purposeful, so willed, so arranged. It was like it kept reminding you that this whole majestic thing we call 'Man,' guided by the human brain, the most transcendent thing in the universe, is nothing but meat, just like everything else. And the expression on the face . . . the piece of the face . . . was just an illusion. It was just a dead piece of meat. But . . ."

"But what?"

"But at one time, it walked around and loved and

talked and hated and thought and suffered. And I couldn't help but wonder every time I passed it whether it still had any capacity to suffer, or whether that part of its brain that was still there could do anything for it, or whether even in death it missed the rest of the brain, which had undoubtedly been incinerated long ago, not being part of the exhibit."

David had to admit he found the whole image a little chilling himself. He stared for a moment out the darkened window and wished he had conducted this discussion during daylight hours. "You were only in medical school a year?" he asked.

"That's right. I got sick in the spring of my freshman year."

"This was the . . ."

"The brain tumor. Oligodendroglioma of the right temporal lobe."

"What do you want to tell me about it?"

"A feeling of total helplessness."

"And hopelessness?"

"Sure. I remember arriving at the Goddard Institute in New York, where the doctors from Yale referred me, and just before I walked in I thought of the line from Dante, written on the gates of Hell: 'All hope abandon, ye who enter here.'"

"How long were you at Goddard, Paul?"

"Almost four months. Although when I got there, I just assumed it was forever, however long that turned out to be. There must have been about fifteen or twenty other patients on the floor, all with what they called 'guarded prognosis.' That meant the doctors wouldn't, or couldn't, admit to us we were all going to die and there was nothing they could do for us."

"Was Norbert Ramsey the neurosurgeon at Goddard yet when you were there?"

"Oh yes. He was already getting a lot of publicity for his daring operations. Most of the other patients revered him like he was God. Their only hope for salvation."

"I take it then you didn't think of him that way?"

"I thought of him as a healthy person when I was sick, and I resented him for it."

"But he did make you healthy again."

"I guess he did." Paul's expression didn't change.

"Of the fifteen or twenty patients you mentioned, how many others survived?"

"Not more than one or two. I'm not sure. I was never much involved with any of them. It wasn't a place where you shared your suffering . . . or your joy."

"Did you have any feelings about coming out of Goddard alive when most of the others didn't?"

"I'm not sure I follow you," Paul said.

"In psychiatry we speak of a condition known as 'survivor guilt,' in which an individual feels anguish over surviving a situation that others close to him didn't. It was a tremendous problem with survivors of the concentration camps, who felt that their own salvation was, under the circumstances, as arbitrary and unjust as the deaths of their friends and families in the same camps."

"I don't know if I've thought about it in those terms," Paul stated. "But as a scientist, I am familiar with the second law of thermodynamics."

"You'll have to refresh my memory," David said.

"Every system, left to itself, will go from a higher energy level to a lower one; everything in the universe moves ultimately toward entropy, toward randomness. I suppose that carries over beyond the realm of molecules."

They continued talking long into the evening, as Paul related with a detachment David found painful the details of his hospitalization and confrontation with the tumor that conventional wisdom said would kill him. He told David about the "bright promise" with which he began his undergraduate career at Harvard, and his acceptance at Yale Medical School. But midway through the first semester the headaches came. And when they combined with the dizziness, with the nausea and the weakness radiating through his arms and legs, he chalked it all up to the pressures of years of academic overreaching and concluded he was probably having a nervous breakdown.

When the brain tumor was finally diagnosed, he was relieved that his psyche was intact and that he was not cracking up. But by the time he left Yale-New Haven Hospital for the Goddard Institute in Manhattan, the relief had turned to despair. And when, after the operation and the weeks of emptiness long past worry, Norbert Ramsey told him the glioma had been arrested, he knew he had already been through too much to rejoice.

"Why didn't you go back to medical school at that point?" David asked.

"After bearing personal witness to the miracles of the healing arts, everyone thought I would dedicate my life to doing for others what Ramsey and his staff had done for me. But nothing could have been further from my thinking."

"So then you decided to go into physics?"

"Yes."

"Why?"

"Because it was safe."

David sat with his feet up on the desk and stared out his office window at the patient who had been washing his Honda for the last hour and a half. The price had been agreed on in advance: one dollar. David had offered more (not a lot more), but the patient, a long-term resident who had his own cottage industry washing cars at the hospital, had carefully determined that the job was worth exactly one dollar. David had the telephone receiver crooked between his shoulder and chin and was waiting for a long-distance line.

He called Goddard Institute's main number and asked the receptionist, "Is there still a Dr. Wendell Fuller on the staff?"

"One moment," came the reply. "I'll connect you."

Several seconds later he heard a pickup and a rousing "Heh-lo!"

"Wendell? It's David Sherman."

"David? Where you been hiding, boy?"

"I'm still here at St. E's."

"They ain't done beat you to the ground there yet?" There was no mistaking Wendell. They had met at Vanderbilt when both men were taking their psychiatric residency. For David, Nashville was a small, provincial hamlet. For Wendell, who had spent all of his formative years in the Pine Mountain community of Jellico, Tennessee, Nashville was a revelation of what life could be like at its fullest and most varied. It was no accident then that the southern mountain boy ended up living and working in New York City. Wendell was the vibrant, high-wired sort that David always lamented not keeping in contact with.

"I wasn't sure if you were still at Goddard," David said.

"Where the hell else would I be? Plenty money here, good facilities, and we's always getting our name in the papers for some new discovery or another." David wondered if it was difficult to maintain the accent and speech rhythm in the decidedly foreign milieu Wendell now found himself in.

"So you get yourself married yet?" Wendell asked.

"No, not yet."

"You ain't queer, are ya? I know about you Yankee boys."

"Not that I know of, Wendell."

"Got yourself a regular girl?"

"Not exactly."

"Well, you oughta hightail it up to the Big Apple, then, boy. I'll get you together with some ladies that'll unravel your socks!"

"Oh yeah?"

"Davey, I'm telling you, these big-city gals is another number entirely. They'll get on you like a heat rash in August; turn you every way but loose!"

David pleasantly imagined himself being turned every way but loose by some tall New York Amazon with a firm stomach.

Wendell interrupted his daydream to ask, "Now what can I do for you, old buddy? Or did you just call to chew the rag?"

"No, there is something. I have a patient who's been through a lot of trauma recently with progressive personality disorder. Recognizing the current stimuli, he still traces his problem back to the time he was hospitalized for a temporal lobe glioma about twenty years ago at Goddard."

"Are you sniffing up some progressive organic brain disease?"

"I don't think so. His IQ is near the ceiling and he doesn't have any orientation problems. I'm convinced the whole thing is psychological."

"Well, what can I do for you, lad?"

"I'm sending him up to see Norbert Ramsey, hoping that talking to his own surgeon can give him some insight. You know all the mystical bugaboo so many brain patients end up with after surgery. And apparently, in all his post-op checkups, Ramsey never offered him much help with his feelings."

"That's no big shock," Wendell commented. "Have you ever met a good neurosurgeon who wasn't an ice man?"

"What I'd like you to do is look up his records for me. I want to know his exact diagnosis, surgical notes, psychiatric comments. He's convinced something happened to him there."

"Well something obviously did."

"And I'm hoping for some clues. I think it might shortcut a lot of psychoanalysis. I just want the guy to be able to function normally without this demon from his past hanging over him."

"What's the fella's name, Davey? I'll get the files out and be back to you in the morning."

David gave him Paul's name and dates of care.

"You'll probably get a pretty florid operative report if Ramsey did the cutting. That son of a bitch writes twelve times as long as the next closest contender. Describes every stitch individually. Writes up an incision like he was opening King Tut's tomb! I swear, he's a damn Agatha Christie. Reading him you're in such suspense waiting to see what he finds under the cranium! Like no one else had done it before."

"Is that how he got so famous? I understand he's something of an egotist."

"Well . . . I guess he's got a right to be. Pretty fair head cutter from everything I've seen."

"My man wasn't overly thrilled with his bedside manner," David commented.

"His privilege, of course," Wendell said. "But from what I've seen of Ramsey, your man might just owe him his life."

Chapter Seven

Chicago

The conference room was rosewood-paneled on one side and glass-walled on the other, and from ninety-two floors up on a clear day, facing the lake was like riding on a flying carpet heading over the horizon. But even though the sky was cloudless and the water a deep azure blue, the effect was lost on the meeting's participants. Since documents were involved, Mr. Kendrick had instructed that the double-backed, light-blocking drapes be drawn shut. Even with the drapes open, the only possible vantage point from which to spy would have been a helicopter with an extremely long lens. But as J. Tyler Kendrick well knew, if it was possible, it had to be guarded against.

As usual, he had the others waiting in the conference room for his arrival so that none of his time would be wasted. If any of the influential guests objected to this arrangement, they could hire someone else to be their watchdog. But so far, no one had complained. He stood over his desk, shoulders hunched and hands spread on either side of the inlaid leather blotter. The desk top was full of written material—letters, memos, statements and reports—all stacked neatly in piles according to urgency, just as compartmentalized as his mind. There were no pictures, memorabilia or other bric-a-brac anywhere on the desk. The numerous gifts and awards he received each year ended up in a cardboard box in his secretary's closet.

A soft buzzer sounded.

"Yes?" he answered.

"The Partners for Progress are ready for you," came

103

a metallic voice from out of the air. Kendrick insisted on an intercom that required no attention on his part. Distractions were always costly.

"Thank you," he replied. He picked up the "Partners" folder from the top of his "Most Urgent" pile and headed out the door and through the outer office, which adjoined the conference room. As he passed his secretary's desk, she spoke into the telephone:

"Universal Oil Corporation. Mr. Kendrick's Office. No, I'm sorry, he can't be disturbed at the moment."

He continued to the conference room without looking back.

As soon as he entered, the uniformed guard on the outside closed the door behind him.

He took his place at the head of the table but did not sit down, knowing he would be standing again in a few seconds. John Christopher, his opposite number at Amalgamated Motors, marveled every time he saw J. Tyler Kendrick. Today he was wearing a trimly cut black three-piece suit with only faintly visible gray pinstripes. Christopher visually followed the line from the gold stirrup buckles on his Gucci loafers to the gold Patek Philippe watch on his wrist, to the gold stickpin in his white dotted tie. From there on up, the dominant color changed to deep bronze, the rich hue of his face and neck, accentuated by steel-gray temples and conditioned by daily exposure to a sun lamp. The Senior Vice-President of the Universal Oil Corporation *looked* like a retouched studio portrait of a corporate executive.

"Gentlemen, and lady," Kendrick began, making sure to acknowledge Thalia Reinhardt amidst the room full of men, "spread out on the table in front of you are photostats of the most important of Dr. Paul Garrett's working papers, taken from his office at the Massachusetts Institute of Technology and then immediately replaced after copying. These papers have been scrutinized by trusted research scientists here at Universal Oil and by other confidential consultants who report directly to me."

Leave it to Kendrick to let everybody know from time to time that he alone runs the show, Christopher thought to himself.

"As we've suspected ever since his twin articles appeared in *Physical Review* and *Annalen der Physik*, Dr. Garrett is making undeniable progress in his attempt to establish a workable and interchangeable relationship between gravity, electromagnetism, and the nuclear forces. This concept, which had eluded scientists since before the time of Einstein, is commonly referred to as the Unified Field Theory. Now let me remind you all, this work is purely theoretical and as much as anything in science, is the work of genius and individual imagination. So while our people can evaluate Garrett's formulas now that they've seen them, they can't work forward from them the way he can. In fact, there probably aren't a dozen physicists in the world capable of picking up on his work."

"Well, if this is so highly theoretical, Tyler, why are we so worried about it?" Thalia Reinhardt asked. She was a formidable, large-busted woman with strong square features and metallic-blue hair, whose soft, rather grating Georgia accent masked her iron will. Of all the people in the room, she held Kendrick in the least reverence.

"Let me back up to give you an example," Kendrick explained. "Early in this century, Albert Einstein came out with his Special Theory of Relativity. At the time, it was startling, even iconoclastic, but it was just an abstract theory of the way things move in relation to each other. Within twenty-five years, scientists had begun to put that theory to practical use; that is, atomic energy. Einstein was also working on the Unified Field Theory at the time of his death in the mid-nineteen fifties, but never made much progress with it.

"But there has been progress since then, most notably from Dr. Garrett. And our experts have determined that if a Unified Field Theory as all-encompassing as Einstein predicted could be worked out, there wouldn't be a twenty-five-year lag time between theory and practical application. We're talking about five to seven years, by our best estimates."

The people around the table began to sit up and listen with closer attention. When Kendrick began giving figures in years, they knew he must be about to speak in terms that affected them directly.

"And equally significant," he went on, "if Garrett is completely successful in his theoretical work, once he publishes his findings, an army of scientists and technicians will begin work on the practical applications of using magnetism to affect and alter gravity."

"And what *are* the practical applications?" Thalia Reinhardt persisted. She was Vice-President for Development of The Marshall Group, an internationally diversified holding company based in Dallas. She was given full credit for personally heading off the recent Justice Department antitrust action against Marshall with her carefully orchestrated campaign of quiet threats and promises. And of all the people in the room, she was the one Kendrick most respected.

He stood rigidly straight to enhance the effect of his delivery while addressing Thalia Reinhardt directly. "That's an extremely complicated question and we're preparing a detailed presentation to the full Partners for Progress meeting in Switzerland. But just to give you some idea, one possible outgrowth is an extremely cheap, essentially limitless, and easily accessible form of energy anywhere in the world, at any time. And as I say, that's just *one* possibility."

The Arab who had been staring at the white drape, imagining Lake Michigan on the other side, suddenly turned toward the speaker, his eyes registering incredulity.

"But how do we know Garrett is really onto something?" John Christopher asked. "You said yourself, physicists have been working on this problem for years."

"Let me call your attention to this document," Kendrick responded, reaching for the photocopy closest to him and holding it up before the assembly. "These are notes found in Dr. Harry Gillette's briefcase at the time of his death in Boston. They represent the transcription of Garrett's latest breakthrough, given over the telephone to Gillette. Next to this is Gillette's own mathematical analysis of Garrett's ideas. In the opinion of all the consultants available to the Partners for Progress, this latest development indicates significant progress. Now, some simple math will give you the seriousness of the problem. If Garrett can complete his work within the next three or four years, and it takes six more to reach the first practical stages, that's only ten years. And since there are at least thirty to forty years of proven oil reserves remaining on this planet—to use an example that affects my own company—that means about twenty years of worthless product and worthless equipment. Of course, we are heavily involved in researching alternative energies that *we* can control and profit from, but there is no way we could assure ourselves of control of something this broad and basic. And make no mistake—this research affects every company and industry represented in this room. And that's why I felt it necessary to put the matter before the Partners for Progress steering committee, even before we convene in Switzerland."

"It was a wise and understandable action," the Arab commented.

"Do I take it that this Dr. Gillette's death falls under the heading of 'untimely'?" Thalia Reinhardt asked.

"It was unavoidable," Kendrick explained. "I don't want to burden the meeting with matters of past procedure. Suffice it to say it was a judgment call with which I happen to agree."

The audience seemed to accept his statement without further explanation.

"Now, to bring you completely up to date, Dr. Garrett's wife, Julia, took her own life last week through an overdose of barbiturates while he was out of town. As far as we know, he has suspended his work since then, has not been to his MIT office or laboratory, and has effectively dropped out of sight. How long this will continue, we have no way of knowing."

The Arab asked, "Why do we not have this man eliminated, if at this stage his work is unique? The Partners obviously have the means at their disposal."

Kendrick sighed and rubbed his chin in thought for a moment. "This is something of a delicate point," he said. "Though the death of Mrs. Garrett appears to be the result of a successful suicide attempt, there may be more to it than we realize. It could mask a more sophisticated motive. Mrs. Garrett—or the second *Dr.* Garrett, more accurately—was also a physicist, connected with Harvard University, and it is quite possible that she was working with her husband. If, in fact, it develops that she was killed by agents of foreign powers, who first learned from her more about her husband's work than we now know, some other nation —most probably in the Eastern bloc—could exploit Dr. Garrett's work even before the United States. And that would be a worse case scenario than even the one we'll face at our full meeting. So to answer your question, sir, at least for the time being, we have to keep Dr. Garrett alive, but closely watched. But the situation remains fluid, and I assure you I'll be on top of it."

Washington, D.C.

David Sherman was in his characteristic pose: shoulders pressed to the back of the swivel chair, feet up on the desk, left hand playing with his hair where it began to swirl at the back of his head, twisting it into a knot that would take both hands to untie. When he realized he'd inadvertently reached that point, he dropped the telephone receiver trying to undo his other finger.

"What the hell's going on down there, boy?" Wendell Fuller demanded.

"No problem, Wendell. Now what were you saying?"

"I been reading the file on your man Paul Garrett, Davey."

"Anything unusual?" David asked.

Wendell paused for a moment, and David could sense him thinking about his answer. "Depends on what you consider unusual," he said at last. "Once you get past the Master's literary style, there's nothing out of the ordinary in the surgical notes except that old Norbert decided to shoot for the moon and take the whole damned glioma. And as you know, Davey, that's one hell of a ballsy move. I guess he figured, what the fuck, you know? If the guy's gonna kick in six months to a year anyhow, why not go for the glory and screw the chance of impairing any other function by killing off surrounding tissue. At that point, what the hell's the difference anyway? No, the operation's pretty normal. It's what happened afterward that gets interesting."

"What do you mean, Wendell?"

"I mean the guy lived."

David was silent, so Wendell went on. "David, you're talking about fully resecting an end-stage oligodendroglioma of the temporal lobe in 1959. Shit, I wouldn't have given you a Confederate dime for the chances. Ramsey took a chance, cut out the whole damned thing, evidently cut none of the healthy tissue, and this guy who's supposed to be a goner gets better and there's no recurrence. None! I'd have to say Norbert hit a grand slam there."

"Quite a piece of luck."

"That's what I said. But then I started getting curious, so I took time out from my own busy schedule of ministering to the sick and confused to see who else was in there at the time with end-stage tumors. And do you know what? I found two more with almost identical circumstances! A ten-year-old girl named Amanda Jane West . . . pretty hoo-hah name, Amanda, don't you think?"

"There must be a lot of girls in New York named

Amanda," David said. Wasn't there an Amanda West at Sandy's party, he thought.

"Ain't none in Jellico. Okay, she had a medullo blastoma; not too uncommon in a kid that age. But try to rip one of those out. How many of them live? Then there's a fellow in his mid-twenties name of Nathaniel Abraham Kagan—gotta be a Jew or a Baptist with a name like that—and he presents with a glioblastoma multiforme."

"What's that exactly?"

"In this case, it's a grade-three astrocytoma of the frontal lobe that's invaded the opposite hemisphere."

"That's bad news."

"About the worst. And yet all three of 'em walk out of the place on their own two feet."

"You get any insights from the psychiatric notes, Wendell?"

"Nothing to write a book about. All three of them were depressed, felt singled out, the whole bit. You don't need Kübler-Ross to figure that out for you. But the point is, you take someone with a cancer growing in their brain—and this Amanda West was only a kid— and you can write up any psychiatric report you please and I'm not gonna tell you it's unusual. Sure your man Garrett's got emotional problems even though it's been twenty-odd years since he did his time here. I'd be sure as hell surprised if he didn't. And, David, you read the same books as me . . . you tell someone for almost sure they's gonna die and let 'em stew with that awhile, then you tell them no, turns out they's gonna live after all, that don't mean they gets over what you told them first so fast. You follow me?"

"Sure, I know that," David replied. "I don't know what I was looking for. Maybe a clue, that's all. I guess I was so thrilled to have an intelligent, complicated patient like Paul Garrett after all this time that I wasn't willing to admit his problem might be as simple as what it's turning out to be."

"That's what we're all looking for," Wendell said

wistfully. "The definitive case. I used to dream of finding a patient with something so off the wall they'd have to call it 'Fuller's Syndrome.' But I'm through with that shit now. Seeing all the rock stars of medicine up here in New York, folks like Ramsey and Morrow right here at Goddard, I decided you can have the prominence for your own self. It don't take much to make me happy anymore. Just eight hours of work, doing my best for whatever patients they throw at me, and bedding down a stewardess at least three nights a week."

"I'm glad to see you've got your priorities so well ordered," David commented. "It's a sign of good mental health."

"Ain't it though?" Wendell agreed. "Listen boy, anything else I can do for you, you just holler now, hear?"

"I sure will. And I'll make sure to see you next time I'm in New York."

"Just give me two hours' notice and I'll get you a stewardess, too. Give me three hours and I'll get you one from SAS. Make your tongue stick to your teeth, I'm telling you."

David's eager grin vanished suddenly as he looked down from the ceiling to see Margie Ferenbach occupying the visitor's chair next to his desk. He hung up and attempted to assume a businesslike demeanor, which Margie saw through instantly.

"And who were you talking to?" she inquired.

"I was discussing a patient," he answered defensively.

"She must be some knockout from that look on your face. What's her problem—nymphomania?"

"Never mind. You want to do something tonight?"

"What did you have in mind?"

"What would you like to do?"

"Do psychiatrists always answer questions with other questions?"

"What do you think about that?"

"David! Come on!" she protested.

"How do you feel about yourself when you talk like that?" he continued.

"I'm leaving." She turned and started for the door.

"Hey, wait! Margie! Come back here." He caught up with her in the hallway. She stood there sternly and rigidly, her arms straight down and tight to her sides. David grasped her affectionately by the shoulders, trying to get her to loosen up, while the normal collection of residents paced by obliviously.

"Sometimes you drive me crazy!" she declared.

"Then you're certainly in the right place," he said.

New York

The *Aurora* office was in chaos. All the color proofs for the next issue had come back out of register and the art director, Jerry Cassell, was running around to anyone who would listen threatening to commit hara-kiri. The majority vigorously encouraged him. Nancy Flanagan even offered to lend him the knife. A contingent of junior high school journalism students just happened to be touring the facilities when a process server arrived to inform Amanda she was being sued for libel by an inventor whose supposed perpetual-motion machine she'd maligned in print. The accountant from the Scientific League had stopped by to go over the books, which were over a month out-of-date. And the receptionist had suddenly become sick to her stomach and run off to the ladies' room, leaving all the telephone lines ringing to no avail. If one more thing came up, Amanda swore she was going to run upstairs to the pastoral offices of *Antiques and Collectibles* and hide out for a while.

In the midst of the bedlam, as she was telling the junior high school kids and their approving teacher that the most important traits they had to acquire were accuracy and reliability, Paul Garrett walked through the front door.

She momentarily lost her breath and felt dizzyingly faint, with a tingling sensation in her fingers as she realized that, yes, he actually was here. Somehow, from somewhere, what she had wanted most of all since that night at the Watergate West had just happened. What he was doing here, for how long, under what circumstances . . . those were all details. They could wait.

She sputtered briefly in the middle of her statement about maintaining concentration, while her mind raced over to the door to greet him, and when she finally recovered her mental equilibrium she abruptly changed pace with, "Ah . . . and now my assistant editor, Nancy Flanagan, will tell you about meeting deadlines."

Nancy, who had been only half listening somewhere in the back while she edited a particularly nonlucid piece of copy from a distinguished contributor, shot her boss a helpless, bewildered look and found the students turned toward her as Amanda made her way over to Paul.

He stood by the empty receptionist's desk, and when she reached him she stared up into his eyes for a moment and said quietly, "It's so good to see you I can't tell . . ." Then she stopped herself, swallowed once and said, "Come on into my office."

He followed her, and when she'd closed the door to the small cubicle she turned and threw her arms around his neck while he hugged her tightly.

"Oh, Paul . . . I was hoping so much you'd call me. I was already worrying about how forward it would look if I called you." She laughed self-consciously and found herself crying at the same time.

"I've been thinking about you ever since you left Washington," he said. "I . . . I haven't been able to get you out of my thoughts."

"I'm so sorry about your wife. So very sorry. I know how you must feel and . . . I just can't . . ."

He held up his hand to silence her, for which she was grateful. "It was terrible . . . unbelievable," he stated in a low voice, and she could tell that he had nothing else to say on the matter at the moment. He smiled painfully in a conscious effort to change the subject. "But tell me . . . how have you been?"

"Oh . . . I've been . . . well, you can see from the office, I guess. I did try to call you, actually."

"Did you? When?"

She thought back to that agonizing hour in the police station, then said only, "All that can wait." Now it was she who was trying to change the subject. "How long are you in New York?"

"I'm not sure. A few days."

"Do you have a place to stay?"

"Not yet."

"Please stay with me."

"All right," he said with the same even tone of voice.

Picking up her suede shoulder bag from the back of a chair, she fumbled through her wallet until she produced the spare key to her apartment. "I'd go home with you now if I could, but I've got an interview this afternoon. An interesting guy I met in the park . . ."

"Oh?"

"Not to worry," she laughed. "He's a rabbi from Long Island who's very involved with Zionism but who's also active in the anti-nuclear movement. We're doing a story about . . ." In the middle of the sentence she realized she was running on. "You should meet him," she concluded. "You'd find him interesting." Why couldn't she think of what to say to Paul? Why was she sounding and acting so nervous?

"Listen, Amanda, I can see that you're busy. Why don't I leave you here and we can catch up around dinner time?"

"No, sit down for a few minutes, Paul. It's not that terrible." She tried hard to keep the eagerness out of her voice. She motioned him to the black wooden spindled armchair with a Barnard College crest on the back. She sat on the corner of her desk. "So tell me in a few words, what are you here for?"

He took a deep breath, which he held for several seconds, making Amanda worry that she'd somehow asked the wrong question. "I don't know if I can tell you in a few words," he said. "But what I came to do, you might want to do with me."

"I don't understand."

"I came to examine my past, help jog some of my old memories, to try to get some insight into what I'm all about now; who I really am."

"I'm afraid you're being very elliptical or I'm being very dense. How can I help you with your memories?"

"I don't know if you can help me with my memories, but you are one; dim, but as I reconstruct it, unmistakable."

The look on Amanda's face indicated bafflement bordering on terror.

"Thinking back on it, I remember a very pretty, very frightened ten-year-old girl, with pale skin and yellow hair. From somewhere in the midwest, I think. Her mother was with her, and her father came to visit often, with two brothers."

As he spoke the incredible realization sank in and Amanda turned to him, wide-eyed with incredulous shock. "How did you . . . I don't understand . . ."

"I was there too, Amanda. I was at Goddard with you. I was one of the survivors."

She just sat and looked at him in stunned silence, grasping the edge of the desk with her left hand for security. Finally, she said, "How did you make the connection? You couldn't have recognized that ten-year-old child when you met me."

"There'll be time for the whole story. But what I wanted to tell you was, I'm going to see Dr. Ramsey tomorrow afternoon, to see what I can uncover about myself. Do you want to come, too?"

"No," she said, almost instantaneously. "No, that's not something I want to experience right now."

"That's okay. Believe me, I understand. I just wanted to ask you."

"Thank you."

Paul stood up. "I've really got to leave now. Shall I just wait for you at your apartment later on?"

"That'll be fine. The address is on the key ring: four twenty-nine East Thirty-Sixth. Just tell the doorman you're staying with me."

"He won't say anything?"

"He never has."

Paul just smiled.

"Oh come on! My reputation isn't as bad as all that." She stopped and they looked at each other. "I'm glad you're here, Paul," she said.

"So am I."

They embraced; a long, passionate enfolding of body to body.

"See you later," he said. "Shall I leave your door open?"

"Yeah, that's good." She watched him walk out of the office.

Her head was swimming with so many conflicting ideas and impressions. His coming in like this was so surprising in itself. And then the . . . the Goddard business. It was so incredible. All they'd had in common up to now . . . that psychic rapport, that emotional empathy, and now this. How unbelievable, that this man, whom she already felt so much for after one night together, should have been associated with the worst, most horrifying experience she was ever likely to live through. Ha. That was a funny choice of words. The most unlikely part of the whole experience was that she *did* live through it. One part of her even wanted to go with Paul tomorrow morning. But she knew she couldn't do it. She knew she couldn't yet—more than twenty years later—face it directly.

And yet time had not dimmed that memory in the slightest. She had been a little past nine. A pretty, yellow-haired, shy, serious girl living with her parents and two older brothers in Evanston, Illinois. She remembered herself as being totally undistinguished in every way. Bright, they all told her. But isn't every proud father's only daughter bright? That's something you just take for granted. She was popular in school, but not exceptionally popular. The boys made lewd comments about her when they huddled together on their side of the playground and the other girls teased her about it. But they talked that way about most of the girls.

No, Amanda recalled, placing herself back in the mindset of the child she had been, the first truly notable act of her life was the growing of a tumor inside her head—a feat she accomplished without even thinking about it. Without even being aware of it. But after the crushing headaches began and her eyesight started getting blurry and she couldn't walk straight anymore . . . and finally, in vague terms, they told her what was going on in there, she couldn't figure out how her own brain—which everybody knew was for thinking—could have done that to her by itself. She *must* have thought that tumor into growing. Why else would it be there? And then if she died, well, that was her own fault, wasn't it?

They had all told her—her mother and her father and all the doctors and everybody—that it had nothing to do with anything she'd thought or done. It was just one of those things that happened.

Just one of those things that happened.

But how, the adult Amanda wondered, how do you explain a fatal brain tumor to a child whose entire view of the world and her own life is based on concrete causality? Something happens because something else made it happen, right? So without benefit of a more compelling explanation, she had concluded that she'd given herself a brain tumor. After all, there were all those new thoughts happening in there. Anger and aggression and longing—deep physical longing . . . not love, just desire, which everybody knew was wrong—

all mixing around in there and Jesus, just taking over her whole brain. Taking it over from all the clean, responsible, respectable thinking that had been there before. No wonder her brain couldn't handle it all. No wonder it had started to rot. There was only one way out. It just popped itself off a tumor.

At the hospital, the doctor had asked Amanda if she'd like to go wait in the other room with the nurse for a few minutes. There were plenty of interesting magazines to read because (he said with a smile) she was too old to want to play with the dolls, wasn't she? Only much later did she find out what the doctor was telling her parents. The best hope, they said, and keep in mind, please, that it's a slim one, is to get her to the best place they could find. One of those centers that sees "a lot of this sort of thing; much more than we do here." And the best hope, they all agreed, was Dr. Norbert Ramsey at the Goddard Institute in New York.

So off they went. Amanda and her mother and her father and, when they could, her two brothers. Everything was going to be fine, her mother had assured her. But the old cliché is true—you can't lie to children. They're too primed for the truth.

And how, Amanda thought back, how can you lie about what she could see was happening? How could you lie about having to puncture this pretty, shy, introspective ten-year-old with countless needles and shove one tube down her throat and another up her rectum and shave the whole side of her head bald like that man Yul Brynner in *The King and I* and deliver her budding body, stark naked and shivering uncontrollably, to that cold porcelain operating room? At that point, *everything else* becomes fantasy and make-believe. That searingly bright room and the doctor who covers up his face with a mask before he cuts you with his knife are the only realities.

In the weeks and months after the operation, the headaches and the blurred vision went away, the bandages came off and the yellow tresses grew back. And the only tangible souvenir of that apocalyptic experience was the scar near her forehead, which was mostly covered up by hair and didn't look so dreadful, anyway.

But of course, everything had changed. Except for the fact that she was still breathing, everything had changed.

"I guess I can tell you now, honey," her father later told her. "I thought we were going to lose you there for a while."

She had thought so too. In fact, she had known so, but couldn't share with them the knowledge they had been too paralyzed by love and grief and terror to share with her.

But that was her triumph. No doubt about it. If she had caused the tumor in the first place, as she knew inside herself she had, she must have cured it, too. Dr. Ramsey had assisted, but only the way a baby doctor assists a mother in getting out a baby she's already grown herself.

"I fixed you up so your head is going to be even smarter than before!" Dr. Ramsey had said when he first came to see her on rounds. But whatever it was, she knew she had done it, not him.

And now, having just had an unexpected and shocking visit from her new love, a fellow survivor of the Goddard horror, she was about to interview another survivor. Jesus! She'd said something to Paul about Rabbi Kagan, but she'd forgotten to tell him the most important thing! How many separate coincidences could be compounded before a pattern started to emerge . . . before it was revealed that they weren't coincidences at all?

Her mind was reeling, and it must have showed, because when Amanda slung her suede bag over her shoulder and walked out of her office to meet Kagan, Nancy Flanagan asked her, "Are you all right?"

"Ah . . . yeah, I guess so," she answered. "Why?"

"You look a little flushed."

"I just saw someone I wasn't expecting. Brought back a lot of old memories."

"Is everything okay?"

"Yeah, Nance, I'm fine. Thanks. I'm meeting Nathaniel Kagan for an interview. I'll be back later on."

She met him in Greenacre Park, the small refuge on 51st Street between Second and Third avenues. He was sitting toward the back, under one of the young sycamore trees that sprouted up through an opening in the maroon brick, watching the clear water cascading down the sculpted rear wall. From there it flowed into a narrow moat that ran along the two side walls of the park, physically separating it from the adjacent buildings. To Amanda, the small area was also separated in spirit. Closed off as it was on three sides, it gave the sensation of being removed from the rest of midtown. The lush potted shrubs and heavy, oak-beamed trellises over the entrance and west side gave the place the peaceful look of a grape arbor. It was Amanda's favorite meeting place near her office, and she scheduled her rendezvous there as often as possible.

"I hope you haven't been waiting long," she said as she sat down next to him at the small round table. Through the trees they could see the sheer aluminum and black face of the Citicorp Center.

"I just got here myself," Nat Kagan replied. "But it's such a lovely setting, I could sit here the rest of the day."

The park was almost empty. One child played with his nanny near the steps to the street, a casually dressed man fed his dog, a beautiful, huge German shepherd, at one of the other tables, and a middle-aged man in a business suit sat reading the newspaper on the ramp by the refreshment window. Other than that, Amanda and Nat had the space to themselves.

"So . . . how have you been since that pleasant afternoon in Central Park?" he asked her.

"I've been well." She smiled. "But I've been thinking about a lot of things. I hope you won't mind talking about them before we get into the actual purpose of the interview."

"Of course not. A good rabbi learns to talk about

almost anything. What's on your mind?" he asked kindly.

It started out with the revelation Paul had just delivered, a fact that instantly bonded the three of them together, as any survivors of life-threatening ordeals always remain bonded together.

"Maybe it wasn't by chance then that the three of us have become aware of each other like this," Nat commented.

Amanda's eyes brightened, intrigued. "What do you mean?"

"Maybe we were somehow directed to each other to provide support and strength." He noticed the glow of excitement fade from her eyes. "You look disappointed by my answer."

"No, not really," she said. "It's just that I thought you were going to . . . to offer some idea, something more concrete that would explain all the other coincidences, too. I guess I was looking for something less 'spiritual' and more down to earth."

"Coincidences?"

"Yes. For example, all three of us are committed to science in one way or another; you and I differently than Paul, but all deeply involved. Or another thing—after we met I looked up some articles that had been written about you. You attended the Bertrand Russell War Crimes Tribunal in Sweden in the late nineteen-sixties."

"That's right. I was a great admirer of Russell's. Had the pleasure to meet and talk to him on several occasions."

"I was there, too," Amanda said. "And I felt the same way about him. Or what you told me about your religious beliefs—the universe based on natural order. I'm not Jewish, in fact I don't have any organized religion, but I feel the same way you do about that. And so does Paul, from what I've been able to gather so far."

"Those are interesting coincidences," Nat admitted, "but . . ."

"I'm sure there's more. Do you play a musical instrument?"

"I used to play the violin, but I haven't had much occasion in the last several years."

"I've always wanted to play the violin," she stated triumphantly. "In fact, whenever I hear chamber music, I always fantasize that I'm playing before an audience. Then . . . we met in the park. I do a lot of walking in the park when I want to be alone. And whenever I have the chance, I like to go hiking in the mountains. Do you?"

Nat grinned. "Sorry to break your perfect score. When I want to be alone with myself and my thoughts, I go sailing. I have my own boat."

"So does Paul! He told me that the first time we met. Then there are lots of little things . . . sentences you both start that I know I can complete; things like that. I'm very anxious to have you meet him. I just know there's a pattern somewhere, an answer of some kind."

"The answers we get are almost exclusively determined by the questions we ask," he mused.

"There it is again. I don't remember ever having heard that statement before, but it sounds so familiar I feel as if I've said it myself. It's like déjà vu, only stronger. The way you said you felt when you came into that knoll in Central Park for the first time—like you'd been led there by your own instincts."

"That's right. I had a mental picture of the place, though I'm sure I'd never been there. And what led me there, out of the whole park to choose from, I have no idea."

The casually dressed man with the German shepherd was stroking and massaging the dog around the neck, and seemed to be talking to him. The child by the front steps was being tugged by his nanny down 51st Street and toward Second Avenue. And the middle-aged man in the business suit had drifted over to the refreshment window, which was built out of a brick wall on the street side of the park. Amanda realized that, selfishly, she hoped no one else would come in and sit down. The opportunity for Manhattan apartment dwellers to have outside spaces to themselves was rare.

The next few seconds were a blur. Amanda became aware of movement around her, and by the time she looked up, the German shepherd was racing toward them, its eerily translucent eyes fixed on them like a homing device. She screamed. Nat looked up and the dog was jumping up onto the chair next to him.

He crossed his forearms in front of his face as the dog, pushing off on its hind legs, lunged for him. He jerked involuntarily back in his chair. But as the dog jumped, the chair skidded out from under it and came to rest on its side. Snarling, the animal fell on its shoulder on the brick pavement, allowing Nat a moment to recover.

But a split second later it had regained its bearing and was lunging for both of them. With the one movement he had time for before the dog reached them, Nat pushed Amanda in the middle of her back with enough force to send her crashing to the pavement. She screamed again as she saw the dog land on Nat's chest, virtually burying him under the surging mass of fur. It was obviously a trained attack dog. It was going right for Nat's neck and looked ready to spring right over to Amanda the instant it had done the job.

Its teeth had already penetrated the rabbi's shoulder and covered his shirt with blood, when they both heard something like a "pop." Suddenly, the shepherd froze in midair, then dropped rigidly to the ground. Its right front leg jerked forward once, then there was no movement at all. The tongue hung limply from the side of the mouth and the eyes were blank. As soon as Nat had recovered enough to stand, he noticed two jagged round holes in the dog's head—one in front above the left eye and the other on the side, forward of the left ear—from which thin streams of blood were trickling. He immediately looked over to where the owner had been sitting, but he was nowhere to be seen. He glanced around for other witnesses, but the middle-aged man with the newspaper could just be seen darting out of the park. The refreshment stand was empty.

He staggered over to where Amanda was still crouching on the ground and bent down to help her. "Are you all right?"

"Yeah, I think so," she said, stunned, brushing herself off. Her dress was torn and both her knees were scraped and bleeding. "What about you?"

"It just got to my shoulder. I'll be okay. But another tenth of a second and it would have torn my throat open. I'm sure of it."

"So am I," she agreed. "It was trying to kill us. But then what . . . ?"

"Shot. By an expert. Two shots, although I only heard one."

"It didn't even sound like a gunshot."

"He must have used a silencer."

"The man with the newspaper?"

"I don't know who else it could have been."

"Could it have been an accident?"

Nat shrugged. "All I can tell you for sure is that someone we don't know almost killed us. And someone else we don't know saved our lives. Should we report this?"

"Something tells me no. I just have the feeling."

"But that man just happened to be there. And he had a gun. Another coincidence?" Nat asked.

She tried to catch her breath. "I don't know."

When Paul heard the apartment door open, he was totally unprepared for the sight that met his eyes. There was the ravishing Amanda, the woman of his obsessions, standing in a torn dress, with bloody knees, covered with dirt, one side of her face bruised and her hair tangled.

"What in God's name happened to you!" he gasped as he raced over to her.

"I almost had an accident," she replied.

Chapter Eight

Operating Rooms 1 and 2 were next to each other on the east corridor of Goddard Institute's surgical suite. They were identical octagons with viewing windows in the ceilings. They shared a common scrub facility and one floor above it was a hallway that connected both viewing galleries. The walls of each room were covered in lime-green tile, which was supposed to be both bright and soothing on the nerves. The floors were covered in deep maroon tile, which was supposed to make dropped instruments stand out and not show blood.

In OR-1, Dr. Alexander Morrow was performing a coronary bypass on a sixty-one-year-old woman, replacing her obstructed left main coronary artery with a section taken from the saphenous vein in her thigh. Morrow stood at the patient's left shoulder, above her gaping chest held open with a metal spreader. The head nurse stood next to him, slapping instruments into his upturned palm on a regular beat. He wore a headlamp over his surgical cap and the cord ran down his back under his gown and plugged into the wall behind him.

His assistant, Dr. Michael Barnett, circulated throughout the room checking each station—anesthesia, heart-lung machine, sponge count, intravenous bottles, X-ray light box—painstakingly contorting himself amidst the jumble of tubes and wires leading from virtually every part of the patient's anatomy to the gleaming array of hardware cluttering the room.

To a casual observer, or even an intern or medical student watching through the soundproof glass panes of the viewing gallery, the greatest danger seemed the possibility that one of the twelve to fifteen participants on the floor at any given time might upset the delicate rigging of tubes and wires and throw off the fragile balance of surgery.

Motion was constant. The room radiated with activity. Morrow stood geographically and focally in the center, orchestrating the many functions being performed with a single goal in mind.

In OR-2, Dr. Norbert Ramsey was resecting an acoustic neurinoma from the brain stem of a twenty-seven-year-old man. It was 2:37 PM and he had been there since 6:22 that morning. He stood contemplatively at the end of the table, his hands held straight up to avoid contamination, while his assistant, Dr. Robert Anderson, adjusted one of the twin optics of the huge, plastic-wrapped Zeiss microscope for him. When it came into focus, the image also appeared on a large television monitor at the right of Ramsey's field of vision.

The small opening in the skull, protected by a sterile field of towels and gauze sewn directly to the scalp, was all that was visible of the patient. In the operating room, at this stage of surgery, he was nothing more than an intellectual abstraction, a disembodied brain that reacted autonomically to the surgeon's probes and cuts. And it was necessary that it remain this way—for both the patient and the doctor.

The bright overhead lights were off and other than the small lamps trained on the instrument table and the anesthesiologist's gauges, the only illumination was a spotlight beaming down on the area around the incision. A tape recorder in the corner was playing Sibelius' Sixth Symphony. Ramsey loved the music. It was spare, cold, and distant, with craggy, aggressive phrasing that underscored both the distance and the agressiveness of the operating room. Hearing it released his adrenalin, began it coursing through his body, signaling that he had achieved once again the edge he needed to face the transcendent challenges of neurosurgery.

Ramsey peered into the microscope, looked up to

check his perception on the TV monitor, then signaled the nurse to flip down the magnifying lenses he wore attached to his glasses, so he could view the tissue directly. The microscope was fine up to a point. But there hadn't been anything like that when Ramsey began operating back in the late forties, and you couldn't *feel* the tissue through a lens. It had to be a live one-on-one, with no technological barriers in between.

He gazed down into the cranial hole, watching the pinkish-gray brain gently pulsating in concordance with the body's heartbeat, and he waited until it felt right to proceed. The visceral feeling—the feeling originating somewhere deep within his own brain—this was just as important as any other factor. Because to Ramsey, as to most of his peers, neurosurgery involved complex rhythms, and everything was part of a unity. And that unity lay ultimately in mystery. The mystery of the brain itself.

The brain—the encephalon, as science called it—was like nothing else, and therefore the ritual of its healing was like no other procedure in medicine. In other types of surgery, if something went wrong, if something unexpected happened, there was a set corrective action to follow. It might not work—the surgeon might still lose the patient—but it was what he tried and he knew he had done all he could.

In dealing with the brain, there was no such comfort or safe harbor. No action had a set outcome and everything was ambiguous. It was even difficult to distinguish between a tumor and healthy neural tissue. It all looked the same. Oftentimes the surgeon couldn't take the whole tumor for fear of damaging the surrounding areas and leaving the patient with insurmountable impairment. Like this acoustic neurinoma. If he got it all and didn't cut up the pons or anything else in the cerebellopontine angle, the patient walked away from the hospital like any normal person. If he screwed up—and there were plenty of ways to do that—he had a dead patient, or a live one with a lot of paralysis and all kinds of other problems.

So he prepared himself with the X-rays and the CAT-scans and the EEG's and the neurological work-ups. But as much as anything else, he went in on instinct, and instinct guided him deeper and deeper into the mystery. And once he got out he often had nothing but that visceral feeling to indicate whether he'd made all the right choices, or taken a single wrong turn, which would ultimately lead to disaster.

Unlike the rest of the body, the brain left no margin for error. It was absolutely unforgiving. A slip of millimeters—sometimes of microns—could destroy unique tissue controlling movement, memory, intellect, vision, anything. And unlike the rest of the body, brain tissue does not restore itself. Once it's gone, it's gone forever.

He either had it or he didn't. And any neurosurgeon who claimed he'd never gotten an erection in the operating room was either a liar or an underachiever. He had made his living and his reputation on his skills, his insight, his amazing dexterity. But there was another factor of equal importance, he knew, and whether or not his patients perceived it on a conscious level, most of them knew it, too.

He was secure with the responsibility of decision.

He generally made the right decision, and sometimes made the wrong one. But once it was made, it became the only decision. The only choice. And everyone around his tables always knew it. ("How can you tell the good brain from the bad brain?" he was reputed to have said. "The bad brain goes up the suction tube.")

No surgeon, intern, nurse, or attendant could remember Ramsey ever losing his nerve in the operating room.

He held his hands up to the light to make sure there were no tiny holes in his bloodstained latex gloves that might jeopardize the sterility the brain insisted upon. Attention to tiny details could often throw the odds the right way.

"I want all these vessels cooked," he said to Anderson. "I want a clean field to work in."

Anderson moved into position with the electrocoagulator and staunched the bleeding where the dura had been folded back. "You got it," he announced when he had finished.

"Elevator," Ramsey ordered as the nurse pressed the instrument into his right hand. Without looking at it he said, "I don't want this one. Something smaller." She passed him an alternate.

He inserted the second Freer elevator and pried loose the surrounding tissue. He glanced up through the viewing window momentarily to let the interns and medical students know he was now speaking for their benefit. "We are attempting to resect the entire acoustic neurinoma while at the same time preserving the seventh nerve. This isn't always possible, but we won't know that until we get inside. We've made a twelve-centimeter vertical incision four centimeters above the superior nuchal line halfway between the inion and the mastoid process. There's no need to extend the craniectomy into the foramen magnum or to remove the arch of the atlas. But it is important to remove the bone up to the transverse sinus, and laterally to the mastoid air cells of the temporal bone. Everybody with me so far? You'd better be."

The occupants of the viewing gallery looked at each other with knowing expressions. Captain Ramsey was definitely in command.

"All right, the cerebellum is gently elevated to expose the tumor. Then, when we aspirate the cystic component over the postero-inferior portion we can establish the limits and size of the lesion and decide how complete a resection we can go for. We'll then enter the tumor in an avascular area, and for God's sake don't forget that or you're in big trouble. I'll use a fairly large curette to gut the tumor. But also keep in mind that since the facial nerve is usually anterior or ventral to the tumor, you can't violate the capsule in this area."

He stopped for what seemed longer than necessary to let his warning sink in. This little bit of drama might save a patient from unnecessary paralysis some day.

"Next we will clip the veins draining from the tumor into the superior petrosal sinus. Or if it looks ripe, we might coagulate them instead. Moving medially now, we clip and divide the arterial branches from the cerebellar artery. We'll dissect the fifth nerve from the tumor capsule and then change the angle of retraction from inferiorly to laterally to carry out the crucial medial dissection.

"All right, ladies and gentlemen, now comes your moment of truth. At this point we have to decide whether we're taking the whole capsule, or leaving a small portion adherent to the brain stem. If we can, we're going for all the goods. But let me emphasize, I want no one proving his manhood in this hospital by how much tumor he takes out."

The two female interns grimaced.

"If you get to the porus accousticus and see that you're flirting with permanent impairment, see that you err on the side of conservatism. Once you start cutting, there isn't anyone in the world who can cover your tracks for you. I want that fully understood and comprehended.

"I hope you've been listening carefully. Now just sit back and watch." His eyes darted around the table. "Everybody ready? Let's move."

When the tumor was finally exposed, there was nothing terribly prepossessing about it—a little yellowish-gray knob in a pool of blood that Anderson was sucking up through the tube. But when Ramsey could actually see it in front of his eyes, he felt his pulse jump fifteen or twenty points. It was a normal reaction. It settled down again as his attention focused completely on the intruder he had invaded this brain to destroy.

The interns in the viewing gallery and the attending staff around the table watched intently as he went after it. But he had no awareness of them or anything else in the world beyond the thirty-square-centimeter opening in the side of the patient's skull.

He worked quickly once he had determined the exact size and expanse of the neurinoma. The cutting stage merely required skill.

When he finished, he placed a section of tissue on a sterile gauze for the pathologist and then let Anderson take the rest with the sucker. When the area was clear, Ramsey surveyed it again.

"I think we've got a leak in this vein," he said. "Close it up."

Anderson inserted the electrocoagulator and was about to press its trigger when the nurse next to him jostled his elbow, pushing him forward enough to press the instrument into the cavity.

A collective gasp went through the operating room and the gallery upstairs.

Anderson instantly pulled out. The forehead of his surgical cap just as instantly soaked with sweat. He was trembling.

Ramsey ripped off his gloves and threw them down on the floor. "Another millimeter on that trigger and you would have fried this kid's whole lower brain stem," he said slowly and tersely. He was not in the habit of yelling. "If you want to know what that would have done, go back to your neuroanatomy book; don't play around on living specimens. We lose enough of them as it is because there's nothing contemporary medical science can do. I don't want to be losing any of the ones we've figured out how to save."

He paused to let his reprimand take its effect on everyone present. He was still the consummate teacher. Anderson's eyes were wide and his mouth, in outline behind the dull green mask, hung slightly open.

The hardness suddenly drained out of Ramsey's face and there was no further evidence at all that anything had gone wrong.

"Okay," he said to Anderson. "Finish up."

Paul Garrett had spent twenty years trying to overcome the fears and the memory of the fears that had gripped him, that had possessed him during those terrible months awaiting the tumor's final victory. And twenty years worth of defense layers, built up one by one at tremendous cost and struggle, all dissolved in an instant as he approached the main entrance of the Goddard Institute.

The gray brick facade had not changed appreciably since Paul had been a patient, but the hospital had grown considerably over those years. Newer wings sprouted from every available wall in the back and on the sides of the building. And once inside, Paul got the full effect.

Floors in the new and old sections didn't match up, so you had to take a ramp to get anywhere. None of the elevators went all the way up. You had to get off and transfer if you came in the front and had to get to a rear upper floor, or came in the back and wanted to get to the top front. If you came in either side you faced the same maze. Corridors went on and on, turning corners that should have ended sensibly with a blank wall or a single door. Windows looked out on two feet of air space and then another wall where a new wing had been added.

The hospital had just kept growing and growing, seemingly on its own and of its own accord; wildly, with no overall plan or focus. It seemed to him at that moment not so different from the malignancy that had threatened to take over his own body. Nothing about Goddard gave him peace.

As Paul expected, Ramsey was late.

"I was hoping he'd be back by now," his secretary explained. "But you can't tell in advance how long surgery will take." She was a short, white-haired woman, probably in her late fifties, with a perpetually apologetic quality acquired over years of having to cover for a boss who could never get to every thing or person he had committed himself to. She wore no wedding ring, and Paul was willing to bet that taking care of Norbert Ramsey was her chief reason for being.

"Would you like some candy?" she asked, extending

a gold-colored box across her desk to him, as if it would help alleviate the wait.

"Ah, no thank you," he replied.

"It's Godiva. It's expensive," she said.

"No. Thanks very much." He sat back down on the facing couch and the secretary went back to opening an enormous stack of mail with a letter opener in the shape of a jewelled dagger.

Ramsey's office, or at least the outer office where Paul was sitting, was richly furnished without being particularly tasteful. It wasn't garish, but it didn't betray any personality, either. The woods and upholstery were all genuine enough, but they had obviously been selected out of a catalogue or by a decorator in some mass furnishing effort.

Every three or four minutes the phone rang and the secretary fended off another demand on her boss's time or energies. By the second call Paul had learned her name was Miss Olson, which confirmed his first deduction about her. There was a generous stack of literature for him to read—most of it out-dated—but he couldn't keep his mind on even the *People* magazines that had lately become the staple of most doctors' waiting rooms.

When he had finally lost track of time Paul heard the door opening and felt a jab of anxiety in the center of his chest. The memories and feelings all rushed past the edge of his consciousness. He wanted to leave.

Norbert Ramsey lounged far back in his chair while Paul sat rigidly forward in his. He seemed to inch up slightly with each added detail of his story. Throughout, Ramsey massaged his chin with one hand. He was still wearing his surgical greens and the Adidas running shoes that dissipated some of the strain of prolonged standing. It had been more than twenty years since the operation; fifteen since he'd last seen Ramsey for a post-operative checkup. But the mind has its own signposts that have nothing to do with time. It had not taken long for the old relationship to be reestablished and Paul had to force upon his conscious will the fact that he was no longer a terminal patient.

"I can appreciate what you've been going through," Ramsey stated. He scanned the folder on his desk. "Now it says here I removed an oligodendroglioma from your right temporal lobe. Apparently—from the fact you're still alive, for one—we were able to get the whole tumor. And from the pathology reports and the post-op tests it doesn't seem that we took too much surrounding tissue. But that's an area we went into that we refer to as the 'interpretive cortex.' That's where you live. And a glioma's a tough tumor, sir. So whatever mental or emotional problems you say you've had, I'm not going to tell you you didn't buy them on my table."

"So whatever I've been feeling since then could just have been a psychological response to the surgery?" Paul asked.

"The traditional response you'll get from a neurosurgeon is, 'Don't ask me about your mind. I had nothing to do with your mind. It was your brain I worked on.' But the truth of the matter is, we just don't know."

"I should be more articulate, I know," Paul said. "One scientist talking to another. But I just feel . . . different."

"You are different. In this business, we're fighting wars of inches most of the time, not miles. By that I mean, if by going in we can buy a patient an extra couple months, or a year without pain, that's often the best victory we can hope for. But you're the big winner here. You're the survivor, and in the kind of war you were fighting, sir, there aren't too many."

Paul thought immediately of the "survivor guilt" David Sherman had mentioned.

"Frankly," Ramsey admitted, "it's conversations like this that got me into the field I'm in. In college—a long time ago—I started out to be a philosopher. But the questions they dealt with were so arcane, they had no relationship to anything as far as I could see. So I went from there to psychology, figuring if I was going to deal with ideas of the mind, I might as well deal with the mind itself. Then I decided to go to medical school and take up psychiatry. But everything was too vague and iffy—'paranoid tendencies' and the like. So I moved over to neurology. But that was like watching the show from the wings. I wanted to touch what I was dealing with. So here I am, cutting up brains to try to make people well. And the only thing I lost along the way is what all of those other fields are all about—the mind. I don't dismiss the concept entirely like a lot of head surgeons. I just can't let it get in my way or I cease to function."

Throughout the meeting, Ramsey had been toying with a silver-plated mallet that had been lying near the corner of his desk. Paul couldn't tell whether the object was supposed to be a gavel symbolizing his directorate of the Neurological Research Unit or a crude joke on the still primitive state of brain surgery.

"Why did you choose now to come see me?" Ramsey asked.

"There were a lot of factors," Paul responded. "But I guess the triggering trauma that made everything else seem all the more unbearable was the death of my wife."

Paul wasn't sure, but he thought he noticed Ramsey stiffen almost imperceptibly. He glanced at his watch for the first time during the interview. When he told the surgeon about the tragedy, Ramsey seemed much more sympathetic, even—was this the word?—more interested.

"That alone would be enough to send most people over the edge," he said at last.

Should he mention Amanda, Paul wondered, and bring up his obsession with her? Wouldn't Ramsey find it strange that after twenty years, two of his "survivors" had stumbled across each other and fallen in love? But he decided against it. That would only complicate the matter further, and it seemed muddled enough as it was. Besides, based on the conversation so far, what could Ramsey possibly have to contribute on that score?

When he looked up, Ramsey was standing, his knuckles pressed against the surface of the desk. "If you continue feeling this way, I think your best bet is to continue with your psychiatrist," he said. "From what you tell me, he seems to have a pretty good grasp on things. I wish I could have been more help, but we're really talking two different languages, here. There's surely a connection somewhere along the line, but you're talking about what's going on in your mind and all I can say for certain—for reasonably certain—is what's going on in your brain, which anatomically speaking is three pounds of fat, water and conductive cells. And no matter what leap of intellectual faith you're willing to make, you can't completely explain something that isn't tangible in terms of something that is."

At that point Paul found himself moving toward the door, as if being eased along by an invisible tide, by the force of Ramsey's will.

He hadn't come away with what he or David had hoped, but since he hadn't defined what that was, he didn't know what could have been expected. It was frustrating that Norbert Ramsey hadn't provided the solution for his emotional problems. But what the former *wunderkind* of neurosurgery was apparently too gracious to admit, the former patient realized, was that if he hadn't at least provided the solution to his *physical* problems, Paul would have been twenty years dead.

Chicago

J. Tyler Kendrick stood in front of the glass wall, hands in his jacket pockets, staring out over the lake. He stood there rigidly, as if transfixed by the expanse of the water; as if contemplating his own insignificance in relation to the scope and power of nature. But John Christopher had never heard a single utterance from Kendrick that would in any way imply a sense of personal insignificance in relation to anything. So he concluded that at most, Kendrick considered nature's scope and power equal to his own.

It was ironic, really, Christopher thought. But in this current situation, Kendrick actually was helping to preserve nature's power, or at least its influence. Because if he was on the mark about this Paul Garrett research, the power and influence of fossil fuel on the world economy was potentially threatened. And as Kendrick had said, that was just one aspect.

"No one's seen or heard from him since his wife died," Kendrick stated without turning around.

"What's that?" Christopher asked, astonished.

"Garrett. He hasn't been back to his laboratory. I don't think he's even in the Boston area."

"As long as he's not doing his research, what's the difference where he is?"

Kendrick finally turned to face Christopher and therefore removed his hands from his pockets. When speaking to someone directly, Kendrick always used gestures. "Garrett's a theoretical physicist. The laboratory only represents a small part of his work. The main thing, the important stuff he can do anywhere he's got a pencil and some paper."

"So you think he's working secretly?"

"There's no reason for him to. Except the murder of his wife still worries me. If he's either been kidnapped or has reached some sort of agreement with the Eastern bloc, we've lost control."

"Maybe he's gone over to the Arabs."

"No. Both the Partners for Progress and Universal Oil have many contacts in the Middle East. I would have heard about that right away. I don't like the vibrations I'm getting lately."

Christopher wondered how Kendrick could get any vibrations sequestered on the ninety-second floor of the Universal Oil Tower. He couldn't remember the last time he'd seen Kendrick outside his own office and conference suite. That was some commentary on modern times. The whole fucking world is being run by men who never leave their secluded offices on the tops of skyscrapers.

"We've got two options," Kendrick said. He was ostensibly speaking to Christopher, but that was merely for the sake of convention. The same thoughts with the same phrasing would have gone through his head whether there was anyone else present or not. "We can either go it alone and just continue monitoring the situation as it happens, or we can call in our friends in high places."

This time it was Christopher who stared out the glass wall. "Who could be in higher places than this?" For the first time that afternoon he noticed Kendrick smile.

"When the status and profitability of every important industry in the western world is on the line, these people can be very sympathetic." Kendrick clearly enjoyed constructing his own hyperbole. "Look what they did for your worthy associates at Chrysler. And if they bought it tomorrow, hardly anyone other than a few thousand auto workers would blink an eyelash. We're talking about high stakes."

He pressed the intercom button on his desk and spoke out into the air. "Get me George Henderson in Langley."

New York

Amanda had had enough experience with investigative reporting to be aware of the cardinal rule for uncovering a hidden trail or theme: Follow the Money. It almost always turned out to hold true. But as she sat hunched over her desk, a yellow legal pad and a typed list of names in front of her, she couldn't see how money might enter this particular equation. Still, she couldn't get it out of her head altogether that whatever the pattern or theme turned out to be, money would have something to do with it.

Though Paul—always the skeptic—remained unconvinced, she was sure there was a pattern and connection to these three lives that had become linked together recently by chance. If she could find the answer, it would certainly explain all of the random traits she and Paul and Nat had in common. And perhaps it would even explain that unpleasant incident at Bloomingdale's, and the more unpleasant one on 51st Street.

Nat had said—and it had been one of those phrases that inexplicably haunted her—that the answer you arrive at depends on the question you ask. She didn't know what kind of answer she was looking for; Paul wouldn't even acknowledge there was an answer to be found. So she wasn't sure of the form her question should take.

She did have one concrete fact, though. All three of them had been patients at Goddard Institute in June of 1959, suffering from the same incurable brain disease. And all had been cured. Whatever the commonality of their experience, it obviously started there. The more people she could find who also shared that rare distinction, the more clues she'd have to work with. At least something might turn up along the way that would point her in the right direction.

The list in front of her had been supplied to Paul's psychiatrist, David Sherman, by a staff doctor at Goddard—Wendell Fuller. It contained all the brain tumor patients at the hospital during any part of her or Paul's stay. There were thirty-four names on the list. Next to eighteen of them was the annotation that they had died in the hospital, and could therefore be discounted. All the others would have to be tracked down.

As she drew a blue pencil line through the last of those eighteen names, the implication of that simple act became clear to her. Each pencil line represented a death—a convenient limitation of the research task ahead, but also an acknowledgment of a grim and helpless death that could have just as easily been hers. She thought back to all the times she had casually added up statistics of any sort and dismissed a death or an injury as a mere abstraction. Detachment. Objectivity. Weren't they the goals a journalist strived for, particularly in science? Or did all of that go out the window when one became personally involved?

The first remaining name on the list was Harry Mervis of White Plains. She called the telephone number printed on the computer sheet, but it was now assigned to a dry cleaner who had never heard of Harry Mervis. She called Westchester County Information, but they had no listing for a Harry Mervis, so she took down the names and numbers of the four other Mervises in the directory. Now came the unpleasant part: calling each of the four and asking—not in so many words—if they know or knew a Harry Mervis and whether or not he survived his brain tumor.

Henrietta Mervis was not at home. William Mervis knew no Harry with his surname. Franklin Mervis said he knew all the Mervises in the area and there never had been a Harry. But Marianne Mervis occasionally used to get wrong numbers several years ago for Marion Mervis whom she believed had a father named Harry. Did she know where Marion lived now? No. In fact, she thought she got married about four or five years ago, so she'd probably changed her name. Did Marianne recall Marion's mother's name? No, but it seemed to her that she got married, too, after her husband died. That answered Amanda's main question, but it was still worth following up. When one doesn't know the specific questions to ask, the answers, if they come at all, are most likely to surface indirectly.

She next called the Westchester County Records Office and got a clerk there to look up a marriage license issued to Marion Mervis. On April 28, 1973, she had married Michael Girard.

Back to Directory Assistance. There were two listings for a Michael Girard and none for a Marion. She called the first and a maid answered the phone. Amanda requested Mrs. Girard and was asked to wait. Mrs. Girard eventually came on the line and Amanda asked if she were Marion M. Girard. No, she wasn't. Did she know Marion M. Girard? No, and who is this, anyway? Did the name Mervis mean anything to her? No. Amanda thanked her for her time and dialed the other number.

As soon as she got a connection she heard a click, then a recording stating that the number had been changed. The new area code was for Lawrenceburg, Indiana. A woman answered the phone.

"Mrs. Girard?"

"Yes?"

"My name is Amanda West. I'm a reporter with *Aurora* magazine in New York."

"Never heard of it."

"Could you tell me, please, are you Mrs. Marion M. Girard; Mrs. Marion Mervis Girard?"

The woman's voice was thick with suspicion. "Ahh . . . yes, I am. What is this about?"

"Mrs. Girard, I'll try to be as delicate as I can. Was your father, Harry Mervis, a patient at the Goddard Institute in New York in the late nineteen fifties?"

The pause was so long that Amanda became consciously aware of the static on the line.

"Yes . . . he . . . was. What is this about?" she repeated.

"I'm a reporter, but I was also a patient there at the same time," Amanda explained, "suffering from the same condition as your father, I believe."

"I see." Her voice had lost some of its suspicion, but none of its hard edge.

"Please bear with me, Mrs. Girard. I know that your father left the hospital. But could you tell me if he . . . recovered . . . from his condition?"

"Why do you want to know?"

"Actually, it affects me directly, and the several other brain tumor patients still alive who were there then. It's a matter of health," she improvised.

"We thought he was getting better for a while,"

Mrs. Girard relented. "But then the . . . the . . . tumor . . ." She had obvious trouble getting the word out.

"The tumor returned?"

"That's right. By the end he was hardly ever conscious. And even when he was, he didn't seem to recognize any of us. He just sort of . . . I don't know . . . went off into himself, I guess."

"Was there anything particular he said or did after he came home from Goddard? Anything you would consider unusual?"

"I would consider everything he did unusual. He was like a different person."

"Could you tell me how?"

"I already did. He wasn't outgoing anymore like he always had been. He was depressed all the time. He hardly said anything, and when he did talk, it was like he would start in the middle of a conversation and nobody would know what he was talking about. He knew he was a burden for the first time in his life. And he knew he was going to die. Sometimes he said he wanted to die and get it over with."

"I can empathize with that, Mrs. Girard. Believe me, I can. But you can't recall anything other than that? New preferences, or insights? Or interests or drives he didn't have before?"

"Of course not. He was the same person as before . . . only worse."

Amanda groped for additional questions, but knew she already understood Mr. Mervis as well as she could. "I'm terribly sorry to have troubled you like this," she said. "But I do appreciate it and you've helped me considerably."

"Okay," the woman said quietly, and hung up.

Almost an hour wasted, Amanda realized, and no answers to show for it. But how can you come up with the right answers when you don't know the right questions?

She stopped short. Why did that phrase seem familiar? Why did she feel she'd heard it before? Or said it before in some important context?

All she had to go on were the vague, visceral impressions that she and Paul had been experiencing. But in her mind, that was definitely something. She checked off the next name on the list and dialed the phone again.

The procedure continued throughout the morning, moving from one blind alley to another. People had died, people had moved away, people didn't remember, people didn't want to remember. Some weren't home or didn't answer and could be called back tomorrow or the next day. But by lunchtime, Amanda had no more to go on than when she began.

In the middle of the afternoon she was going over the graphics for the story on black holes with Jerry Cassell, the gratingly fussy art director. "What do you mean, 'Take the red and the blue out'?" he screeched.

"Jerry, the whole idea of a black hole is that its atomic structure is so dense that its gravitational pull doesn't even allow light to get out. Without light, there's no such thing as color."

"Well, why do they call it black, then?"

"Black is the absence of color. It's black because it's not anything else. Theoretically, you can't see it at all."

"Then how am I supposed to draw something that can't be seen?"

She smiled and tapped him on the forehead with her pencil. "I don't know. Use your imagination."

Nancy Flanagan called her from across the room. "Phone call for you."

"Thanks. I'll take it at my desk."

The caller identified herself as Mrs. Esther Radner. At first the name meant nothing to Amanda, then something clicked. "Was your husband Abraham Radner?"

"That's right. You called this morning and left a message." She sounded to be in her sixties or seventies, which would be in keeping with her husband's age according to the Goddard records. She had a soft, sympathetic voice, and Amanda began her much-rehearsed explanation of why she had called, ending with the question about any unusual behavior. She steeled herself for the agonized response, but distance and age had apparently blunted Mrs. Radner's anguish. She was calm and deliberate.

"There was one thing, Miss West."

"Please call me Amanda." She almost felt her heart leap at the promise of the first marginally hopeful offering of the day.

"Very close to the end, when we both knew what was inevitable, Abraham made an unusual request. He told me he wanted to be buried in Berlin, in—what was it now?—*The Friedhof der Jüdischen Gemeinde*. I asked him why, but he never told me. He was very insistent on this, you see, and it worried me. But I knew his brain had been affected by his illness, and so I tried to forget about it. All these years, though, I still can't get it out of my mind."

"Can you think why he would have wanted to be buried there? Was he from Germany?"

"No. Both his parents were born in this country and he was never in Germany, although that's where his father's parents were born. I suppose this is where they were buried; that's the only thing I can figure out. And when he was so sick in his brain, returning back there where he came from must have seemed very important to him. But of course, I couldn't go along with such a wish. How could I? I buried him right here in New York."

"Anything else you can think of to tell me?" Amanda asked.

"There is one more thing. I was with Abraham when he died. He was delirious, I know. But I was trying to listen to what he said. I can't be sure, now, but I believe he was saying something to me in German at the end."

"Well, that would fit in, it seems to me," Amanda said. "Especially with what you said about his grandparents and his family heritage. Why do you find that unusual?"

There was a slight pause on the line.

"My husband couldn't speak German," Mrs. Radner responded. "I'm sure of it."

Bernadette Olson knew that Dr. Ramsey wasn't in the habit of being interrupted for any reason during rounds, so when the intense, determined-looking visitor arrived in his office, she asked him if he had an appointment and when he said he did not, told him he'd have to wait until Dr. Ramsey could squeeze him in.

"I'm sorry, but I don't have the time to spare," the visitor explained. "I have to see him right away."

"If it's a medical emergency, I suggest you go down to the emergency room," Miss Olson said, "because Dr. Ramsey is with his residents on the neurosurgical ward at the moment."

"All right, then. Just tell me where the ward is, and I'll go find him myself."

"No, sir, you don't understand. You can't go down there," she stated, trying to control herself in the face of his unbelievable audacity. Who was he to question her authority? And he didn't even have an appointment. "Perhaps you'd like me to make you an appointment and you could come back at a more convenient time," she offered, trying to be more conciliatory than the man had any right to expect.

"Never mind, I'll go get him."

Before she could yell, "You can't do that!" he was out the door.

This was intolerable. She picked up the telephone and punched four buttons. "Security? This is Miss Olson in Dr. Ramsey's office. There was just an intruder here . . . that's right, an intruder. He insists on seeing Dr. Ramsey and is on his way to the neurosurgical ward to look for him. About six feet tall, thin, gray hair, about fifty-five. Oh yes, I got a good look at him. Yes. Call me back when you find him." She hung up the phone with the satisfaction that comes from a necessary task, efficiently performed. He'd see how far he got, behaving that way.

"What the hell's going on here!" Norbert Ramsey thundered as two blue-uniformed hospital security men bolted through the double doors to disturb the peace of the ward.

The guards slowed down with respect when they saw him. "We got a call that someone's coming for you here," one explained.

"Is he suffering from a gunshot wound in the head or does he have a pickaxe sticking out of his brain?" Ramsey grilled him.

"Ah . . . I don't know, sir," the guard stammered.

"Then if it's only a tumor, it won't get appreciably worse before I finish rounds."

The interns in his entourage turned to each other and chuckled, delighted and relieved to see Ramsey's wrath directed at some other innocent for a change.

"Whoever it is, pick him up and drag him out of here," the surgeon commanded. "Only do it quietly."

As he spoke, the double doors at the other end of the ward swung open and the determined visitor stepped into the ward. Two other security men could be seen coming around the corner in pursuit.

"That's him!" one of the guards in the room shouted to the other. They sprang for him, but stopped in their tracks as Ramsey said:

"Hold it!" The guards turned to each other with surprise as the visitor smiled knowingly.

Ramsey turned to his assistant, Robert Anderson. "You're in charge. Try to teach these people something." Then he marched over to where the visitor was standing, grabbed him by the arm, and escorted him out of the ward.

Once beyond the double doors he positioned the man in the corner of the empty waiting room, next to an enormous plastic fern whose white pebble filler had spilled over onto the green tile floor. "Henderson! What the hell are you doing here?"

George Henderson rubbed his arm lightly where Ramsey had grabbed him, but did not lose his knowing smile. "Sorry to interrupt you, Doctor. Can you spare a few moments?"

"What's this all about?"

"I'd rather not discuss it here. I'm sure you agree. Why don't you take a brief walk with me. Your patients seem to be in good hands for the moment." When Ramsey didn't budge, he said it again, this time more firmly. "Let's take a walk."

They went across the street to a small luncheonette and sat in a booth in the back. "Now for God's sake tell me what this is all about," Ramsey demanded. He was still scowling.

"Norbert, I don't like this whole business any better than you do," Henderson assured him. "But it's something we've got to follow through on. And since you may have to become materially involved again, I wanted to keep you apprised of the developing situation."

"Look, George, I find this whole matter extremely distasteful. I don't want anything more to do with it."

"I'm afraid it's beyond that, and I think you know it. You made your choices twenty-five years ago."

"Let's not go over old territory," Ramsey said. "You're wasting my time. What the hell's going on. Is this about Paul Garrett?"

"Of course it's about Paul Garrett. I certainly wouldn't drag you away from your work for any of the rest of our mutual business."

"He came to see me this week."

"I'm not surprised. He's somehow met up with Amanda West. I'm not sure how; it may have been coincidence, it may not have been. And she's met up with Nathaniel Kagan. We've got pictures. Now let me ask you a question. Is there anybody on your staff— now or then—who could have put them together?"

"Absolutely not."

"You're sure?"

"Completely."

"All right. Could they have gotten together on their own?"

"What do you mean, on their own?"

"I don't know; that's your territory. Something like a homing instinct . . . I don't know what you'd call it."

"I can't say," Ramsey replied. "That's a purely theoretical area. There's no data on it."

"All that money and no data?"

"Don't give me any shit, George," Ramsey said wearily. "Just get on with what you came to say."

"Garrett's closest associate, Harry Gillette, died recently. It may not have been from natural causes. It's essential that we find out if this death is connected to the meeting between Garrett and West or West and Kagan."

"How the hell should I know?"

"I don't expect you to know," Henderson said sharply. "But I do expect you to assume a more constructive attitude about the problem."

"George, it's not my problem anymore. Garrett hasn't been my patient for fifteen years. He's completely cured."

"When you spoke to him the other day, did you get any sense that he was nearing . . . a realization . . . about himself?"

"No. And I'm afraid I didn't help him much."

Henderson smiled sardonically. "Thank you for your cooperation."

"He came to me because the psychiatrist he's seeing recommended it."

"What's the psychiatrist's name?"

"I don't know. It's none of my business."

"Come on, Norbert. We need to know things like that. Why is he seeing a shrink?"

"Combination of things, I gather. Mainly he was upset about his wife's death, I think."

"That was unfortunate, but it couldn't be helped."

Ramsey grabbed the edge of the table with such force that the water glasses rattled. "What!" he yelled.

"Keep your voice down. This is a public place."

"Are you saying that Mrs. Garrett didn't kill herself? That the Agency killed her?"

"It was a matter of national security."

"You're a bunch of fucking animals!" Ramsey seethed.

"Don't go getting moralistic on me. You know the guidelines."

"You pull this off yourself?"

"Of course not."

"Who'd you get? Your Jack the Ripper lookalike?"

"It was done very humanely."

"Humanely! You killed an innocent woman!"

Henderson sighed. "Norbert, you're growing tiresome. And we have reason to believe she was not an innocent woman."

Ramsey turned his body to the side, clenched his jaw and hammered his elbow on the table in frustration and disgust. "I'm a doctor. How do you expect me to react to this kind of shit?"

"You're also a scientist . . . and obviously a damn good one. Sometimes those two callings bring one into personal conflict."

"I refuse to have to be a party to this madness. If you know what's good for you, you'll leave me out of it."

Henderson smiled again at Ramsey's demand. "I'm going to have to ask you to reconsider. You see, in your own way, you're a vital part of our team. And you're a sophisticated thinker. You must realize that everything is linked to everything else. You wouldn't be able to eliminate one aspect of your 'work' without irreparably harming all the others."

"I'm not so sure."

"Trust me, you wouldn't. But why take the chance? I'm not asking you to get your sensitive and talented hands dirty. Just play along with us. Everything else will stay the same."

Ramsey rose slowly, staring straight through Henderson the entire time.

"I'll keep you informed of developments," Henderson said, remaining seated.

"I'm sure you will," Ramsey stated, and walked out.

Chapter Nine

During the night, Paul had awakened suddenly with sweat beaded on his forehead. He had been dreaming of the anatomy lab again, methodically removing pieces from the open cadaver spread out on the shiny table in front of him. But the pieces would not stay still on the sideboard. Instead, they turned into little gray lumps that scuttled silently like crabs along the floor of what became a smoky black cavern that had no walls. And he knew they were ready to spring on him and devour him with their mouthless heads. When he woke up, he felt like a car whose engine is idling near the red line. And in his chest he felt that familiar, constricting tightness that he'd had to convince himself before was not actually his heart.

Amanda had clutched his trembling hand and softly reassured him that everything was all right, turning her face away from his so he wouldn't detect the fear that was plain in her eyes. Now, in the morning, she stood by the bedroom door watching him pack his suitcase. She was still wearing the "Aurora Illuminates!" T-shirt she'd slept in, as if her unwillingness to get dressed would deter him from completing his task and intentions. But he kept wedging socks and shirts into the corners of the bag he'd purchased the day before. As each pile of clothing left the bed, she felt another jab of tension in her stomach, and a welling heaviness in the floor of her mouth that made her want to cry. But that wouldn't have accomplished anything, she knew, and so she struggled to restrain herself.

For Paul, the act of packing—of picking up his

clothes from the bed and putting them in the suitcase—
evoked uncomfortable mental associations. Last time it
had been leaving Cambridge rather than going back,
and last time the woman who watched him had been his
wife and emotional sparring partner, rather than this
golden-haired object of his adoration. But last time,
when he returned, he'd come back to chaos and horror,
and nothing had been the same since then. Perhaps this
ritual would signal the end of the horror, just as it had
signaled the beginning. As he glanced up at Amanda—
the gray cotton shirt just reaching to the tops of her
long, smooth, tightly muscled legs—he was overcome
with a sense of loss and regret that couldn't be fully
explained by either the trip back home or the anxiety of
this latest conjuring of the recurring dream. But he
knew it was time to leave.

Despite his misgivings, he had to go back. As she
came over and sat on the corner of the bed, one leg
tucked under her, he knew what she was thinking
before she said it. That had happened often between
them, right from their first meeting.

"What's so important that you have to go right
away?" she asked.

"My life and my work are up in Cambridge," he said,
suspending his packing and turning to her. "I have to
go back at some point, and whenever I do, it would be
just as painful as now."

"You've only been here a few days, really."

"I didn't plan to become your permanent house-
guest." He smiled, trying to get her to do the same.

But she bowed her head, looked down toward her
lap and sighed. "I thought I'd reached the point where I
wasn't dependent on a man any longer. But facing the
prospect of you leaving makes me . . . I guess I wasn't
as far along as I thought."

"Hey, it's not like this is the end of our relationship,"
he declared, as much for his own benefit as for hers.
"New York and Boston are less than an hour's plane
ride from each other."

"It's not the same as actually being together every

day, though." She hesitated for a moment, then said,
"Don't you feel like we *belong* together?"

"Of course I do, but . . ."

"I haven't figured out what the pattern of our
meeting and attraction to each other is all about yet,
but I feel like we're *supposed* to be together; like we're
part of the same entity."

He slid over next to her and put his arm around her
shoulders. "Amanda, can't we have it the way it was
before I came to New York? The way we both would
have been content to keep it after that first night we
spent together at your apartment at the Watergate?
That's all that my going back home means. And there's
really no way around it. I have to do my work. I want to
do it. And I have a grant for the summer, so I'd better
get something accomplished or no one will give me
another penny for scientific research." He saw he was
making little headway. "Look, you know this is an
artificial situation for me, staying at your apartment
while you work all day. I wouldn't ask you to give up
your job and come live with me in Cambridge. It
wouldn't be fair."

"Maybe not, but I wish you would ask me," she said
tearfully.

"And what would you say?"

"I don't know. I guess you'd better not ask me. Right
now, I'd probably say yes."

"Well, that indicates a fair degree of insight into
yourself."

She ignored the compliment. "But when will I get to
see you again?"

"Whenever you want."

"I still don't see why you have to leave right now. I
wanted you to meet Nathaniel Kagan. If you'd just talk
to him and see how much *all three* of us have in
common, you'd be staggered. I'm telling you, Paul—
there's something to all this."

"All right," he said, taking both of her hands in his.
"I'll be happy to meet him if it'll make *you* happy." She
nodded her head affirmatively. "When is that anti-

nuclear rally you've been telling me about that he's supposed to speak at?"

"A week from tomorrow evening."

"I'll be back," he promised.

"And you'll stay here?"

"Certainly."

He stood up and finished off the last few articles that needed to be packed.

"Paul," she said, still watching him from the corner of the bed, "I worry about you. You will be careful, won't you?"

"You're the one who's got to be careful," he warned. "I know you well enough to know how inquisitive and resourceful you are. And I know how wound up you are in this 'search for the elusive mysteries' about the three of us. So for God's sake don't do anything crazy. If anything was to happen to you . . ." He let his voice trail off.

"Well now." She finally smiled. "We've each got a responsibility to the other, don't we?"

Amanda wanted to come along in the cab to LaGuardia, but Paul said it would be better if she didn't. He couldn't stand to string out a temporary parting into an agonized, emotional excess, he told her. Actually, he was afraid she might not be content simply to ride with him in the taxi, and would insist on going into the Eastern Shuttle Terminal. And if that happened, she would see him head not for the Boston plane, but the one to Washington. Not that he was trying to keep any big secret from her, he assured himself, but since she was one of the reasons he was going there and not directly home, it would be better and less complicated if he kept it to himself. In a way, he was sorry he'd even mentioned that he was seeing David at all.

She still hadn't made any move to get dressed, even though she had usually left for the office by this time. He hoped it wasn't a sign of depression, similar to staying in bed all day rather than facing the problems and challenges of one's life. God knows he had enough to feel guilty about without this additional burden. He hugged her tightly to him, and during their long kiss her eyes remained constantly open, staring into his. That, it seemed to him, was a healthy sign.

"I'll call you tonight," she said when he had taken his hands from around her waist.

"No, I'll be in and out. I'll call you," he countered.

As soon as the cab pulled up in front of the Eastern terminal, Paul had the money ready for the fare. The driver thanked him profusely for the generosity of the tip, then changed his tone abruptly as Paul was getting out of the car. He shouted an epithet in the general direction of the dark green sedan that had pulled up from behind and swerved into the "No Parking" zone in front, wedging the taxi in. But the sedan's driver seemed oblivious to the cursing, leaping out from behind the wheel and running into the terminal building. It looked like the same car Paul had noticed in front of Amanda's building when the cab picked him up, but he hadn't been paying that close attention. If it was the same one, he could have hitched a ride with him and saved the thirteen dollars.

While Paul was filling out his boarding pass in front of the Washington gate, he noticed the man standing at the telephone bank in the middle of the long, low-ceilinged hall. It must have been an important call to risk tangling with a New York cab. Paul expected the man to divert his eyes as he looked over at him, but he gazed straight back, as if stating his defiance to anyone who disapproved of his driving techniques. A lot of good that'll do him, Paul mused. The cops are probably towing his car away even while he stands here talking.

As usual, the shuttle was packed, and Paul ended up seated next to a nineteen- or twenty-year-old kid who kept unwrapping and eating hard-boiled egg quarters. When he got to his seventh, Paul couldn't contain himself any longer and asked for an explanation.

"There's a lot of summer flu going around," the young man said. "Keeping healthy is all a matter of eating the right things; putting the right things into your body. Every food has a specific scientific purpose. It's all very logical. For example, you want to keep from getting the flu, eat eggs," he advised, holding up the last quarter in a sort of salute.

"But I hate eggs," Paul said.

"That's okay," the kid assured him. "You can use Brazil nuts instead."

Paul grimaced and moved himself slightly away. The kid smiled benignly.

He was typical of many of the college-age kids Paul had observed the last couple of years, though not so much at MIT as in other parts of Boston. He was friendly enough, but with a kind of detached glaze to his eyes that made talking to him like picking up a conversation in the middle of a stream of consciousness. He wore a University of Southern California T-shirt, which at least gave Paul an entry into a dialogue.

"You go to U.S.C.?"

"I did."

"Did you know Professor Stephen Hastings?"

The kid shook his head blankly. "What department was he in?"

"Physics."

He continued shaking his head. "I wasn't into anything heavy like that. Sorry. As it is I had to get out."

"How come?"

"I don't know. College was doing a strange number on my head, y'know? It was all so artificial and make-believe. I had to get out and work and see what the real world was like."

"So what do you do?"

"I'm a guide on the Jungle River Cruise at Disneyland."

Paul nearly choked on the watered-down coffee he'd brought on board with him. For a fleeting moment he yearned to explore further into the youth's perceptions of reality, but almost as quickly realized he'd be wading into an intellectual morass that neither of them would find profitable. Instead, he asked, "What are you doing in the East?"

"I went to a wedding in New York. Now I'm going down to D.C. to see some other friends who're thinking of tying the knot, too." He clicked his tongue against the back of his teeth. "It's really getting unnerving. All the time more and more of my friends, people I know, are getting married on me."

"Wait till you get to be my age," Paul said, "and they start dying on you."

The Eastern baggage claim area at National Airport is a vector of floorspace formed by the intersection of two long concourses. He was waiting for the conveyor belt to begin whining and spitting suitcases out from the giant mousehole in the wall when he heard, "Paul! Paul Garrett! Is that you?"

It was Charles Hollister, carrying an expensive leather briefcase and wearing a Brooks Brothers suit that looked slightly too heavy for the weather. He got closer and said, "Yes, it is you, isn't it?"

"Evidently," Paul replied, a bit self-consciously.

"Waiting for your bag, I see." He made even the most obvious, obtuse remarks with a heartiness and prep-school enthusiasm that prevented one from responding with the kind of withering sarcasm they would have merited coming from someone else. "I'm just back myself," he explained, indicating his briefcase. "Overnight to Atlanta. I've got my car here. I'll take you wherever you're going."

"That's very kind but . . ."

"No trouble. I insist."

"Ah . . . sure, Charles. Thanks very much." It was easiest to accept. Hollister was clearly the type who didn't take no for an answer.

They dodged traffic across the four-lane loop in front of the main terminal entrance and headed for the short-term lot where the hourly charge kept piling up with no maximum. But when Paul saw the car, he understood why Charles shelled out for a premium parking space. They walked over to a Rolls Royce Corniche Coupe, finished in two gleaming shades of brown; a deep coffee color below the horizontal midline, a rich bronze above. Other than books, automobiles were the only physical objects that held any attraction or fascination for Paul, and this was one of the most breathtaking ones he'd seen. Perhaps Charles had more taste and substance than his "Old Boy Network" exterior indicated.

The attorney swung behind the wheel and asked, "Where are you headed?"

Having Charles drive him meant changing his plans slightly. "Ah . . . the Jefferson Hotel at 16th and L."

"How long will you be in town, Paul?"

"Just a day or two."

"Look, tell you what. Why not stay with us in Georgetown?"

Paul offered the perfunctory, "No, I couldn't. I've already taken advantage of your country hospitality," and expected to be let off with that.

But Charles insisted, "So now you'll see how we live in the city. I mean it. We've got plenty of space. And we're always looking for someone interesting to brighten up our household. You wouldn't even have to eat with us if it wasn't convenient."

"You haven't even asked Sandy . . ."

"No problem, I assure you. She loves company. We'll be extremely insulted if you say 'no'."

Paul couldn't figure out why he was being so insistent. They actually hardly knew each other.

They went back and forth for several more rounds before Hollister wore him down sufficiently to extract an acceptance. Charles picked up the telephone receiver from the console between the two seats, cradled it on his shoulder and punched the buttons. "Hello, Sarah. Tell Mrs. Hollister that Dr. Garrett will be staying with us for a few days. That's right. She is? Good. Thank you. We're on our way back from the airport now." He replaced the telephone and turned his full attention back to the airport road, a look of satisfaction on his face as if he'd just achieved an unexpected social triumph—a date with the homecoming queen, for example.

Then he said no more until they had pulled onto the George Washington Parkway toward Memorial Bridge. Paul also sat silently, his mind temporarily diverted from the concerns of his life and work by the car's leather-encased luxury until Charles said, "I can't tell you how shocked and sorry we were to hear about Julia. Unbelievable—that's the only word for it. I wish there was something we could do."

"Thank you. I appreciate that."

"It must be a terrible burden for you. I know . . . everybody knows how close you two were. The Scientific League would like to start a memorial scholarship in her name at Radcliffe, if you wouldn't object, of course."

"Uh . . . not at all. That would be very moving." He wondered if the League took this much interest in each of its members.

"Well, enough on that," Charles announced with a decisive change of tone. "But if there's ever anything we can do, you will let us know, won't you?"

"Yes, of course."

"I'm not just saying that, Paul. I really mean it."

"I know you do, Charles."

"Good. Now, tell me how your work is going. I want all the details."

From Memorial Bridge they turned onto Rock Creek Parkway and then took the Whitehurst Freeway access ramp to lower K Street. The Hollister home was near the corner of 31st and Dumbarton Streets, a huge, three-story red brick Federal with Victorian additions; a bay-window alcove on one side and a two-story wing on the other. The house was set back from the street on a five- or six-foot elevation and surrounded by a low brick wall that ran to a driveway on one side. To Paul, the house was as impressive as the car.

The driveway led around back to what had once been the carriage house. Just inside the gate Charles stopped the Rolls and said, "Here. You get out and I'll pull the car around back. The front door will be open; they'll have seen me coming. Leave your bag here. I won't be a minute."

"No problem," Paul replied. "I can ride the rest of the way with you."

"No, no. Not necessary. Go on up the steps. I'll meet you inside directly and get you squared away."

When Paul stepped out of the car, Charles drove around back and pulled into the carriage house. He switched the ignition key from the ON to ACC position and opened a leather-covered panel at the front of the center console. He pressed, in sequence, buttons marked STOP and REW, then after a short interval during which he visually followed the number counter spinning backward, another button marked FWD. From the car's right stereo speaker he heard his own voice saying, "I wish there was something we could do."

A few moments later: "I really mean it."

"I know you do, Charles."

"Good. Now, tell me how your work is going. I want all the details."

After he heard Paul's voice say, "It's a complicated puzzle, but I've had an important breakthrough that I want to follow up on," he smiled with satisfaction and shut the machine off.

He pressed the EJECT button, slipped the tape cassette into his inner jacket pocket, retrieved his briefcase and Paul's bag from the back seat, and went to join his guest inside.

Washington, D.C.

"I happened to run into your brother-in-law at the airport," Paul explained to David Sherman in the living room of the psychiatrist's house in Foggy Bottom.

"I'm hardly surprised," David replied. "He always seems to be at the right place with the right people."

Paul smiled caustically. "I don't see how I qualify with either."

"You must. Charlie has an unfailing instinct for this sort of thing. He's built his career on it. You haven't told him you're seeing me, have you?"

"No. I just said I was in town on Academy business. And I probably will stop in there before I leave. He and Sandy have a beautiful house, by the way."

"It is nice," David agreed. "The Establishment certainly rewards its own; especially in this city. How about a drink?"

"Vodka would be fine." Paul looked stunned, as if he'd surprised himself by what he'd said.

"Is anything wrong?"

"No. It just got me thinking. Thinking about what I'm here for, I guess."

David paused in the process of opening the Smirnoff's bottle. "Do you have a drinking problem?"

"No, nothing like that. Just the fact that I drink vodka and so does Amanda West . . . it was just one of the many things we have in common. If that's the word for it."

David set the drink on the coffee table in front of Paul. "I gather that's what you came to talk to me about."

Paul nodded. "I stayed in New York for a few days after I went to see Dr. Ramsey. I stayed with Amanda. All right so far. But when it came time to leave and go

160

back to Cambridge to pick up my life again, it was almost as if . . . I can't describe it precisely."

"This isn't the laboratory. You don't have to describe it precisely."

"It was almost as if I didn't feel that I belonged back in Cambridge, but that I belonged with Amanda, wherever she was. And I know she was just as desperate for me not to leave as I was to stay."

"Then why didn't you stay?"

Paul groped for an answer. "I'm confused. It's happened so quickly that I decided if I didn't step away and think about it, it would be beyond my control. I don't know why it's this strong. One thing I can tell you is that after only a few days, really, I love her more than any woman I've ever known."

David shrugged and offered a lighthearted grin. "Why shouldn't you feel that way about her? From everything you've told me, she's intelligent, beautiful, sensitive, passionate, loves you in return, has an interesting, influential job, and can empathize with your particular emotional problems because she's gone through many of them herself. That's a pretty compelling list of attributes."

"But why do I feel this way *now*, for God's sake? I mean, right after my wife kills herself, I'm back chasing skirts. A normal person wouldn't even be thinking about that now. I thought I'd outgrown that. And even if I haven't, I could have at least waited a decent interval. But when you come right down to it, I was already emotionally involved with Amanda before I knew Julia was dead."

"Please don't burden yourself with that, Paul," David counseled. "It's perfectly normal for healthy men to be attracted to good-looking women. Seeing Amanda on the tennis court at Shorecliffe, it would be difficult not to be attracted to her. If you were going to condemn every man at that party who made a habit of looking at women other than his own wife, you'd have the complete male guest list."

"But it isn't just sexual attraction," Paul asserted. "That part's easy enough to understand. I guess I've been to the well with enough of my co-eds over the years to be at least an informed amateur on the subject. But those relationships were strictly physical. That was the understanding at the start and that was the reality at the finish. And because of that they were all self-limiting. There was never any emotional attachment to speak of. I got the physical kick of a beautiful young body and they got the ego kick of fucking the professor. A simple value exchange."

"But with Amanda it's different?"

"That's right. With her there's an emotional commitment and a sense of longing there that I know I've never experienced before. Not even with Julia during the best of times."

"Maybe then you're just maturing in your ability to conduct relationships," David suggested.

"But I don't understand the whole thing. Look at both of us. When you stop to consider it, neither Amanda nor I has ever been seriously involved with the opposite sex on a deep emotional level. I've been married, we've each had our share of flings, and she's had any number of men who wanted to become seriously involved with her. But for whatever reason, neither one of us ever had been . . . until now. Maybe we're each too self-interested or self-involved."

"Maybe."

"But now that we've found each other, that's all somehow changed. And I don't know how to handle such a sudden alteration in my own emotional reality."

"And you feel guilty about this 'first' for you. You feel guilty about this deep emotional commitment to another woman when you never had it for your wife. And now that wife has been conveniently taken off your back . . . through your own negligence and insensitivity, you think."

Paul looked stunned. "I . . . guess that's . . . right."

David waved his hand across the air space in front of

him. "I don't want to sound harsh or cruel. I'm only trying to paraphrase what I think is in your mind."

Paul shook his head. "I guess you've summed it up pretty well. I feel like my emotions have taken over for my senses."

"We'll try to work through those feelings," David said, "and let you feel comfortable about normal drives and desires."

"It would be nice if you could convince me of that. Because all this has left me feeling decidedly *ab*normal."

"How long have you felt this way?" This might have been the most utilitarian of all David's psychiatric stock phrases.

"On this level, ever since Julia died. But on a larger level, ever since the surgery, I guess. And from what Amanda's told me, she feels the same way, too. Being able to pick up on her mental wavelengths and her being able to do the same to me is only symptomatic. I guess I'd have to say that nothing has felt really secure for twenty years, in the same way that it did before my brain tumor developed. I feel like I know things I haven't learned, I sense things that seem to be coming from outside my mind. I have terrific doubts about myself."

David rested his elbows on the arms of his chair and clasped his fingers together. "From outward appearances, you're one of the most successful, authoritative people I could imagine. But tell me about these doubts."

"Some of them I can't articulate. Some are personal matters, like not believing I could have more than a physical relationship with a woman; that I could do no more than envy other men their emotional attachments. I've felt that particular kind of incompleteness ever since I came out of the hospital. Lately, I've begun to question other things. Since my most recent scientific breakthrough, for instance, I've begun to question why I became a physicist in the first place after the operation; why I didn't go back to medical school. At first it was just an idle speculation that crept into my mind from time to time. But it's been growing steadily larger and more haunting."

"Have you come up with any tentative answers?"

"None that I find personally very flattering. I mean, what was it that changed about my personality or was taken away after I left the hospital? Was not wanting to be a doctor anymore something about not wanting to directly help other people, or be responsible for them? After what I'd been through, was I not willing to put myself out for anyone else? And if that is the case, it goes back to what I was just talking about—my emotional detachment from other people, particularly women . . . even my own wife."

"Maybe after all the trauma you'd been through in hospitals and with doctors, you just couldn't stand the emotional pressure of being around them through the rest of medical school and what came afterward. You were just too emotionally vulnerable, and the study of medicine would naturally trigger all of those negative connections. But looking back on it now, twenty years later, do you regret not going back to medical school?"

"Not really," Paul admitted.

"Would you like to be a doctor now, instead of a scientist and teacher?"

He thought for a moment. "No. I can't say that."

"All right, then. Let's approach it from the positive perspective. What is it that appeals to you about being a physicist?"

"The kick of discovery. Just like the cliché about climbing the mountain. I guess that's the real motivation for all science. It may not be as mature or altruistic or noble as curing a sick person the way a doctor does. But that's the reality. That electric moment when something comes together in your mind and suddenly you see it clearly, and everything else seems obvious and natural in light of what you've just figured out; that's really what it's all about. The sober rationale and justification for why you attempted it—that comes later, to explain and support the kick. If I can solve the Unified Field Theory, and pick up where people like Einstein and Bohr left off, that would be the greatest kick I could possibly imagine. Whatever happens to it afterward, or even if nothing happens to it, won't matter at all. As long as it's accurate, that's all I could possibly want."

"That sounds pretty down-to-earth to me."

"But up until I met Amanda, I'd have to say that pretty much represented the total scope of my life . . . at least the important part of my life. But since I've been with her, so many other things keep intruding. How shall I say it? I feel like I'm being 'completed' by her, just like I was able to complete the first part of my theory by being around her."

"What you're doing, Paul, is just offering a rationalization for being in love with her. And you don't need to do that, any more than you have to keep torturing yourself over Julia's death."

"But I still can't escape the feeling that something isn't right," he stated. "I don't feel normal. Ever since that surgery I've felt different, and meeting Amanda only confirms that for me."

David nodded with recognition. "There's nothing unusual about feeling that way. But keep in mind that none of us is the same person as an adult that we were as children, or before and after experiences in combat, or whatever. You would be a different person now than you were twenty years ago whether or not you'd had the brain tumor! I'm not the same person I was before I had my appendix taken out. But the point is, I'm *essentially* the same person. And you're essentially the same person, and just as good a person." He picked up a manila folder from the end table next to him and opened it. "Maybe this is as good a place as any to start."

"What's that?" Paul asked.

"The results of some of your tests when you were at Goddard. Some of your psychological tests. I had Dr. Wendell Fuller look them up for me. I just want you to know what the staff psychologist at Goddard found out after your surgery. I think it'll give us some common ground to talk about you.

"On the Wechsler Adult Intelligence Scale—that's an IQ test—you scored one eighty-four. That's considered in the genius range. The Bender Gestalt Test showed no evidence of neurological dysfunction. On the Minnesota Multiphasic Personality Inventory you were within every norm of behavior. The Thematic Apperception Test showed you were extremely creative, with a visionary sensitivity. The Rorschach Test indicated an imaginative integration of perception and understanding. And then there's the Rosenzweig Picture-Frustration Study, which showed that you were so completely acclimated in traditional stress situations that you considered them normal occurrences. That could have been the result of coming to grips with having to live with a brain tumor. But the point I'm trying to get across to you with all this is that you did come through the operation and the whole experience with both your mind and your psyche intact. It's perfectly natural that you should have the kinds of emotional feelings you do about the operation. But you're not psychotic. You're rational and highly intelligent."

"But I can't get over the sensation that somehow my mind was altered during that operation. And again, meeting Amanda has only intensified that sensation. Like the fact that so often we're able to finish each other's thoughts. You saw it yourself during the bridge game at Charles' and Sandy's."

"That was rather extraordinary," David admitted.

"Like the fact that we're both interested in science and both so obsessively involved in our work. That operation had some kind of similar effect on both of us, and on this Nathaniel Kagan, too, from what Amanda tells me."

"We're all the products of our emotional conditioning. Our reactions to everything are based on it. The three of you all went through the same experience and so have had a degree of similar emotional conditioning. It's not that surprising that you all react in similar ways."

Paul shook his head. "There has to be more to it than that. I tried to get it across to Dr. Ramsey but I don't think we were operating on the same wavelength. But since the operation, I just don't feel completely . . ." He shrugged and cast his hands out in frustration. "I don't feel completely whole. That's the best I can define it. My mind is playing games with me."

David sat back in his chair with his legs crossed and exhaled. He held his own drink up and swished it around in the glass. "There's been a lot of speculation over the years, but we still don't know exactly *what* the mind is. Every indication, of course, is that it's directly related to the brain. But just what that relationship is, we have no idea. Have you ever heard of Wilder Penfield?"

"The name sounds vaguely familiar. Who is he?"

"He's dead now, but he was a neurosurgeon, head of the Montreal Neurological Institute. He studied with Sir Charles Sherrington at Oxford and did some of the pioneering work in epilepsy. He should have won the Nobel Prize in Medicine; I don't know why he didn't. He spent his entire career speculating on the mind-brain connection, and since he had living brains of conscious patients to work with—a lot of that type of surgery is done with the patient awake—he had incredible opportunities for first-hand research. Eventually he came to the conclusion, or maybe 'impression' is a better word, that the mind and the brain were two separate entities, and that the brain was sort of a 'receiver' for the mind; which could itself be defined as a kind of psychic energy rather than physical tissue. We know that if you damage or destroy certain areas of the brain you lose certain functions. If we damage areas of the cerebral cortex we can stop thinking and reasoning, but that doesn't mean that thinking necessarily happens there."

"I don't follow you."

"All right, let's say I'm here talking to you on the telephone and you're home in Boston. If someone cuts the line in Philadelphia, the connection might go dead, but that doesn't necessarily indicate that either one of us was in Philadelphia. The cerebral cortex tissue might just be a *conductor* of this psychic energy the same way that the telephone line is a conductor of our voices. The fact that the line was cut doesn't mean that our voices cease to exist. It only means that they can't be conveyed that way until the damage is repaired. So that was one of the ideas Penfield and his associates were working on. But even after all their work in trying to physically localize the mind, we can still only talk about it in terms of effects, not of causes. So in psychiatry, since we don't understand how the mind works, we just try to rechannel it into happier, more productive areas. What I'm getting at is that at our primitive stage of understanding, a lot of what we conclude is going to depend on our definitions. Whatever you feel you've lost during and after that brain operation—whatever kind of psychic energy it is—might still be there just waiting for the right 'conductor.' And in psychiatry, we hope that the mind is resilient enough to find it."

"So the mind may be a 'natural force' unto itself?"

"That's right," David said. "In your work, you've explained to me that you're trying to relate the powers of the universe to each other; to see if there's some fundamental relationship between gravity and magnetism. People like Wilder Penfield have been trying to figure out some fundamental relationship between mind and brain, and how they interact. Penfield, for example, theorized that somehow the mind might be able to exist separately from the brain, such as after physical death."

"That's an incredible concept for a serious scientist," Paul commented. "It's the kind of thing you think of as belonging more to religion."

"Religion and science get very close sometimes, as you well know," he answered. "But he wasn't dealing with faith. This was sound physiological theory. And do you know who is one of Penfield's leading and most accomplished followers?"

"Who?"

"Norbert Ramsey."

New York

"Now try to push my hands together, as hard as you can."

Norbert Ramsey held his arms in front of him, about two feet apart, pressing his balled fists out as the young Spanish woman labored to move them closer together. She didn't really understand what he was saying, but from his gestures she could tell what was expected of her. Her tongue pierced through her pursed lips with the tension of the effort, but she finally did manage to move the fists.

"Very good!" Ramsey commended her. She broke out in a broad grin, having obviously pleased the surgeon. It was very important to please the man who took your life in his hands, especially when you had no money to pay him. For the many who could not afford to pay, Ramsey accepted no fee. From the many wealthy he treated from all over the world he asked for—and received—three or four times his normal payment.

He walked over to the table where Robert Anderson was sitting with manila file folders and a blank chart pad and dictated a few notes. The assistant then handed him the next open folder. Ramsey scanned the first three entries, handed it back and called out, "Miss Tracy?"

Another young woman, blonde and fearful and not more than twenty-four, stood up meekly from the row of upholstered chairs that lined one wall of Norbert Ramsey's personal consultation room. Every afternoon at this time, the postoperative outpatients sat as long as necessary and waited for the doctor's judgment. The room adjoined his office suite to simplify his daily movements as much as possible. While the exam session was taking place, Miss Olson was lining up all the phone calls Ramsey would be returning when he finished with the last case in the room. The calls would be set up so that as soon as he completed one, the next would be on the line waiting for him. After he finished with the calls, an intern would come in to bring him up-to-date on current medical literature. Any minutes he could save from procedural work could be devoted to more productive endeavors.

"How are you feeling today?" he asked the young blonde woman.

"Um . . . okay, I guess," she responded, as if afraid to be at all negative in the surgeon's presence. Somehow, it might break the spell.

"Well, let's take a look," he said, not unkindly. He picked up an ophthalmoscope from the examination table, held it up to her eye and instructed, "Okay, now look up at the ceiling." Holding her still with his hand on the top of her head and squinting into the instrument, he said to Anderson, "Optic nerve looks good. No pressure. Now we'll check out L-3."

He motioned her to sit on the side of the examination table, raised her knee-length hospital gown to her mid-thigh, then tore open an envelope containing a sterile needle and proceeded to jab it lightly into the girl's leg. She winced, but said nothing. He pricked her several more times in the same general area, then asked, "Does that hurt?"

She nodded.

"Good. That means the nerves are working. You can let your gown back down. I'm very happy with your progress." Miss Tracy beamed, just as the previous patient had done.

Within twenty-five minutes Ramsey had seen thirteen patients. It was a good day—all were recovering well and there were no complications. And each patient greeted the doctor's pronouncements with the same mix of awe, reverence, and fear. He was the one who had laid hands upon them and brought them back from the proximity of death; in many cases after other doctors had written them off. Ramsey didn't encourage his patients to think of him as a god or superhuman. But he did not discourage it, either. Faith—in anything —can be one of the most important aspects of the healing process.

When he returned to the office, Miss Olson could tell the patients were all doing well. If a tumor was growing back, or paralysis returning, he would have been in a black, uncommunicative mood. As it was, though, today he took the taxing administrative and paperwork routine in stride.

The first three calls were to other doctors, so even though the connection was made on the secretarial level, once Ramsey was ready to speak, he had to wait a few moments for the other man to come on the line. The next four calls were refusals of speaking invitations, though, and these were much easier to get through, with Ramsey explaining that at this stage of his life he had had to make the choice of whether he was going to spend his time speaking or operating and . . . The inviting parties always seemed to understand and selflessly agreed with the choice.

"Who's next?" he asked into the intercom box.

"Her name is Marion Girard. She says her father was a patient of yours. She called yesterday afternoon."

Armed with that much information, Ramsey punched the line-3 button and began, "Mrs. Girard? Norbert Ramsey here. Sorry I couldn't get back to you earlier. What can I do for you?"

"My father was a patient of yours back about twenty years ago," the woman explained. And even after she left verbal space for Ramsey to speak, he knew better than to ask how her father was doing before obtaining more information or recalling the specifics of the case. "He died of a brain tumor not too long after leaving Goddard," she filled in when he failed to speak.

"Yes, I remember," he said. "I'm very sorry. Your

father was a very kind and sensitive man. How can I help you, Mrs. Girard?"

"Something happened . . . I got a call the other day. I just wanted to make sure it was legitimate. A woman called who said she'd also been a patient of yours at the same time and wanted information about my father. She asked some personal questions and I just thought you ought to know about it . . . you know . . . in case it wasn't on the level or something."

"I see. Did you catch her name?"

"Yes. It was Amanda West."

Ramsey was silent for a moment. "Amanda West? Okay . . . ah, I'll certainly look into that, Mrs. Girard. Thank you for bringing this to my attention. And how is the rest of your family doing?"

"Very well, thank you. My mother's remarried."

"Very good. I'm very happy to hear that. And if anything else like this comes up that you're not sure about, you know to call me. Right?"

"Yes, of course, Dr. Ramsey. Thank you."

As soon as the light on the telephone went out, Miss Olson was back on the intercom announcing the next call.

"Ah . . . could you hold that one a minute?" Ramsey asked. He rested his chin on his fist and tried to rapidly think the situation through. Finally, he said, "There's another call I have to make first."

"Shall I get it for you?"

"No. I'll dial it myself." He pressed the button for the one line that didn't go through Miss Olson's phone in the outer office. He reached for the rolodex on the corner of his desk and turned the tab to the H's for the card with George Henderson's number.

Chapter Ten

Cambridge, Massachusetts

Going back to the apartment was like returning to the scene of an ancient tragedy. It was quiet and ordinary-looking now, and there were no visible traces that anything unusual had taken place. But the memory of the event pervaded the atmosphere and made everything seem garish and slightly skewed; not quite right. Paul felt a chill between his shoulder blades and a twisting in his stomach as soon as he opened the door.

For one thing, the place was unnaturally clean. After the police had finished up, the landlord had thoughtfully sent in a professional cleaning crew who must have scrubbed every inch of floor and wall, as if they could physically remove the taint of suicide. They'd been so complete they'd even smoothed over the indentations in the carpeting made by the chair legs. All in all, it looked to Paul like a museum reconstruction of his recent past. He hung his coat in the hall closet instead of tossing it onto the side chair as he usually did, and even sitting down in the living room felt strange and awkward.

Thankfully, he wouldn't be spending much time here—sleeping and occasionally eating; the rest of his day would be devoted to his lab and office at the Institute.

He brought his suitcase into the bedroom, thought about unpacking it, then decided to leave it next to the dresser for the time being. He loosened his tie, pulled off his shoes, and stretched out on the bed with his fingers clasped behind his head. He thought of Amanda. She'd probably been trying to call him up here the last two days and must be worried at not being able to get him. As he thought about her, he desperately wanted to see her, to have her lie next to him, to touch her. He tried to remember in order all the things David had said during their long session together; how he shouldn't torture and castigate himself for loving her. But then his eyes traveled down from the ceiling to the floor, just at the edge of the bed, and he visualized that scene that assaulted him when he opened the bedroom door not very long ago. And a choking sob welled up in his throat as he contemplated all the ways he had failed Julia.

He stood up again and began pacing around the bed, his hands thrust tensely into his pockets. He had to stop thinking this way. He felt as though he was existing in a kind of limbo now, outside his marriage, his classes, the serenity of his professorial life—all the anchors that had helped him to continue functioning on a relatively normal level. Before, when he felt this way, he would have called Harry Gillette and asked him to go have dinner with him and talk it out. But now, even Harry was gone.

Sitting down on the edge of the bed again, he reached for the receiver to call Amanda. At least he would tell her where he was. But as he started to pick it up, the phone rang. He jumped slightly. It had to be Amanda. That would be so predictable—they were always anticipating each other's thoughts. But after he expectantly said, "Hello," the voice at the other end said:

"Paul? This is Charles Hollister. How are you doing?"

"Oh . . . ah . . . okay, Charles. What's going on?"

"Look, I just wanted to make sure everything was all right. When you left, both Sandy and I thought you looked kind of strange; preoccupied or something. I said we were probably reading too much into it, but I just had to be sure that's the case, right?"

"Sure, Charles. Everything's okay. I was just kind of immersed in my work. That's all."

"Well good. I told Sandy that's all it was. You're sure everything is all right?"

"Yes. Absolutely."

"Fine, then. I won't keep you. I know you must be tired. But you know to call if anything comes up. You do know that, don't you?"

"Certainly."

"Very fine, Paul. Take care."

Had he seemed that out of it when he left the Hollisters' house? He didn't think so, but maybe he had. And why was Charles, only a casual acquaintance, really, so concerned with his well-being? Having had Paul stay at his house, perhaps he felt somehow responsible for his condition.

He was about to try for the phone again when his stomach once again tightened up and began to rumble. It couldn't be nerves, could it? Not for calling Amanda. Then he realized he hadn't eaten anything since early morning, and then only half a grapefruit and a piece of toast. That's all his stomach was trying to tell him, he reassured himself.

He went into the kitchen for an inventory. As he suspected, the refrigerator was completely empty. The cupboard offered a few cans of tuna and salmon, but nothing more substantial than that. He wanted something emotionally more satisfying to eat.

He'd go have dinner at Legal Seafood in Inman Square and then call Amanda as soon as he got back. He'd be more relaxed that way. He put his shoes back on and was on his way out the door when he stopped and recalled that he didn't think Legal Seafood took credit cards. He checked his wallet, but after the cab ride from Logan he had less than ten dollars, and he couldn't get a check cashed until morning. Shit.

Then he remembered. Ever since the rash of break-ins in the neighborhood the year before, Julia had kept a hundred dollars in twenty-dollar bills in an envelope in the drawer of her night table. The detective they'd happened to talk to told them that thieves were much less likely to harm a person who could give them some cash and let them get out quickly. So since that time they'd kept that hundred dollars there—absolutely not to be touched for anything other than discouraging a burglar. But now the situation had changed, and Paul felt no compunction about using some of the money to buy dinner.

He went back to the bedroom and opened the night-table drawer. But the money was gone! The white legal-size envelope Julia kept it in was still there, but it was ripped open and crumpled instead of being new and uncreased. He opened the other drawer just to make sure. The money wasn't there, either.

The cleaning crew must have taken it; that was the only possible explanation. He couldn't imagine the police or his landlord having stolen a hundred dollars from him, and they were the only other people to have been in the apartment since Julia died. It had to have been the cleaning crew. He couldn't decide whether to wait and report them in the morning, or disturb his landlord right now. What the hell? He was angry enough. If his landlord got angry, too, he might do something about it; not that he ever expected to see that hundred dollars again.

But wait a minute! Something didn't quite add up. If they happened upon the money—and they'd have to really be looking for it since it was in the back of a drawer between the pages of a book—why did they just tear open the envelope and leave it as evidence? Even the most careless of thieves would have to realize that taking the envelope along with the money would mean a much smaller chance of detection. The package might not be missed at all, while the torn envelope was a dead giveaway.

Maybe they figured what's the difference, Paul reasoned. But they had to be concerned with that. They were the regular cleaning crew for the building and the theft could easily be traced back to them. No one is going to risk losing his job on an obvious crime like that.

Could someone else have broken in and taken the

money? No. There was absolutely no evidence of anything else missing or any forced entry. There had to be some other explanation.

Think logically, think like a scientist, Paul prodded himself. If the envelope was still there—torn and crumpled—but the money was gone it must mean that . . . God, was it possible? . . . Julia must have opened it herself. And if she took it out, especially since she obviously *tore* it out, she must have been using it for the purpose for which it was originally intended! Someone had broken in and she was trying to get them to leave! That had to be it!

Feverishly, he tried to mentally reconstruct the entire scene as he came in and discovered her body. There'd been no indication of anything other than a suicide. Of course not. If someone was that skilled, they wouldn't leave any traces of a murder. They would have had to take the money if it was offered, but if they didn't see where it came from, they wouldn't have known about the envelope to destroy it. That much made sense.

But get ahold of yourself, Paul kept thinking. Are you jumping to conclusions? Could there be some other explanation? You wouldn't accept this as absolutely conclusive evidence in the laboratory. Maybe grief, fatigue and hunger have affected your reasoning processes.

He sat down and went over every possibility again. But no other one made any sense. Amanda would certainly agree with this beginning of a theory. She was always looking for hidden patterns.

He went into the bathroom, fished through the medicine cabinet for Julia's eyebrow tweezers, and carefully picked up the torn envelope and laid it on the top of his dresser. If the police could find fingerprints from anyone in the cleaning crew, he would rest a lot easier.

New York

Moshe Baruch was early, which didn't surprise Nathaniel Kagan in the least. The Israelis were always there when they wanted something from you. And the situation wasn't going to go away, so he might as well deal with it.

"Why isn't there any security in here?" Baruch demanded as he invited himself into Nat's cramped and disheveled office. "There's no guard or anything."

"There is so a guard," Nat protested.

"In that case, I got by him."

"It's your business to get by guards."

"It's also the business of the people the guard is supposed to keep out."

"I'll see what I can do about it then," he promised.

"Please do. You make me nervous this way."

The feeling was unquestionably mutual, the rabbi assured himself.

"Well, Moshe, let's get down to business. Today is my only day in the Committee office this week. And I have to make the speech at the nuclear rally tonight, and I'm meeting Eleanor for dinner first. By the way, how was your flight?"

"You know El Al," he laughed. It had become a standard joke between them.

Baruch sat down. "Why do you waste your time on all that nuclear energy business? There's plenty of people running around *haking a chainik* about it already."

"What's it to you?" Nat snapped. "I happen to feel very strongly about it. You don't seem to mind the time I spend on Zionist issues."

"That's different. We need all the help we can get. What business has a rabbi to talk about scientific issues?"

"It's a moral issue."

"I wonder how moral you'll think it is when Israel's getting all its power from nuclear reactors."

"Not to mention atomic bombs," Nat added sardonically.

Baruch arched his eyebrows and smiled. "Come now, Nathan. You know we don't have the Bomb. But enough talk of irrelevant matters." He placed his battered Samsonite briefcase across his knees. Though it looked like something an airline claims representative wouldn't allow five dollars on, it was actually more expensive than Nat's leather Hartmann attaché. Because unlike the ones sold over the counter, this one was fitted with a complete steel shell on the inside and two locks that could neither be picked nor broken.

He was just about to open the case when he looked up, set it down and crossed over to the window. Through it there was a marvelous view of the Chrysler Building. "There are at least five hundred vantage points out there from which I could use a high-powered telescope to pick out every blood vessel in your eyeballs." With that he ceremoniously pulled the blinds shut and returned to his chair and briefcase.

"This is the list we've made up of your main contacts and representatives overseas," he stated, handing the two stapled pages across the desk to Nat, who took them, read them over, and was unnerved by their completeness.

"It looks accurate to me," he said.

"Now, the nitty-gritty, as you say." He paused long enough to extract a pair of reading glasses from his jacket pocket and with a snap of his wrist to open them, fitted them on his head. Nat couldn't recall having seen him wear glasses before, so he took the gesture as a sign of the seriousness Baruch was trying to impress upon him. "The Committee for Jewish Unity is a well-respected international organization. And your friends back in Israel want to commend you for all you've done as director."

"My friends in Israel want to take over the Committee and use it for their own purpose," Nat stated.

"Use some of its resources and connections," Baruch clarified. "That is all we're asking. Of course, there would be no direct contact between us and your representatives; at least not at first. And anything that had to happen later on would be through you and with your approval."

"What assurance do I have you'll hold to this?"

"You have our word. That's all you need. Look, Nathan, if we wanted to play those kinds of games we wouldn't bother with you at all. You saw how we got your list. We could have just as easily free-lanced the rest. But what appeals to us is that the Committee is *not* a secret organization. It's aboveboard and out in the open. So its affairs—the individual comings and goings—nobody pays much attention to."

"I'd like you to be more specific," Nat said, even though by this point he knew exactly what Baruch had in mind.

"All right. The Committee for Jewish Unity tries to see to the welfare of Jews in countries where they have traditionally been persecuted, or you have reason to believe they might face persecution because of a change in political climates."

"Yes. Go on."

"These countries coincidentally happen to be—by and large—the same ones that the State of Israel sees as threats to its own security."

"What makes you think my contacts can tell you anything you don't already know? They're mostly rabbis and businessmen, and a few professors."

"People who are there all the time can read the mood of a country, notice subtle changes and developments that wouldn't be obvious to the one-time observer, no matter how well trained he was."

"So you just want me to tell my foreign contacts to be alert to that sort of thing."

"That's right," Baruch confirmed.

"And that's all?"

"No, of course that's not all!" Baruch threw the papers he had been holding across the desk. "If that was all, you wouldn't have been playing games with me all this time. I also want to use your contacts as couriers, to get information in and out of those countries . . . and just as often, through them."

"But, Moshe, don't you see what you're asking?" Nat protested. "These people aren't trained for missions like that. Look how easy it was for you to find flaws in our security here. You're making these people extremely vulnerable."

"We have couriers all over the world, Nathan. Most of them are ordinary businessmen who travel a lot in their work. All this project would be is an extension of that arrangement."

"Yes, but in hostile countries."

"Let's not have to go back to the beginning. Life has never been easy for Israel, just as it hasn't been easy for Jews in general. But you can rest assured that without Israel, it would be a lot more difficult. And we all have to do what we're in a position to do."

"I forgot you came from Eastern Europe, Moshe. You're still a skilled practitioner of the Jewish art of guilt. I thought the Israelis were past that stage."

"We're a very utilitarian people. I'm just asking you to meet us halfway . . . for the sake of the country you profess to love."

Nat sprang to his feet and slammed his palms down on the desk. "Look, Moshe!" he shouted. "You know that I'm as committed as anyone to the principles of Zionism. My record goes back twenty years if you care to check. So don't try to use that kind of *mishegas* against me!"

Baruch put up his hands in a "back off" gesture, turned his head to the side and chuckled. "Okay, okay. So I went too far just now. I was just trying to push you a little, that's all. You know . . . whatever works."

"That's your guiding creed, isn't it?"

"You know as well as I do, Nathan . . . it has to be."
He snapped his briefcase shut and stood up to leave.
"So I'll see you later on then?"

"Where?"

"At this fancy speech you're giving."

"You're coming? After all you said before?"

Baruch grinned. "I wouldn't miss it for the world."

"So I put the ripped-open envelope in one of those
seal-lock plastic kitchen bags and took it to Lieutenant
Kennedy at the police station," Paul explained in the
cab heading for Wall Street.

"And what did they find?" Amanda asked.

"The only fingerprints anywhere on it were mine and
Julia's. And the specific ones on the end where it had
been ripped were her right thumb and index finger."

"My God," she pronounced. "What are they going
to do?"

"Kennedy said they'd reconsider the whole thing,
although the coroner said she definitely died from a
barbiturate overdose. He said there were a lot of
possible explanations for the money being missing, like
the fact that she could have spent it herself while I was
gone. He said if she was intending to kill herself, it
wouldn't matter whether she had money by her bed for
an emergency or not."

"Do you agree with all that?"

Paul stared at her for several seconds. "No," he said.

"Now do you believe me that something's going on?"
she demanded.

"I don't know what to believe. But since there's
really nothing I can do about it . . ."

"One of these days you're going to lose some of that
scientific detachment and . . ." She saw that he was
ready to snap at her and quickly nipped her lecture
short. "We don't have to talk about that now. I just
have to tell you how good it is to see you, Paul. I
haven't stopped thinking about you since you left. I
thought that maybe once I was alone again I'd realize it

was all just a passing infatuation. But . . . it's not, as it turns out."

"I'm glad." He smiled. "Because, as it turns out, it's not with me, either."

"And I'm glad you decided to come with me tonight."

"As long as you understand it's *only* for you," he said. "Do you know how many anti-nuclear demonstrations I've had to suffer through on the MIT campus alone?"

"But this one will be different," she promised.

"That's what all the organizers always say. 'We've got Jane Fonda,' or 'We've got George Wald,' or 'We've got a trained monkey who became sterile at Three Mile Island and has written an epic poem about it,' or 'We've got an agnostic Zionist rabbi who's an expert on the negative aspects of plutonium.'"

"Don't make fun. Rabbi Kagan is an extremely intelligent, sensitive man."

"Whose opinions you happen to agree with. I've seen what *Aurora's* written about the intelligent, sensitive people you don't happen to agree with."

"You'd agree with him, too, if you'd stop and think about the issue," she asserted, knowing she was moving them closer to another confrontation just when she was rejoicing in having him back again.

"Don't you think he's spreading himself a bit thin?" Paul asked. "I mean, between his congregation in Long Island and this Committee for Jewish Unity I keep reading about and this anti-nuke gadfly stuff. Sounds like a strong measure of dilettantism thrown into the equation."

"I'm not going to let you bait me like this," she resolved. "Just listen to what he—and everybody else —has to say with an open mind. Stick by me long enough and I'll expand your horizons no end."

"That's what I'm afraid of. I'll lose my scientific objectivity." He smiled, leaned over the seat and kissed her.

"You could stand to lose some of it. You guys are all the same."

"You just got through telling me how different I was from all the rest," he protested.

"Do you know how many times I've sworn I'll never date another scientist?" she said.

"Come on now. We're much more interesting than lawyers."

"And totally full of yourselves," she added.

Paul feigned an injured expression. "Oh no, my dear." He threw his arms out expansively. "We're full of . . ." He hesitated, as if grasping for just the right word, but when he saw her open her mouth into a mischievous grin he barked, "Don't say it!"

The cab let them off at Broadway and Exchange Place and they walked down the shadowed granite corridor to Federal Hall.

"We're just in time!" Amanda said, pulling him along faster as she saw Nathaniel Kagan step up to the microphone on the makeshift podium.

They edged their way through the throng of people to get close to the front. Paul half-listened to the speech, his eyes periodically darting over to Amanda, who was listening intently. The rabbi was saying nothing he hadn't heard before. He could practically predict what each new point would be.

"We're past the era of second chances in our history. Technology has taken care of that," Nathaniel Kagan concluded his speech. "There will be no more opportunities to be wrong and live to correct the mistakes."

There was some polite applause and a few cheers and whistles, almost identical to those for the other speakers. The television news crews were now packing their equipment into the line of vans and station wagons parked illegally along Broad Street, and with their departure, the crowd was beginning to dissipate. The entire Wall Street area promised to turn into the deserted canyon it became every night.

"Come on," Amanda said, taking Paul's hand. "I want to introduce you to Nat." They climbed the stairs toward the George Washington statue. On the way up he turned his head to see a fistfight that had broken out on the other side of the steps and crashed into a hawker selling buttons and other anti-nuclear souvenirs from a large felt-covered easel. The buttons and the hawker clattered to the granite stairs.

"Hey, Jack! Why the hell don't you look where you're going?" the vendor yelled. Paul tried to spit out his apologies as he lifted the man up by the elbow, but he refused Paul's arm and fell back on his side. He screamed.

"Oh God," Paul said, figuring the man had broken his hip. But when he looked closer he saw a button that read "Split Wood, Not Atoms," impaled in the man's thigh. Paul pulled it out.

"Gimme my damn button back, Jack," he growled.

"Sorry. Just trying to help."

"Yeah, well you helped enough already. I'm just trying to make an honest living and . . ."

Paul grabbed the first thing he could reach from the vendor's easel—a pennant bearing the legend, "No More Nukes!" and a beautifully rendered drawing of the bomb dropping on Nagasaki—and asked the hawker, "How much?"

"Two-fifty."

"Here." He pressed three dollar bills into the hawker's bruised hand and walked quickly up the remaining stairs. "He had it coming," he said to Amanda, "trying to profit from a situation like that."

Amanda could no longer contain herself, and burst out laughing.

"Yeah, very funny."

There was still a small clutch of people around Kagan when they reached him, but when he saw Amanda he waved and signaled her over.

"Wonderful speech," she said. "You really drove home the point. Nat, I'd like you to meet Paul Garrett, who I told you about."

Nat extended his hand. "You must be a real true believer," he said.

"What?" Paul responded, then looked at the pennant he was still carrying. "Anything for the cause," he recovered.

"Paul, Amanda . . . this is my wife, Eleanor. And an Israeli friend, Moshe Baruch."

Amanda was surprised by Eleanor, though she didn't know exactly what she was expecting. Maybe a rabbi's wife was supposed to be plainer, or more retiring. Instead, she was pretty, vivacious, and looked a good deal younger than Nat. She was particularly surprised, she guessed, because Nat had mentioned that Eleanor's father had been a rabbi, too.

"So, what do you think of your crusading husband?" Amanda asked her.

"He's always crusading for something," Eleanor replied. "Sometimes I can't keep track. When he's not in Israel," she turned with a look of reprimand to Baruch, "he's in his office in the city or at the synagogue or out on his boat. I keep telling him he's become a jet-age rabbi." Everyone chuckled.

"Well, would you all like to go out somewhere for a bite to eat?" Nat offered. "I don't think there's anything open in this area, but I've got my car here. We could drop you off afterward."

"That sounds fine," Amanda said. "Paul?"

"Sure."

"Good."

They started walking toward the Kagans' car, which was parked around the corner on Pearl Street. "I guess this is like a reunion, in a way," Nat said. "A rather small graduating class, but an extraordinary one, under the circumstances. I wouldn't have recognized Amanda, she was just a child at the time and has changed so much . . ."

"I hope so," she broke in.

"But now that I see you, Paul, you do look familiar. I remember. When Dr. Ramsey would come by on his rounds, almost all the other patients would clamor for his attention. But you would sit back, not say anything, and wait until he came to you. It was as if you wouldn't give him the satisfaction of worshiping him."

"I guess I've always disliked authority. In any form," Paul said.

"A wise stance to take."

"I'm very happy to meet you, Dr. Garrett," Baruch said. "I've heard a lot about your work."

"He probably hasn't," Eleanor suggested. "He's just trying to make more contacts."

"That's not true." Baruch laughed. "We Israelis are very much interested in science. Technical know-how is one of our leading export items."

"I'm afraid I don't do anything anyone would bother to export," Paul said. "Except perhaps in arcane physics journals."

They reached the car. "Look how tightly we've been parked in," Nat exclaimed. "We'll never be able to get out of that space."

"What did you expect?" Eleanor said. "This is New York City. Give me the keys, I'll get it out."

"We each have our own strengths," Nat commented. "It's one of the things that makes the marriage work so well. And one of Eleanor's strengths is getting us out of tight squeezes." He handed her the keys to the Oldsmobile.

"This won't take but a minute," she assured them.

She opened the driver's side door, sat down, and put the key in the ignition.

Paul noticed a strange expression on Moshe Baruch's face. It almost looked like he was confused and didn't know whether to admit it openly. Finally, Baruch said, "Eleanor, just a minute. I want to . . ."

"It's all right," she called back. "Believe me. I can handle it myself. I've seen the way you Israelis drive, anyway."

Baruch smiled appropriately, but there was still something in his eyes that was unnerving. He heard the car's starter click and suddenly his expression changed to one of determination and purpose.

"Eleanor, don't turn it on!" he screamed as he rushed toward her.

As he said it, they were all knocked to the ground by the force of the shock waves and a huge ball of yellow flames exploded from the Oldsmobile's hood, engulfing the entire car in less than a second.

Chapter Eleven

The previous several hours registered as a hazy nightmare in Amanda's mind: the shattering explosion and screams of agony, the almost instantaneous sound of fire engines and police sirens, the ambulance, the manic madness of the Bellevue emergency room, the resident trying to force a needle of some sedative into her arm while a police officer continued hammering her with questions, her unwillingness to leave Paul's side, even when they wanted individual statements from everyone. She didn't know how many times she'd been through the story now; how many times they'd all been through the story. All except Nat Kagan, who'd been considerately left to his own grief.

Throughout it all, she moved through the entire range of emotions, from shock to panic to fear to horror to sorrow. But the only sensation that stayed with her constantly was a dull ache near the base of her skull; the abstract registering in her brain of having been involved in yet another act of violence.

They were sitting now in a police security room in the hospital's emergency suite. She and Paul and Moshe Baruch. They hadn't brought Nat in. Maybe he was sleeping. Or maybe they'd taken him home. Moshe Baruch had seemed just as unwilling to let Nat out of his sight as she'd been to let go of Paul, but there wasn't much he could do about it. They assured Baruch he'd be safe. In this room a police guard was posted at the door and another was in the hallway that provided the only access to the room. Baruch paced restively around the windowless chamber, his face locked in the same grim expression he had had all evening.

"Moshe, I know what you're thinking. Please stop blaming yourself." The voice was Nat's. The guard at the door stepped aside to let him in.

"How could I have missed anything so routine?" Baruch answered.

"How could you know? Who could have expected anything like that?"

"We should always be expecting something. A momentary lapse. And it cost a life."

Amanda stood up from the vinyl couch she shared with Paul. "Nat, how are . . . how are you feeling?" She came over to him.

He offered a weak smile.

"I just can't believe it. After everything else that's happened." She wanted to do something . . . to reach out to him, to touch him, to communicate her empathy.

Recognizing her distress, he gave her the opening, extending his arms for her to rush into. She put her arms through his and held him in back by the shoulders, softly sobbing.

"I wish there was something I could . . . I could do for you," she cried.

Nat struggled to restrain his own tears. "I know," he whispered. "I know exactly."

"Thank you." She gradually released her hold.

"That bomb was clearly meant for me," he said. "Such a chance thing. She happened to be better at parking the car, that's all. And because of that insignificant talent, she's dead and I'm alive. I don't know how I can go on, knowing she died in my place."

Paul thought immediately of David Sherman's comment about survivor guilt. Then he thought about Julia.

"She died *l'kiddush Hashem*," Baruch said.

Amanda looked perplexed.

"In the Jewish religion," Nat explained, "when an innocent person dies for his faith or to save the life of another person, it is said that he died *l'kiddush Hashem*

—for the sanctification of the name of God. And for them is reserved a special place in the hereafter. It's one of the most important concepts, and even people who believe little else believe it."

"Does it give you any comfort?" Amanda asked hesitantly.

"As a rabbi, you can imagine how many times I've had to provide comfort and solace to others who'd just . . . suffered a loss. And almost all of them look to me for answers."

"What answers do you give them, Rabbi?" Paul inquired.

He shrugged. "I tell them to look inside themselves for the answers. I tell them that because there are no other answers. The best we can hope for is to be 'bound up in the bond of eternal life.'" He glanced around the room for something to fix his gaze on, but there were no windows and nothing on the walls. "I wish I could be reasonably certain even of that. But now that I face this tragedy myself, and I look inside myself for the answer, I have very little to offer."

"Your faith must support you, as you support others," Amanda said.

"My faith consists of a humble admiration of the infinitely superior spirit that reveals itself in the little that we, with our weak and transitory understanding, can comprehend of reality. As to whether that spirit works individually on our behalf, either here in this world or in the next, is something I can't really speak about. I've always been much more comfortable working with values than with beliefs. Morality is of the highest importance—but for us, not for God. So it would be intellectually and emotionally dishonest for me to suddenly embrace a kindly and benevolent God who is working through His own purpose. It would be comforting, but it wouldn't work."

When Amanda happened to look at Paul, the color had drained from his face. "Is anything wrong?" she asked.

"No. I don't know what to say," he responded. "But while Rabbi Kagan was talking just now, I got the feeling that I'd heard it all before."

"It's not exactly an original idea," Nat admitted. "You very well may have heard it before."

"But it was more than that. I can't exactly articulate what I mean except that I felt as if I'd *said* it before. And in just about those exact words."

"What is it you say, Paul? 'Life is full of mysteries.'" Amanda stated.

"The most beautiful thing we can experience is the mysterious," Nat went on. "It's the source of all true art and science."

Again, Paul looked stunned. "That too. It sounds like something I recognize from inside my own mind. I don't know where or when, Nat, but I know I've said that."

"Maybe we're just on the same wavelength. Some people are, you know."

"But at a time like this?" Paul asked.

"We've both lost our wives to meaningless, senseless violence. Maybe that kind of stress brings people together. I don't know. I guess I'm just going on like this to avoid looking inside myself; because I know I can't face what's there."

The door opened and Lieutenant Bartlett came in. He was the detective from the First Precinct who'd been assigned to the investigation. "I'm sorry to keep you all here so long," he apologized, "but in a case like this, it's better to be complete and thorough right up front. Rabbi, are you comfortable?"

"Reasonably so, yes. Thank you."

"Mr. Baruch, I've contacted the Israeli Consulate, as you asked. Rabbi, Nassau County police have been sent to your house and will remain there while the investigation takes place. And as soon as we finish here, my men will take you wherever you want to go."

"He'll be going with me tonight," Baruch stated.

"As you wish. Just be sure we have a number where you can be reached. Now, I have two more people here who'd like to talk to you." The door opened again, as if on cue, and the two men—one middle-aged and gray-haired, the other younger but bald—entered the room. "This is Lawrence Klein of the Nineteenth Precinct," Bartlett said, indicating the bald man, "and George Henderson of the FBI. Rabbi Kagan, Paul Garrett, from MIT, Amanda West, the editor of *Aurora* Magazine, and Moshe Baruch . . ."

"He's an economist with the Bank Leumi of Israel in Tel Aviv," Nat said.

Baruch appeared to flinch as Henderson was introduced, but said nothing. Seeing Klein, Amanda smiled slightly and relaxed, as one often does when a familiar presence lessens a particularly stressful situation.

"I came over as soon as I picked your name up on the police teletype," Klein explained, taking her hand. "Did you notice anything, or anyone in the area of the car? Anything that might have seemed similar to anything you saw in Bloomingdale's?"

She shook her head. "I'm afraid not. Do you think there's any relationship?"

"We don't rule anything out without evidence one way or the other. So far, the only relationship is you. Neither one of these incidents is routine, even by New York standards. And so we try to look for things that are out of the ordinary. Sometimes they lead us to the answer."

"Has anyone made any threats against you lately?" Henderson asked Nat.

"Occasionally we'll get a crank letter or phone call at the Committee for Jewish Unity office. But never anything for my statements on nuclear energy."

"It's doubtful that whoever placed the bomb was interested in that," Henderson said.

"Wait a minute!" Amanda exclaimed, looking at Nat. "What about the dog in the park?"

Both Henderson and Baruch turned right to her.

"What was that, Miss West?" Henderson asked.

She told him the story, how they had been sitting there peacefully for some time, and then suddenly, with no warning, the dog attacked, only to be killed just before it killed them. "We were very lucky that time."

"Too lucky," Klein commented. "It's absolutely beyond the realm of coincidence. Why didn't you report it?"

Amanda shrugged and Klein didn't pursue it. She thought for a moment, then said, "Since I was there at both of these incidents, do you think it's possible that I was the target, not Nat?"

"Why would anyone want to hurt you?" Paul asked.

"I have no idea. But do you think it's possible?"

"It's certainly possible," Klein said. "But improbable."

"I agree," Henderson said. "Mr. Baruch, you're from Israel. Do you think you could have figured in this somehow?"

"I don't see how," Baruch responded. "True, I'm an Israeli, but I'm here as an economist. And people don't murder over money . . . at least on this level, not directly."

Amanda thought back to her own attempt to apply the "Follow the Money" rule. Still, she came up blank. "But just before . . . just before the explosion, you said something," she noted. "Like you were trying to stop her from turning the key. Do you remember?"

"I must have had . . . I don't know, I just at that moment had a premonition that something was going to happen. I get that every once in a while."

"Did you see anything?" Klein asked.

"No. I just had a feeling. That's all."

"All right, just a few more routine questions, please, and then we can wrap this all up," Henderson announced. "Where were the five of you going when the explosion occurred?"

"Just out to dinner," Paul answered.

"What had brought you together?"

"Paul . . . Dr. Garrett and I had come to hear Rabbi Kagan's speech," Amanda said. "This is a very important scientific issue and much of what Rabbi Kagan believes represents my magazine's official position."

"How did you three meet?"

"Amanda and I met by chance in the park. In Central Park," Nat said.

"By chance?"

"That's right."

"You're sure you didn't know each other before?" Henderson persisted.

"Well, as it happens, we did sort of know each other before. In fact, all three of us did, which is what makes the story somewhat unusual. We were all in the hospital together, more than twenty years ago."

"I see. So you got together as sort of a reunion?"

"No. It was nothing like that," Amanda explained. "I happened to run into both of them, and introduced them to each other."

"Very interesting," Henderson said, writing the answer to each question in a green, government-issue notebook. Amanda couldn't figure out what this line of questioning could have to do with his investigation. "How exactly did you and Miss West meet, Dr. Garrett?" he continued.

"Ah . . . it was a party on the Eastern Shore of Maryland," Paul answered.

"It was given by the attorney for the Scientific League," Amanda added. "They publish my magazine and Dr. Garrett is a member. But I'm afraid I don't see where all this is leading."

"We just have to take all possibilities into consideration," Henderson said. Amanda detected his annoyance at the challenge.

Lieutenant Bartlett looked over to Lawrence Klein, his eyes raised in a question. Klein nodded silently in response. "I think we've got all the information we need for the time being. Mr. Henderson, is there anything else?"

"No, I guess this'll take care of it for the present, as long as we know where to reach everyone."

"I'm sorry we've had to keep you here this long," Bartlett went on, "but I'm sure you understand. It's a case with international overtones, so . . ."

Moshe Baruch rose immediately from where he'd positioned himself near the door. Paul and Amanda followed suit and so, finally, did Nat Kagan.

"Can I take you home, Miss West?" Klein asked, but before she could answer Baruch said:

"The bank's provided me with a driver and it'll be no trouble for me to take care of everyone. I don't want Rabbi Kagan to be alone tonight."

"Of course," Bartlett said.

"Let me just make one quick phone call and have the driver come round."

"I hope you don't mind," Baruch said, turning from the front seat to face Paul and Amanda in the back, "but I'd like for you to stay with me this evening. I have a house outside the city."

"But . . . I don't understand," Amanda said. "I can see that you'd want to have someone with Nat, but we'll be fine by ourselves."

"I'm just trying to make sure of that, Miss West. We can stop at your apartment for your things. And I believe Dr. Garrett has been staying there with you."

Amanda flinched at this; not the indelicacy of his mentioning it in front of a rabbi, but the fact that Baruch had the piece of information at all. "I just don't know what you're getting at."

"We don't know exactly what happened this evening," the Israeli responded. "And until we know a little more, I'd feel more secure if you'd both agree to come along. Just for one or two nights, please."

"You're asking us to go who knows where with you. This whole thing is really crazy. I don't see what an economist has to do with . . ." She turned to Paul for confirmation, then to Nat.

"Moshe, I think you'd better tell these people who you really are," the rabbi said.

Westchester County, New York

From the outside, the house looked like a venerable, comfortable Tudor, encircled by a chest-high stone fence and sitting at the end of an established, tree-lined street. That the owners were well-off and took pride in their home was apparent at first glance. Not so apparent until one stepped inside was the bulletproof glass fitted into each window opening, the security console in the front hall that indicated when anyone set a single foot on the property, and the telecommunications setup in the metal-lined attic that provided a direct, noninterceptible link to an even more secure building in Tel Aviv.

Moshe Baruch sat in the walnut-paneled den, his view of the street obscured by the light-blocking drapes. He was working the many facts and possible facts through his mind, waiting for calls from the operatives who by now had fanned out throughout the New York City area. He kept a bottle of Jack Daniels close by, and every so often he reached for a thoughtful swallow. When he was fatigued, he found that a moderate amount of alcohol kept him thinking clearly after his normal mental reserves would have been depleted. Good liquor was a luxury in Israel, but traveling overseas as he did offered certain side benefits, such as duty-free purchasing and no customs inspection.

When he arrived at the house with his three guests, the two-man permanent staff (a husband and wife, actually) were prepared, Baruch's driver having alerted them by restricted channel radio-telephone on the way up. They put Nathaniel Kagan in the room at the end of the hall, where it was quietest and where he wouldn't be disturbed. It was unlikely that noise would bother him in any event tonight, since Baruch had insisted he take more than one Dalmane capsule.

He played the events of the evening over and over, trying to isolate any specific point where he could have anticipated trouble. But no matter how many times he went through it all, he came up empty. His business was to plan for contingencies, but the crime just didn't fit into a standard pattern. It just didn't fit into the operating patterns of the PLO or its sister organizations to make this kind of political statement at an event that had nothing to do with its cause. If Nathan had been addressing an Israeli solidarity rally, for example, Baruch would have instinctively checked out the car for explosives before he let anyone turn the ignition key. Or even if they'd wired the rabbi's car as it stood out in front of his house overnight . . . that would follow the pattern. But at a rally against nuclear reactors? Who could figure it?

Then he thought back over the discussions with Nathan about his plans for the Committee for Jewish Unity and the possible danger to some of the members. It had all seemed abstract, even during the talk that very afternoon. But now, right at the beginning, the very worst had already happened. Nathan would certainly hold this up to him from then on; that is, if he got beyond his grief enough to even talk to him. And he supposed he didn't really blame him. Not after the death of his wife.

Maybe if he had a stronger or more orthodox faith in God he would just say it was God's will. But Moshe knew him better than that. No, Nathan wouldn't understand, and he wouldn't put it in perspective. He was a Zionist and a patriot, to be sure, but he wasn't a soldier. He didn't have a soldier's mentality.

He hadn't had to fight the same way Moshe Baruch had had to fight. For Nathaniel Kagan, Israel was an ideal, the historical realization of a Biblical memory, a place of unity for all the members of the Jewish faith scattered throughout the world. For Baruch, it was nice to think about those things, but to him, Israel was a means to personal survival. It was, more than anything else, a haven for which he longed after seeing his parents and two sisters butchered in the camps at Buchenwald and Mauthausen. For him, the existence of the State as a place to receive homeless and displaced Jews was not enough. It must also be strong enough to destroy anyone or anything that might try again what was done to his generation. That would never happen again—regardless of the consequences, regardless of the price in lives. From now on, in the mind of Moshe Baruch, every Jew must be a soldier.

"Anything come in yet?" he called to the "housekeeper" standing watch and monitoring the communications console in the front hall. The man shook his head negatively. Baruch hoped for some clue tonight, something on which to base a search. The chances of an early break like that were slim, but the effort was worth it. The PLO operatives were highly mobile, and in another eight hours they could be back in the Middle East or Europe. Or, they could stay right here in the area, and this worried him just as much. He could hold his guests a day or two at the most. Then, they would be at the mercy of whoever decided they wanted them. And Baruch still wasn't convinced Dr. Garrett and Miss West didn't figure in somehow other than coincidentally.

He brought the bottle up to his lips again. He had taught himself to relax, even in the midst of the greatest pressure and stress. For the moment, there was nothing else to do.

As he tipped the bourbon back, he detected a slowly moving form diffused through the brownish glass. He moved the bottle to one side and saw Amanda standing near the double walnut doors that led into the den. She was wearing an embroidered, high-necked nightgown that came down to the floor, covering her entire body. She was standing very still.

"Care to join me?" he asked, extending the liquor out toward her at arm's length. But she didn't answer. "Is anything wrong?" Still no response. "Having trouble sleeping?" She wasn't looking at him, he realized, but about three feet beyond. He turned to see what was there, but it was only a blank wall.

He set the bottle down on the end table and went over to her, taking her hand in both of his. "Miss West. Amanda. What's wrong? Are you all right?"

Her eyes darted around the room and blinked in obvious confusion. Her breathing was shallow and labored. She reminded him of his own little girl waking up from a nightmare.

"What is it?" he pressed. He clasped her by both shoulders, then with one hand moved her chin so that she had to face him directly. She was breathing even faster now, but he couldn't tell whether the look on her face was of fright or . . . or what?

"Is it Dr. Garrett? Is something wrong with him?" Maybe she was just shell-shocked. He'd seen it from time to time in battle, especially in the 1948 war when they were using women fighters along with the men. "I'm going to take you back upstairs to your bedroom," he articulated, in case she was having trouble hearing as well. "All right?"

"Yes, all right," she said distantly, though she still did not acknowledge him with her eyes.

With one hand around her waist and the other guiding her arm, Baruch walked with her toward the hallway and then slowly up the staircase. She took each step individually, planting both feet before moving on to the next.

At the top of the stairs Baruch thought he heard a noise, almost a whining sound, coming from the end of the hall. He halted the procession a moment and listened more intently. It was wheezing, or choking, and it was coming from Nat Kagan's room. He started to rush down the hallway toward him, but decided he couldn't leave Amanda just standing there in her condition, especially so close to the stairs. So he tried to hurry her along in the direction of the noises. Several times she stumbled as her legs refused to move fast enough, but he held her firmly.

Baruch pushed open the rabbi's bedroom door, quickly positioned Amanda to one side and hurried over to the bed. Nat's face was drained of color and sweat flowed from his forehead and neck. Baruch couldn't tell whether he was asleep or awake but he was gasping for air. Beneath the blanket his legs were stretched out rigidly and his feet were pointed. Could he be having a heart attack? Baruch pressed his fingers to Nat's neck. The pulse was normal. Asthma? What could he do? Did he need oxygen? He'd have to call a doctor or an ambulance.

But there was something about the look on Nat's face that made him stop, at least for a moment. He couldn't figure it out exactly, but there was a look of intent and purpose. Was he trying to tell him something? Moshe Baruch tried to understand.

It entered his mind in the midst of a dreamless sleep. "There is a unifying sense to everything," Nat Kagan was telling himself. "God does not play dice with the universe." It was the kind of trance in which he was both participant and observer; when he was inside his brain and outside of it at the same time. He felt as if his mind was approaching a vision of infinity. And he felt, very possibly, that he was approaching death.

The insights were coming to him that way, the way he'd heard people describe the final ecstatic playing out of lifetime images before the moment of death. They were coming from inside his mind, but they were coming from outside it, too. From the room, which he could only make out and remember as a hazy perimeter, from other rooms, from the air. And they weren't merely words, but pictures. Straight lines in a perpendicular grid that began to curve, first all together, then around many invisible circles in a blackened field. And in this vision, he instinctively knew that he was looking at everything at once—the stars and planets, himself as an individual entity, every atom of matter.

But it was all together somehow. He longed to understand in the time remaining to him the unity between matter and the field surrounding it. Can the existence of matter be deduced from the field itself? And can the field be represented by an expression of words or numbers so that the mind of man can even comprehend it? Is matter merely the region of the field that is the strongest? In his haze, the question struck him as all important; the answer as sublime. What holds true for one field, must it then hold true for every other field in the universe? How could it work for some, but not for others? God is subtle, but He is not malicious. The laws that govern the planets around the stars must also govern the electron around the proton. Only then is there unity.

In one distant part of her consciousness, Amanda was aware that she was standing up, gazing at a gasping form, covered except for its head. But her overwhelming sensation, much more vivid and actualized, was of floating through a blackened field of curving lines that all pulled toward invisible circles that appeared up to the horizon and beyond. Each one exerted its attraction, but the repulsive force was greater still, and so she continued floating. It was both matter and that which surrounded it, and she knew that to know either, it was necessary to know them both. Neither could be assumed independently.

A progression of ideas, of impressions, flooded through her mind. At first they were visual, geometric, the intersecting of lines that represented both physical direction and abstract thought. Then the ideas became words, sentences, mathematical expressions. And still she continued to float through the blackened field of curving shapes that had no end and no boundaries. It was pure existence—basic and simple—and she felt the presence of superior reasoning power; one in which all forces would come together in unity. In which matter and field were the same, and in which the physical geometry of the universe remained constant.

The forces that had just been pictures before became now discernible concepts, and she began to understand their relation to each other. The gravitational field is influenced not only by the moving gravitational masses but also by the electromagnetic field itself. The electromagnetic field is characterized by six functions in space and time. The gravitational field is characterized by ten functions changing in space and time. The ten functions that characterize the geometry of our physical world are the same ten functions that characterize the gravitational field.

She knew she was beginning to understand and that was all that mattered in the midst of the timeless moment. It was emanating from within her brain, she knew, but also from outside, as if she were part of a larger mind, as if she were only one of the centers of force in the middle of the endless field. She was part of it, and she was watching, both at the same time, and time itself meant nothing.

Paul had dreamed he was back in the anatomy lab, but this time the cadaver being dissected was him. Still, he was able to feel every slice of the novice medical student's scalpel and see with his own eyes every brownish-gray organ as it was removed from his gaping chest cavity. As the young man picked up the cranial saw, Paul tried to recoil, knowing all the while that his body would not move. But as the top of his head came off, instead of the dreaded agony he anticipated from previous dreams, he was suffused with a feeling of serenity.

"The most beautiful thing we can experience is the mysterious. It is the source of all true art and science." It came to him from inside his head, but he did not think it was himself saying it.

He was walking down a corridor—a hallway—it seemed to him, but at the same time he was floating above a curving force field of intersecting lines. He had been there before in his imagination, but now it was just as real as walking down the hall. And he was seeing it from a new perspective, from several perspectives simultaneously. And he was picking up thoughts he had

had years ago and still had, only they were coming from somewhere else.

"The electromagnetic field is characterized by an antisymmetric tensor with six components. The gravitational field is characterized by a symmetric tensor with ten components. And the geometry of the universe is characterized by a general tensor of the second order with sixteen components."

This was familiar to him; it was not new. But it was pointing him in a new direction, he sensed, toward an answer he had long pursued. An answer inextricably tied to the unity of all forces and all matter, which is the unity of everything. An explanation of the whole of physical reality.

He was standing still, he knew; not walking anymore. There were others around him. But he was also floating through the curving force field and was an integral part of it. Everything was part of everything else, and he knew he was not alone.

Suddenly, Nat Kagan opened his eyes wide, and for a horrifying moment Moshe Baruch thought he was about to submit to death. He bent down and checked his pulse and breathing. Both had relaxed. The rabbi, too, was staring right through him, and when Moshe turned around to look in the same direction, he saw not only Amanda, but Paul Garrett standing still beside her. He was wearing only his shorts, and like Amanda, his piercing eyes were locked on Kagan's recumbent body.

Baruch glanced from one to the other. They all bore the same expression, a combination of serenity and understanding.

"Are you all right?" he asked them. "I don't know what's going on."

"Yes, I'm all right," Amanda answered calmly. "But I think I have to sit down." She went over to the corner of Kagan's bed.

"What about you?" Baruch demanded of Nat.

"Okay. I've just had the most astounding experience. I think we all have."

Ten minutes later they were all four sitting on the two facing couches in the den; Paul and Amanda on one, Moshe and Nat on the other. The Israeli could see that the other three sat limply, slouching on the seats, as if they had just completed a marathon race.

"What happened?" Nat asked. "I don't know what it was, but I know you were both sharing it with me."

"How do you know that?" Baruch inquired. Nat shrugged.

"It's true," Amanda said. "But I've never known anything like it before."

"I have," said Paul, and the others looked at him. "Not exactly, but it was similar. It was like that moment after the bridge game at the Hollisters', when we went walking outside together, and I had that sudden, unexplained inspiration that set all my work of the past several months into perspective. Only this time it was even more intense. I feel like I have a complete understanding of where I have to move in my work." He looked at Nat and Amanda. "And somehow, I got it from you."

It *was* like something she'd experienced before, Amanda finally comprehended. It was like the first time she and Paul had made love, but she didn't know why. It occurred to her to be ashamed that her personal analogy was so much less spiritual and intellectual than Paul's, but it was what she thought of, and she knew she was right. She realized that under her nightgown her legs were spread apart. She demurely pressed them back together and folded them under her on the couch.

"This is obviously your field, Paul," Nat said. "What were we doing?"

"'Field' is a good word to describe it," he replied. "Somehow, our three minds were moving together from the same point in pursuit of the Unified Field Theory, the scientific concept I've been working on for years. I could sense you were both going through some of the basic considerations—the idea of matter being merely a point in the surrounding field where the energy level is the greatest, for example—and then coming up to the ideas I had that night with Amanda." He paused and breathed in deeply, as if he needed the richest possible oxygen mixture to continue. "And then at the end I felt a kind of energy pattern coming from both of you, like a wave motion, but it was purely intellectual. I can't describe it any better than that, and I know it doesn't make much logical sense."

"That was the time when I felt like I might die," Nat stated.

"You looked like you might," Baruch said. "I was terrified."

"Paul," Amanda asked, "why haven't you run to write everything down the way you did last time?"

"It's not exactly the same," he explained. "Last time I was dealing with specific mathematical expressions of relationships I'd been trying to establish. Here it's more a matter of seeing everything clearly and in a different perspective. What I learned tonight I'll apply to everything from here on in. But there's one thing . . ."

They all waited for him to complete the thought, but he said nothing further.

"What is it?" she asked.

"I don't know how to say this, or exactly why, but now I know that I need you both to help me."

Chapter Twelve

Tel Aviv

The headquarters of the Mossad is in a nondescript government building whose location is a state secret. It is perhaps the most secure structure in all of Israel, but Moshe Baruch proceeded directly to the Deputy Chief's office without being stopped. He was expected.

When he arrived in the small, drab room, its one window overlooking the concrete inner courtyard, Yoshua Shlomo had both the *New York Times* account of the car bombing and his own telex report laid out on the wooden table in front of him.

"Shalom," they said to each other without shaking hands.

"I see you were busy in New York," Shlomo commented. "At least you managed to keep your own name out of the papers."

"Just barely. The police questioned us for three hours."

"What do they think?"

"Probably a Palestinian group."

"They caught on to our plan for using the Committee?"

"I doubt it. There's no way the information could have leaked out unless the rabbi's office was bugged. And I had it swept myself on my last trip over."

"But the fact remains, Moshe, Rabbi Kagan is a well-known Zionist. So the bombing could have been nothing more than a simple political statement."

"That is true. Still, I don't believe it fits into their pattern, as I wrote in my initial report."

"Do you have any better explanations?"

"No. But there is an added element. The New York police brought in an FBI representative to ask questions when they were finished."

"So? There's nothing unusual about the FBI being brought into an investigation of terrorism."

"Does the name George Henderson mean anything to you?"

"He's with the Agency," Shlomo responded. Baruch just shook his head affirmatively. "Why would he go through a ruse like that?"

"You tell me. Unless the Agency has some interest in Rabbi Kagan beyond his being a target of extremists."

"Henderson didn't recognize you, did he?"

"No. There's no reason he should. We've never met."

"Do you think Rabbi Kagan is still in serious danger?"

"I can't be sure as long as the case is open. I was hoping to pick up some information that first night, when I had him and the other two at the safe house in Westchester. But nothing turned up. He's staying with them for the time being. I couldn't get him to come back to Israel with me, so under the circumstances, this seemed the next best thing."

"Ah yes . . . the circumstances." Shlomo sighed. "How is he taking it?"

"Not well, but he's managing. Aside from his terrible grief, he blames himself. Not only for letting her get in the car before him, but also for getting involved in the kinds of activities that would put himself and his family in jeopardy. He told me he came through a supposedly terminal brain cancer when he was a young man, and that should have told him not to tempt fate any further. He also wanted assurance that his two children would be protected."

"Of course."

"Both are in college. I had the Embassy alert the local police."

Shlomo paced around to the folding table behind his desk that had become the repository for his current files. The table was piled nearly to the window ledge. "I noticed in your report this curious incident involving Kagan and the other two, Paul Garrett and Amanda West."

"Yes, and that's why I think more than mere coincidence might be at work. The woman was with Kagan in that small park on 51st Street when the dog attacked them. If David Bar-Din hadn't been tailing him at the time, they both would have died; no question about it. That dog was trained to kill on command."

"Thank God David's a good shot."

"And thank David that he thought to carry a .357 magnum. I don't know if the Beretta would have made a dent in that animal's skull."

"So you think the same party was behind both attempts, Moshe?"

"I don't know. It can't be ruled out. Nor can it be ruled out that Miss West was also a target. Except for the fact that the bomb was placed under the driver's seat. With the explosive charge that was used, there was only the assurance that the driver would be killed. And even if the bomb's planter knew that she would be with Kagan that night, there could be no reasonable expectation she would be driving."

"Yes, I quite agree. Which brings us back to my main concern," Shlomo declared. "They've been threatening for years to launch a large-scale campaign against American Jewish leaders."

"I can't believe they'd begin with Rabbi Kagan, and expend so much effort," Baruch said.

"Let's hope you're right."

Baruch stood up and stretched his beefy arms. As short as they were, this just had the effect of making his chest appear broader. "I'm going to get some sleep," he announced. "The El Al plane was full when I called and I had to sit in coach." The official insistence that people in Moshe Baruch's position fly the national airline had nothing to do with Israeli pride. Rather, it was the only carrier militarily prepared to resist a hijacking attempt.

Shlomo rose with him but made no move toward the door. "There is another possibility," he said pensively.

"I thought the same thing at first," Baruch acknowledged.

"What if Amanda West is the setup? How do they know each other?"

"They met accidentally in Central Park. But they'd also met about twenty years before. In the hospital. But the woman was only nine or ten at the time. I've never heard of planting a nine-year-old as a sleeper agent." He forced a laugh.

"It does seem a bit far-fetched, doesn't it. Well . . . I still want to know everything we can about her. And what about the other one—Paul Garrett?"

"A very distinguished physicist. I understand they follow his work at the Technion and the Weizmann Institute. That was what the whole business that night was about. We still don't understand exactly what happened. By the way, he lost his own wife very recently in Boston. A suicide. And he was in the same hospital with Kagan and West."

"A scientist of his reputation would have access to many international contacts without arousing suspicion," Shlomo suggested.

"Except that the Agency apparently *is* suspicious," Baruch added.

Shlomo took a legal pad from his desk and began making a list. "All right, I'll have our researchers here prepare dossiers on both Garrett and West. But I'd also like to know more about his work, and especially whatever it was you saw happening there. So I'll find out who at the Weizmann Institute knows the most about what he does. Garrett apparently is carrying on the kind of work Einstein was doing, and the Weizmann has the Einstein archives. So someone there should be able to explain this to us." This time he walked with Baruch over to the door. "I guess that's it, Moshe. Go and get some rest."

On his way out, Baruch picked up his bag and attaché case in Shlomo's secretary's office. He used her phone to call his wife in Ramat Aviv, and told her he would be home after a while.

"No more calls?" the secretary asked him.

"No, that's it," he said.

When he got down to the lobby, though, he went to the pay phones in the middle of the corridor, dropped his tokens in the slot and called Ariel Herzen. He was delighted to find her at home and said he'd be there as soon as he could.

London

Nigel Dunninger was lunching in his favorite pub on Shaftesbury Avenue when Walter Oppermann slid into the hard wooden bench opposite him and thrust folded copies of the *Times* and *Standard* over his plate of sausages. He looked up calmly and, since he could no longer see his food, put down his fork.

"Have you seen this?" Walter asked urgently.

"I got a call this morning, if it's what I think you're referring to. Would you care for something to eat?"

"No. I've already eaten."

"How about a pint, then? You really oughtn't take up a place during lunchtime without buying anything."

"Very well," said Walter impatiently, snapping his fingers for the serving girl and then pointing to Dunninger's foaming glass on the varnished plank table. It must have been very dusty when they did the varnishing. Tiny flecks could be seen underneath the coating.

"All right," said Dunninger, satisfied. "Let's have a look at your stories."

"They're nearly identical. Accounts of a terrorist car bombing in New York City. Involving both Paul Garrett and Amanda West, and a rabbi called Nathaniel Kagan. His wife was killed."

"Yes. That *is* what I'd heard."

"Don't you have any reaction?"

Dunninger refolded both papers with their front pages once again on the outside and placed them on the side of the table so he could resume eating. "I find the food very good here, and quite reasonable by today's standards. Even something as ordinary as sausages always shows pride and care. You ought to eat here yourself."

Walter's face displayed mounting consternation. "Nigel, I'm really not concerned with the sublime amenities of your pub at the moment . . ."

Dunninger raised his fork in one hand while daubing the napkin to his lips with the other. "See? They still use cloth napkins here. I don't believe there's been a single compromise of quality since I first patronized the place, and that has to be fifteen years. Yes, yes . . . I know what you're trying to say. But you really have to learn to be more contemplative. The one thing my scientific background has taught me is not to make precipitous judgments on the spur of the moment. It's always better to take one step back. Oh, good, here's your beer."

The waitress set the pint down in front of Walter. He nodded to her.

"But you must realize the spot this puts us in," he persisted. "God knows we don't want a replay of what happened to Julia Garrett."

For the first time during the meeting, Dunninger seemed genuinely sad. "How very, very unfortunate. But the situation isn't exactly analogous. If it turns out that her death was not a desperate act of suicide, then I'm assuming that it was in response to our *approaching* her. We haven't directly approached Paul Garrett, and there is no need to directly approach Amanda. I just want her looked after for her own good."

"Which is getting more and more difficult all the time. We were lucky to have someone near her when she was threatened in Bloomingdale's; someone handy with a knife. We weren't as on top of things as we should have been when *this* happened." He drummed his fingers on the folded newspapers. "She could have just as easily been killed as Mrs. Kagan. More to the point, Garrett could have been killed, which would have meant the end of the project, just like that."

"Quite true," Dunninger admitted. He glanced down at his plate, pushing the last bit of sausage onto his fork, putting it in his mouth and then taking the time for a long quaff of beer. When he'd finished with the glass, he hunched forward and stroked his chin with his left hand. "I have been giving the matter some thought; trying to see it objectively, without preconceived notions. At first, we considered the fact that Amanda and Dr. Garrett came together as they did a fortuitous circumstance. It gave us more direct access to Dr. Garrett's thoughts, every time she wrote down anything he'd told her. But the fact that they now seem so—how shall I say it?—closely aligned, leads me to believe there must be something else operating here."

He signaled the serving girl that he wanted another pint. "And I would dearly love to learn what it is."

Rehovot, Israel

Yakov Perlman sat for a while in the garden of the Weizmann Institute of Science, after all these years still unable to quite believe that this refuge of peace and beauty actually existed in the heart of this embattled country. As he pushed the hand lever that guided the wheelchair over the uneven flagstone path back toward the long, low, white building, he struggled to tilt his head enough to see the tops of the shading palm and acacia trees. Yakov Perlman, who had been the prized student at the Kaiser Wilhelm Institute in Berlin, who had dazzled his peers at the Institute for Advanced Study at Princeton, finally felt that he belonged. And as he cruised slowly up the ramp and then rammed into the door with sufficient force to open it, he was happy once again that he was able to finish out his career, and his life, at such a place. Here, he was finally free. Despite the amyotrophic lateral sclerosis that wracked his body and limited his voluntary motion to the gross movements of his left forearm, Yakov Perlman felt free.

Inside his first-floor office, he skimmed the article from *Annalen der Physik* that his assistant had removed from the files for him, turning the pages with the aid of a rubber-tipped wand. Then he wheeled around to the other side of the table to look at the newspaper accounts the Mossad agent had left. Unfolding a newspaper was out of the question, so the agent had thoughtfully cut them out and pasted them onto pieces of cardboard.

He knew Paul Garrett's work well. He had been following it for years now. He couldn't say enough for the man's intellectual grasp. He did not recall the name Amanda West, though he had read *Aurora* magazine from time to time. And while Nathaniel Kagan meant nothing to him, he could appreciate his devotion to Zionism and the halt of nuclear proliferation. And if he was important to the Mossad—for whatever reason— he was clearly important to Israel.

Perlman studied the newspapers and the file the agent had left with it and began mentally cataloging the information together with his own knowledge. A crime was committed in New York City, which had as its targets the woman who was killed plus three others: a Zionist rabbi who spoke out against nuclear power, a science writer known for her political stands and her advocacy of pacifism, and a leading physicist working on the relationship between gravity, electromagnetism, and the nuclear forces. The two men were in their forties. The woman's age was given as thirty-two. After the incident described, they were taken to a Mossad safe house outside the city and in the presence of one of its agents, they extraordinarily came together with the same visions and mental processes and expanded upon Dr. Garrett's understanding of the components of the Unified Field Theory. Garrett has asked the other two to accompany him up to Cambridge, Massachusetts.

He was weaving in his head a pattern of familiarity and long-established connections. Whether the pattern was actually there, or whether he was only wishfully imposing it, he could not be sure. But it was tantalizing; of that there could be no doubt. Somewhere in the back of his mind he had always figured this might happen, and his only hope was that he would be alive to see it, if and when it did. The implications, if this is what it was, could be incredible . . . or devastating.

He would like to speak to this Dr. Garrett.

King's Point, Long Island

"Off the top of my head, I can come up with at least a few explanations or hypotheses," David Sherman said. "None of them are particularly enlightening. Moving from the most hard-headed on out, I could discount the whole thing as a rather elaborate coincidence of dreams. Or I could suggest that you three—possibly through the physical trauma of intricate brain surgery —have tapped into some unknown reserve of energy within each brain that we haven't discovered yet. Or possibly that the universe is full of rhythms of all sorts and somehow you happened to be at the intersection of several of those rhythms."

"Do you believe any of those, Dr. Sherman?" asked Amanda.

"Please call me David. And I don't believe or not believe. I'm speculating. You're way beyond my professional competence as it is."

They sat in the study of Nat Kagan's house, at the end of the *shivah* week, the first seven days of mourning in Judaism. David had agreed to make the trip at Paul's request and Nat had told them that during this period, all friends and well-wishers were welcome in the house of the bereaved. He had taken them into the study for privacy, but told them he couldn't remain away from those who had come to call for long. In the living room, he had been sitting on a low, hard chair, as is customary for mourners. But in here, he sat next to David on the couch, so as not to make anyone feel uncomfortable.

"So something just clicked when we all got together?" Amanda went on.

"Possibly."

"But could the brain suddenly 'assert' itself that way just because the three of us were in the same room?" Nat inquired.

"Again, I don't know. Perhaps the stress . . . the acute stress of . . . the tragedy triggered this episode."

"But is that possible?" he pressed on. "It just seems absurd."

"If you told my great-grandfather, who was also a doctor, that the salvation from the scourge of infectious disease lay in a piece of bread mold, he would have laughed you out of his office. Today, we try to be a little bit more open to such possibilities."

Nat drummed his fingers on the arm of the couch and pursed his lips. "Is it possible that this represents some kind of mass hypnotic suggestion we, and who knows how many others, were put under?"

"But when?" Amanda challenged.

Nat shrugged. "Maybe when we were at Goddard—that seems the most likely time—and maybe it's taken this long to surface."

"You read about that happening in novels," David commented, "but I've never heard of a hypnotic suggestion laying dormant and then surfacing twenty years later in real life."

"Also," Amanda added, "from what I know about it, hypnosis can alter behavior to a certain extent, like getting people to stop smoking or whatever, but it can't alter or add to basic intelligence or knowledge, can it?"

"No," David agreed.

"And we've obviously got a situation where at least Nat and I have called up some intellectual insight that we really can't account for." She moved around on her chair a quarter turn to face Paul. "Well, whatever's going on, you can't still deny it's something. The three of us meet by chance, we all have the same medical history, we share numerous traits and interests, someone is out to get one or more of us, and now we find our brains somehow operate on the same scientific wavelength. Eventually, it's all got to come together?"

"Yes. But how?" the rabbi asked.

"This is all speculation," Paul interrupted. He turned to acknowledge Amanda. "Obviously, there's something going on. I admit I was skeptical, and I still don't feel comfortable dealing with events I can't explain. But the one thing we *do* know is that among the three of us, we seem to have the intellectual resources to complete the most significant problem in physics since the General Theory of Relativity. This is the work that Einstein, had he lived another ten years, might have developed. After the experience the other night, I just feel intuitively that if this much of it works, there must be more."

"How can you figure that?" Amanda asked.

"Because what we came up with is simple."

"Simple?" She rolled her eyes incredulously.

"Yes. Simple and symmetrical. It's one line of reasoning from beginning to end. That's the whole point of physics—to uncover the simple relationships that must exist between everything. And I think we've begun doing that here. I don't know why it's taken me this long to see it this far, now that I know where we've been."

"The typical lament of the scientist," she retorted. "Simplicity always seems obvious in retrospect. But simplicity is always the most sublime form of mystery."

"I'm beginning to think that beneath that vociferous *Aurora* stridency lies a genuine scientific sensibility." He laughed, then kissed her on the forehead.

"But what exactly are you asking from us, Paul?" Nat's expression was one of confusion.

Paul rose, as if he was about to give a lecture. "I want you both to come back with me to Cambridge and work with me on the Unified Field Theory."

"But we're not scientists like you," Amanda protested. "We can't all of a sudden walk into a lab and just start solving problems. Or are we just going to sit around and wait for more supernatural dreams?"

"You're not scientists," he admitted, "but you've obviously got some kind of profound scientific insight. You could orient yourselves to the work in the field in a couple of weeks, and then, playing your ideas off against me, I know we could make significant progress."

Nat Kagan sighed and hunched himself forward on the couch. For the first time the ravages the last several days had inflicted upon him were plain to see. He appeared smaller than his normal robust stature. And more vulnerable. "Even under normal circumstances you'd be asking us to suspend our jobs . . . our lives, really, for a scientific shot in the dark which you admitted yourself even eluded Einstein."

Paul started to interrupt but Nat held up his hand and continued. "But with what's just happened to me, how could I, how could I even think about such arcane things, I couldn't . . ."

This time Paul broke through. "But you obviously have been thinking about these things, Nat. It was in your bedroom that we found ourselves. I know what you must be going through. Look, my wife died, too . . ."

Amanda immediately shot a reproachful glance in his direction.

"The circumstances were somewhat different," Nat said icily, "as well as the relationship." He looked over at Amanda. "And you have a substitute."

"Forgive me. I . . . I never should have said that. I guess I was caught up in my own enthusiasm because I believe so strongly in this."

"I don't see how I can help you. While I sympathize with what you're trying to do, I'm more concerned right now with comprehending God's pattern of life and death than I am with comprehending His arrangement of the elements of the universe. And trying to figure out just what it is I do believe. Maybe He was trying to send me a message through my wife." He paused and wiped away the moisture from the corner of his eye. "I hope not."

"Will you at least think about it?" Paul pressed him.

He stared at him for several seconds in silence. "Yes, I'll think about it." He stood up. "And now I have to get back to the others and accept their consolation. This *shivah* week is one of the most enlightened aspects of Judaism, I think. It lets us deal with our grief in stages, when to do otherwise would destroy us." He extended his hand out to David. "Good to meet you. I hope we'll be able to talk again."

"I hope so," David confirmed, and Nat left the room.

As he opened the door, Amanda could see the gilded mirror in the hall, its glass covered by a white sheet in another expression of mourning.

"Well, what about you?" Paul said to her. "Can you make arrangements with *Aurora* so you can come up with me to Cambridge?"

She shouldn't give him an answer right away, she knew, but she knew something else, too. He had asked her to be with him; not in the way she'd imagined it would happen, but now he genuinely needed her. Now, she could be sure of having him and for a while, anyway, they would share everything together.

"Yes," she said softly. "I'll make the arrangements with *Aurora*."

He smiled gratefully at her and she knew that her fears were unfounded. It was ironic, really, just the opposite of what she used to worry about with men.

But looking into his eyes, she could tell that Paul didn't just love her for her mind.

He turned to David. "I can't thank you enough for coming up."

"That's quite all right. It's worth it. You're proving to be a fascinating patient."

"And you're proving to be a good friend." They shook hands, then spontaneously clasped each other around the shoulders and embraced.

"One thing interests me," David then stated.

"What's that?"

"No matter what you've told me about your attraction to physics, and the kick of uncovering the laws of existence, this Unified Field Theory has to lead somewhere, it seems to me. Einstein, as brilliant as he was, must have realized that special relativity was going to lead at some point to atomic energy. You must have done the same with your work."

"When you're doing research, it's easy to lose sight of the end result. You get so bound up in the next step and whether it's going to work out or not. But sure, I've thought about what the Unified Field Theory could lead to, if we can construct one at all and it turns out to be what we hope it is. If we can actually set down, as simply as Einstein did with relativity, the basic relationship between the forces of nature, we could conceivably use them to affect each other; manipulate their properties at will."

"And just what does that mean, for instance?"

Paul smiled again, his eyes beginning to sparkle with visionary zeal. "Pick your favorite dream," he said.

Chapter Thirteen

Zurich

J. Tyler Kendrick had worked out every detail. As each member's private jet touched down at Zurich Airport, it was met by an armored Mercedes-Benz 300 which radioed verification upon first visual identification of its assigned passenger. Customs clearance had been arranged in advance so the car, with its escort vehicle maintaining a distance of no more than twenty-four inches from the rear bumper, proceeded directly to the Dolder Grande Hotel. There an experienced functionary who knew all the members by sight cross-checked the arrival against the radio call, handled the front desk formalities and sent word up to Mr. Kendrick's suite.

In any other city, the coming together of so many powerful and influential people amid such elaborate and apparent security would have provoked curiosity and the attendant risk of international publicity. But not in Zurich. It was for its unrivaled powers of discretion, rather than its picturesque beauty and fabled charm, that Kendrick chose the city for the meeting of the Partners for Progress.

There were no meetings scheduled for the first day. Despite the fact that members traveled under optimum conditions of comfort and convenience, Kendrick made it a habit never to conduct business in a new time zone without a night's sleep, nor to deal with anyone who had not had the benefit of that same night's sleep. And for that reason there were no dinners or social functions scheduled for the first day, either. At this level, there is no effective difference between a business meeting and a social function. They both share the same intended purpose.

The diversions provided for the first night were more individual in nature, intended to compensate for the hardship of being away from home and office. These, too, were arranged by Kendrick's staff, based on carefully researched and continually updated files. For example, two strikingly blond Swedish boys in their early twenties were dispatched to Thalia Reinhardt's room along with freshly cut ostrich feathers and a large bucket of ice. An equally striking blonde German girl arrived at the room of Terence Gleeson of the British Mining Group with nickel-plated wrist shackles and a braided whip.

Everyone arrived at the opening session the next morning well rested and ready to take on the complex issues that faced them.

After a brief greeting from Kendrick, the matter of territorial market disputes was taken up and a set of guidelines established for settling future disputes. Next was a report on double taxation of multinational corporations and the ways of shifting declared income to circumvent it. Third was the presentation of a study on terrorism and kidnapping for profit in the more volatile European and South American countries. All of the issues had been dealt with before and while the members listened attentively, they displayed no great or overt absorption in the discussion. The management council's recommendations were overwhelmingly and perfunctorily accepted in each case.

It was after lunch that the opulent hotel's gold and crystal ballroom became a theater of high technological drama.

Kendrick ascended the podium and announced, simply, "We will now take up the Garrett Project."

The audience listened to him through individual headsets even though each person in the room spoke fluent English. The hotel was old, and whereas near-perfect security could be guaranteed, sound-deadening acoustics could not be.

"To lead the scientific portions of this discussion," the chairman continued, "I'd like to introduce Dr. Ian Ludlow of the Osric-Duvall Labs, who is the head of the scientific evaluation team for the Partners for Progress and a recipient of the Nobel Prize in Chemistry."

Ludlow climbed the several steps to the podium, passing Kendrick, who disappeared into the shadows of the darkened room. He was a tall, gaunt man, well over six feet tall with stringy brown hair and a shaggy beard which somehow still managed to come to a perfect point. He cleared his throat several times, each time making his prominent Adam's apple stick out even farther than normal. He wore a long white lab coat, but this was clearly more for credibility than any practical purpose. When he finally spoke it was with a definite Cambridge accent, though his origins in the American Midwest came through on certain consonant sounds.

He gripped the sides of the lectern as the single spotlight formed a nimbus around his shoulders and head.

"For centuries, ever since Isaac Newton first accurately described its properties, scientists, writers and ordinary men and women have dreamed of ways of overcoming and utilizing gravity . . ."

The spotlight grew dimmer and a huge screen behind him lit up with a period engraving of Isaac Newton sitting under his venerable apple tree. In animated fashion, one piece of fruit suddenly broke from its stem, and with a whistling sound, sailed down to hit the scientist on the head, leaving a dotted line trail to mark its descent. Instantly, a purple bump appeared on Newton's brow. He looked up in consternation, scratched his forehead, and then his eyes lit up with a beatific glow. The audience tittered warily.

". . . The concept of controlling gravity for one's own purposes is neither new nor uncommon. Manifestations in the popular imagination have ranged from H.G. Wells' 'Cavorite'-powered space ship to Walt Disney's 'Flubber' . . ."

Newton's image dissolved into a scene of the lunar surface approaching in the 1919 film version of *The First Men in the Moon,* to be replaced moments later by Fred MacMurray piloting his winsome Model T above the Capitol dome in *The Absent-Minded Professor.*

". . . But these, and most other unattainable dreams of altering gravity, depended on some nonexistent material or substance that in a small, compact form, had incredible buoyancy; enough to make any object float." His lip curled slightly in a derisive smirk. "And I can assure you, no such material exists. If it did, the companies represented in this hall would surely control the world's supply."

Now he stared straight out into the middle of the audience, seeming to cut the gathering in two with his gaze. "But now we come in real life to the work of Dr. Paul Garrett of the Massachusetts Institute of Technology. From his private papers, eyewitness accounts by other scientists of his experiments and other vital data, we have strong reason to believe that Dr. Garrett may be on the verge of figuring out a way to conquer gravity, not by coming up with some mythical substance, but by unlocking a force that might be an inherent property of all matter."

Ludlow paused for what seemed like more than a minute, but the audience remained raptly attentive. "Garrett proposes to do this by means of what we have come to call a Unified Field Theory; that is, a formula or set of equations that describe the unified behavior of all the natural forces. Like the dreams of controlling gravity itself, this scientific goal is not new. It was proposed by the German mathematician Hermann Weyl as early as 1918 in reaction to Einstein's theory of relativity. And Einstein himself worked on the theory for decades, in fact up to the end of his life. In the years since then, the concept that such a theory is even *possible* in the natural world as we know it has fallen into disfavor among most scientists. Until Paul Garrett. His work, as we shall see, shows not only that such a theory may be possible, but that it is even likely."

The screen now filled with Paul Garrett's equations, in his own handwriting, since they were reproduced directly from the papers that had been taken from his office. Chuckles again erupted throughout the room. The notations were so complicated they appeared to be a parody of cheap science-fiction stories.

"One of the reasons scientists have despaired of eventually constructing a Unified Field Theory is because of the fundamental difference between two of the forces—gravity and electromagnetism. Electrical charges are both positive and negative; that is, they have the potential to attract and to repel. Gravity, on the other hand, is only an attractive force, so far as we know. But keep in mind that thus far, ever since the time of Newton, our knowledge of the powers of gravity is purely empirical. We know *that* gravity works in a certain way, but not *why*. But if we *could* construct a theory that would understand and take all of the properties into account, we could conceivably construct negative 'gravitons' analogous to electrons, and find the equivalent of negative gravity. And once this is possible, the next step becomes the regulation and manipulation of this force through the introduction of another force, namely electromagnetism."

A montage backed by upbeat marching music flashed across the screen, composed of pictures representing all aspects of member companies' activities. Wells pumped crude oil from the deserts of Arabia. Assembly lines turned out endless processions of automobiles. Airplanes soared through the clouds. Harvesters plowed through vast fields of wheat. Power generators churned out electricity. Communications satellites floated through inky space. It was a sequence designed to evoke a misty sense of proprietary pride among these people who controlled the industrial muscles of the western world. And if the lights had been turned up, there certainly would have been revealed more than an occasional moist eye in the gathering.

Suddenly, the screen went black and the music stopped abruptly. There was murmuring in the audience. But then Ludlow broke in with, "Now what does all that I've said mean to you?" He brought his arm back in a grand gesture toward the empty screen. "Just this," he rhetorically replied.

From the base of the podium, J. Tyler Kendrick smiled with satisfaction. The little audio-visual presentation was having its desired effect.

"Quite simply," Ludlow continued, "a workable Unified Field Theory has the potential to supplant the current methods of delivering most of the goods and services represented in this room. From what we can see so far, Garrett's thinking is that the suspected negative gravitational force could be amplified through the interaction with electromagnetism to make it, when desired, more powerful than the dominant positive force. Now what does *that* mean?"

On the screen the Matterhorn appeared, looking very much like the Paramount logo. But then slowly the snow-capped mountain began rising above its eternal setting in the Swiss countryside and floated across other mountains, cities, ocean, more cities and more mountains before coming to rest in the middle of an exceedingly flat Kansas wheat field. A cartoon farmer looked up from his sowing at the intruding formation and shrugged.

". . . Now this is not to imply that Dr. Garrett is setting himself up to go into direct competition with all of you. Our detailed psychological profile on him shows him to be influenced by the traditional scientific motivation of uncovering the truths of existence for the simple satisfaction of doing so. This might have been the motivation for Albert Einstein also—with whom Garrett has often been compared—when he formulated his special theory of relativity which set out the theoretical framework by which small amounts of matter could be transformed into vast amounts of energy. However, as we all know, there were plenty of other applied scientists and technicians waiting to take up where the theoretical scientist left off."

Behind Ludlow, a mushroom cloud billowed up against a blood-red sky.

". . . We are facing the same type of potential with the Garrett Project. Once such a theory is devised, the practical applications become almost limitless. Let us begin with transportation and fuel."

An aerial view of the Los Angeles freeway downtown interchange dissolved into a cutaway animation of an internal combustion engine.

". . . At this stage of his work, Garrett anticipates using a magnetic coil in a highly specialized pattern to control the characteristics of the particles of the matter that is subjected to it. Presumably, once that coil is designed, it would be submerged in liquid nitrogen at a temperature of minus two hundred seventy degrees Celsius, or three degrees Kelvin, to boost its electromagnetic properties tremendously. The coil would have the effect of transforming the subatomic particles into negative mass. Now, if a large enough region of particles could be uniformly affected—say, the size of an automobile or an airplane—it could be moved through the air without the resistance of gravity and guided through its electromagnetic component to the desired destination. And the only fuel that would be necessary is what is needed to cause the initial activation!"

A scene from a Buck Rogers serial showed a swarm of personal-size flying saucers crossing each other in midair as if it were a downtown intersection.

". . . Imagine all of these vehicles operating not on a *new* source of fuel as some scientists predict, but *without* an external fuel supply. Or another alternative, since the earth rotates once in a twenty-four-hour period, any large mass that was activated with negative gravitational force could be kept aloft until the earth underneath moved to the desired spot of relocation. In other words, by standing still above the earth's surface, an object could effectively be moved at more than a thousand miles per hour! In that case, the mountain truly could come to Muhammad, or the Matterhorn to Kansas, for that matter."

An audible, collective gasp filled the room, dying off into numerous variations of "Is he serious?"

". . . When perfected, this technology eliminates the need for fossil fuel of any sort. This in itself poses a major dislocation for the world's economy and just as easily implies possible realignments in strategic positions. But there is more to it, my friends. The implications for defense are just as great. Through the control of electromagnetism, enemy surveillance satellites could be removed from space simply by rearranging their subatomic force fields."

On the screen, a "killer satellite" with the earth in the background was seen to break apart, not in a violent explosion, but just matter-of-factly, with all the pieces floating off into the void of space.

". . . By accelerating the antigravitational force, guided missiles could be directed with incredible speed —and again with no great amount of fuel—to their targets overseas. But this would probably be a waste of time and effort, because from a laboratory high overhead, any desired target could be atomically 'rearranged' out of existence. And this could be done so selectively that the White House could be obliterated without jarring a picture on the wall of the Executive Office Building next door."

The view of Pennsylvania Avenue minus the presidential mansion dissolved to shots of a hurricane battering the Florida coastline. The winds literally tore houses from their foundations, bearing grim witness to the awesome, unforgiving power of nature. The scene then shifted to the parched, dry Great Plains. A film of dust covered the bleached white animal bones, and when the camera panned up, not a single cloud was visible in the unrelenting sky. Just watching the screen made the climate-controlled ballroom seem sweltering.

". . . 'Everybody talks about the weather but no one does anything about it.' That's the old cliché, isn't it? It will also come to have as much relationship to reality as the geocentric view of the universe. While we can't touch it or hold it, a storm cloud is composed of matter—that is, atoms—the same as anything else. Therefore, by flying an airplane equipped with the magnetic coil I just mentioned next to the cloud, it could be moved to a spot where the rain would be beneficial. Or, in the case of a violent hurricane, the cloud could be dissipated to the point where it could not do any damage. The effect on world agriculture should be obvious. Optimum growing conditions could be maintained from sowing to harvesting and then when the crop is ready for market, it could be transported there cheaply and easily. No longer would a bushel of corn destined for Europe have to be placed in trucks, then transferred to other trucks, then transferred to trains, then transferred to ships, then transferred to other trains, then transferred to other trucks before reaching its eventual destination. It could be loaded right at the place of harvest after a shorter and ideal growing season, and moved electrogravitationally directly across the ocean. Consider if you will the number of steps and services which would no longer be required."

The room lights came on and Ludlow said, "Before proceeding any further, I'd be happy to answer any questions. And since I know this is difficult to comprehend, please feel free to stop me at any further point in the presentation."

The president of a German munitions works which achieved international notoriety during the second world war rose to his feet. "These technologies you describe are dazzling, to be sure. And if you are correct, they do make many of our current practices and products obsolete. But with the power and international cooperation represented in this room, why could we not assure ourselves of an equally strong lock on the outgrowths of this Garrett work?"

Heads throughout the room nodded in assent.

Ludlow nodded slightly himself while the man spoke, as if he had been anticipating this question. "Einstein's scientific quest throughout the later portion of his life was for a simple expression of the interrelationship of the universal forces. Though the applications I've described seem highly complicated and are, so far, still impossible, with the knowledge of how to manipulate the negative gravitational force by means of electro-magnetism, the process becomes as simple as the mathematical expression of it. To put it simply, this is not the type of technology that can be exclusively controlled. Once perfected, it is open to virtually anyone. Let me give you an easy example. May I have tape number twenty-five, please?"

It was another animated cutaway, this time of a stone about the size of a baseball, which floated up to a height of about three feet and then fell back to the ground, only to rise up again. Connected to the stone was a cable running to a cam in a generator.

". . . What we see here is our conception of a simple home-power generator utilizing the Unified Field prin-ciples. Left to its own devices, the stone falls to the ground; this is obvious. But when that stone's positive-negative gravitational orientation is rearranged as we've described earlier, it floats up to any given height. Since just a slight amount of activation energy is used, as soon as the stone reaches three feet, the orientation wears off and the stone falls again. The falling of the stone generates its own energy as naturally as water falling over a dam, but in this case on a much smaller scale. But enough energy is provided with each fall to provide activation for the next orientation reversal and to run the generator to which it is attached. All of the home's heating, air-conditioning, and electrical needs are met essentially for free by this arrangement and with no pollution. With the new knowledge, such a generator would be relatively simple to build, every home or public building would have one, and there would be no need for the likes of Con Edison; no need for centralization. We go back in one step to the self-sufficient village concept, yet it is all the result of scientific breakthrough. There is no way a major power company could compete with this, and no way the technology could be kept out of millions of hands."

Another man stood up and Ludlow acknowledged him. "My name is Hans Steinbrunner."

"Yes, Doctor," Ludlow said with respect.

"Your little diagram and demonstration is quite nifty, to be sure. But it seems to me that no matter how incredible Garrett's theory may promise to be, you aren't suggesting, I don't believe, that it can violate the laws of physics as they exist today?"

"Certainly not."

"Then how do you account for this home generator you've just described? If you'll admit it, Dr. Ludlow, the simple truth is that any machine that powers itself internally, even after the initial activation, without outside fuel, has to violate the law of the conservation of matter and the first law of thermodynamics!"

Numerous eyebrows raised throughout the ballroom as the eyes all focused back on Ludlow.

Without raising his voice he replied, "With all due respect, Dr. Steinbrunner, neither law is violated. In fact, it demonstrates quite nicely the *second* law of thermodynamics. The energy for the movement, if you'll think about it, actually comes from the nuclear dissociation of the atoms of the *stone itself*. So on each transaction up and down, the rock actually *loses* matter, which is converted to energy and then given off. Each time the rock rises and falls it becomes smaller and lighter as a result of the energy loss. But since the rock has approximately ten to the twenty-sixth power atoms, and using Einstein's conversion ratio for the transformation of matter into energy, we can see how a minute amount of matter—a relative handful of atoms —becomes a huge amount of energy. So it's going to be a long time before we have to get a new rock!" Finally, Ludlow allowed himself a satisfied grin. Steinbrunner had sat down as inconspicuously as possible halfway through the explanation.

"Keep in mind, ladies and gentlemen, that we are dealing not only with gravity and electromagnetism, but also with what we call the weak and strong nuclear forces. These forces, which actually hold the atoms of our beings together, are far stronger than either gravity or electromagnetism and also come into play significantly in this discussion. For example, ever since the advent of atomic energy, scientists have been trying to figure out how to maintain a controlled fusion reaction. Through the Unified Field Theory we should be able to come up with a way to use an amplified gravitational force to hold together the electrons that naturally want to repel. Also, since a fusion reaction would be too hot for any known substance, it has been theorized that the best 'container' for it would be a magnetic field. So far we have not been able to come up with one that is sufficiently 'leakproof.' But once we understand the actual dynamics and properties of magnetism, this should be a natural outgrowth.

"What we're talking about in all cases is using *natural* energy in ways that up to now it has been impossible to harness and exert selectively. The amount of gravitational energy represented by the earth itself is inconceivably enormous, if it could only be used." He paused and gripped the sides of the lectern tightly again. "But if it could be used in the ways I've described, it would cause the most massive cultural and economic dislocation the world has ever known. There is not an industry or way of life that would remain untouched."

This time it was Thalia Reinhardt who shifted her substantial weight to her orthopedically shod feet. Her blue hair glistened in the semidarkness. "Are you saying that one man holds the key to all of this? That if we don't do something, within the next five or ten or fifty years the world as we know it will be totally obsolete?"

Ludlow appeared as solicitous of Thalia Reinhardt as Kendrick was. He mechanically brushed his hair back as she spoke, as if she'd made him self-conscious of something and the only thing he could affect was his appearance. "Let me clarify that. I'm not saying all of this is going to grow out of a successful Unified Field Theory, and even if it does, I'm not saying it's going to come overnight. It could take, as you say, fifty years of application before we achieve this sort of 'brave new world.' It might take more like a hundred and fifty years, for all we know. But judging from past scientific breakthroughs, especially the special and general theories of relativity, and Garrett's own experiments so far, we have reason to believe there is strong *potential* for some or all of these applications to come to pass. Eventually, I feel confident in saying, all of the things I've described will be commonplace. But without the one quantum breakthrough that an Einstein or a Garrett represents, we might be looking five hundred years in the future.

"So as I say, Garrett might hit a dead end just as Einstein himself did, or he may come up with a workable theory, win the Nobel Prize in Physics, and have nothing of a practical nature arise from his work. He could end up finding out that there is no way to control the negative gravitational force, or that there is no such thing to be controlled. The Unified Field Theory could then be relegated to an interesting intellectual exercise, like so much of pure mathematics. But on the other hand . . . Well, you've all just seen the other hand. What you have to decide is whether you're ready to face that risk, and to thrust on society at large a power it certainly isn't ready to handle; not now or in the foreseeable future."

"But I can't believe that so much could come from one man," Thalia Reinhardt persisted. "If this is ready to be discovered, won't it be someone else if it's not him?"

"That's an interesting question, and it gets right to the heart of the age-old notion of scientific determinism. It's the same as asking, 'Had Beethoven not lived, would someone else have eventually written the Ninth Symphony?' We can't say for sure, but the history of science is made up of the stories of men and women who saw what no one else saw. And had each of them not been born, it's highly questionable whether their discoveries would have been made. Just as we wonder whether the Ninth Symphony would have been written had Beethoven never lived, we have to wonder how many great works of music *never were* written because their composers never lived.

"So, yes . . . I would say that one man can have that much influence, and in a relatively short time. During the miraculous summer of 1665, having retired to the country to avoid the plague, Isaac Newton conjured up the basic laws of mechanics, gravitation, and integral and differential calculus. This was probably the most stupendous feat of concentrated mental acuity in the history of civilization. And it changed the world from that point on. We may be on the verge of another such breakthrough right now up at MIT."

The murmur buzzing through the crowd steadily grew in intensity, and even the commanding presence of Ian Ludlow pounding with the flat of his hand on the surface of the lectern could not restore quiet to the room. He understood, though. The people he addressed were used to ultimate control, straight-line problem-solving and comfortable, predictable planning within the cozy and well-defined parameters of conventional wisdom. And he was confronting them with the unthinkable; for most of them—the unimaginable. These were people who lived by forecasts and projections that ranged far into the future, and they measured their successes and failures by how much or little they deviated from them. He was forcing them to abandon their traditionally successful linear thought patterns, to deal with a fluid, unpredictable, evolving scientific x-factor. The managerial mind, he knew, even at the tops of its field, was not accustomed to dealing with real fluidity. The best it could do on that score was to deal with "contingencies" and "scenarios." But that was not the same thing. It was still traditional, linear thinking.

And if there was one thing his years of experience had shown him, it was that you cannot deal with an intangible in terms of a tangible; you cannot deal with the abstract when your only frame of reference is the concrete and already existing world.

"I have one other thing to talk about," he announced somberly when the noise had finally died down. "We've prepared a cute little film clip from *The Sorcerer's Apprentice* and some rather touching illuminations from the Bible, but I think I'll dispense with all that and just get to the meat of it. Slide number fourteen, please."

A periodic chart of the atoms flashed on the screen. Next to it appeared an H_2O molecule.

". . . This, as we all know, is water. There is essentially an unlimited supply of it on this planet. And if we follow the Unified Field Theory to its natural conclusion, the ability to completely disassociate subatomic particles and restructure them electrogravitationally means that we should eventually be able to make anything out of anything else since, as you see, everything is composed of the same subatomic particles, only in varying distributions and arrangements. It will be no harder for us to turn water into wine than it was for Jesus Christ! We will be able to do what the alchemists of the Middle Ages only dreamed of: we'll be able to turn lead into gold! And we'll be able to do it using almost no energy.

"And if we then reach the point where gold is so easy to manufacture that it becomes worthless, we can begin making anything else we want. The point is, natural resources cease to matter when everything can be made from sea water! At that point, no nation has any advantage or leverage over any other nation and the science of economics becomes nothing more than an historical curiosity."

The agitation in the audience was nearly uncontrollable. People stood up and sat down aimlessly, mouths hung open and heads swung back and forth in disbelief.

So the return of J. Tyler Kendrick to the podium came almost as a rescue for them, a reassurance that they could now return to their familiar worlds.

"Thank you, Dr. Ludlow, for a most enlightening presentation."

Ludlow nodded solicitously and quickly descended the stairs.

"Again, ladies and gentlemen, let me remind you, as the doctor already has, that everything he's told you here today is merely scientific speculation, though based on the best information at hand. We can't say it will come to pass, or even what the percentage chances are that it will. But if any portion of it does, I think you can see that we're not just talking about an alternative to fossil fuel. We're talking about a new order that destroys all of the conventions of society as it has built up since the Industrial Revolution. Paul Garrett does not represent the magician or god who is going to make this all happen. But he might represent the triggering mechanism that sets in motion an inexorable process that no one will ultimately be powerful enough to halt.

"I will now entertain discussion on what action, if any, the Partners for Progress should take."

Part Two

Chapter Fourteen

Cambridge, Massachusetts

They had been in Cambridge almost three weeks now, but Amanda couldn't get over the feeling that she was sharing her bed with a ghost. With all the other men she'd slept with, their previous bedmates hadn't concerned or interested her in the least. She was fully confident in herself, and so there was no need to worry about how she compared to each partner's former lover. Also, she had to admit, she'd never been so deeply involved or committed to a man that she genuinely cared. But now, as she lay next to Paul, every time he put his arms around her, ran his fingers gently through her straight blonde hair or pulled her over close to him, she felt the presence of the woman who little more than a month before had occupied the same space and tried desperately to occupy the same affections.

Paul loved her, she knew, and loved her in ways he had never loved Julia. But he was living under a burden of guilt, she also knew, bound up in all the ways he thought his life had been a failure up to that one day—the day he came upon his wife sprawled lifelessly upon this very bed. When he told her about coming back and finding the hundred dollars missing, Paul had said how much he hoped it was a false clue; that it didn't point to anything more than met the eye. But deep down, Amanda suspected he hoped the missing money did point to foul play. And after spending her first night in Julia's bed, she knew she did. That would open up a whole new floodgate of anguish and place them perhaps in greater jeopardy than they might already be in, but if it would release Paul from that blinding guilt of feeling he killed Julia himself, it would be worth any risk to her. And then, perhaps, he could begin to see that he was not a failure as a human being; that he was, in fact, an extraordinarily warm and gifted human being, and on the verge of unimaginable success.

If people could only see themselves rationally, she thought, lying on her back and staring silently at the ceiling while listening to Paul's rhythmical breathing next to her. Not that she was any more a model of how to act than he was. Shortly after he came back to her in New York, he'd admitted thinking of her as what he called a "total being" when they first met. It was meant as a compliment, but it seemed almost touchingly naive to her. Camus once said something to the effect that we always look at other people and envy them because they seem to be more complete than we are, she remembered. Whatever they are, they appear whole and unified as we see them from the outside. But we see ourselves from the inside, and what we see is an amalgam of bits and pieces that don't go together or add up to a unified whole. And as much as she liked herself, as much as she acknowledged her own talents and accepted her own beauty and charm, she had always felt that Camus must have written those lines with her specifically in mind.

The irony, of course, was that *together*, she and Paul were adding up to something approaching a whole. At least as far as his scientific accomplishments were concerned. He had been right. By explaining to her what he was looking for, she could come to understand it and then help him complete his own thoughts. It hadn't seemed like she was doing much, especially at first. But he had assured her that the kinds of questions she was asking him, the kinds of criticism she offered when he described a new line of reasoning, the kinds of suggestions she made when there was one variable left to fill in, all contributed toward slow but steady progress in assembling the components of his theory. To Amanda, it seemed that what she was doing was just simple logic and common sense, but he claimed no one else had been able to zero in so accurately on his thoughts and ideas and make him understand the subtleties of his own reasoning; not even Harry Gillette.

"Physics is like sex," Paul had commented to her with some seriousness in his voice. "It's easy enough to describe the physical procedure to someone who's never experienced it. But the important part is the nuance."

She wondered if the work would move any faster if Nat Kagan had agreed to come up here with them. Because whatever that magic connection was that brought her and Paul together as both lovers and thinkers, Nat was definitely part of it, along with who knew who else? It had to have something to do with the coincidence of their hospitalization together at Goddard, but beyond that the mystery only intensified in Amanda's mind. Somehow, they had been driven toward the greatest challenge in the realm of physical science, and in the relatively small community that followed such work closely, Paul was already being compared to Albert Einstein and Niels Bohr. And for the first time, instead of being a commentator and sidelines reporter, Amanda was part of the main action. She was not only describing the physical procedure, but experiencing the nuance as well.

But to her, the human mystery was just as important as the scientific one. While Paul sat in his office or adjacent laboratory with his feet up on the nearest chair, smoking the pipe that came as a surprise to her when they reached Cambridge, staring transfixed at the blackboard containing his own scribblings, Amanda sat nearby, trying to mentally approach the circumstances of their mutual experience from as many perspectives as she could, hoping that one of them would finally make everything fall into place.

She turned on her side and propped her head on her

folded arm so she could look at Paul. Despite her movement, he was still sound asleep. She didn't want to bother him. Since they'd arrived in Cambridge, he'd been coming home exhausted every night, but he had been sleeping better. There'd been none of the nightmares he'd had before—the twisted visions of the medical school anatomy lab. Maybe, she hoped, they were gone for good. Maybe David Sherman had been able to exorcise them from his psyche.

She swung herself around lightly and got out of bed, glancing at the digital clock on the way. It said 5:36 A.M. She padded into the second bedroom that served as a study and opened the top desk drawer that she'd claimed as hers. Several worn yellow legal sheets lay on top. She removed them and spread them out across the top of the desk, seating herself backward on the chair and wrapping her arm around the chair back. As always in such a posture, she had to periodically brush back the strands of hair that had a habit of falling in front of her face. She focused on several sheets of paper at the same time. Across the top of the first page she'd written, "Coincidence Factors," under which were listed:

1. All three in Goddard Institute at same time for same condition.
2. All three survived extremely low-percentage brain tumors.
3. All three operated on by Norbert Ramsey.
4. All three have same unexplainable vision at same time.
5. All three meet within a few days, twenty years after leaving hospital.
6. All three have episodes of anticipating what other is thinking (similar to ESP).
7. Both men's wives die mysteriously/accidentally within short time.
8. Two attempts made on Kagan's life. Two possibly made on West's.

9. All three somehow involved in science. Beyond that, all three have extraordinary insight into components of Unified Field Theory, on which Garrett is already a leading expert.

This last point brought her eyes and mind over to the second sheet, which she'd titled, "Personality Traits." Down the left-hand side, in no particular order, was her subjective distillation of the things that struck her about each of them. Across the top she had written the three names. And under each name there was an "X" corresponding to the traits she thought fit with that person. It wasn't the most scientific method, but all she was looking for was a trigger.

	GARRETT	KAGAN	WEST
Sailing	X	X	
Chamber Music (esp. Bach and Mozart)	X		X
Hiking/Mountain Climbing		X	X
Distrust of Authority	X	X	X
Dislike of Germans		X	
Pacifism (Bertrand Russell)		X	X
Zionism		X	
Problems with Spouse/ Opposite Sex	X		X
Interest in Science	X	X	X
Capacity for Science	X	X	X
Intellectual Skepticism	X	X	X
Periodic Emotional Detachment, Moodiness	X		X
Religious Philosophy Based on Natural Order (Spinoza)	X	X	X
Obsessive Involvement with Work	X	X	X
Against Nuclear Power		X	X
Interest in Philosophical Writing		X	X

She could go on listing traits forever, she realized, growing increasingly more arcane: Paul's and Nat's pipe-smoking, the fact that Paul played the violin at one time and she had always dreamed of doing it, Nat's perfect mental memory of the knoll they'd met at in Central Park even though he was sure he'd never been there before. But the important thing was that in her mind, she had a specific profile. She reached for Paul's volume of *Scientific Biography* to check her memory, but it was only for confirmation. In her position she'd often written about the most famous personality in twentieth-century science. And so it was off the top of her head with only occasional glances into the book that she wrote:

Albert Einstein, who was born in Germany, renounced his German citizenship early in life, and after being forced to leave his post at the Kaiser Wilhelm Institute in Berlin after the rise of Hitler, maintained a life-long hatred of the German people. He was, throughout his adult life, an ardent pacifist and Zionist, and was deeply troubled when those two philosophies came in conflict. Though married twice, he admitted that both were marriages of physical convenience and always had problems relating on a deep and committed level to members of the opposite sex. Such interest distracted him from his work. When not working, he was an ardent sailor, mountain climber, and chamber-music devotee, especially of the works of Bach and Mozart. He played the violin extremely well for an amateur. He shared with his close friend, philosopher Bertrand Russell, a healthy intellectual skepticism and distrust of authority, and spent his life pleading for an end to the excesses of nationalism. He was often moody and withdrawn, frequently depressed and plagued with self-doubt, and consumed by his work. Though his General Theory of Relativity laid the groundwork for the development of the atom bomb and atomic energy, and though at the urging of Leo

Szilard and Eugene Wigner he wrote a famous letter to President Roosevelt advocating intensive nuclear research during World War II, he was appalled by the use to which atomic energy had been put and became strongly opposed to its proliferation. Though he was Jewish, a Zionist, and was even offered the presidency of Israel by David Ben-Gürion in 1952, Einstein was an agnostic whose personal religious philosophy was based on a natural order as set forth by Spinoza. His own philosophical writing is among the most articulate on the subject. He spent the latter portion of his life attempting to construct a Unified Field Theory of universal forces, which would have the same type of comprehensive effect on explaining the behavior of fields that the General Theory of Relativity had for time, speed and mass. He died in Princeton, New Jersey, in 1955 without having completed the theory.

When she finished writing, she took in a deep, slow breath and realized her heart was pounding. Unless she was totally misinterpreting the evidence, the connection was unmistakable. She shifted her attention back to the list and stopped to consider every entry for which she'd put an "X" under her own name. When had it started? When did she first become interested in classical music? When did she first start dreaming about playing the violin? When did her religious views become clear? When did she become a pacifist? The questions pounded through her mind.

She got up and turned the chair around so that she could sit on it properly, then extended her bare legs and rested her feet on the edge of the desk to think about it. This was the same posture she always saw Paul assume in his office, she noted—one more subconscious similarity. She couldn't remember exactly—maybe her mother would—but of all the traits she'd listed, she couldn't remember one from before her operation. Obviously, an eight-year-old kid isn't going to appreciate chamber music or read Bertrand Russell, and problems with the opposite sex are the norm rather than the exception. But trying to evaluate her own personality as an entity, Amanda realized that she had always considered herself a different person before and after her tumor. It was natural, all the doctors had said, and of course, she'd agreed with them.

What about those two entries near the middle of the list: "Interest in Science" and "Capacity for Science"? In elementary school she hadn't had the slightest interest in anything technical. By twelfth grade she was the outstanding science student at New Trier High School. Had she just blossomed all of a sudden, as her teachers had said? The case for some type of determinism was growing too great to ignore.

She rose again and ran back into the bedroom, rousing Paul from his sleep.

"What is it?" he asked groggily.

"Paul, wake up! I have to ask you a question."

He opened one eye wide enough to see the clock. "Can't it wait?"

"It's waited long enough already." She paused while he opened the other eye and clasped his hands behind his head. "When you got out of Goddard, you didn't want to go back to medical school after the experience you'd had. Right?"

"Right."

"So instead you became a physicist."

"Right again. So what's your question?"

"My question is, why?"

Langley, Virginia

"So how was the Partners meeting in Switzerland?" George Henderson asked.

"I expect you already know," J. Tyler Kendrick responded, a wry smile crossing his lips. "I assume you had a representative or two there."

The Agency man returned the smile and walked over to the walnut bar against the wall. He extracted a bottle of Glenlivet and two glasses. "How do you like it?"

"Neat," said Kendrick.

Henderson wasn't surprised. He scooped ice into one glass and poured the other straight, handing it over. "Cheers. Now, what can I do for you?"

"As you undoubtedly know, the Partners for Progress are extremely interested in the work of Paul Garrett. For reasons which were made clear in Zurich, there is considerable economic implication, and since it potentially involves not only this country's standing in the world market but also the collective strength of the Western Allies, I thought it proper to discuss the matter with the Agency. I was frankly surprised to learn that your file on him was already rather extensive." He downed his Scotch and handed the glass back to Henderson.

"A refill?"

Kendrick waved him off. "That would be excessive. But back to the file . . ."

"Yes. People tend to underestimate the effectiveness of the government. We are, in fact, looking out for the best interests of our citizens and our national friends." He moved a few paces back toward the window, stopping next to a framed photograph of himself with "Wild Bill" Donovan in front of the Houses of Parliament right after the war. The profile hadn't changed much in thirty-five years.

Henderson was Old Agency. He had been tapped from Army Intelligence by Donovan's group during World War II—the one that people of his generation would always refer to simply as *the* war. When the OSS evolved into the Agency in 1947, the then Major Henderson stayed on board, first working in London and eventually going to Brussels as station chief. He had relished his work; he could honestly say that. It had been much simpler in the old days, much more clear-cut. We had known who was for us and who wasn't, and what to do on the inside regarding the ones who weren't. Half the staff came from Yale in those days, and the quality of the work was first rate. Now, nobody gave a living shit about anything.

When he got back from Brussels they moved him from Area Concentration to Plans. And somewhere along the line, from that point forward, it wasn't the same anymore. He couldn't say exactly what or when; maybe during all the weird crap in the 1950s. But the reality remained. He was an old barnstormer, and the closed cockpit and single wing had become the norm. There wasn't any room for free-lancers these days.

"I sent along our evaluation of Dr. Garrett's work," Kendrick told him.

"I've read it," Henderson said. "An interesting analysis, with quite a bit of imagination. From looking at it I'd have to say it would be in your best interests if Garrett—how shall I put it?—weren't working any-more."

"What's the phrase the Agency uses—'terminate with extreme prejudice'?" Kendrick's wry smile was noticeable again.

"We don't use that term much anymore. People tend to laugh at it now . . . ever since the Watergate fiasco to which our name was unfairly affixed. But to give you our position right off the top, we have a vested interest in seeing that Paul Garrett's research be allowed to develop. Some of the reasons are obvious, some are more delicate." He saw that Kendrick was about to protest, so he continued. "Now please believe me that I understand fully the implications for your energy, communications, and high-technology associates if your worst-case scenario is accurate. Contrary to popular misconception, we do think it would be economically disastrous to take the world off traditional technologies cold turkey. In your own company's case, for instance, we wouldn't want to see the world go off the 'oil standard' when we control almost all of the refining capacity. So, to put your mind somewhat at ease, we do not at this point want to see the outgrowths of the Garrett theory come to fruition any more than you do. Except in one instance."

"And that is?" Kendrick prodded.

"War. In most cases, though it might sound like a haunting paraphrase of 'Engine Charlie' Wilson, we do believe that what's good for the big corporations is good for America."

"Very patriotic of you."

"But as I said, there is an exception. In the event of major war, according to *our* worst-case scenarios, foreign oil sources would dry up, communications satellites could be shot out of the sky, the need for massive rapid material transfer and strategic missiles becomes acute, etc. etc. At that point, the applications of the Garrett theory, which would have been developed secretly and kept hidden for such an eventuality, take on tremendous leverage. I'm sure you can appreciate that."

"Yes, of course," Kendrick said tersely. "Assuming you could gear up to the new systems almost instantaneously. But you can't read an intelligence report that says the Russkies are going to attack tomorrow and then go out that night and develop a missile system based on the Garrett work."

"Very true," Henderson agreed. "But as you acknowledge in your own report, much of the theoretical application of this work does not involve complicated systems. It's merely using natural forces against each other. Part of the attractiveness of the whole package is its simplicity. So we think it is workable under the contingencies I've just outlined. At the same time, I realize how important the continuation of present methods and practices is to your member companies. As the operating representative of the Partners for Progress, your opinion obviously carries considerable weight in strategic policy circles. So keeping in mind our mutual—and largely overlapping—interest in this matter, I've worked out an informal arrangement, which I think should be acceptable to you." Henderson paused for emphasis, and saw Kendrick's eyes rivet on him uncomfortably. The man clearly didn't like suspense.

"Go on," he said.

"We will continue monitoring Dr. Garrett's work, which is, I believe, the function for which you came to us in the first place."

"Correct."

"And when it reaches the stage where it can be successfully interpreted and completed by others, it will be taken out of his hands . . . by whatever means necessary. There is extensive precedent for this kind of action and it won't be a problem. From then on, it will be developed 'on the inside' and kept on ice until such time as it is strategically necessary—the contingency I outlined earlier—or until the various technologies naturally catch up in a linear fashion as the result of normal developments."

"But the aspect that has always troubled us is the matter of accessibility," stated Kendrick. "Once Garrett reaches that certain stage, the scientific principles become accessible to a large number of skilled scientists and technicians. And then, regardless of what happens to Garrett personally, the situation is out of our control."

"Yes, I understand, and we've considered that problem carefully. And it comes down to a question of timing. We will have to take over the work at such a stage that its practical applications are already feasible, but not widely disseminated. At that point we can have one of our brethren clamp a military security label on it, which essentially takes it out of circulation. That's what we did with the laser principle, and that was extremely successful for twenty years. Even the inventor lost his right to continue research."

"A scientific theory and a technological application are two different things, but it sounds as if you've come up with the best possible working plan, assuming it remains fluid enough to deal with contingencies, of course."

"Of course."

"And the disposition of Dr. Garrett himself?"

"In dealing with matters of national security, we have a certain flexibility unavailable to other government agencies."

"Someone might have been exercising flexibility if Mrs. Garrett's death turned out not to be a suicide, for instance?"

"Yes. It was a very unfortunate event," Henderson said. "We've been looking into it."

"Needless to say, I'd be most interested in the results of your investigation."

"We're also looking into the death of Garrett's colleague, Harry Gillette." He stared straight at Kendrick, evaluating his reaction. But the oil executive returned the gaze with equal intensity.

"I understood that to be a heart attack," he said.

"That was the official report," Henderson agreed.

"Assuming that either of these deaths is directly related to Garrett's work, do you think the bombing of the car in lower Manhattan is also part of the picture?"

"I don't think so. From what we can see, it was an Arab terrorist action against a prominent advocate of Zionism, Rabbi Nathaniel Kagan. The fact that it took place at an anti-nuclear rally was merely circumstantial."

"As was the presence of Dr. Garrett at the scene?"

"Presumably so. The FBI is going through its data on Palestinian groups. Hopefully, they'll come up with something."

"I'll try to put out some inquiries with our contacts in

the Arab world," Kendrick offered. From the tone, Henderson couldn't tell if it was meant to be a threat.

The Agency man walked back over to the bar, dipped his glass in the ice chest, then poured another two inches of Glenlivet. "Change your mind?" he asked.

"No thank you. Now that we've reached a tentative understanding and agreement, I'll be going."

"Are you staying over in Washington?"

"No. I have a meeting this afternoon in Chicago."

"Too bad you can't stay. The city is quite beautiful and the weather has been unusually pleasant for this time of year."

Kendrick shrugged. "We all have different concepts of beauty, I suppose. To me, one office looks the same as the next."

He stood up to leave at the same time that the intercom buzzed. "Martin is here to see you, sir."

"Send him in." When he'd entered Henderson said, "This is . . . Doug . . . Martin," struggling a moment with the first name he seldom used. After they exchanged greetings, Henderson extended his hand. "Thanks for coming by. I think things will work out to everyone's benefit. My secretary will see you out."

When Kendrick was gone, Henderson leaned against his desk and folded his arms across his chest. "He went for the plan, but I don't completely trust him. He's brilliant, but I know that type of corporate mentality. Its brilliance is based on perfect control and not taking chances or letting things get out of hand."

"You didn't tell him . . . ?"

"No, of course not. And all things considered, I'm glad the Partners for Progress decided to come to us. That way, we can keep closer track of what they're up to."

"Any other impressions?" Martin asked.

"I think he's suspicious that we murdered Mrs. Garrett. I could see it in his eyes."

"What about the bomb in Rabbi Kagan's car?"

"I tried to pin that one on the Arabs. I don't know

whether he bought it or not. But frankly, that's a minor issue. He's certainly not going to go around advertising his suspicions."

"Especially when we got the wrong person."

"Yes," Henderson rejoined grimly. "We're getting quite a bit of experience killing wives."

Martin looked down at the floor and sighed.

"Look, that's past history now. I'm more concerned with the present and future. That bombing could prove to be costly. With the stunts we've pulled so far, our exposure is dangerously high. And I don't have to remind you that the sole purpose of this exercise is to avoid the kind of exposure which, in light of previous revelations, could cripple us."

"Yes, I know. That's why we bent over backward to do the Mrs. Garrett thing up right," Martin reminded him.

"What worries me now is that somehow they've maneuvered themselves into the right position to pry the lid off the whole thing. How, I don't know. It may all be by chance; it may not be. But the less contact all three have together, the better."

"We think Garrett and West are still together, but not Kagan."

"That's at least good news." He closed his eyes and massaged his temples with his thumb and forefinger. He'd followed the Paul Garrett file for more than twenty years and during that time he'd half convinced himself the matter would take care of itself. But now, Henderson would have to deal with him. Eventually, everybody had to be dealt with.

The Cadillac limousine swung around in back of the Page Terminal at Dulles International Airport and out onto the tarmac behind the building, pulling up right in front of the Grumman Gulfstream III. National Airport, where Universal Oil also had hangar facilities, was a good deal closer to Washington and Langley than Dulles was, but J. Tyler Kendrick liked the convenience of being driven right up to the plane, which could only be done here. And for Kendrick, sitting in the back seat with a stack of confidential reports and a mobile telephone next to him, the extra time in the car was not wasted.

Inside the Gulfstream cabin, John Christopher was waiting for him, alone with the mauve and gray ultra-suede decor. A lithe and comely hostess, attired in a jumpsuit of complementary colors, appeared from behind the front bulkhead.

"Can I get you anything to eat or drink, Mr. Kendrick? We have Clams Casino, Beef Wellington and Caesar salad today."

"No thank you. Just a ginger ale, maybe. Mr. Christopher and I have to talk."

"Very good, sir. We'll be taking off in three minutes." After delivering his ginger ale, she followed his implied order and disappeared back behind the bulkhead again.

"How did it go with our friends at the Agency?" Christopher asked.

"Reasonably well. But what they propose is too much of a holding action. The time might come in the very near future when we have to take matters into our own hands . . . beyond accountability, of course."

"What do you have in mind?"

"It is conceivable that Garrett's work could benefit us, if it could be channeled quickly and appropriately. I might not even be beyond making him an offer."

"That would have to be done with discretion, I would think."

"With the utmost discretion," Kendrick agreed.

The jet taxied to the end of the runway, radioed its readiness for takeoff to the tower, then turned on its engines full throttle. J. Tyler Kendrick didn't like to be kept waiting any longer than absolutely necessary.

Cambridge, Massachusetts

Amanda spent the morning in the MIT library, the accumulated evidence gnawing at her mind, pushing her logical processes beyond their resiliency points. The elusive puzzle challenged her intellect beyond its experiential reserves. If she was to meet it, it would have to be through instinct.

Something had to have happened to each of them during their operations at Goddard. She proceeded from that premise as the least unlikely. Something had happened to direct their intelligence and emotional development along complementary channels. And somehow, the outlines of Albert Einstein's personality and even his scientific work had been impressed on them in ways that made them seem willful imitations. If she believed in such things—which neither she, nor Einstein did—she would have concluded that his soul had been split and transferred into their bodies upon his death. There was plenty of literature to support such a phenomenon. Certain Eastern religions brimmed with it. But for a more rational, scientific explanation, she found the great library devoid of sources. She would have to come up with this explanation on her own.

What she did find, though, was an extensive medical collection detailing the current level of understanding of the human brain. And what struck her over and over again as she skimmed one volume and then another was the repeated disclaimer about how little we actually know of the brain's makeup and function. But somewhere, there had to be a logical answer. If you could only find it, there was a logical answer to everything. It was Einstein himself who said, "The mystery of the world is its comprehensibility."

She caught her breath. Had she read that statement somewhere, or did she just . . . *know* it?

The written material was overwhelming, but Amanda was an extremely rapid reader and, through years of deadline-prodded research, a good "extractor." She went through most of the important works on the subject, from Hughlings-Jackson and Pavlov up through Cushing and Sherrington to Penfield and Jasper. She also found, to her amusement, that two of the most distinguished English neurologists had been Lord Russell Brain and Sir Henry Head! If that doesn't support the theory of scientific determinism, she thought, I don't know what could. And she read with special interest, *Localization and Correlation of Interpretive Neurological Function* by Norbert Ramsey, 1962.

The specific cerebral areas responsible for motor function had all been mapped out for decades, she found. And the cranial nerves were even named according to what they controlled. The first is olfactory, the second is optic, the third is oculomotor, the seventh is facial, the eighth is acoustic, and so on. But what was far less clear, even in the lucid and penetrating writing of Penfield and Ramsey, was where thinking, reasoning, memory, and emotion happened. There was strong circumstantial evidence that much of it took place in the temporal and prefrontal cortices. The limbic system, and specifically the hypothalamus, was thought to be the location of emotional characteristics, and both reasoning ability and creative thought seemed to reside in the frontal and temporal lobes, anterior to the precentral motor area. The research had all been empirical, generally the result of observing which functions or abilities were lost when a particular part of the brain was damaged or destroyed. But the empirical study could only reach a certain level, beyond which there was only vague and tentative theory, so speculative as to be tinged with religious belief. No one had been able to show that what happens in the mind actually has a physical correlative. No one had been able to observe the brain through a microscope, point to a specific chemical or electrical activity and say, "This is a thought taking place." No one had been able to directly associate the tangible brain with the intangible mind, leading Wilder Penfield to ask, "Can there be energy without structure?" As she read, Amanda was struck with the paradox of trying to use the mind to comprehend and interpret itself.

Struggling to hold all the concepts she had just learned about in some kind of mental equilibrium, she pushed herself for a logical explanation. There was the possibility of mass hypnosis, or brainwashing, but how could that account for the specialized ability they each seemed to have? What were the other possibilities; the physical possibilities?

She tried to catalogue in her mind all the different types of therapy used on the brain. Radiation was used on brain tumors. Could it have caused some of the cells to mutate? Could an electrical implant cause the tissue to reorient its energy patterns, thereby increasing intelligence? Some researchers suggested that the brain actually is constructed like a super sophisticated computer. If that was the case, could electric shock therapy alter the magnetic field of the memory bank? Recently, a lot of work had been done with chemical neurotransmitters. Introducing a foreign chemical into the brain might increase its power or change its character. Or maybe the simple act of cutting tissue during surgery, of creating new lesions, had altered their brains somehow. Amanda sighed with frustration. Everything was possible, nothing was probable. One explanation was as logical as another and the frontier was completely uncharted.

But even if it were not possible to localize a specific thought or emotion, suppose a surgeon such as Ramsey did something to certain parts of the frontal and temporal lobes while he was operating that did cause them to change characteristics. Let's say it was electrical stimulation, for instance, as was widely used during the 1950s. And suppose by "adjusting" these generalized areas he was able to increase their capacity, as a grow light speeds up a plant's development. After all, it was well known that the average individual only uses between five and fifteen per cent of his or her brain potential. Suppose this adjustment helped "actualize" the brain potential of those it was used on. That might even explain the miraculous curing of the deadly tumor. Now Amanda felt she was making progress.

But what about the Einstein tie-in? She squirmed in the hard wooden chair, not wanting to lose her momentum. But even that could be explained, though it might be far-fetched. Certainly she'd have to search for independent evidence. Maybe as a young man in Germany he had had the same type of operation from a surgeon equally as gifted as Norbert Ramsey. Maybe that accounted for his incredible and otherwise unexplainable mental capacity. But if this could be done, she went on, why wouldn't these surgeons have made the operation routine? And why wouldn't they have published their results? Unless the whole thing was just a shot in the dark. Maybe they couldn't predict in advance what the results would be in each case and some of the patients died, or ended up as vegetables. Maybe Norbert Ramsey was just extremely lucky to have had three successes at the same time. Maybe he tried it on all the tumor patients at Goddard while they were there; Harry Mervis and Abraham Radner and all the others. Maybe Ramsey was still doing the operation, and maybe others were as well.

Her mind raced with possibilities. What other geniuses of the world might have had it? Did the Nazis or the Russians try it? There had been rumors for decades that Ivan Pavlov had a secret laboratory in the Ural Mountains where he experimented on human beings. Could he have been doing something like this? The flight of imagination veered off into a detour of paranoia. She could feel her armpits dampen and a frosty sweat form along her hairline.

Her first inclination was to go right to Dr. Ramsey

and spill out her suspicions to him. But she quickly accepted the impracticality of that idea. He wasn't about to hand over any secret he'd managed to keep for twenty years. And confronting him might alert him to cover any existing trails, driving the truth that much further off. And if she was completely off the mark, this little encounter could be embarrassing in the extreme. She would have to do more research and more thinking on the subject. She had to be patient.

But her patience was wearing thin. Much as she loved Paul, the living arrangement she'd had such mixed feelings about in the first place was getting to her. She'd already used up her vacation time and would soon have to go back to New York, whether Paul needed her to stay or not. She was able to keep up with some of her professional responsibilities through her assistant, Nancy Flanagan, who was the only one she had told where she was going. Being able to trust Nancy took at least that burden off her shoulders.

If Paul's theory did work out, though, all the inconvenience and dislocation would be worth it. Anticipating the exclusive syndicated series and the best-selling book that would follow was a delicious exercise, even as a casual daydream. The mind is so fluid. It was funny how quickly it could shift from such deep and troubled speculation about its own functioning to these carefree thoughts of fame and fortune.

She glanced at her watch. She'd gotten carried away with her research. It was time to meet Paul for lunch. And since he was in his laboratory setting up his experiment, he would undoubtedly be just as engrossed in what he was doing and work straight through if she didn't drag him away for an hour.

She walked down the steps of Hayden Library, along Memorial Drive, and crossed the grassy, tree-lined Killian Court. Even during these summer months, the campus was full of activity—from people playing Frisbee on the lawn to others sprawled idyllically in the sun, engrossed in aero-dynamics journals. But here,

Amanda knew, the kids flinging the Frisbees could explain in clear mathematical terms to the ones reading the journals exactly by what laws of dynamics the platters flew.

In college, she'd had a boyfriend at Harvard and had spent a good deal of time in Boston one year. MIT was just thought of as the other kingdom of Cambridge. The kids might have been as smart as those at Harvard, but they were considered much weirder. The boys, it was said, were all myopic dwarfs with slide rules. And the girls were just boys who'd worked their balls off in high school. She laughed to herself as she thought back twelve years.

But in the weeks she'd been here with Paul, Amanda had changed her opinion of this place everyone referred to simply as "the Institute." There were plenty of tall men and attractive women, and the "nerd" element was greatly overplayed. The intellectual atmosphere was staggering, no more pompous than what she remembered from Harvard, and one couldn't help feeling that some of the most advanced and fascinating work in the world was going on right inside these somber gray buildings.

Even in the heart of teeming Cambridge, right across the Charles from Boston, MIT still succeeded in maintaining the trappings of a traditional undergraduate college. The feeling was relaxed. Every day Amanda either jogged, swam, or played tennis, and without fail some student or young faculty member would try to make a date, or ask her out for coffee. And feeling no disloyalty to Paul, she would often accept. The whole atmosphere was different here and the situation so much less threatening than it would be in Manhattan. You could be freer here, more spontaneous, without worrying about the social or physical consequences. She thought about what it might be like to be a professor's wife at the Institute. But the idea of leaving New York permanently, or leaving the job she'd worked so hard for, for that matter, was something she wasn't prepared to deal with. And anyway, just thinking about it was assuming a bit more than she felt comfortable assuming at this point.

Paul's lab was on Vassar Street, in a run-down section of the campus next to the railroad tracks. The style of the red brick building was Dickens Gothic, and it easily might have been a warehouse at one time. Inside, the brick warehouse motif was continued. The ceilings were an open gridwork of exposed beams, pipes, and wiring. The windows along the Vassar Street side seemed not to have been cleaned in Amanda's lifetime. The only obvious modernization was the concrete flooring which increased only the structure's efficiency, not its charm.

Walking down the hall toward Paul's door, Amanda resolved to outline her whole theory to him before his contagious enthusiasm for his own work seized the moment away from her. But as soon as she knocked once and then opened the door, she knew she'd already lost.

She'd hardly kissed him and gotten out, "Honey, I had some new ideas this morning," before he countered with:

"So have I!" and led her by the hand to the corner of the room where she could fully appreciate the Byzantine apparatus he'd constructed.

"What is that?" she exclaimed, detecting from his look of boyish delight that maximum enthusiasm was expected.

To her left was a waist-high, gray metal bank of capacitors, extending most of the way across the room, connected in series to a large cylindrical electromagnet. A second, equally long capacitor bank connected to eight pulse lasers mounted on metal brackets. Beyond them, ringing the entire core of the experiment about six feet out, were six more massive magnets hanging on chains from the ceiling at a level of two feet off the floor. They were connected both to a third capacitor bank and a series of liquid nitrogen canisters stuck behind them, as out of the way as it was possible to be in the cluttered lab.

Amanda inspected the lasers, certainly the most intriguing pieces of equipment in the room. A plate on the side of each one read, "Property of U.S. Air Force."

"Did you steal them?" she challenged playfully.

"No, they're surplus. They'd cost a fortune new. Even the Institute has to economize where it can."

"Would you like to explain all this to me?" she asked, knowing he'd like nothing better.

"Okay. Very simply . . . and I'm leaving out a lot . . . gravity, so far as we understand it at all, is the effect of an attractive force between two objects, and it's dependent on their total mass. Now, though it's been speculated, no one has so far been able to produce concrete evidence of a corresponding *repulsive* force like the one in electromagnetism."

"You mean like when I try to push two magnets together with their same poles facing?"

"That's right. But if, as I suspect, there is a unity between gravitational and electromagnetic fields, I should be able to unlock the resistive power of gravity."

"You?" she said, trying to cover her smile.

"Me," he answered, beaming. He pointed to the equation-covered blackboard. "With this latest tensor I worked out, it all fits together mathematically."

"What about in real life?"

"Let's keep our fingers crossed. There's a hell of a lot I still haven't been able to work in yet, which is why I've set up this experiment. But the way I figure it, the resistive, or repulsive power is a very weak force as it normally exists in nature and is therefore masked by the attractive force, which is what we commonly refer to as gravity. You can't even tell the weak force is there. The key is to either amplify it or rearrange it."

"And how do you propose to do this, my dear?"

"Well . . . I'm going to start off by seeing if I can disrupt the nuclear gravitational force holding together the subatomic components of a few hydrogen atoms."

"Why only a few?"

"Think back to your special relativity. Even a few atoms hold an incredible potential of energy. We'll get into the bigger numbers once we know we can control it. But right now, with the equipment I have, I should be able to reverse the gravitational force."

"So what are all the batteries for?"

"Capacitors, not batteries. I need them to store up the huge amount of power I'll have to have as the instantaneous activation energy. See, the equations say that a vast supply of energy's needed to activate the repulsive force, but once that's attained, the energy from the atomic dissociation becomes the *supply* and feeds on itself. The lasers direct the collision of each subatomic particle with its corresponding repulsive component, while also helping to begin the dissociation by heating up the atoms to create the proper environment. And this electromagnetic coil surrounding the field is supposed to control the reaction."

"So what happens if it all works?"

"We should be able to detect and measure some type of energy release from the atoms dissociating. But exactly what types and amounts, I'm not sure."

She walked over to a fortified steel shield in one corner of the large room. "I see you're not taking any chances, though."

He laughed. "This is completely new ground. I just can't be sure how much energy we're talking about. It could be quite a lot."

She smiled sardonically. "You sound like the guys who did the first atom bomb test at Alamogordo. Since they'd never done a chain reaction just like that one, they couldn't be sure it was going to be finite. They figured it was remotely possible the fission would never stop and eventually spread all over the world. But they did it anyway. And look at you, standing behind your shield just itching to throw your switch."

"Thank you, Dr. Einstein. But I believe I've already read those remarks in *Aurora*."

"Don't make fun. Somebody's got to keep you from going off the deep end." She continued her circuit around the room. "So that switch box behind the shield is what triggers the whole thing?"

"Presumably. We'll know later on in the afternoon."

"And what's that for?" she asked, pointing to an aluminum ladder near the capacitor banks.

He pointed up to an empty light socket in the ceiling. "Changing bulbs."

"Oh. I thought maybe it was to climb out of the way if it got too hot for you."

"It's not a thermal reaction. There shouldn't be any heat beyond what the lasers generate."

"Very reassuring. Let's go to lunch."

"You go without me," he said. "I don't want to take the time."

"You can't skip lunch, Paul."

"Why not? You don't stop to take a nap when you're halfway up a mountain. If this works out, I'll take you for a big fancy dinner tonight. That should more than make up for it. You go on ahead. Come back for me about six."

When Amanda returned to the laboratory late that afternoon, Paul's buoyant optimism had been replaced by a pervading sense of depression. She could tell as soon as she saw him, hunched up on a wooden stool, staring blankly at the magnetic coil.

"It's not working, is it?" she asked with the empathy of a mother who knew her son had just dropped the game-winning fly ball.

"I don't know what's wrong. I've set it up four different ways. I throw the switch each time and nothing happens."

She glanced over to the area behind the steel shield. "Do you know you left the switch on?"

"It doesn't matter," he replied forlornly. "I had to recharge the capacitors so the lead from the terminal pole to the switch box is disconnected."

"That's still careless," she chided. "And look, both open terminal poles are uncovered."

"What's the difference, it's not doing anything. We might as well get out of here."

She could imagine what his mood would be like until he got back to the lab again, so she said, "Are you set up to try it again?"

"Well, I have to hook up the capacitors again, otherwise the circuit isn't complete. But other than that . . ."

"Then why don't we give it one more try? Your work seems to go better when I'm close by."

"That's true," he allowed. She could sense his mood lifting. "Okay. Let's give it a go. I've changed around a few things that could make a difference . . ." He was back in his element again. He'd often said that a scientist's ultimate success was largely determined by his resilience to failure. Now he was attempting to prove it. "Move that ladder to the side," he directed, "and I'll connect . . ."

He had just picked up the cable lead when the door to the lab slammed open.

"What the hell . . ." Paul looked up to see two men holding automatic rifles. They were both short, dark, and in their mid to late twenties.

"Are you Paul Garrett?" one of them demanded, his weapon trained directly at Paul's head. He had a slight accent that sounded faintly Slavic, but they both looked as if they were from the Middle East or Turkey.

"What do you want?" Paul responded.

"We want you to come with us." The other one aimed his gun at Amanda, who stood midway between the capacitor bank and the protective shield.

"Where are you taking us?" she asked.

He waved his free hand in the air to silence her. "Where is the rabbi?"

Paul turned his head to Amanda, stunned.

"What are you talking about?" she said.

"We have no time for this! Is he with you here?"

"No," she responded.

"Good. Then this is all," he said to his companion.

"But he's expecting us!" Amanda added quickly. "If he doesn't hear from us within the hour, he knows to call the police."

The gunman seemed unimpressed. He motioned with the end of his rifle toward the door. "That way, come with us."

At first, neither Paul nor Amanda moved. Then she started inching slowly toward the shield.

"Stop!" the intruder yelled. "With these guns we could kill you both in less than a second without even aiming. And even if you reached that shield, it wouldn't help. The bullets can rip right through it. Now come!"

Paul nodded slightly that she should comply. He started toward the door. She glanced once more toward the shield, noting that the switch box was still in the on position.

They walked gingerly forward. Paul's eyes never left the determined faces of the two gunmen. Amanda's eyes darted everywhere around the room.

She took a deep breath and tried to keep her hands from trembling. Paul reached out to her but the gunman grunted him away.

As they passed the aluminum ladder, Amanda suddenly bolted and grabbed it, throwing it with all her strength into the gap between the capacitor pole and the terminal leading to the switch box. In the same motion she dove toward Paul's knees, tackling him and sending them both skidding along the floor in the direction of the steel shield. She felt the skin tearing from her knees and elbows as they slid.

At the same moment, sparks crackled out from the two terminal poles as the ladder banged against them, completing the electric circuit.

The lead gunman heard the sound, turned his head and uttered a growl of anger. It took him less than a tenth of a second to recover his senses and whip his weapon around to Paul and Amanda on the floor and begin cocking his index finger to pull the trigger.

But it was the last action of his life.

There was a staccato of sonic booms coming from all

directions at once. A strong, cool wind rushed by like a sudden vacuum and Paul and Amanda could feel the air pumping from their lungs. An explosive force rocked through the lab, making them flatten their faces to the concrete floor. Large chunks whizzed by their heads.

Within a second it was over. They looked up. The lab was destroyed. Not merely wrecked, but totally obliterated. The roof was gone, having blown straight up and out. Nothing was left in its previous form. Everything had disintegrated to pieces of rubble. And most terrifying, above a two-foot level, the steel shield they had counted on for protection was nonexistent.

They looked over in the direction where the gunmen had been standing and saw only four independently standing legs going up to just above the knee. Beyond that, nothing. Like a clean, sharp, guillotine cut. A second later and the disembodied legs thudded randomly over onto the floor. There was no sign of the rest of the bodies, the weapons, anything. The massive capacitor banks also looked as if they'd been sheared in half lengthwise, like a soft slab of butter.

"Good God!" Amanda breathed when she had recovered her senses enough to react. "Why weren't we killed?"

Paul slowly rose to his knees, and then even more slowly to his feet. "Look, everything from two feet above the ground on up was destroyed; everything below untouched. Pulling us to the floor like you did saved our lives."

She rolled over on her back, trying to ward off delayed hysteria. She knew she'd have to get up momentarily.

"It worked!" Paul stammered. "This time it worked! We finally got the repulsive gravitational force to assert itself!"

"We certainly did," she said drily. "Now come on, we've got to get out of here!"

"Do you realize what this means?" he asked, pulling her to her feet and throwing his arms around her.

"It means someone wants to kill or capture us and we've got to get the hell away."

"No, I mean this shows that atoms can be completely dissociated through the repulsive force." He spread his arms in triumph. "Look around the room. Everything above the two-foot level is broken apart. This is incredible!"

"So are you. Now come on. There'll be people here any second."

"You're right. Let's go." He focused on her long enough to realize her arms and legs were bleeding, and there was a small gash on her forehead. "Are you okay?"

"For the time being. Now move!"

They stumbled out of the rubble through the back of the building and along the railroad tracks. They could already hear sirens coming closer on Vassar Street. Bits of debris from the lab were scattered across their path as far up as Main Street. They continued along the tracks and circled around behind Technology Square, the four-building corporate enclave where Polaroid maintained its headquarters. They ducked into a deserted loading dock. It was after six, so there wouldn't be any more activity there.

Amanda leaned against the concrete wall, trying to catch her breath.

"We've got to get out of town," Paul said. She nodded, still breathing furiously. "We'll go back to my apartment and patch you up. Then you can change clothes."

"No," she panted. "There's liable to be people there waiting for us. We don't know how many others there were besides the two in the lab."

"But you can't go like this. How's it look—a middle-aged man dragging a young bleeding woman onto a plane. Okay, listen. We'll have to buy you some clothes. Long-sleeve blouse and pants. We'll go to the Harvard Coop. The Square is always so crowded we can get lost there and I can use my Coop card to pay."

"Good. By the way, Paul. Even if we weren't blown

to smithereens, why weren't we fried in that explosion?"

"I told you before, it wasn't a thermal explosion; there wasn't any heat generated. The sound wasn't even what you'd expect. It was more like a fission reaction without the radiation. The atomic particles were just separating with incredible power."

"Why wasn't it an even bigger blast, then?"

"The range of the explosion depends on how many atoms are involved in the first place. It can only react with its own energy."

"Then why did it leave that line of devastation starting two feet off the ground?"

"There were magnets set up at that level, but they weren't hooked up to any energy source. But possibly . . ."

"Okay," she interrupted. "Enough science lesson for the time being. I'm ready."

They walked briskly down Main Street to Kendall Square and caught the "T" to Harvard Square. During the ride Amanda sat in the far corner of the car and Paul stood in front of her, hanging onto the horizontal bar and trying to block a clear view of her body.

At Harvard Square they ducked into the alley between the Coop and its annex. "Do you have something to write on?" he asked.

"No. My pocketbook must have been blown up in the explosion."

Paul fished through his jacket pockets and finally extracted a scrap of paper. "Here. Write down your sizes for me."

He went to the clothing department while she waited for him in the alley out back, sitting with a newspaper so as to shield the sight of her injuries. He bought the first things he could find in her size, a dark blue slacks and blouse combination. As an afterthought, he added a handbag to his purchases, realizing she'd be conspicuous without one.

He met her back outside and handed her the shopping bag. "Go change in the ladies' room at the

Holyoke Center. Throw what you're wearing in the trash. Oh, and wash your face."

She looked at him admonishingly. "Don't worry. I won't embarrass you in public."

"Yeah? Well, you already wrecked my lab. What are people going to say?"

"Cute, Dr. Garrett. Very cute."

She dodged the eternal traffic crossing the square and headed for the Holyoke Center. He went back down the stairs of the MBTA station and over to the wall of telephones. He dialed 411 and asked the operator, "Do you have a listing for a Bertram Kennedy, please?"

The call was answered on the first ring. "Kennedy here."

"Lieutenant Kennedy . . . this is Paul Garrett."

"Garrett! Where are you? Are you all right?"

"Yes . . . yes . . . I'm all right."

"I just got the call not five minutes ago. I was heading out the door for the station when you . . . What the hell happened?"

"Two people tried to kidnap me and my . . . friend. There was an explosion, and . . ."

"Garrett. Tell me where you are. Let me come pick you up. I've got a lot of questions to ask you; things we need to know." His voice was urgent, imploring.

Paul was silent for a long time; thinking, weighing options, trying to account for contingencies. "Ah . . . let me call you back, Lieutenant. I have to sort a few things out."

"No, wait! Garrett! Let me . . ."

Paul hung up the phone, slowly climbed the steps and crossed over to the Holyoke Center.

Only when Amanda emerged from the ladies' room could he see that the impact of the horror had finally reached her. She was pale, almost ashen, and as she walked she tried to mask an unsteadiness in her legs. Paul pulled her gently by the arm.

"How are you doing?"

"Okay," she replied bravely. "Just all of a sudden in there, I started thinking about everything . . . and it just all came down on me. I thought I was going to be sick."

"As soon as we get where we're going, you can let it all out. But you've got to be strong until then. Can you do that?"

"I'll try."

"I know you will. Just like you did back in the lab. You saved our lives."

"I think I used up all my heroism for the day. Where are we going?" she asked.

"Washington. Someone's there we can trust. But there'll be people looking for us together, so we have to go separately." He took two hundred dollars from his wallet. "Take this. I just got a check cashed this morning. I've kept enough for cabs and I'll pay for my ticket by credit card."

"We should take the shuttle to New York and then to Washington. That way we don't have to risk making reservations, which could be traced."

"Good thinking."

"Where shall we meet?"

"Tomorrow morning at St. Elizabeth's Hospital, Alfred Noyes Division. Ask for David Sherman."

"Okay." She felt a new surge of adrenalin and her eyes grew wider and clearer. "I guess this is good-bye, then."

"Only for tonight."

She looked at him plaintively.

"Are you afraid?" he asked her.

"Terrified."

"Me too. But we've got to get out of here so we can sit back and figure things out. Maybe there's even a logical explanation to all this," he grinned.

"I'll bet." She put her arms around him and squeezed tightly, blinking back tears. "Good luck," she whispered, trembling.

"Same to you."

"Oh, and one more thing."

"What's that?"

"We've got to contact Nat Kagan as soon as we can.

You heard those men ask for him. I hope they haven't gotten to him already."

Then they parted, reluctantly but hastily, each heading in a direction to hail a cab to the airport, trying to evade a vague enemy whose identity and motives they did not know.

Chapter Fifteen

Washington, D.C.

For the rest of his life, the moment would be fixed in David Sherman's mind.

It was after eleven and he had settled into his comfortable daily wind-down pattern: his shirt off, a glass of Irish Mist in his hand, watching the local news in his living room, the only space in the house long enough to afford a comfortable viewing distance from the television. The weather segment was on, and mentally he had just about drifted off into the billowy white clouds that provided the backdrop for the next day's forecast.

The doorbell rang and he nearly jumped through his skin.

He warily opened the door and Paul Garrett practically slumped into his tiny front hall, a look of dazed anguish in his eyes that David had seen in battle-shocked soldiers in Korea. He quickly slammed the door and put his arm around Paul's waist to steady him, moving him to a sitting position on the steps.

"What in God's name . . . ?"

"Someone tried to capture us . . . in my lab," he quavered. "Me and Amanda. We killed them."

"Holy shit!" David exclaimed, his head reeling. "Amanda . . . is she all right?"

Paul nodded his head. "People are looking for us . . . I'm sure of it. I told her to come separately. She's to meet us at St. Elizabeth's tomorrow morning." He lowered his head between his knees in fatigue.

David waited until he looked back up again and then said, "Come on, let's get you into the other room. Then

273

you can give me the details." He reached for Paul's forearm.

He poured him a double Scotch and brought it over to the sofa. "I'll give you something stronger if you need it." He listened in silence as Paul related as coherently as he could the events of the day.

". . . And when Amanda pushed over the ladder to complete the activation circuit, if the reaction hadn't occurred successfully, they would have killed us. The first one already had his machine gun whipped around at us. I could see the muzzle pointing at my throat when the explosion blew them to bits."

David let out a nervous sigh. "Then she was taking a hell of a chance, since you say the reaction hadn't worked the four previous times you'd tried it."

"That's right, I guess. But for some reason, I knew in my mind it would work this time. I guess I'd eliminated all the variables. I certainly didn't know it would be that powerful an explosion, but I knew it would be something pretty dramatic, at least enough to divert attention for a while."

"So you're saying in that split second before she decided to do it, Amanda somehow sensed your confidence that it would work this time . . . enough to risk both your lives for the chance?"

Paul shook his head slowly in bewilderment. "I guess that's what I am saying. We've been getting these sensations, picking up these vibes from each other right from the beginning; ever since the bridge game at your sister's. Then of course you have to keep in mind that these people looked like they were playing for keeps. I think there's a good chance they would have killed us anyway. So the risk seemed worth it at the time."

"Sure. So who knows about this now?"

"Half of Boston, I suspect. When the roof blows off your lab, it's pretty hard to keep it a secret. But nobody knows I'm here, or even in Washington. At least I hope nobody does."

"You were wise to pick someone as obscure as me."

Paul dragged his front teeth across his lower lip and

swished the liquor rhythmically in his glass. "I'm terribly sorry to have dragged you into this. But you were the only one I could think of; who I knew I could trust." He looked up and his eyes were welling up with moisture. "I just want you to know I appreciate that, even if you didn't have a chance to back down or say no."

"Forget it," David said. "We'll figure out exactly what to do in the morning, after you've had a chance to sleep. I have one idea. At least it'll buy us time until we decide our next move. Only you're going to have to trust me to trust someone else, Paul."

"Whatever you say. At this point, I'm all used up."

David crossed back to the front hall and dialed the telephone. He was silent for what must have been four or five rings, then said, "Hello, Margie? It's me. Sorry to call so late, but I need your help. That's right. Leave earlier in the morning so you can come here before you go to the hospital. I'll explain it all then. Thanks. Yeah, everything's all right . . . I think." He hung up the phone and turned to go back to the living room. "Now, it's time for bed."

But Paul had bolted up and met him halfway back. "Jesus! I just remembered, I have to call Nat Kagan!"

Amanda arrived at Washington National Airport on the last Eastern Shuttle of the night. It got in after eleven, and the only reason she made it was because it had been delayed by weather at LaGuardia. Coming down the exit hallway at Gate 18, most of the other passengers were grumbling about the wait, the crowd, the continually revised takeoff announcements, the turbulent pounding the plane took in flight, and the threat it might not get off at all because they missed National's eleven P.M. landing curfew. But Amanda wasn't thinking about any of that at this point. All she was thinking about was dragging one foot in front of the other to keep moving someplace . . . any place.

She couldn't remember ever having been this tired. With all the overnights she'd pulled with the magazine to make deadlines, no matter how exhausted she'd gotten, there was always that jolt of adrenalin somewhere in reserve. But not now. This time she knew she'd used up every last ounce of her energy. She'd expended most of it in that one moment in the lab and she knew that the aftermath of stress was exhaustion. Well, the aftermath of incredible stress must be complete and total exhaustion.

All she wanted as she slowly ascended the stairs and trudged across the gently curving concourse was for someone to find her there and take care of her. She surveyed the thinning crowd through watery eyes and hazily thought, wouldn't it be nice if her mother was here to meet her and put her arms around her and take her home for the night and take her clothes off and tuck her into bed. That was all she could think of that she really wanted out of life. Nothing else really seemed that important. She could see now why some of the prisoners of war in Korea and Vietnam had been willing to collaborate and sell themselves out for the price of a blanket, a quiet place to rest and a few good meals. Right now, it seemed like quite a bargain to her, and she empathized with the lack of understanding that had met their return. She understood.

She kept telling herself she had to stay awake and cogent long enough to find someplace to spend the night. She couldn't sleep on a chair in the passengers' lounge, although that certainly looked inviting. She would certainly be picked up; if not as herself, then as a derelict. Huh. Imagine that. The sophisticated and glamorous New York career woman picked up as a derelict in an airport in Washington, D.C.

For the last hour and a half she'd been periodically digging her thumbnail into her wrist in an effort to jolt herself into alertness. But the last several applications of self-punishment had been less successful. Her black and blue wrists were growing increasingly numb, and her brain increasingly fuzzy. There was a dull buzz in the back where her neck joined her skull, and the room was starting to reel.

The important thing was to get out of here, find a cab while there still were a few to be had and check into one of those cheap tourist motels along Route 1 in Virginia where they won't ask questions if you come in without luggage and nobody's likely to spot you. She'd just tell the cab to stop at the first one with a vacancy sign lit up.

She wanted to at least buy some candy; the sugar could give her a momentary lift, enough to get her through this immediate crisis. But at this hour, the vending areas were all shuttered for the night. Maybe she should at least go into the ladies' room and wash her face with cold water. But no. She'd better not waste the time or stand around here any longer than she had to. Go out to the curb and find a taxi.

She was walking past the United counter and about to step on the rubber mat for the automatic doors when she heard from over her shoulder, "Amanda West?"

She jerked her head around and saw two men in brown suits.

"Amanda West?" the man repeated.

Her eyes widened but she remained silent as both men pulled small leather billfolds from their jacket pockets and in one simultaneous motion whipped them open to reveal gold badges about the size of quarters. She dully made out a blindfolded figure holding the scales of justice on each one.

"Miss West, I'm Guy Hackett and this is Stan Burwell. We're with the FBI. Come with us, please."

David and Margie Ferenbach sat in the front seat of his Honda. Paul rode in the back.

"I want him admitted as a voluntary patient under my signature," David instructed her. "We'll give him a made-up name and an untraceable history—no fixed address and all that shit. Say he's been traveling around the country the last couple of years doing odd jobs and has a history of alcohol and drug abuse."

"Thanks a lot," Paul broke in.

David glanced at him through the rearview mirror. "By the way, don't shave. It's better for the image.

Okay, and I want you to go work your charms at Central Admissions, Margie. Take care of the paperwork without us actually sending him through there."

"Think that'll work?"

"With those irresistible eyes? Of course it'll work."

By midmorning, Margie had brought the admissions forms over to the office at Noyes Division and David ushered Paul into his office, ostensibly for his initial psychiatric evaluation.

"I figure this is the last place in the world anyone would think of looking for you," the psychiatrist commented. "You should be safe, as long as you can stand the food. In the meantime, we've got to decide on your next move."

Paul kept looking up at the large electric clock on the wall. "She should have been here by now. I don't know what's wrong."

"Maybe she missed the connection at LaGuardia and had to spend the night in New York. In that case she could show up any minute."

"I never should have left her alone."

"From everything you told me, you had no other choice. It would have been too easy for you both to be spotted together."

"I should have risked that. It would be better than this not knowing. I can't even decide what to do next until she gets here."

"Do you want me to put out a psychiatric advisory to the police that we're looking for someone and then give Amanda's description? I can say that they're just supposed to report to me if they spot her, not pick her up or take her in."

He shook his head. "No, too much of a risk." He stood up and began pacing back and forth. "All I wanted was to be left alone to do my work," he said. "Just to be a hermit in my lab."

"That's not entirely true," David corrected. "If it was, you wouldn't be so worried about Amanda right now. In fact, you never would have gotten involved with her in the first place. And you never would have felt the way you did about Julia's death, which means you never would have come to see me."

He stopped pacing and turned. "Why are you telling me all this?"

"Because I know what's going through your head right now and I know what you're feeling about yourself. So I want to remind you that you are not a hermit, that you care deeply about other people, and whatever problems or anxieties you face are not the result of lapses or flaws in your personality."

"Why does everything have to be so fucking complicated?" Paul sighed. "Why can't I figure out what's happening to me? Why can't I figure out what's going on inside my head, inside Amanda's head, why people are trying to kill us, etc., etc., etc. Maybe I should have stayed in medical school instead of going into physics and none of this would have happened."

"And maybe I should have gone into dermatology," David said. "We all think there's answers somewhere just over the horizon of our understanding. And sometimes we think we've learned and experienced just enough to get them into sight."

"How do you mean?"

David shrugged. "You know, when I was in the army, a group of us psychiatrists once decided over a table of Singapore beer that if you got a guy in to see you at the dispensary and he has 'Mother' and a heart with an arrow through it tattooed on his arm and 'L-O-V-E' and 'H-A-T-E' tattooed across his knuckles, the chances were ninety-five percent he was a psychopathic personality."

"And reflecting upon it in your more sober moments, do you still think it's true?"

"Probably," he replied. "But you know something? Nothing has ever seemed as clear-cut to me since."

Paul looked up at the clock again and tried to smile.

London

The news had reached Nigel Dunninger before dawn and he had wasted no time in summoning Walter Oppermann to his house in Curzon Street. By the time Walter arrived, Dunninger was already dressed in a dark blue Saville Row suit and bowler to keep the London dampness off his balding head.

"Let's walk to the office," he said curtly as he met his young associate in the double-story marble foyer. He selected one of three identical-looking umbrellas from the brass stand near the front entryway and pushed open the oak door with the stained-glass inset.

They had passed Brown's Hotel on the way to New Bond Street before Dunninger had worked up to his comfortable walking stride and opened up the conversation. "I'll give you the outlines now, Walter. When we get to the office we can fill in the details. There was some sort of explosion last night in Paul Garrett's laboratory. The police reports don't say anything about its nature—they obviously don't know—but I'd be willing to bet it was the result of a successful, though uncontrollable, electrogravitational rearrangement."

"Then it works . . ." Walter responded in wonderment.

"If that's what it is, yes. At least it means the positive gravity force can be gotten to."

"Then all your hunches were correct. All your pleadings for support from the board—it was all worthwhile. You called this one absolutely right on the money."

"Thank you for such a glowing testimonial, especially this early in the dreary morning. But it's rather best left for my retirement ceremony, when they hand me the inevitable gold watch. And it'll be just my luck that synthesizing gold becomes the first practical application of the Garrett research! But the situation's gotten away from us."

"I assume Garrett wasn't hurt in the explosion or you would have said something right off."

"No, thank the Lord. But he's disappeared, and Amanda West along with him. The Cambridge and Boston police are looking for them, but they don't think they're still in the city. God knows where they ran off to."

"But why would they try to escape after an incident like that?" Walter asked. "I'm sure the MIT establishment is enlightened enough to realize what the explosion means, and not hold it against him too terribly much."

Dunninger held up his finger for emphasis. "Ay, there's the rub, as our venerable countryman used to say. In a brief call he made to a Cambridge police lieutenant Garrett said, 'Two people tried to kidnap me and my friend.'"

"Good Lord. Someone obviously wants him to fail as much as we want him to succeed. You were right on that score as well."

Regent Street was already filling with its normal contingent of well-heeled shoppers and black Austin taxis whizzed past, daring pedestrians to set foot off the curb. With his slow, methodical pace, Nigel Dunninger seemed out of sync with the hurried surroundings. But Walter Oppermann had never heard him deliver a more urgent message.

"I want you to leave for the States on today's Concorde," he told the younger man. "You'll have full discretionary power and the full resources of the Foundation behind you. A personal letter of credit will be waiting for you at Citibank in New York in the sum of one million dollars. Call immediately if you need more. All of our agents will be notified of your arrival. The main thing is, we have to find Paul Garrett."

"And when we do?"

"I think the time has come to let him in on the role destiny has chosen him to play."

"He'll be offered membership?"

"Exactly."

Washington, D.C.

They had taken Amanda not to the main, mausoleum-like FBI headquarters on Pennsylvania Avenue, but to a small suite of rooms in some downtown office building. It was so late and dark when they brought her in, and she was so tired beyond exhaustion that she hadn't even noticed what the front of the building looked like.

She had been ushered into a good-sized room with an oak desk and a long, old-fashioned leather couch, its rich upholstery cracking in places. Before she'd had a chance to look around, Stan Burwell had handed her an assortment of towels along with a washcloth and a wrapped bar of soap. "There's a pillow and blanket on the couch," he'd told her. "Right through that door is the bathroom. This is the only entrance, so you don't have to worry about anyone barging in on you. If you need anything, just holler or knock on the front door. Someone'll be outside all night."

It had occurred to her that she should have demanded to see her lawyer, or something like that. Didn't they have to read her her Miranda rights? But what could be the harm of letting all that wait till morning? She told herself she'd be able to think more clearly after several hours of sleep. It wasn't as if they were going to keep her up, shine a bright light in her face and force a confession out of her. They hadn't even asked her any questions beyond the routine, "Where have you been?" "Where are you going?" and "Who are you doing it with?" And when she'd just idly shaken her head and refused to answer, they hadn't seemed particularly surprised or upset. And now they were going to let her sleep, which was all she really wanted, anyway.

In the morning they started in on her.

They sat her on a hard wooden chair in front of the oak desk and paced around in their rolled-up shirt-sleeves, pivoting around to face her every time they asked her a question.

"We'd like to make this as easy for everyone as we can, Miss West," Guy Hackett announced. "But there are certain things you have to tell us."

"Are you going to beat me with a rubber hose if I don't?" she asked. She thought it might add a note of levity to the proceedings, but immediately thought better of it when she saw the reaction from Hackett.

"Come on, Miss West. You know we don't do things like that. And certainly not with a woman. But we can make it pretty uncomfortable for you . . . in other ways, if you don't cooperate."

She decided not to inquire into the "other ways."

"All right, Miss West. Let's go over what we know so far. Maybe you'll decide to enlighten us along the way." He flipped open a notebook and began reading from it. "There was an explosion of considerable force at a physics laboratory at the Massachusetts Institute of Technology assigned to Dr. Paul Garrett. This laboratory was located on Vassar Street between Main Street and Massachusetts Avenue. After the explosion, a man matching his description and a woman matching your description were observed fleeing from the scene. Found on the scene were parts of human bodies, totally dismembered, which forensic pathologists believe belonged to at least two people, most likely Caucasian men in their mid to late twenties. Now what do you have to add to that?"

"Nothing," Amanda whispered.

" 'Nothing,' you don't know any more, or 'Nothing,' you're not going to tell us any more?" Burwell grilled her.

"Just nothing," she said again.

Hackett walked back toward her, half sat and half leaned against the corner of the desk, and took her right hand in both of his. "Look," he said, trying to sound understanding, "I don't know exactly how you got yourself involved in all this, but I can't believe you'd have any part in a crime. Something obviously happened, and we just have to find out what it was. We don't believe you personally did anything wrong—other than not coming forward to the police or us to begin with, of course—so it makes perfect sense for you to tell us everything you know so we can get to the bottom of this. I mean, doesn't it make sense that way to you?"

She looked down at her lap and tried to pull her hand free. But Hackett tightened his grip; not enough to hurt her, but enough to let her know he was capable of hurting her if he wanted to. Finally he stood up and let go. "You know what it seems like to me?" he said to Burwell with the flourish of a stage interrogatory.

"No, what's it look like to you, Guy?" came the equally rehearsed rejoinder.

"It looks to me like Amanda and Dr. Garrett are minding their own business in his lab, he's setting up an experiment of some sort, you know the way scientists do . . ."

"Sure."

". . . And Amanda here is keeping him company. And all of a sudden two or three guys bust in with guns and say they're gonna kill both of them. So Garrett throws a switch, or tosses two chemicals together or something, and the whole place blows up. That's what it looks like to me. And so in actuality, Dr. Garrett and Amanda here are just innocent victims, and whatever they did, it was only in self-defense."

"Sounds like a good explanation to me," Burwell agreed.

"So tell me, Miss West. Am I on the right track?"

She wanted to tell him that yes, he was on the right track, but once she told them one detail, they would press her for all the others. And eventually, whether she meant to or not, she would end up revealing the details of Paul's experiment. And that couldn't get into any other hands for the time being; not even the FBI's. If she could just stonewall it long enough. They couldn't hold her here forever.

But they kept hammering at her without letup. They gave her a cup of coffee in the morning and a ham and cheese sandwich and a Sprite at lunchtime and let her get up every time she said she had to go to the bathroom—which was more and more frequently as the afternoon wore on. But except for these occasional and preciously savored breaks, they kept throwing questions at her, forcing themselves into her face, standing directly in front so that no matter where she turned her head, she still saw them. The dull buzz of fatigue that had permeated her body the night before had been replaced by the throbbing ache of having to sit in one position on a hard surface for too long. Her neck ached, her shoulders ached, her lower spine ached, her backside ached and her thighs ached where the edge of the chair cut into them.

Throughout the interrogation she kept thinking of Paul—where he was and how frantic with worry he must be by now. He must be imagining all kinds of things that could have happened. If only she could get a message to him and let him know she was still in one piece. Then it struck her. Maybe they'd picked him up, too, and were grilling him in another room. If that's what was happening, then she definitely couldn't tell them anything, in case he didn't, or told them something different. She couldn't risk getting him into trouble with a conflicting statement.

"Look at it from our perspective, Miss West," Hackett said while kneeling down next to her chair. "We figure, if someone's innocent, they're gonna want to tell us that, and if they can, to tell us who the guilty one is. But if people just clam up and won't say anything to us, what are we supposed to think? I mean, think about it. We know something happened, right? There's a building without a roof on it and a bunch of random bodily parts to show for the trouble. This is the kind of thing that's usually considered an incident worth investigating. Now you're obviously materially associated with this incident in some way. At least, there's an eyewitness account, and let's face it, Miss West, you haven't denied anything . . ."

"Would it matter if I did?" she interjected.

"Well, I guess that would depend on how convincing your denial was. I'd be happy to listen."

"Never mind," she replied sullenly.

"Now when I say denial, I'm just talking about you denying you were at the scene. As far as denying a part in a crime, we really don't believe you had a part in a crime."

"Then why are you holding me here like this?"

Hackett was growing increasingly exasperated. "Because you won't tell us anything, for Christ's sake! All I'm saying is, tell us you didn't do anything, tell us what happened in there, tell us why you think someone wanted to kill you and Dr. Garrett. Tell us anything!"

She noticed he didn't ask her where Paul was. That must mean they had him there, too. Well, she'd stonewall it as long as they did. She just hoped they'd keep their promise and not get physical with her. She didn't know how she'd react if they did.

But as the questioning persisted over the hours, she found she was no longer agitated or nervous. She was merely exhausted again, having entered into that "come what may" phase of stress. So far she was holding up all right, and she owed it to Paul to keep holding up as long as she could. Her love for him would help her along, she assured herself.

They brought in dinner around six o'clock— hamburgers and soggy french fries. And after they finished eating the ritual continued.

Can they go on like this forever, Amanda wondered. Why not? This is their job. They probably get in training for it, the same as anything else. It looked like they were going to make her spend another night there on the couch, and the prospect of the third day running out of touch with the world, sleeping on a makeshift bed, wearing the same clothes that didn't fit her too well to begin with, made her realize her resistance was wearing thin. That was obviously what they were counting on.

The food, unpalatable though it was, gave her a small burst of energy and cleared her mind. Surely they couldn't keep her here indefinitely without notifying someone. Even if they considered her a national security hazard, there had to be some due process involved. Well, it was time to make the play.

"I demand to speak to my lawyer," she stated.

Hackett looked up from the floor, turned on the chair he was straddling and replied, "You demand what?"

"You heard me. Whatever this investigation's all about, I know I have a right to contact my attorney. In fact, anything you would have gotten out of me up to this point would be considered tainted in court. I suggest you read the Miranda Decision if you don't know what I'm talking about."

Burwell looked over at Hackett and grinned. "Well, look who's the jailhouse lawyer."

"You can kid around as much as you like," she said firmly. "But that's the law." Had she pushed them too far?

Hackett turned back to Burwell. "What do you think?" The other agent shrugged disinterestedly. Hackett licked his lips, wrinkled his chin and finally said, "Okay, Clarence Darrow. Who's your lawyer?"

"Do I get to call him?"

"There's no phone in here and I can't let you out. Orders from above. Give me his name and Stan'll call him."

Is this a trick, she asked herself. Is there any way they could turn this against me? She didn't see how. The worst they could do was not call and say they did. But she would have lost nothing. "Okay," she agreed.

But then there was another problem. She didn't have a lawyer in Washington. Who did she know in this town? There was one! Charles Hollister. He'd come.

He handled all the business for the Scientific League. She knew him well from all the *Aurora* business.

"Charles Hollister," she announced.

"Go call the shyster," Hackett directed. Burwell left the room.

"And I'm not answering any more questions until he gets here or I get to talk to him," she went on.

"You can't answer *more* questions, lady. You haven't answered *any* yet."

In her sudden burst of sunny optimism she thought about responding by correcting him with "I *can* answer *more* questions. I just can't answer any *fewer*." But if he hadn't read *Alice in Wonderland* he wouldn't appreciate it much. And even if he had read it, he still struck her as the type who might not appreciate it. So she kept her mouth shut and awaited a word from Charlie Hollister.

He arrived less than half an hour later, striding into the room with a confused and appalled look on his face.

"Amanda! I couldn't believe it when they called me. How long have you been here?"

"Who even knows anymore?" she responded. "It seems like forever."

"Have you told them anything?"

"She's told us nothing," Burwell offered.

"Why wasn't I notified immediately that she was being held?" Hollister snapped.

"We never *denied* her the right to counsel. This is the first time she asked."

The attorney eyed him disdainfully. "You know as well as I do you'll be laughed out of court if you try to pull that one. Where can I talk to her? Alone."

"Right here is fine," Hackett suggested. "We'll leave."

"That's not good enough," Hollister countered. "I assume the place is equipped with listening devices." He looked around. "What's that lead to?"

"The bathroom."

"Fine. We'll go in there."

He led Amanda into the bathroom and closed the door, trying to lock it but finding the mechanism had been removed.

"I found that somewhat disconcerting myself," she commented.

He turned on both the sink and shower taps and then walked around the room, surveying every inch of wall space, looking behind exposed pipes and in corners. "All right, now what happened?"

She gave him the outlines of the story, which basically amounted to what the agents had read off to her. "And what I'm worried about," she concluded, "is that they've got Paul, too."

"They don't. That's the first thing I asked them. And if they lied to me on something like that, they know they'd not only blow their case out of the water, but probably open themselves up for criminal prosecution at the same time. As it is, I'm going to file charges for what they've done to you."

Amanda was grateful to finally have someone come to defend her and take care of her. She was so weary of having to exist by the end of her wits at the time that her physical and emotional reserves were at an all-time low. Thank goodness she'd thought to call Charlie. He would make everything all right.

"Okay, now tell me: Did they threaten you at any point?"

"No. Not directly, anyway."

"I can't believe this happened. Did they ever charge you with anything?"

"No. Charlie, I've got to get word to Paul of where I am and that I'm all right."

"Okay. Where is he? I'll tell him and also say we're going to get you out of here."

"They can't force you to tell them, can they?"

"Absolutely not. This is strictly privileged conversation."

She paused a moment, thinking. She pursed her lips,

then said, "He's at St. Elizabeth's Hospital, Alfred Noyes Division, in care of Dr. David Sherman."

Hollister looked stunned. "That's my brother-in-law. Sandy's his older sister."

"Yes, I know."

"I wasn't aware Paul knew him. But yes, wait a minute! I introduced them myself at the party at Shorecliffe! Funny the way these things work out. I wonder what they have in common. Oh well, none of my business, really." He put one hand in his jacket and scratched his head with the other. "Amanda, you wait here."

"Where are you going?"

"To see if I can get you sprung."

He closed the bathroom door after him and Amanda stood waiting, listening to the competing sounds of the two running taps. When he returned there was a look of triumph in his eyes.

"They're releasing you, right now."

"Oh Charlie!" she practically exploded. "How'd you manage that!"

"I said they'd better either charge you and bring you before a magistrate, release you, or I'd call the Attorney General myself. Now, you must be terribly tired and overwrought. How about coming home with me? Nobody will bother you and you can relax and sort things out."

"Thanks. But I have to get to Paul. You understand."

"Yes, of course. But stay in touch with me, Amanda. I want to get a statement from Paul as soon as he's ready to give it to me in case we run into any more difficulties. And if you have any trouble, you know where to reach me."

"Thank you so much."

"Can I at least drive you someplace?"

"No, I'll be fine. Really."

"Very well. Shall we?" He motioned her toward the door. When he opened it, Hackett and Burwell were standing near the desk.

"Sorry for the inconvenience, Miss West. It was nothing personal, I assure you," the first agent said.

She strode toward the door without acknowledging him. "Are you coming?" she asked Hollister.

"You go on ahead," he replied, glaring at Hackett. "I'm going to take care of some paperwork here to make sure we don't mess up *our* case the way these gentlemen have theirs."

"Okay. And thanks again, Charlie."

Hollister watched her walk out the door and listened for her footsteps clicking down the hall toward the elevator. He was silent for several seconds after they stopped, then said, "It worked out perfectly, just the way we figured it."

"I'm just glad she asked for you as her lawyer," Hackett said.

"Yeah," Burwell added. "If she hadn't, we would have had to say whoever she asked for was out until she finally came up with your name. And that might have blown the whole operation."

"And you had no trouble convincing her you were agents?" Hollister asked.

"No." He pulled out his leather billfold. "These badges were cast directly from the real thing."

"They ought to be, for all the money this thing's cost us. All right, we don't have a lot of time. Let's get down to business. Garrett can be found at St. Elizabeth's Hospital, Alfred Noyes Division. Let's not waste any time."

Langley, Virginia

George Henderson threw the teletype report down on his desk and shot up with such force his desk chair toppled over backward. "What in the fucking hell is going on?" he demanded of the five operatives standing in a semicircle in front of him.

"All we know is what's in the report," Martin explained. "It's taken right from the Cambridge police."

"Well Jesus, we might as well just publish the whole story on the front page of the fucking *New York Times* and be done with it. If there's any Agency involvement with this explosion in any way, I'm going to tack that man's balls onto the threshold of the Intelligence Oversight Committee."

"George, I assure you, we had absolutely nothing to do with this stunt."

"Do I have to call fucking Jack Anderson to get the real story of what's going on in my own shop?" he ranted.

"I'm telling you, George. This is strictly an outside action."

"All right. Give me some answers. If Garrett's just mixing around his chemicals and suddenly they go 'Pop!' that's one thing. But pieces of bodies were found at the site, and the one telephone communication with Garrett mentions people trying to get them. I want to fucking know who they were, who they worked for, and what the fuck they wanted. Immediately!"

Washington, D.C.

Except for the exposed fluorescent bulbs hanging down from the faded ceiling, the ward looked the same as it must have when the Victorian reformers deemed it an enlightened and humane way to care for society's emotional misfits. But now the scene was a good deal less encouraging and represented not enlightenment but a turning away.

Sixteen beds and sixteen lockers were arranged in two straight rows facing a center aisle. The noises coming from each metal cot ranged from light, wheezing breathing to snoring that sounded like a manhole cover being dragged across rough concrete. Some of the men talked to themselves in their sleep—disturbed, frightened monologues—even less coherent now than they were during their waking hours. Even with its nineteenth-century high ceilings and tall, open windows, the ward was stifling hot and the air heavy with the odor of sweat, urine, and unwashed men.

A man emerged from the top of the stairwell opposite the door. He was wearing dungarees and a threadbare gray tweed jacket. His shoes were of ragged blue canvas, with crepe soles that did not betray movement across the slatted wooden floors. He took a deep breath and tiptoed across the hall to the ward, knowing that once he had reached this third floor, his actions were no longer as easy to account for should he be spotted. He glanced quickly in both directions and saw no one.

Once inside the ward, it was even more vital that he disturb no one. He studied the shadow line where the cloudy moonlight spilled in from the windows and stepped to the darker side of it. He then moved carefully from bed to bed, getting as close as he could to each sleeping head, maneuvering himself into a position in which he could see the face.

At the first bed he extracted a small photograph from his inner jacket pocket. It was a color head and shoulders portrait. At the bottom was printed: PAUL GARRETT. He compared the sleeping man to the picture, allowing for longer hair and several days' growth of beard. Satisfying himself that it wasn't his man, he moved to the next bed, and when he had examined all the patients on that side of the room, he ducked under the window sill, where it was dark, and crept to the other side.

It was at the third bed in the row that he found the sleeping man who matched the photograph. He did have the beginning of a gray-black beard, and his hair was matted with sweat and tangled in small ringlets. But he was definitely the man.

He stirred as the intruder came closer, forcing him to flatten himself against the side of Garrett's locker.

Garrett half snorted and jerked spasmodically around, facing him, before uttering a hollow sigh and once again clutching the dirty pillow in repose. It was just as well. This way, it would be an easier shot.

The man reached into the opposite pocket of his coat and removed a wooden-handled ice pick, which had just been stolen from the St. Elizabeth's cafeteria. It had to look like an inside job, preferably by another deranged inmate. That way, there would be a cursory investigation, some name-calling, mutual recrimination, and editorials decrying lax security at St. E's, and then the whole thing would die down without further fuss.

He experimented with several grips until he found one that felt comfortable. It should really be done with a single blow, if possible, so he could get the hell out of there right afterward. He had been careful to observe everything on his way in. He had a clear exit through the staircase. He could be off the grounds before anyone knew what had happened. No, all things considered, this would be one of the easier ones.

He came close enough to the bed so he could reach the sleeping man's throat and jugular right at the end of his downward extension. That gave him the most power and leverage. It would also put him in position to see Garrett's eyes pop in that instant of horrible recognition that then melts harmlessly into death. Well, it wouldn't bother him . . . not nearly as much as it would bother Garrett. He smiled and took one last deep breath to steel himself.

The ice pick was raised and began its downward arc. Suddenly, Garrett rolled to one side and propped himself on his left arm. The intruder's hand continued its downward course involuntarily, imbedding the metal point in the lumpy mattress. He gasped in terror as for one instant he fleetingly focused on Garrett's other hand and the gleaming silver surgical scalpel it held. Garrett brought it down with one quick thrust.

Paul's gaze traveled from the blank eyes to the

crazed, contorted mouth to the scalpel sticking out of the bloody chest. The single wound had been anatomically precise. The man died without a sound.

Paul glanced to his left and his right. One neighbor grunted, but was still asleep. The confrontation had been quick and quiet, hardly heard above the cacophony of noises that routinely filled the ward. He let the man down to the floor, then got out of bed and got a better grip to lift him back up. With a single heave he was able to sprawl him across the mattress, then with further refinements got him into a normal lying position and covered him up to the waist with the blanket.

He put on his shoes and belt. All other personal items were in David Sherman's safekeeping. He extracted the scalpel from the corpse's chest and examined the wound opening. Now came the distasteful, but necessary touch. He picked up the ice pick from the floor, inserted it into the chest cavity, and twisted it around, enlarging the wound to look as if it was made by that weapon. He left it in, then used his handkerchief to wipe off any possible fingerprints. He also ran the cloth along the bedrails, locker, and any other smooth surface the police were likely to dust. Then he pulled the blanket up over the body.

He surveyed the scene quickly to make sure he hadn't left any traces. Everything looked all right. Even the tight features on the man's face were starting to relax.

He stealthily eased down the aisle and out the ward. As he reached the final bed, its occupant opened one bleary eye and muttered, "Wha' hoppened?"

"Nothing," Paul whispered. "Go back to sleep."

The eye snapped shut and Paul continued out of the room.

He spotted Margie Ferenbach's Opel in the parking lot, right where she said it would be if he needed it. The key was resting on the top of the right front tire.

As he drove through the gloomy darkness of Southeast Washington headed for David's house, he had to confront within himself the reality of the third death he had caused in as many days. But unlike the others, he was directly responsible for this one. And even though he realized the intruder would have killed him first if he hadn't been quick enough and alert enough, he had now taken a life with his own hands. And he had done it in as cold-blooded and savage a way as he could imagine.

Chapter Sixteen

"Thank God you asked me for that scalpel," David Sherman attested when he had heard the gory conclusion of the story. "But how in hell were you able to strike that accurately? You must have gone right through the aorta."

"I did," Paul stated neutrally. The edges of his mouth twisted downward, forming a half-smile, half-grimace. "From his instantaneous paralysis, I'd say I ripped through the ascending arch of the aorta and sliced the sinoatrial node."

"But how . . . ?"

"As you might recall from our previous conversations, the one thing I remember from my year in medical school is anatomy."

It had happened less than an hour ago, but the acute reality had already receded. It had to, Paul realized. One couldn't keep that image vivid and actual and still continue to function. One couldn't maintain that close an emotional proximity to one's own narrowly missed death.

In the face of that prospect, David's living room became both physical sanctuary and psychical haven. And with Amanda now sitting closely beside him, not yet willing to let go of his bloodstained right hand, his relief—though he knew it was temporary—was total.

"I was so worried about you," she said, tenderly spreading his fingers out between her own, "and I see I had reason to be."

"I lost a couple of minutes' sleep over you, too," he returned.

"I had no way to contact you after the FBI picked me up, until Charlie Hollister showed up."

"And he certainly worked fast."

"Are you sure it was he who set you up?" Margie Ferenbach asked. David had called her right after Amanda showed up at his front door, just as Paul had the night before.

"It had to be," he stated. "No one else knew where I was."

"I feel so . . . responsible," Amanda stammered. "To think that I was the one who told him . . . that you were almost killed because of my stupidity." The tear that trickled down her cheek was followed by a steady stream as she pressed her head against Paul's shoulder, sobbing. He reached over to stroke the back of her neck comfortingly, knowing that no words were called for.

"I never did trust Charlie," David commented. "Not that I suspected him capable of anything like this."

"It's getting so you can't trust anyone," said Paul.

David rose to his feet and began pacing nervously around the room. "All right, let's try to deal with practicalities. Paul, did anyone see you tonight?"

"I'm almost sure they didn't," he replied. "Certainly no one saw me closely enough to make an identification. But what about when they find the body in my bed in the morning?"

"It really isn't your bed," Margie pointed out. "It's the bed of Richard Talbert, the identity we made up for you. If they look for anyone, they'll be looking for a man who doesn't exist, assuming you took care of fingerprints."

"Yes, I did. But what about the physical description on the records? Won't they be able to trace me from that?"

Margie grinned with satisfaction. "I don't think so. The records I wrote up for Central Admissions give your eye color as green instead of brown and your height as five-ten, instead of six-one. I altered your weight and I added a couple of scars and identifying marks that you really don't have. I figured that while you were at the hospital, no one was going to actually compare you to the written records, and after you left, there was no sense leaving accurate information about an identity we wanted to keep hidden."

"Good for you, Margie," David said. "Only I'm starting to feel responsible for this progressive loss of innocence in you. I remember what you were like when you first came to work at St. E's."

"Spare me the tender details, if you don't mind. I've been trying to move away from that phase of my life."

"So what are we going to do now?" Amanda asked. As usual, her bout of tears and self-pity was short lived, and now her bright blue eyes displayed renewed determination and, if Paul was not mistaken, enthusiasm.

"Well, we can't go back to Boston . . ."

"And now that Charlie Hollister's been tipped off, we can't stay here. But where does that leave you, David? He's your brother-in-law and he knows you're somehow connected with us."

"Let me deal with that," he said. "I'll figure out something. But right now, we've got to figure out how to keep both of you safe."

"And Nat Kagan," she added. "Were you ever able to reach him?"

"No," Paul answered. "I've been trying since changing planes at LaGuardia. But I've never been able to get an answer."

"Me neither. I hope to God he hasn't been . . ."

"If we don't get him soon, we're going to have to go back to find him."

"I'm glad you feel that way," said Amanda softly. "I was afraid you wouldn't." She shifted her position on the couch, and changed her tone at the same time. "But if we go back to New York, we have to be careful."

"We have to be careful anywhere, for God's sake."

"No, but listen. If Charlie is actually working against us, since he's the counsel for the Scientific League, then who knows how much of the League is also with him? Maybe the whole organization, for all we know."

"I find that hard to believe," Paul stated.

"But it's possible. Even if it isn't, though, if it's infiltrated as high up as Charlie's level, we can't take a chance on trusting anyone there. Which also means I can't trust the people at *Aurora*, other than Nancy Flanagan, of course. I know I can trust her." She suddenly jerked her head upright and swallowed hard. "Oh Jesus!"

"What is it?"

"Ever since I first spent that night with you after the concert here in Washington and up until a week and a half ago when I just let it get by me, I've been filing memos on your work."

"You've been doing what?"

"It's a routine procedure. I write memos on all the scientific trends I come across to be used later for stories. In fact, I've gotten some of my best leads on dates. People are much looser and more willing to talk."

"Well I certainly feel used," Paul said caustically.

"Oh, you're a big boy. You knew exactly what you were getting into." She paused abruptly, blushed, then continued. "I didn't think anything of it until just now because those memos are for my personal file. That's where Nancy puts the only copy. But if someone's infiltrated the organization, they could get into those files and read the memos, and they'd be tipped off as to what your next move was going to be. Several people in the Scientific League have keys to the office. In fact, the lease is in their name."

"You're still assuming that whoever is out to get us is interested in my work. Maybe they're interested in something we're overlooking."

"I don't think you can keep your head in the sand, Paul. It has to be your work, especially after that epiphany in the house in Westchester. I'm convinced of it. There may be other complicating factors, too, but that has to be the main one."

"I agree," said David. "Amanda's right. Everything

points to it. It's not you so much as your knowledge that they want."

"But why? It's so arcane, the only people who'd be impressed by it are other physicists."

"Not true," Amanda noted. "Blowing the top off a brick building with a new kind of energy reaction is not exactly arcane."

"But that's just the first experimental step, honey. You saw as well as I did that it can't be controlled yet. I've got to do a lot more work. As it is now, the only thing it's good for is explosions. And there are already plenty of efficient ways of making explosions without adding another. The work is good to no one unless I can move farther ahead with it."

"Maybe that's just the point," David said. "Maybe they don't want you to move ahead."

"You know yourself what the Unified Field Theory could mean. It could be monumental. And there are a lot of powerful people around with a vested interest in keeping things the same," Amanda said.

"But even if it works, it'll be years, decades before anything practical comes out of my research."

"Large corporations plan decades into the future. They could just be protecting themselves."

"So I, and you and Nat Kagan because you're now associated with me, we're all in danger for our lives because of some scientific secret locked inside my brain . . . and yours, too, it seems."

"That's the way it looks to me, Paul."

"Then what do we do? We can't just keep running from everyone the rest of our lives. Unless those lives are going to be extremely short."

David's jaw was grimly locked in a tight clench. He pounded one fist into the other, continuing to pace. "There is a way out!" His expression changed as he stopped moving around and held his hand up for attention. "It's not so much you they want to kill as your knowledge."

"What's the difference?" Amanda asked.

"The difference is that if you can make enough progress to actually publish a viable theory, which means it's available to anyone who wants it, there's no reason to kill you anymore. Once your theory is out, you personally become insignificant as far as these people are concerned."

"That makes perfect sense," she said. "We've got to find a place where you can continue your work without being threatened and then publish it. That's what you want anyway, isn't it?"

"That's what I've always wanted. But maybe we should just go to the police and try to explain everything."

"You had the chance to go to the police up in Cambridge. You even called them. But some instinct told you not to go through with it, right?"

"I . . . I guess so," he admitted.

"Paul, we don't know who's in on this. It's obviously not any small-time operation. Look at what they've tried already. Look, for all I know the FBI is involved. Maybe that's why they picked me up in the first place. The Scientific League has been infiltrated. We're dealing completely with unknowns. So we've got to play from the only strengths we have—the knowledge in our heads."

David asked, "Where will you go?"

"I'm not sure," said Paul. "It all depends where we can get the right equipment. I know they have it at Cal Tech, Stanford, but I don't think we should stay in this country."

"Wherever you go, you know I'll do whatever I can for you. We both will."

"That's right," Margie confirmed.

"I know that." His eyes began misting with gratitude; he tried to continue several times, then stopped himself.

David finally rescued him. "All right, enough of this sentimentality. Let's make a plan."

"The first thing is, we still have to find Nat Kagan,"

Paul stated, rapidly regaining his composure. "He's probably in danger, and we owe it to him."

"There's even more to it than that," Amanda said. "I can't explain it exactly, but ever since that night in Westchester, I've felt as if he's a part of us. We have to find him for our own sakes."

"I'm going to New York right away," he declared.

"It's too dangerous!"

"It's less dangerous than staying here. In fact, the more we move around, the safer it is."

"Then I'll go with you."

"No you won't! That would be *really* dangerous. And we'd be too easy to spot. You stay here until I get back or call you."

"You can stay with me," Margie offered.

"That's a good idea. I don't think anyone will look for you there. I'll rent a car first thing in the morning. I don't want to take the chance on a plane or train—if I'm spotted there's no way of escape."

"Wait! There's a problem. If you rent a car, even if you pay cash, they make you give them a credit card as security on returning the car, which immediately puts you into a central computer that the police and God knows who else can tap into."

"Take my car," Margie offered again. "It's right here and you can leave before dawn if you want."

"That would be the best idea," he agreed, "if you're sure you're willing."

"Of course. When this is all over, you can buy me a new one with all the money you're going to make from your formula or theory or whatever it is."

"I'm not counting on making any money, but buying you a Ferrari will be one of my top priorities."

"Where will you stay in New York, honey?"

"I'll call Wendell Fuller, my psychiatrist friend at Goddard," David said. "We can trust him, I know. I'll write down his address. By the time you get there, he'll be expecting you. Call me from somewhere on the turnpike to make sure I've been able to reach him."

"Good enough. Because I want to go back to Goddard anyway while I'm in New York."

Amanda suddenly turned pale. "What for?" she gasped.

"After everything you've put together while we were up in Cambridge, I think the time has come to pay another visit to Norbert Ramsey. Find out what the hell he has to tell us."

"No Paul! Not now. This isn't the time. That's hanging yourself six feet over the edge."

"She's right, Paul," David insisted.

"It's something we have to know."

"As soon as you're safely out of the country, I'll investigate myself. I promise. And I can do it with a lot less suspicion being aroused. Please, leave that to me."

The look of gratitude showed again in Paul's eyes. "All right, then. Believe me, I'll . . . we'll never forget all you've both done for us. Somehow we'll figure out a way to repay this."

"All I'm hoping for is a new car," Margie piped in. "I never really liked that Opel anyway."

"Okay, let's all try to get a couple of hours' sleep," David said. "We're going to need them. You've got a long trip ahead of you. And we'd better make sure we get to the hospital on time. Because when they find that body in your bed, the shit's really going to hit the fan."

In the few hours he had to sleep, Paul dreamed almost continuously. It was one of those dreams that though he couldn't remember a single specific detail upon waking, its mood and discomforting aura reverberated through every action and feeling of the day. By the time the sun came up he was on the Delaware stretch of I-95, acutely alone with only his emotions and his hazy plans for finding Nat Kagan.

On and off for years he had had that vague feeling that he was losing control of his own situation, his own life. But it was nothing compared to what was happening now. What was the expression? He was merely being carried along by the tide of events, and they determined his course. Three unknown, faceless people had tried to kill him, and he had killed each of them. Through no conscious wish or identifiable action on his part, in these last several weeks his life had changed forever. The prominent, learned Paul Garrett, who many said was in line for the Nobel Prize in Physics, was now reduced to the status of fugitive on the run. He finally—with the help of Amanda and David—had an inkling of why, but the *who* and the *how* remained an elusive and threatening mystery.

Maybe that was why he was speeding toward New York with such urgency, he thought. Maybe subconsciously he wasn't only racing toward Nat Kagan—if, God help him, he was still alive—but also to an answer, a spiritual redemption of some sort. What it was, or where he might find it, he had no idea. Or even why he was pursuing it in New York. What was there that was special in New York? Nothing, he thought. Nothing except the Goddard Institute. And with that image he felt a cold droplet of sweat trickle down his spine.

Jesus Christ! He'd killed three people! And God knew how many more were still trying to get him. That just isn't normal, he said to himself. Then he smiled so broadly he almost laughed out loud. The whole idea of "normal"! He'd never been normal. He'd survived a brain tumor that was supposed to kill normal people, for one thing. And then he'd begun devising a scientific theory that normal people couldn't understand, much less care about. And now, evidently, other people wanted him for that theory and the distinctly abnormal things it might cause to happen. And once he found Nat Kagan, assuming he even could, what was he going to tell him? That his life was also in danger so he should come with them where they would pursue a scientific puzzle that had eluded Einstein, with the hope that in its solution lay peace and security? It all sounded like a Kafkaesque nightmare.

When he reached the last rest stop on the New Jersey Turnpike, he pulled in to make his call and refill the tank. While the car was at the pump, he went to the men's room, got enough change to make the long distance call without his credit card or calling collect—both of which would have left a computerized record—and dialed David's number.

"Is everything all right?" the psychiatrist asked him. He sounded relieved to hear Paul's voice.

"Yeah, so far, so good. How's Amanda?"

"She's all right. She's at Margie's and has promised not to open the door for anyone."

"I just hope she doesn't get brave and inquisitive. Did you talk to Wendell Fuller?"

"Yes. Everything's fine. If you stay over, he's expecting you."

"Good. Well . . . I guess that's it, then." He realized he didn't want to hang up the phone, as if terminating this conversation with David was cutting off his last contact with the comfortable and rational world. Now he was heading toward a menacing, irrational realm that, even if he did not pursue it, would ultimately catch up with him.

"Paul . . . take care of yourself," David said. "Call me again as soon as you can."

"Sure, David. Thanks." He hung up the receiver of the pay phone and walked slowly back to the car.

He had visions of coming back to the gas pump to find the vehicle surrounded by a contingent of New Jersey state troopers in Smokey-the-Bear hats and FBI agents in no-nonsense gray suits, and he wondered what he would do. Bolt and run? That didn't make any sense. Maybe try to steal another car? Maybe just make another phone call and elude them until one of his confederates could make it here in another car.

But when he did get back to the pump, he found only a young attendant in greasy overalls enjoining him to move his car out of the way so the next guy could pull up. His body relaxed and he could feel his heart slow down again, but he was alarmed that his mind had worked up this paranoid fire drill at all. He had to remain alert and unemotional, he sternly told himself, so far as that was humanly possible. When he climbed back into the car he was tempted to give the boy a dollar or two as compensation for his aggravation and as a token of Paul's own relief, but then realized the gesture would make him stand out in the young man's mind, should he ever be questioned. So he just drove off.

He came into Manhattan by way of the Lincoln Tunnel and found a deserted phone booth under the elevated roadway on the West Side. He dialed the number of the Committee for Jewish Unity and got through to Nat's secretary.

"No, I'm sorry, Rabbi Kagan isn't in the office. May I help you?"

"When do you expect him back?"

"I'm afraid I couldn't say, sir."

"Is he in town?"

"I'm afraid I couldn't say, sir."

"Do you know if he's at home, or at his synagogue in Long Island?"

"I'm afraid I don't know. Would you like to say who's calling, please?"

"Ah . . . just a friend. I was in town so I thought I'd call and say hello."

"Well, if you'd like to leave your name and a number where you can be reached, I'd be happy to give it to Rabbi Kagan if he comes in or calls."

"Do you expect that might happen?"

"I really couldn't say, sir."

Paul wrestled with whether he should leave a number or not. But whatever number, and whatever name he left could be easily traced. He couldn't risk that.

"Ah . . . no thank you, ma'am. Maybe I'll try him again later some time."

"Very well then, sir. Have a good day."

He hung up the phone, got back in the car, and stared at the steering wheel, thinking. Then he got out again, went back to the phone booth, and called the synagogue. Kagan hadn't been in for several days and they didn't even know if he would be back for the weekend's services.

Paul wished he had some psychic urge or suggestion, like the ones he'd already experienced with Nat and Amanda, to tell him what to do next. He tried to relax his mind and body, even going so far as reclining the seat all the way back, hoping an impression would simply take over. But nothing came.

Well, he thought, what was he going to do now? And again the absurdity of the situation struck him. He'd been a target of at least two murder attempts, and so had Amanda and Nat, he was scared out of his mind, wrestling constantly with that all-pervasive anxiety, and what was he doing about it? He was sitting in a borrowed car under the West Side Highway, having driven most of the night to get there, and what was he going to do now?

There were no other options. He would drive out to King's Point and knock on the rabbi's door. Assuming he wasn't home, he'd have to start playing detective— going to neighbors and asking when was the last time they saw him, was he acting strangely, did he say where he was going and all the rest. At least he ought to be able to pick up some leads that way.

He wished he had Amanda with him. She was much better at this sort of thing than he was. That was part of her job, being a professional snoop. What if whoever had tried to kill him had Kagan's house under surveillance? Well, that was a chance he'd have to take. There just weren't any other ways.

He started up the car and began driving crosstown. Every two or three blocks he made a mental survey of the other cars in the immediate vicinity to make sure he wasn't being followed. He wasn't, but he realized the paranoia was becoming reflexive, almost second nature. God, how long would he have to live this way?

It occurred to him to swing downtown and drive by the Goddard Institute. Maybe that would give him the inspiration he was looking for. After all, wasn't that what he and Nat had in common? Wasn't that, in a sense, the "source"? But as he was waiting for the light to change so he could turn right, the image of the medical school anatomy lab came vividly into his mind and along with it, that slice of head and brain that graced the display cabinet outside. And even though he told himself the scene he pictured was at Yale, and not at Goddard, when the light changed to green he shut off his blinker and headed straight for the Queens-Midtown Tunnel.

King's Point, Long Island

The tree-shaded blocks of well-tended Tudor manors and well-manicured green lawns constituted another world. It was almost incomprehensible that they could exist on the same planet with the dismal repository of psychiatric wreckage where Paul had so recently sojourned. The suburban serenity seemed out of place, out of keeping with his mission of protecting one of its natives from violent harm, as if the lifestyle of heated swimming pools and four-car garages provided its own ample protection.

But he knew this was all facade, not just for the danger he sensed threatening him around every corner, but also for the complex and unhappy lives of many of the prosperous residents. Many belonged to Nathaniel Kagan's synagogue. He had reason to know them. Now, if Paul could just find him, together the three of them could decide on their next move, whatever that turned out to be.

Nat Kagan's house was smaller than those of most of his neighbors, but no less stately. It had a low stone fence in front, a couple of tall oak trees drooping over the front lawn, and a brick path leading up to the front door. The only other time Paul had been there, it had been a house of mourning, and he had noticed few of the details. But now it looked inviting. He supposed he still subconsciously hoped he could walk through the front door and disappear.

He drove around the block several times, trying to case the house from all angles, making sure nothing looked suspicious or out of the ordinary. He saw no signs of life anywhere, except for a group of children merrily splashing away in a backyard swimming pool two houses down. So he came around front again, parked and started up the brick path.

He thought he should probably be having a "This is it!" sensation as he neared Kagan's front door. But after all the calls, the notion that the rabbi might actually be home was so remote that he thought of the exercise as little more than a formality. He looked first right and then left, trying to decide which neighbor he was going to question first. Then he looked once again over his shoulder, back toward the street. The paranoia was an instinctive part of him now.

He rang the doorbell and for good measure rapped the heavy brass knocker set into the middle of the door, stepping back to see if he could spot any movement through the upper-story windows. He waited silently for several seconds, and when the door opened he was so startled he jumped back and bent into the beginning of an instinctive defensive crouch. He recovered just in time to avoid looking like a total fool.

A young, dark-haired woman answered the door. Even in his weakened and exhausted state, Paul could see she was gorgeous. What in God's name would she be doing in Kagan's house? She looked as if she was slightly surprised that anyone had come to call, but she smiled graciously and when Paul said nothing, asked, "Can I help you?"

"Oh . . . ah . . . yes, I'm looking for Rabbi Kagan. Is he home?"

"May I say who's calling?"

"I'm uh . . . tell him a friend from Boston, if you don't mind. I think he'll know who I am."

"Would you mind waiting here a moment?" the woman asked. "I'll see if he can see you. You can wait in the front hall if you like."

Paul was about to say that he'd prefer to wait on the front step if she didn't mind, but then decided he didn't want to remain exposed outside at any one place any longer than he had to. So he stepped inside as the woman disappeared down the hall.

The house looked the same, except it was so quiet now, that it seemed more deathlike than when it had been the scene of Eleanor Kagan's mourning. The hall mirror was now uncovered again, but other than that, the place had not changed. Why should it, Paul found himself asking. It's only been a few weeks.

The woman returned a few minutes later. "Rabbi Kagan says he'll see you in the den, if that's all right."

"Yes, fine." You mean he's here? He's been here all the time without answering his telephone? Maybe he was afraid to. Maybe he's been waiting for me or Amanda to come for him. Or maybe the whole thing is a trap. But it was too late to do anything about that now. The events he had considered on the trip up had already begun to unfold and he was already caught up in them. There was nothing left to be done but follow the young woman into the den.

She led him down the hall and pointed to the door. "Just go right in there," she instructed.

Hesitantly, he continued the additional steps on his own, gripped the knob firmly and pulled open the door.

There was a man standing in the middle of the room. But it wasn't Nathaniel Kagan.

"Dr. Garrett?"

Paul's eyes darted around the den and fixed on Moshe Baruch.

"My God! What are you doing here?"

Baruch calmly sipped from a glass of Jack Daniels. "Waiting for you. I'm glad you finally showed up. If you hadn't come here, we would have had to go out looking for you. Nathan Kagan insisted upon it. And that would have been quite a bother."

"Nat . . . is he all right?"

"Yes. He's safe. And now I see you are, too."

"Just barely. Someone tried to kill me last night."

The expression of subtle amusement left Baruch's face. He set down the liquor glass. "Who?"

"I don't know. But I was set up. By a man named Charles Hollister." He told Baruch the whole story. The Israeli listened silently with his jaw set grimly.

"We'll take care of the Hollister matter," he said gravely. "Now let's get out of here. You and Amanda aren't safe as long as you remain in this country until we can figure out what's going on. Where is she?"

"In Washington."

"I'll have her picked up and flown to New York at once."

The door to the den opened and the woman who had let him in reappeared. "But before we go," Baruch continued, "let me present Ariel Herzen—my professional associate . . . and my good friend."

Washington, D.C.

Charles Hollister got off the elevator on the first garage level of his L Street office building and headed across the concrete floor to his reserved parking space. He inserted his key in the handle, pulled, and the massive, walnut-paneled door swung open with little effort. Both the Rolls Royce and Charles Hollister were the epitomes of their own particular class of established solidity. Before slipping behind the wheel he tossed in the newspaper he had been carrying—the *Washington Post* Metro section folded to reveal the story about the murder at St. Elizabeth's. He started the ignition and pulled the Corniche out of the garage heading for Georgetown.

The story had rocked his sense of quiet, dignified assurance as few things ever had. A man had been killed with an ice pick in the sleeping ward of the Alfred Noyes Division, but the authorities were unclear as to whether the victim was a patient or an intruder. If not a patient, then how did he come to be found lying dead in a patient's bed? Hospital authorities had no explanation or motive at this time.

Jesus Christ! They'd killed Paul Garrett. He couldn't believe it. And worst of all, he had been the key to the whole thing! The Partners said they wanted his whereabouts as soon as possible, however possible. So old Charlie had gone to work, just like always. Anything for a client. As soon as he'd picked up Amanda West's trail the "FBI" ruse had come to him like an inspiration. And it had worked perfectly. They kept her incommunicado, sweated her all day long until she finally begged for deliverance, and then when he showed up and got her sprung from the trap of his own device, she'd practically eaten out of his hand. But God! What they'd done with the information.

He had genuinely liked Paul Garrett, he had to admit, and had ever since the party he'd been told to invite him to, where he'd really gotten to know him. In a way, he even felt responsible for him and Amanda getting together. After all, they'd met at Shorecliffe. The business about David threw him a little, and he'd have to get to the bottom of that rather delicately. He was Sandy's brother. And as much as Charlie loved her, he had to admit she had a mouth as big as the Tidal Basin.

But now Paul was dead because of him. He tried to reconstruct the entire progression in his mind, ending up with his call to the Partners after Amanda told him where Paul was. He had been triumphant in getting the information so quickly and conveying it to his biggest—and only important—client in such a timely manner. But what had he really expected them to do with it? Did he think they were going to rush over to St. E's and throw him a surprise birthday party? The fact is, he never even considered what they were going to do with the information. That was beyond his realm; beyond his need to know. He felt absolutely sick to his stomach at his own unwitting complicity; at being a pawn for the estimable J. Tyler Kendrick and his kind. He was just as bad as they were. He couldn't tell himself apart from them anymore.

And what if Amanda had put two and two together and figured out his complicity? He could never stand to face her again. She had to think the worst of him. She had to think he'd personally ordered Paul killed. He had been completely used by the Partners. They hadn't even opted for subtlety.

He had just turned off M Street onto 28th when he felt something graze against the front of his neck, sharp and metallic. It pressed into his flesh. He felt it tearing his skin and cutting off his breathing. He gasped in fright as in the rearview mirror he saw two hands reach over from the back seat and pull the length of piano wire absolutely taut across his throat.

"I'll loosen the wire enough for you to breathe and drive," came the muffled voice, "but I think I've already proved its lethal potential, so just be very, very cooperative."

"Yes, yes . . . of . . . course," Hollister spat out. Sweat was rolling from every pore on his body. "Who . . . who are you? What do you want from me?"

"Talk clearly, talk straight and talk fast," the voice ordered. "Why did you try to have Paul Garrett murdered? Who do you work for? And who else is in on this?"

"I . . . I don't know what you're talking about," he stuttered as the wire noose once again drew tighter around his neck. He felt a drop of blood trickle down his Adam's apple and stain the Windsor knot of his tie.

"We're professionals, Mr. Hollister. And taking you out would be a very routine assignment."

"Paul Garrett is a friend of mine," he protested. This time the wire pulled him straight back against the hand-rubbed leather seat.

"As I said before, Mr. Hollister, we're professionals. We don't enjoy inflicting pain; it's undignified for both of us. We'll only kill you."

"I was just told to find out where Garrett was. It was

important to my clients to know. I had no idea they'd try . . . they'd try to kill him." He was speaking in quick, shallow bursts, afraid to stop talking long enough to take a deep breath. "I didn't find out about the murder until . . . until . . ." He groped with his right hand for the newspaper, his head still pointed straight forward. "I read about it in the paper." He gripped the steering wheel tightly and summoned enough courage to ask one question in return. "How . . . how did you find out?"

"Garrett told us."

A mixture of shock, terror, and relief flooded over him—shock at what he was told, terror of his own established complicity in the attempt, relief that despite himself, he hadn't caused Paul's death.

"Now suppose you fill us in on the rest of the story," the voice from the back seat suggested. "And anything you don't say will be held against you . . . immediately."

Chapter Seventeen

Israel

It might have been nothing more than a reaction to the trauma they'd just been through, but to Amanda, Israel was like a homecoming. It was not a graceful or relaxing country; a sense of tension and compulsion permeated the air wherever people congregated. Dizengoff Street in downtown Tel Aviv had seemed as crowded, frantic, and garish as Times Square, and just as impersonal. But in this land, for some reason, she felt alive and happy; at least as happy as she could be with their very survival so much on the line.

Nat Kagan had been waiting for them in Tel Aviv, and seeing him was like becoming whole again. Why that particular metaphor came to mind, she couldn't tell. She hugged him tearfully and joyously, then Paul embraced him as Moshe Baruch looked on.

"Nathan has always been an ardent supporter of Israel and Zionism," the Israeli said. "He founded the Committee for Jewish Unity, which gave us even more reason to be interested in him. But now he's brought us something even more valuable than the Committee; something even more important for Israel's greater security."

"And what's that?" Paul had asked.

"You."

Paul's mouth opened slightly and stayed in that quizzical position, saying nothing while Baruch continued.

"I'm not a physicist. That night, when the three of you came together in Nathan's bedroom, I had no idea what was going on. But I've learned about you since then, through Yakov Perlman and others as well. And though I don't understand exactly what it is you're working on, I do understand some of the implications. And let me say that those implications are very interesting to Israel. Very interesting. A laboratory will be set up for you at the Weizmann Institute of Science in Rehovot. At our request, Dr. Perlman has been studying your work and will be able to assist you."

"You said Yakov Perlman?"

"Yes. Do you know him?"

"Not personally, but I certainly know of him. A brilliant physicist. He was with Einstein at the Kaiser Wilhelm in Berlin and then again at Princeton. I didn't realize he was still alive."

"Just barely alive, I'm afraid. He is very crippled, and from what I am told, speaks often of his own death."

"It'll be a great privilege to work with him. And a great advantage as well."

"Paul—the Weizmann Institute," Amanda said. "That's where Einstein donated most of his scientific papers."

"Yes, I was just thinking about that."

The Weizmann Institute of Science in Rehovot is like an oasis, a respite and visual reprieve in the midst of the harsh and unrelenting desert. Most of the rest of Israel is rugged, jagged, dynamic, masculine. The Institute is serenely beautiful, immaculately manicured, pristine in its sense of order. Amanda found it as different from the surrounding Judean countryside as Yakov Perlman was different from the rest of the Israelis. Perhaps it was because he was not a native Israeli, but a fairly recent immigrant. But in a country full of hard, practical, aggressive people, he was gentle, sensitive, contemplative.

"I am not surprised you speak of this spiritual rapport with Dr. Einstein," he told them in his still-thick German accent, slurred by his lack of fine control over his tongue and jaw. "I see much of him in all three of you. And it is fitting that you should come to the place named for Chaim Weizmann, Albert Einstein's good friend; a man who combined the highest ideals of science and statesmanship. Did you know that after Dr. Weizmann's death, Ben-Gurion offered the presidency of Israel to Dr. Einstein?"

"Yes, I think I did know that," Amanda said, mentally registering one more strand to the tapestry of mutual emotional ties.

"Why didn't he accept it?" Paul asked.

"He was too smart for that," Perlman answered with a glint in his eye, as Nat laughed along with him. He punched at the control button with his gnarled, rigid left hand that sent his wheelchair headed toward the laboratory set aside for Paul. His three guests followed him.

Amanda could not reconcile the idea of that brilliant, sensitive mind locked in that dying, nearly useless body. His condition, commonly known as ALS or Lou Gehrig's disease, involved loss of power or control in the brain. Yet how could that brain, still capable of such transcendent and inspired feats of intellect, be incapable at the same time of the comparatively simple task of making the body move and function properly? From what she knew from her own research at MIT, the brain stem, or "reptilian brain" was infinitely primitive compared to the frontal and temporal lobes—the interpretive cortex. Why couldn't these advanced and mysterious hemispheres exert their rightful dominance and "compel" the lower brain to function properly?

At dinner that night, Paul was quiet while Amanda busily related all of their recent experiences to Nat. When they realized he hadn't said a word, she asked him, "Is everything all right?"

He continued playing with his fork as he responded, "Yeah . . . I've just been trying to . . . figure things out."

"What do you mean?"

"We've gone far enough along so that even if we don't get much farther, I have something to show.

Even if the Unified Field Theory can't be carried to any more basic level, we've still proved enough about the relationship between gravity and electromagnetism in the atom itself so that anyone who's interested can take the work from there. The World Congress of Physics is meeting in London in less than a month. We're going to be there."

"And once you divulge what you've done, there's no point in anyone trying to kill us," Nat said. "'The Secret' will already be out."

"That's what I'm hoping for. Then we can live happily ever after."

"That's not the end of your statement, though, is it?" Nat challenged him.

Paul played with his fork, trying to shift it between the outer two and inner two fingers on his right hand. "I am asking you to work with us again," he acknowledged with hesitancy, his fork clattering to the table.

"Nat, he's making tremendous progress," said Amanda. "It's going to come together; I know it. And with your help it could happen even sooner, which would be good for everyone."

"I'm not so sure," the rabbi said. They both looked at him, stunned.

"What are you getting at?" Paul challenged, knowing how important it was to keep his emotions under control at this moment.

"There's an old joke in Israel about how times were so hard and the living conditions so bad that a great debate on what to do about it was called in the Knesset—the parliament. The arguments went back and forth until one young delegate got up and suggested that Israel declare war on the United States. That's ridiculous, everyone jeered. We would lose in a matter of days, maybe hours. A tiny country like us is no match for the United States.

"'But that's just the point!' the young delegate said. 'We'll lose the war and then the United States will take care of us and build us up, like they did to Germany and Japan.' And then everyone thought it was a marvelous idea and in their euphoria they were all ready to go out and sign a declaration of war until one old man got up in the back row and said, 'That's all well and good. But what happens if we win?'

"This is what concerns me, Paul. What happens if we win? I've been doing a lot of thinking about this since you came to my house during the *shivah* week. I've been doing some studying, too. And if the practical applications of your theory are only a fraction of what they might promise to be, I wonder how we're all going to deal with it. I wonder if society can accept that kind of mind-bending change."

He wanted to respond to Nat, but couldn't bring himself to say anything. A couple of months ago, he would have shot back with an answer before Nat had finished speaking. But now, having lived with Amanda and coming to be a part of her outlook and beliefs, he knew there was some truth in what the rabbi was saying. This perception had come to him late in life, this cognizance of the idea that no scientist can work in a social vacuum, no matter how rarified his subject matter. Fermi and Hahn, Meitner, Szilard, Einstein and Bohr had all come to grips with that reality, and in the most wrenching and agonizing fashion possible. And now, just as belatedly, Paul Garrett had experienced his own private intellectual dawning, and he had Amanda to thank for it. Without her prodding and influence, and without her loving and caring, he might never have reached it. He might have been just as accomplished a physicist, but only now was he beginning to realize how greatly diminished he would have been as a human being.

And so he just looked down at the table and let Amanda change the subject of conversation.

Washington, D.C.

"You sent for me, Chief?" Margie Ferenbach cheerfully asked as she closed the door to David's office behind her.

He looked up from the admissions report he was writing and asked, "Is the door shut?"

"Of course the door is shut. It's that big vertical wooden slab about five feet over in that direction," she said, pointing. "That thing over there that breaks up the monotony of the wall."

"I'm sorry, Marge. I've been kind of distracted the last couple of days."

"I should say you have. You're like a mother hen whose ducklings have just flown the nest, if you'll pardon the mixed metaphor. What's gotten into you? Is it Paul?"

He raised his feet to the desk top in his characteristic pose. "I guess so. I just can't get him out of my mind. I wish I knew what was going on."

"You'll hear something soon," she reassured him. "He told you he might not be able to get any word to you for a while."

"I know that."

"Have you heard any more about your brother-in-law?"

"No, and that's very strange. I got a call from Sandy saying he was going to some spa or other in Europe for about a month, and that was the last of it."

"Did she go with him?"

"No. He was going with some 'business associates,'" she said. "She didn't seem to know much more than she was telling me, if anything. The whole conversation was kind of awkward. I didn't want to let on that I knew anything, and I couldn't tell whether she was trying to say something to me. I'll have to call her again."

Margie crossed over to the window wall and leaned against the radiator, positioning a volume of *Modern Clinical Psychiatry* between it and her backside for support. "Now, what exactly can I do for you?"

"I want you to call the National Library of Medicine in Bethesda. Tell them it's a confidential inquiry. Use our Secret Service clearance if you have to to keep the thing bottled up. But I want a computer search run on all brain research conducted between 1950 and 1960."

"That's a pretty broad field, Captain. Can you give me some key words or phrases they can flag?"

He leaned his head back and thought for a moment, then began striking them off on his fingers. "Okay. Grade three and four tumors of the frontal and temporal lobes . . ."

Margie rummaged across the desk for a clean scrap of paper. "Yeah, go on."

"Goddard Institute, Norbert Ramsey, postoperative results and cure rates."

"Okay. Anything else?"

"One more thing . . . and I hope they don't look at you like you're crazy when you ask them—maintenance of living brain in vitro."

Langley, Virginia

George Henderson was at the top of his sarcastically abusive form, which meant that the traschcan-kicking phase would probably be next. Douglas Martin, on the receiving end, sat slumping miserably in the white linen sofa against the paneled wall. The others in the room felt for him, but knew better than to offer any solace, even to the extent of a sympathetic glance, while the Boss delivered his tirade. That was just one of the unwritten rules.

"They show up in Boston, the Partners for Progress find thcm. Shit, anybody could find them, they blew up a fucking building, for Christ's sake! Now how'd *we* miss them?"

"There was nothing to follow, George. By the time we found out about them, it was too late."

"The Partners had the bright idea of going to where the man worked. Did that one ever cross your mind?"

"We knew they were there," Martin said. "But we were just supposed to watch them. And that's what we did—watch them."

"Who was watching them the night of the explosion?" Henderson demanded.

"Ah . . . I'm not sure. It was a . . . slip-up."

"Martin, you wouldn't know to cover your dick if a chippie you were *shtupping* told you she had V.D." He stood up and kicked the trashcan once on his way around the desk.

"All right, gentlemen," he said, now addressing the group as an entity. "We had our chance and we blew it! I don't know if we're going to get another one. So we're going to have to do it the hard way. The more time those people spend together, the more chance something comes together. I want that stopped, even if it means Paul Garrett's life. You understand? The summer's almost over. That means Garrett's got to go back to MIT if he wants to keep his job. I want you guys to start snooping around there, see if anyone's talked to him. See if he ever called that Lieutenant Kennedy again. I want a general name-flagged computer search run on every airline ticket anywhere in the world. I want you to alert Interpol that we want a high-confidentiality fugitive priority on Garrett, West, and the rabbi. I want all Customs passport records gone through since the explosion. I want the Goddard Institute put under twenty-four-hour surveillance and I want Norbert Ramsey followed to make sure he's not in on this. I never completely trusted the bastard. Is everything I've said so far understood?"

The heads nodded in unison.

"And everyone in this section better be alert to any reference to the Ramsey project. Any nuance, anything, could blow the whole fucking thing out of the water. I want the lid on that story no matter what. If it gets out, it could wreck the Agency. I kid you not. No fucking joke.

"Find those three people."

New York

As soon as he saw the fountain of blood, Norbert Ramsey knew he'd lost the battle, but he wasted not an instant as he tried to prove this judgment wrong.

He rushed with both hands into the surgical field, shouting, "Clamp!" as the head nurse rushed one of the silver clips to him. "Let's get some blood in here!" he ordered as the hemorrhaging geyser splattered his arms and forehead.

Robert Anderson pushed in next to him, their shoulders pressing, two more clamps ready.

"It's the anterior cerebral," Ramsey stated tersely. "The whole thing's ripped to shit."

He'd been operating to repair a cherry-sized aneurysm of the anterior communicating artery in the Circle of Willis, the critical area near the base of the brain from which it receives its blood supply. The aneurysm —probably congenital—had shown up on an arteriogram after the forty-six-year-old male patient had complained of searing headaches. What the test had not shown was a second, even more devastating weakness in the anterior cerebral artery. And this was what had burst just as he finished sewing the delicate resection he'd gone in to perform.

Ramsey glanced at the red fluid moving through the IV line into the brachial artery in the patient's arm. "Can't you move it any faster than that?" he demanded, knowing the answer before he heard it. He was losing the race against time. There was just no way to replace the spurting blood quickly enough. It had already formed a deep pool in the exposed brain.

"Bring the sucker in here!" he barked to Anderson. "I can't see a goddamned thing." A steady whine, meanwhile, was emanating from the anesthesiologist's console, attempting to warn the surgeons of what they already knew.

Anderson evacuated the useless blood from the cavity while Ramsey groped with his fingers for the outer parameters of the new aneurysm. "I ain't doing it, Bobby," he said. "As soon as I get a clamp on, it bursts farther up."

The fountain had tapered off into a steady flow, at least twice in volume what the IV transfusion was pumping back in. Ramsey grasped furiously for an arterial section firm enough to attach a clamp to, but all he had in front of him was a two-centimeter length of punctured balloon. There was no way to survive that massive a rupture. There was nothing left to work with.

Even the suction tube couldn't keep up with the rate of hemorrhaging. Ramsey was feeling his way through a bloody swamp. "I'm going to try to pull the two ends together," he said, "then you see if you can tie them. It's our only shot." He jammed his fingers underneath the damaged vessel, prying it loose from the surrounding tissue. "This is as good as it gets. Now go on in there!"

Anderson jabbed with the needle, but it just pulled away from the destroyed vessel wall. And the bleeding continued. He looked to Ramsey for the next order, another hopeless fling made credible only by the surgeon's history of accomplishing the impossible through the sheer force of his unyielding will. He had opened his mouth behind his mask to announce the next move when the anesthesiologist, Milton Younger, quietly murmured, "That's it, Chief. The ballgame's over."

Ramsey's fingers went lax and he withdrew his hands, uniformly red up to the wrists, from the open wound. He peeled off the latex gloves, then his green cap, and threw them decisively to the floor. The rest of the team stood by rigidly, in awe and terror of their leader, as he marched over to the light box and squinted at the X-rays. "Now why the hell didn't we find that one along with the other?" he asked.

. "Could be any number of reasons," Anderson responded. "Sometimes they just don't show up."

Ramsey just shook his head. "I want an autopsy. See if we fucked up . . . or the brain did."

There was no need to go through the ritual of covering the deceased, only of covering the small surgical field. The ritual of draping for the operating room had already taken care of the rest of the body.

Ramsey turned back toward the table. "Thank you for your efforts, everyone." With that, he had given them leave to move, and they began the clean-up process that would prepare the room for the next case. The scrub nurse came up behind him to untie his blood-soaked gown. From experience, he knew exactly how long he had to stand still. When she finished he continued toward the door, passing the anesthesiologist's station.

"Good job, Chief," Younger said.

"Not good enough for our friend here," he replied, indicating the corpse on the table with a sweeping arc of his arm.

"I don't know of any other surgeon who could have pulled it off; who would have even given it the shot you did."

"I'm not any other surgeon," said Norbert Ramsey as he left.

Up in the viewing gallery, Wendell Fuller sat alone, and when Ramsey walked out, so did he. It had been a long while since he'd taken the time to watch the Chief operate, and after watching this losing effort he chided himself for not having availed himself of the opportunity.

Even when he came up short, there was something

about Ramsey's performance at the table that was impassioned, provoking, thrilling. He was utterly fearless. And this kind of outcome showed off the Ramsey style even better than a victory. Fuller remembered having heard somewhere that the truest test of character was the way a man behaves and fights when he's absolutely sure of losing. He couldn't remember the last time he'd seen an aneurysm rip that bad. No one in the world would have blamed Ramsey for folding his hands right after he tried the second clamp. But that wasn't his style. The man may be an abrasive son of a bitch to work with, Fuller thought, but he's a guy who's actually properly defined only by action. It was by demonstrations like this one that he defined himself every livelong day. He was right about not being any other surgeon. He had a style that was all his own. And Fuller couldn't think of anyone he'd rather have messing around inside his skull in the event that—Good Lord forbid it—it became necessary.

Fuller came down the stairs from the viewing gallery just as Ramsey was coming out of the scrub room. He'd planned it that way. The surgeon was still wearing his greens and track shoes, both of which were stained with blood that had seeped through the gown. He nodded to Fuller as he turned the corner, and Wendell doubled a step to catch up with him.

"I saw the show, Chief."

"Did you? How come?"

"Just decided it was time to take advantage of one of our natural resources here at Goddard."

Ramsey seemed more amused than touched. "Don't tell anyone I lost. It's bad for morale; especially the morale of whoever's next." Fuller chuckled grimly and continued to walk with him. "It's a good thing I don't believe in streak-hitting. Otherwise, I'd have to spend some time on your couch."

"I guess so, Boss, only I don't use a couch."

"Oh really? I guess we all have to watch each other work more often."

"Listen, Norbert, there's something I want to ask you about."

"What's that?" he queried without breaking his stride.

"You remember Paul Garrett? Came to see you a couple of weeks ago."

Ramsey suddenly stopped, blinking once. "What about him?"

"Well, sir, you see, I'm not exactly sure. But it seems he's missing, see . . ."

"What do you mean, missing?"

"Well, his psychiatrist's a friend of mine, and he tells me Garrett's just up and left, so far as he can tell. Doesn't know what it's all about. And when he came to see you, I looked up his record ahead of time, saw you took a pretty goddamned big glioma out of his head."

"Yes? So?" he prodded impatiently.

"So as a psychiatric question we could speculate from now till the cows come home. But I was wondering, from your surgical experience, is there anything in the postoperative literature for this sort of thing that covers amnesiac or aphasiac episodes, or episodes of acute depression?"

"The postoperative literature for the type of glioma Paul Garrett suffered covers funerals and burial," said Ramsey curtly.

"Yeah, that's kind of what I thought," Wendell replied. "The case just kind of interested me is all, being so rare. And see, the devil of it is I came upon three people you brought back to the land of the living at the same time back there, and now suddenly they've all three of 'em just dropped clean out of sight. They'd gotten friendly with each other is how it was put to me."

Ramsey stopped moving and turned full face to Wendell. "I'm afraid I can't help you much and I don't really know what you're driving at. But let me give you a word of advice, Wendell. Lay off of those cases. All three are flukes and are in no way instructive of the normal care and maintenance of end-stage brain tumors."

"Well, but you see, that's why they were so interesting . . ."

"Please listen to what I'm telling you. You could get yourself . . . you could get all of us into a lot of difficulty by being too curious. I can't tell you any more than that, but there's no way you can help here, so you've just got to believe what I tell you. Leave it alone, Wendell."

"I . . . uh . . . guess you've made your point, Chief."

"It's out of my hands."

"Yeah . . . well, thanks for your time. I've enjoyed our little chat. And it's always inspiring to see you work."

"Thanks for the encouragement," Ramsey said. "Sorry about all this."

"Sure. That's okay." He headed back in the direction he'd come from and Ramsey continued on toward his suite.

When Fuller got back to his own office, he closed the door and locked it, then dialed his telephone for a long-distance line.

"Hello? David, boy?"

"Yeah," David Sherman responded. "How you doing, Wendell?"

"I just talked to himself. Used your suggestion about trying to draw him out by saying Garrett and the others were missing."

"How'd he react?"

"There's something going on, Davey. He told me to lay off."

"Did he tell you why?"

"'Course not. I don't know if he knew I was on a fishing expedition—he probably did—but as soon as I mentioned Paul Garrett's name, he looked like I'd just accused him of sticking it to my prized sheep under the light of the full moon."

"Okay, Wendell. Let me figure this all out and get back to you. But one way or another, I'm going to need your help."

"Sure thing, Davey. Only the whole thing kinda gives me the feeling of swallowing raw fish."

He hung up the phone and went down to check out the new girl in Medical Records and try to get his mind off the dark cloud he'd just seen form around one of the greatest surgeons in the world.

Rehovot

While Paul spent his days sifting through Einstein's personal physics notes, which the scientist had bequeathed to the Weizmann Institute, Amanda sifted through the country, a place small enough to be easily traversed by car, yet so complex and layered as to offer ever-expanding meaning and subtlety. With Ariel Herzen as her guide and companion, she visited many of the physical monuments to Israel's historical and spiritual past. And everywhere she went, her sense of identification with the country and its people unaccountably increased. Though she had no idea why, now she understood what the agnostic Einstein had found so compelling about this place.

She was also, in these last few days, feeling a growing affection for Ariel who, as her constant guide, she associated with the country itself. She was, as she had said, a Sabra—a native-born Israeli, the name coming from the tenacious local cactus that is hard and prickly on the outside, tender and sweet on the inside, supposedly an analogy to the national character. Ariel was strong and simple, unplagued by the doubts of intellectualism Amanda recognized and grappled with in herself. In Ariel's mind, ideas either resolved themselves into concretions or faith. There was no middle ground. She admired Ariel's joyful spontaneity and the beauty that was so different from her own. Whereas Amanda possessed a sophisticated, blonde "tennis player" beauty, Ariel had the type of blooming, radiant sensuality that seems almost primordial in its allure. And recalling the few occasions during these past days when she had seen her undressed—the loaded Beretta never far from her side—she could easily see how Ariel would appeal to a man like Moshe Baruch.

When she returned to the lab, only Nat was there. It was late afternoon, so Perlman was taking his mandatory nap, but she was surprised not to see Paul.

"He's still in the archives room," Nat reported. "He's been there all day."

"That's surprising," she commented. "I've never seen anyone who likes that kind of research less than he does. Maybe he's on to something."

"I hope so," Nat said.

"Nat, it's been so nice having all of us together again. And I'm so glad you decided to work with Paul on the theory."

"I hope I don't live to regret it," he tossed off lightly, then looked into her eyes and saw the tears of genuine emotion. He couldn't tell whether she was looking at him, or right through him out the window toward the palms and evergreens that sheltered Chaim Weizmann's grave.

There was a knock on the door, but then the visitor didn't wait for a reply. The door opened and Moshe Baruch entered.

"What are you doing here?" she asked. "Ariel dropped me off. She didn't stay."

"No, I came to see you three," he said. "I wanted to give you a progress report."

"On what?" Nat asked.

"We've finished interrogating Charles Hollister."

"Interrogating?" Amanda repeated warily.

"Yes," the Israeli said brusquely. "Don't worry about it. It turns out he represented a group known as the Partners for Progress. They're an international cartel made up of some of the largest and most influential corporations in the noncommunist world. We've suspected their existence for years but were never able to prove it. They were the ones who tried to have you both kidnapped at Paul's lab at MIT, and they were the ones who murdered Paul's friend, Harry Gillette."

"And then tried to kill Paul at St. Elizabeth's?" Amanda added.

"Yes."

"What about Paul's wife? He still thinks that was a murder. And the dog attack on us at Greenacre Park?"

"We don't think so, if Hollister's leveling with us. And at this point . . . we think he's now leveling.. He says they have no idea about those."

"But why would these corporations want Paul and whoever works with him dead?" Nat asked.

"Figure it out," Baruch said.

The archivist at the Weizmann Institute had obviously given the Einstein papers the attention and deference they deserved. Everything was arranged in meticulous chronological order and cross-referenced by subject, a welcome change for Paul, who was accustomed to poring over the feeble organizational efforts of fellow physicists that could best be described as scattershot. But any scientific breakthrough is a series of linear steps over time, each a positive or negative reaction to the previous one, and so to see them all laid out in the sequence in which they occurred gave the body of work an easily discernible symmetry.

There were fascinating details about Einstein's personal life, in addition to his scientific work. Correspondence with Friedrich Adler and H. A. Lorentz around 1918 showed him to be suffering from severe stomach upset that convinced him he had terminal cancer. Paul thought back to his own agonizing time in the Goddard Institute and the horror of living under a medical death sentence came vividly back to him. The stomach upset was later diagnosed as acute nervous distress and marked the onset of Einstein's emotional breakdown.

Again he could empathize, and took some vicarious comfort from the physicist's ability to rebound so completely from his illness. Aside from everything else, the man was incredibly resilient, both physically and mentally, having withstood not only the scurrilous attacks of scientific reactionaries, but the anti-Semitic hysteria that drove him out of his native Germany at the height of his prominence. This human side became so diverting that Paul had to consciously keep his mind on the technical papers. Time was growing short before the World Congress of Physics convention and there was much left to try to do.

The clarity of the archival organization also helped him evaluate what he did not need. All indications from his previous research suggested that the serious Unified Field inquiries began in the late 1920s, after the general theory of relativity was more or less entrenched in the main line of scientific thought. Then, once the laws of Newtonian mechanics had been shown to be less than universally applicable and the entire concept of space and time redefined, the idea that all force fields might be governed by the same set of determinants no longer seemed beyond the range of logic. And so it was Einstein's years at the Kaiser Wilhelm Institute that Paul first focused on, hoping to uncover some original spark that perhaps even the physicist himself had let slip in favor of an ultimately erroneous line of reasoning.

"The answer you get is determined by the question you ask," he heard Einstein telling him, mentally recreating the soft German accent from newsreels he'd seen. Sitting here among all the papers, immersing himself in the man's work and ideas, he couldn't deny the transcendental power Einstein exerted over him. Had it only been recently, since Amanda started pointing it out, or had it been going on for years, subtly, without his even being aware of it? Had he been influenced after he started his own Unified Field work, or had he taken on the work as a result of Einstein's psychic influence? Like the origin of the cosmos itself, the question was circular, endlessly tantalizing and ultimately unanswerable. But the kinship and . . . yes, the affection he felt for the long-dead scientist at this particular moment was undeniable, eerie, and quietly unnerving.

There was a reference file of longhand essays, some of which Paul had read and some he hadn't. But seeing them for the first time in Einstein's tight, tentative script added a dimension of personality, which made them seem even more eloquent. He paused in his quest long enough to read through "The Goal of Human Existence," "Human Rights," "The Pacifist Problem," "Our Debt to Zionism," and "To the Heroes of the Battle of the Warsaw Ghetto." Each of these pieces showed a side of the man that many people could infer from the sensitive, melancholy photographs by nearly all the world's leading photographers. But it was a side of Einstein that Paul could discern from the sensitivity and nuance of the general theory of relativity itself. No physicist can mask his true personality, even in his equations.

He forced his brain back to science. Unfortunately, in the days he'd spent in this brilliantly white, ultra-modern records room, he had uncovered nothing from the Kaiser Wilhelm period that seemed remotely promising. The records pointed to the probability that Einstein was absolutely justified in abandoning all of his earliest suppositions. Paul had read the Unified Field Theory he had published in 1929 in the *Proceedings of the Prussian Academy of Science* and later retracted. And he had studied the 1949 theory given before the American Association for the Advancement of Science. But there were serious gaps and loose ends in that one as well, and it never made much of an impact on the academic community, even as a takeoff point. So there was little point in concentrating on Einstein's prime years at Princeton. Paul wasn't sure why, but his strong hunch was that those final five or six waning years before he died held the promise of an entirely new approach that would have reached marvelous fruition had Einstein been given the additional five years of life he would have needed.

The material from that final period was sparser, partly because of the physicist's failing health and partly because of his increased commitment to the world peace movement. Paul came across the drafts of the public declaration on nuclear armament that Einstein published with Bertrand Russell, the mathematician-philosopher with whom he shared so much. And this was just one more evidence of the spiritual connection between the three of them and Einstein, Paul realized. He had always been an admirer of Lord Russell's logic and powerful prose, and both Amanda and Nat had been at his War Crimes Tribunal on Vietnam.

He had started out to contemplate Einstein's work and here he found himself contemplating Einstein's soul. The sense of identity with him was almost stifling. It was as if he were reading over his own notes, and in these papers of the final years, as if he himself were preparing for death. A breathless surge of anxiety welled up from under his rib cage and he felt his chest hairs matting with perspiration. He had to make a conscious effort to breathe deeply. Trying to stem his discomfort and the dredged-up memories of Goddard that began freely associating in his mind, Paul tried to laugh at the utter pretentiousness of identifying himself with the greatest mind of the twentieth century, the greatest scientific intellect since Newton.

But the feeling was growing stronger rather than receding. So the only way to deal with it was to face it head-on rather than trying to ignore it. Leaving the scientific papers for the time being, he immersed himself in the mundane procedural documents of the final years, many of them relating to Einstein's instructions for the period following his death.

One note instructed the Princeton administration that his office at the Institute for Advanced Study not be preserved as a memorial but given routinely to the next arriving scholar. Like Moses, he wished to leave no physical monuments.

That brought up an interesting question. Where was Einstein buried? Paul didn't think he'd ever known where he had been laid to rest. Wherever it was, maybe when they got back to the States, the three of them could make a pilgrimage to the site. Perhaps that morbid communion would offer further clues to their strange obsession with him.

The last document in the file was the will, filed for probate in Mercer County, New Jersey, in the summer of 1955. There was little property to dispose of and most of the bequests concerned his scientific papers, the bulk of which came right here to the Weizmann Institute. And the question of the gravesite was also answered in short order. Dr. Einstein had instructed that his body be cremated, and the ashes scattered at an undisclosed location so that no one could come to pay him homage. If he were remembered at all, he seemed to imply, it should be solely for his work. His abiding interest, in death as well as in life, was the advancement of science.

It all fit in with that overwhelming intellect and fiercely humble personality, Paul thought, though he did feel a twinge of disappointment knowing there would be no grave to visit. Nothing tangible remained. Every saint should leave a relic, and the first saint of the age of science should be no exception.

He skimmed down the narrow, typewritten columns, more out of curiosity than a compulsion to know anything further. He would have to make his peace with Einstein the man if he was going to objectively take off from his work. And with the reading of this document that legally concluded his earthly affairs, Paul decided he would put the scientist out of his mind in favor of the science.

He was about to refold the will and return it to the file when one word in the middle of a paragraph caught his eye. Was it possible? Suddenly, he was riveted to the page. Connections began forming in his mind. Had he been overcome by delirium, or could it have . . . ? What other explanation . . . ?

Now he really felt as if he couldn't breathe, and his accelerating pulse thundered in his temples and pounded across every surface of his skin. He stood up abruptly, almost swooning with lightheadedness, grabbed the will off the table with trembling fingers and strode quickly out of the library and down the long hall to Yakov Perlman's ground-floor office. He was vaguely aware of other faculty members waving and asking if he was well as he walked by, but they were like a continuous blur and he didn't answer any of them. He forced himself not to think until he reached his destination. He didn't want to be alone if and when the concrete realization hit him.

In the office, Amanda was sitting on a wooden stool next to Perlman's wheelchair and Nat was standing behind him. She was wearing shorts and a Tel Aviv University T-shirt and looked as relaxed and happy as he had seen her in weeks. A shabby leather-covered photo album rested on Perlman's withered knees and the old man was smiling wistfully as Amanda turned the stiff pages. She looked up when Paul entered the room, but was too engrossed in the nostalgic exercise to notice his flushed complexion and fixed stare.

"Paul, you must look at these pictures!" she called over to him. "Yakov must have posed with all the great scientists of Europe at one time or another."

"When I was strong and could walk, look how handsome I was!" Perlman proudly proclaimed, pointing to a photograph of himself taken in Amsterdam with H. A. Lorentz. "And here is one of me with Dr. Einstein himself, when we were both very young; when he still remembered to cut his hair once in a while!"

But as Perlman brought his palsied hand over close to the photograph, Amanda went silent, her exuberant mood vanished and the color drained totally from her face. Nat bent down to look, and when the image registered, he gasped and his eyes opened wide in stunned, anxious amazement. They both stared at the photograph as transfixedly as Paul had stared at the will just minutes before.

It showed the tall, broad-shouldered Yakov, no more than twenty-two or twenty-three, his arm wrapped around the shoulder of an elegantly dressed and neatly mustached Albert Einstein, perhaps fifteen years his senior. They are standing amidst the green forests of the Swabian Alps, Einstein's homeland. They are in a knoll insulated from the rest of the terraced slope by a high stand of oak and evergreen trees, and from many angles it is even difficult to see the tops of the towering mountains. At the top of the knoll where the grass is the thickest, a large, almond-shaped rock juts out defiantly to form a promontory on which one could sit and gaze and contemplate the miniature valley it overlooks. It was spring in the photograph, and the dark wildflowers were out, and the setting looked as serene and lovely as any place Amanda could imagine.

It was identical in almost every respect to her favorite knoll in Central Park; the place where she had first met Nat.

"I . . . I don't believe it. It could be the same spot, it's so close. And when you first came there, when we met, you said you *remembered* it, that you had it in your mind even though you'd never been there before!" She stopped and took in a slow, deep breath and looked for a moment as if she might fall off the stool.

"But look," Nat said. "I *had* been there before. At least part of me had. This is the image I had in my mind that led me there. This very image!"

"Life is full of strange connections," Perlman said, trying through the lightness of his tone to relieve their obvious confused distress. "The job of the scientist is to observe and interpret those connections, and try to make some sense out of them."

"And I've just observed one of those connections," Paul said, walking from the doorway to where the two of them were sitting. He held up the blue-covered document he carried. "Albert Einstein's body was cremated when he died, all except one part. One part was saved."

Amanda and Nat and Yakov looked at him in bafflement.

"His brain."

Chapter Eighteen

New York

"Davey, I just hope you got this caper thought through," Wendell Fuller whispered hoarsely while one part of his common sense tried to tell him it was still possible to back out.

"I hope so too," David Sherman whispered back at him, adding, "In school you were always the wild one, the daring one, not me."

"I know. And that's what worries me. You shy guys who've been holding it back all these years sometimes let it go in one grand explosion; shoot your wad on one roll of the old dice."

He still wasn't sure how David convinced him to go along on this crazy raiding party. But somehow, here he was . . . or rather, here they both were, in Norbert Ramsey's inner office in the middle of the fucking night, dressed in baggy gray custodian uniforms that had "Goddard Inst." embroidered in red above the breast pockets, wearing latex surgical gloves, having crawled through the transom to get in, and now scared shitless they were going to get caught in the act of breaking and entering. "I still don't know why you're trying to be such a goddamned detective hero," he went on as David continued scanning the tab headings of a drawerful of file folders. "I could offer you a passel of psychiatric explanations, but back down in Jellico, we'd just say you was taitched in the head."

"This was the only way I could think of to get to this information," David said. "Unless of course you wanted to put some of that self-proclaimed macho to the test and seduce Ramsey's secretary."

"Miss Olson? I'd have a better shot seducing my old catcher's mitt." He thought wistfully about how he could be home in bed, his arms wrapped around some gently purring stewardess.

David closed the drawer with a slam of disgust. "Nothing in this whole cabinet," he announced. "Nothing in any of them. We've been over the whole room now. The material's got to be in here somewhere."

"I'll take a look in the closet," Wendell offered. He opened the door and saw three spare shirts and a set of greens hanging on the rack, and against the wall in the corner a two-drawer fire-resistant file cabinet with a combination lock. "Over here," he called to David. "But how are we going to open it?"

David came over and contemplated the cabinet, stroking his chin as he thought about it. "When's Ramsey's birthday?"

"How should I know? He's never invited me to a party."

"Well see if you can find his curriculum vitae somewhere around here."

Wendell went away muttering about how David had taken advantage of the southern code of chivalry by asking him to do this and how if they ever got out alive he was going to owe him one hell of a big favor.

The resumé was in the second drawer of Miss Olson's desk, and Wendell came back announcing, "December 12, 1918."

"Twelve, twelve, eighteen," David repeated, translating the numbers into coordinates on the combination dial. He pressed the release latch on the drawer and it slid open effortlessly.

"Now how did you figure that one out?"

"I figured a man like Ramsey would be too busy and preoccupied to keep numbers in his head, unless it was one that was automatic for him to remember."

"Pretty up and walking impressive," Wendell admitted.

A quick scan of the first drawer revealed nothing.

"It's probably a code of some sort," David said, "so I'll take this drawer and you take the bottom one."

"But if you have the top one open, that covers up the bottom one," Wendell pointed out.

"You're right. We'll have to do them one at a time together."

Wendell's faint hope that David had everything worked out in his mind sank.

"I think this is it!" David said after a few minutes of searching. He pulled out a file marked ARTICHOKE and brought it over to Ramsey's desk. He sifted through several pages, finally stopping at a handwritten yellow sheet headed, "Technique," and read:

> "Through means of lowering the body temperature substantially at the moment preceding death, the metabolic rate was reduced to a manageable level and the body was placed in a state of physiologic suspension. A heart-lung machine maintained blood circulation. In practice, there was no noticeable deviation from the tests performed on rats, the gorilla, and the chimpanzee."

He flipped over to the next page.

> "Once the craniectomy was accomplished, the brain was placed in a glass environment of completely sterile nature and with rigidly controlled temperature and humidity. Nutrient materials were perfused constantly and an electroencephalograph producing alpha rhythms at the rate of ten per second verified the viability of the brain during the in vitro state. Auditory and visual stimuli drove the alpha rhythm up to fourteen per second, which we found quite encouraging and in keeping with the animal experiments.
>
> "After the craniectomy was performed, the body was returned to the custody of the Princeton hospital for cremation in keeping with the terms of the will."

"Listen to this!" David stated. " 'The brain appeared to suffer no ill effects during the *four years* it was kept in vitro.' Is this guy serious?"

Caught up in the suspense now, Wendell took the file from David and scanned through it himself. "Holy shit!" he gasped, and held up a page marked, "Implantation."

"Tumor specimens from all of the grade three and four patients in our care were taken and cultured. It was decided to attempt the implant on all those where tissue matching with the brain indicated a reasonable chance of acceptance. Though the brain does not manifest the same rejection characteristics as the rest of the body, it is not without its defenses against foreign invaders, so a regimen of steroids and other immunosuppressant drugs was instituted on all candidates.

"In our opinion and experience, none of the candidates had even a moderate chance of survival and in fact, since the experiment had to be performed secretly, only terminal candidates were considered for so unlikely a procedure. It was my opinion that if anything, the implant could only produce salutary results, as it has long been a theory of mine that introduction of healthy tissue in the area of malignancy could counteract the tumor growth and effectively 'take over.'

"In any event, if successful, these implants would, in the remaining weeks or months of their lives, demonstrate the effects of two brains—and presumably two intellects working in tandem, or perhaps conflicting with each other. Whatever the case, the experiment should contribute incalculable new information on the physical and organic basis of mind. And the results should prove particularly fascinating when one considers that the implanted brain section corresponds to the greatest mind of our time."

David and Wendell looked at each other in stunned silence. "It's true, then," Wendell murmured. "This is the most incredible thing I've ever seen."

"I wouldn't be surprised if it's the most incredible thing anyone's ever seen." They continued reading.

"There was no point in implanting sections of the lower brain stem or motor areas. So far as we can tell, these areas have nothing to do with mind or intellect. But by implanting sections of areas thirteen, fourteen, and fifteen of the frontal and temporal lobes, the areas Penfield referred to as the uncommitted or interpretive cortex, I believe we can go a long way toward establishing the relationship between physical brain, and ephemeral mind. That is, since we have determined that the brain was kept alive and functioning in vitro, is it possible by implanting physical tissue to transfer intellectual powers along with it?

"If the intellect is actually contained electrochemically in specific tissue, it might be possible to do this. If the specific tissue instead acts as a receptor for 'intellectual energy' as Penfield suspects, it still might be possible to transfer whole or partial sections of mind. But the only way to tell for sure is through implantation on one or more human patients. And the only way this technique is ethically thinkable is with a candidate who is going to die anyway.

"ARTICHOKE Control has suggested that healthy candidates be considered, but this is out of the question. Neither I, nor any of my colleagues, will be a party to such an attempt."

"What's ARTICHOKE?" Wendell asked.

"Beats me."

"David, if this is true, old Norbert Ramsey is not only the best head surgeon around, he's a fucking pioneer."

"It's true, Wendell," he answered solemnly. "Look

at this one." He spread out a sheet headed, "Procedure."

"The brain was not sectioned off until the last possible moment before surgery so as not to take a chance on damage. We felt we had the best chance with the first three operations because of the time consideration. The first patient, a twenty-two-year-old male suffering from a grade four oligodendroglioma, was prepared and the surgical field exposed. Only after the resecting was underway was the donor cortical section brought into the operating room . . ."

Rehovot

Paul lay back on the deeply padded couch while, through the subdued light, Moshe Baruch and Yakov Perlman looked on. Zvi Netzer, chief of the Weizmann Institute's psychology faculty, slowly rose from beside the couch and quietly padded over to where Moshe was standing.

"I've taken him up through college, medical school, and the onset of his illness. Now I'm ready to take him into the operation."

"But how can he recall any of that?" Moshe asked. "He was asleep during the whole thing."

"It has been proven experimentally that the subconscious mind records much more than the conscious mind is aware of. I've gotten witnesses under hypnosis to remember license plates of hit-and-run drivers that they had no recollection of awake."

"But hearing something when you're asleep?"

"We hear quite a lot when we're asleep, actually. Now many researchers believe that somewhere in the brain is the complete record of all life experiences, and all we have to do is figure out how to tap it. We can't do that with complete effectiveness yet, but we've had some very good results with deep hypnosis where we approach the subject in question gradually, rather than just get right to it. That's what I've been doing here. He'd been under more than three hours already when you both came in."

"Well, if hypnosis can tell us so much, why wasn't Dr. Garrett just hypnotized in the first place after he began to have suspicions? Couldn't that have cleared up some of the questions without everything he's had to go through since?"

"Yes and no," Netzer responded.

"That's what I like about you scientists," Moshe commented. "Always decisive."

"It is true that whatever information is recorded in Dr. Garrett's brain now was there a month ago, or two months ago, or whenever. But there was no way for him, or a hypnotist, to get to it. We have to prime the pump, so to speak. We have to have some surrounding information to trigger the recall, which is what we got from Dr. Sherman's phone call to Dr. Garrett."

"And what about Miss West and Rabbi Kagan?" Moshe asked.

"We'll try with her, too, but I'm not as optimistic about the results. She was a preadolescent at the time of the surgery, so her subconscious attention and listening skills wouldn't have been as developed. But if my feeling is correct, the same procedure on Kagan should also work." He walked back over to the couch and sat down beside it. When he spoke again, his voice was low, mellow and professionally soothing, exactly the tone calculated to elicit a relaxed response. "Now Paul, you were put under anesthesia at seven-fifteen by Dr. Seymour Hamlyn. You fell asleep quickly and the nervousness and tension you'd been feeling all night gradually began to leave you. Do you remember that feeling?"

"Yes," Paul replied calmly, his eyelids closed but fluttering lightly.

"Then when you were asleep they wheeled you into

the operating room. You didn't see anything because your eyes were closed. But you heard the wheels of the stretcher and you heard voices. Did you hear anything else?"

"Music," Paul said.

"Yes, that's right. Music. It was Sibelius, wasn't it? Cold, icy, distant music. Isn't that right?"

"Yes."

"Good. Now, tell me in order, right from the beginning, just what you heard the voices saying."

Paul said nothing for several seconds and Netzer nodded over to Moshe that this was nothing out of the ordinary. When he did begin to speak, it was with a calm, deliberate tone, totally devoid of emotion; an objective observer to a proceeding from which he was one step removed. " 'Is the positioning all right?' " was the first thing he said, then he quickly followed with, " 'Yes, that'll be fine. I assume the vital signs are stable. All right, I'm making four burr holes which I will then rongeur between, making sure to keep the head positioned with the petrous ridge on the side of the tumor in a straight antero-posterior direction . . .' "

Every once in a while Netzer prompted him with a low but forceful, "Yes, then what," and then he would resume his subconscious narrative; all the way up through the removal of the skull section.

" 'Okay, ladies and gentlemen, there it is, an oligodendroglioma here in the middle of the right temporal lobe, clearly a grade four. Let me have the scalpel . . .' "

"Let me have the scalpel. All right, I don't want any blood. Get in here with that suction. That's enough. How's he holding up? Blood pressure?"

"One thirty-five over eighty."

"Pulse?"

"Ninety-two."

"Good enough. Let me have the specimen dish. This goes to pathology."

"Right."

"I think I can get it. I'm going for the whole damn tumor. . . . That's it. We're clean."

"Do you want the thread?"

"Not yet. Just staunch the bleeding and give me an extra unit of blood for good measure. When I finish cutting here, I want you to come right in with the clamp and hold it there until I tell you to let go. Do you understand?"

"Yes, Dr. Ramsey."

"If the lesion opens up you have to be ready with another clamp 'cause I don't want to sew yet."

"All right, keep that clamp in place. Okay now . . . the tumor's free. Get it out of here. We've got all we need. Now let me have the donor section, and for God's sake be careful; you drop it and the ballgame's over. Measure this out for me. I want one millimeter on each side of the cavity for suturing, but no more. I want a snug fit. How's that?"

"Perfect. Conforms exactly."

"Good. No margin for error on this one. I don't want the brain itself to notice anything's different."

"Dr. Ramsey, I'm approaching with the donor section on your right."

"Good. Does it look okay?"

"No change since you saw it."

"Fine. I really think we're gonna pull this one out. Now, everybody ready. Just like we practiced it. Put it right in my left hand."

"Do you have it?"

"Yeah. You can take your hand away now. Okay, clean out the blood again. I want it completely dry when I go in. And get ready with the clamp."

"You're all set."

"So . . . let's do it. Ladies and gentlemen, the four of you will never be able to tell anyone outside this room, but you're looking at a piece of the brain that made atomic energy possible; the brain that changed the way we think about the universe . . ."

* * *

Paul slept for four hours after Netzer concluded the session. But when he awoke, still exhausted and drenched with sweat, he insisted on hearing the tape of his narrative right away. Netzer and Moshe both suggested he wait until the morning, but when he persisted with his demand, Netzer ran the reel back to the beginning of the surgery sequence and Paul listened wordlessly, gripping the arms of his chair for support.

"So it is true," he said when the recorder automatically shut itself off.

"Yes," Netzer replied. "You and Amanda and Nathaniel Kagan and Abraham Radner and perhaps a few others are each carrying in your skulls a piece of Albert Einstein's brain!"

"I thought something like this might be tried," Yakov Perlman said. "But that it actually worked . . . who could have imagined such a thing?"

"I . . . I just have no response," Paul began. "I'm just numb. You haven't said anything to Amanda yet, have you?"

"No," Moshe said.

"Don't. I have to figure out a way to tell her myself. But good God, how do you explain a living dream . . . a living nightmare, in anything approaching rational terms?"

The four men sat silently for many minutes, each looking at the floor and turned inward on their own thoughts.

"You know," Paul said at last, "in the past few weeks I've faced things I never even considered before. People try to kidnap me and kill me, my lab blows up as a result of a new kind of energy release that I've discovered, I kill a man in cold blood while lying in bed. But none of that is in any way as terrifying as what I've just heard on that tape and found out about myself."

Now, finally, he understood the significance of the image that had plagued him for twenty years. He understood why he had empathized with those cadavers in the anatomy lab, why he had envied them the deference Professor Hardy always displayed. Months after their deaths, those corpses had been accorded a consideration he and the others had been denied in their living primes.

And who was there to lead the class in a moment of silence for the souls of the people they used to be? No one, because those souls could no longer be clearly discerned. They were bound up in the mutant transmigration of scientific adventurism.

"Any student misusing an anatomical specimen, treating it with disrespect, or removing it from the lab . . . will be dismissed from the course." That was rule number 4 on Professor Hardy's list.

"You know your responsibility and obligation. There will be no exceptions or warnings." And that was rule number 5.

His mind reeled with the other image, the slice of Negro head in the glass case, on display for all the curious. And then it came to him—his feeling of agitation, his racing heartbeat every time he went through the lobby. He and that head had something in common, it turned out. They had something rather important in common, it turned out. Both were on neurological display, undignified, against their will, and ultimately, not even being aware of it! There were differences, too, of course. The slice of head was dead. And it was there for the benefit of anyone who cared to look. Paul was still alive, and he was there for the personal vocational amusement of Norbert Ramsey, M.D.

So who the hell was he? That seemed to be the operative question at the moment. Dropping out of medical school to go into physics, marrying another physicist with whom he never got along, pursuing the Unified Field Theory, enjoying chamber music . . . it was all part of the package. All preordained. So Albert Einstein was not dead after all. But was Paul Garrett?

His head throbbed intensely and he knew it wasn't

from the rigors of the hypnotic session. It was the revelation that session only confirmed. It was the knowledge that he, Paul Garrett, Ph.D., Distinguished Professor of Physics at the Massachusetts Institute of Technology, potential Nobel laureate, was the greatest medical guinea pig in the history of science. He, who had spent his professional life questing after knowledge and physical truth, did not even possess the knowledge of his own being, so everything he thought he had come up with had to be called into question. Nothing was sure anymore.

"Whoever undertakes to set himself up as a judge in the field of truth and knowledge is shipwrecked by the laughter of the gods."

The phrase came to him from somewhere outside, just as similar phrases had been coming for so long. But now he knew where it was from. That was Einstein talking to him. Or rather, that was Einstein remembering something he'd said long ago.

How could anyone do this to him? When Barnard first started doing his heart transplants some of the patients worried that they'd become different people, that their emotional centers would be altered. And the heart is no more than a fancy pump, for God's sake. But what are you, if not your brain? And now Paul had to backtrack over twenty years of life and growth and try to figure out what it all meant.

Nat was in the next room. Through the glass panel in the door Paul could see him switching off the tape recorder that had replayed his own hypnotic session. The room was soundproofed, so he couldn't tell what Nat was saying to the other psychologist, but he looked like a man who had just confronted death. He looked so terribly old and frail. God knew he had a reason. This was a man whose profession it was to give solace to others in time of crisis. What possible solace could now be offered to him?

Paul found Amanda out in the garden. The sun was just setting behind the silhouetted palm trees and she was staring off blankly into the gloaming distance, seated cross-legged on a marble bench. He sat down next to her. She turned her head toward him but offered no greeting.

"The hypnosis was the capper. Both mine and Nat's. It confirmed everything."

"I knew it would. Once we saw the photograph that looked so much like the knoll in Central Park, it all came clear." She bent her head down and clasped her hands around her dirty bare feet. "Oh Paul . . ." she said mournfully, "how do I know who I am anymore? How do I know what is me and what is . . . him? I feel as if someone is spying on me from the inside." Her tone was quiet, sullen. There were no tears, although her upper cheeks were blackened from previously running eye makeup. She was past the point of hysteria, a point all the more terrifying for its misplaced peacefulness.

"Didn't you sometimes suspect something like this?" Paul asked. "With all the evidence you uncovered, you must have. I must have."

She shrugged weakly. "I never had to face it as a reality." She raised her shoulders in a gesture of helplessness and desolation. "I feel so . . . so violated. Maybe I should be feeling grateful. After all, it's not just any brain we're sharing our heads with. We've been given a unique gift, I suppose. But then no matter how many times I go over it, I keep feeling that so much more has been taken away from me than I can ever get back. Paul, my *self* has been taken away from me. Albert Einstein's already had his 'selfhood.' Amanda West never intruded on that. How could she? And now I find out that I never had a chance with mine. Everything I am, everything I've ever been since I came out of the operating room—is it me . . . or him? Or does the independent 'idea' of Amanda mean anything anymore?"

He wanted to put his arms around her and pull her over close to him, to shelter her from the terror of her own mind. But something restrained him. Perhaps it was the utter equality of his own terror.

"Well," she said, just as quietly, "I guess this explains our strange affection for each other, right from the beginning, right from the party at Shorecliffe."

"What do you mean?"

"Just like Einstein, neither one of us could develop a deep and satisfying relationship with a member of the opposite sex. They say Einstein never could because he was so absorbed in his own intellect and emotions that there wasn't room for anyone else. And we must have inherited that trait from him along with all the others we each got. But when we met *each other,* it was like my intellect and emotions fell in love with *themselves,* and so this Einsteinian self-absorption was merely transferred to another part of the same entity. Which also explains all of our supposedly 'chance' meetings. They weren't chance at all. I met you at the concert, I met Nat in the park because each of our brains were working on the same 'cerebral clock.' The same as the body's biological clock."

"You've been thinking a lot about this."

She smiled sadly at the naivete of the observation. "I've been thinking about nothing else. I wonder if I'll ever think of anything else again."

He brushed the yellow hair away from her forehead, revealing the scar that ran diagonally along her left temple. He moved his head over, placing his hand behind her head, and delicately brushed his lips along the scar's length. "You can say what you want about the reasons we were first attracted to each other," he whispered. "But I still have enough of a grasp on my psyche to know that it's you, Amanda West, that I love. And that 'I' is Paul Garrett. Einstein's brain might have influenced the course of our lives, it might even have saved our lives. But it's only an influence. We remain individuals and we still have a free will."

"*A* free will?" she questioned.

"Two free wills," he corrected himself. "Amanda,

we're two different, distinct people. We're both interested in science, perhaps extraordinarily gifted in science, and now we know why. But remember how different our outlooks were—how detached I was and how polemic and utilitarian you were, and how we've both influenced each other. That's two people each affecting the other," he emphasized.

"Or one brain in conflict with itself."

"No! We're not going to think that way! We can't. If we have nothing else, we have our love, which is stronger and more powerful than any sensation either of us has ever had. And we have more than that. We have our work, which is as important as anything Einstein himself did." He spoke forcefully, almost commandingly, struggling not only to get through to her, but also to dissuade himself from the identical black thoughts he had just been thinking before he came out to her. He held her firmly by both shoulders and lifted up her chin with his hand so that she looked him squarely in the eyes. "Amanda, we'll go on because that's all we can do. Maybe it's too pretentious to think that as scientists we'll ever find truth, but if we keep at it perhaps we will find meaning. So we have to go on. The only alternative is to lay down and die, and that would be meaningless."

"You didn't realize how accurate you were being when you said that we'd be playing out our destinies. Well . . . we're certainly doing that now." She reached around him and brought her hands up behind his shoulders and pulled him over so that his chest pressed against her breasts. "Paul . . . please . . . don't ever leave me!" She laid her chin down on his collarbone and began weeping, as bitterly and pathetically as he had ever seen her. "Don't ever leave me!" she continued sobbing.

He stroked the back of her head and rocked her gently back and forth, but didn't try to reason with her any further or stop her crying. What comfort can you give to a person facing what no one in history has ever faced before, and sharing it with no one else in the world . . . other than you?

By the time Moshe Baruch came out to the garden to look for them, Amanda was quiet again. But neither one had moved from the marble bench, nor showed any signs of ever wanting to move again, as far as Moshe could tell.

"I . . . uh . . . you didn't come in for dinner," he said. "We got a little worried about you."

Paul nodded his head appreciatively. "It's okay. We just had to be alone for a while."

"Of course. Do you want me to leave you again?"

"No, that's all right," Amanda told him. "I guess it's time we learned to face the world again."

"There's no need to face it all at once. You'll take some time off, relax . . ."

"No," she interrupted. "We're going straight forward." Paul looked up at her in surprise. "We're going to make the conference in London. It's the only thing we can still be sure of in our lives. I need to have something tangible to hold on to." She offered a brave smile. "We might as well play to our strengths."

"Moshe," Paul asked. "In his phone call, David mentioned ARTICHOKE. Do you have any idea what that means?"

"I've had our people find out. It was the code name for the CIA's Office of Security mind-control and research program in the nineteen fifties. That was the new age of science and technology back then, and the Agency was fascinated with all the possibilities and how they might apply to them. I'm sure you've heard about the drug programs, and how people died or went insane after being given LSD without knowing it. But they were also involved in hypnosis, mental reprogramming to try to make people into 'robot' assassins, and research into extracting information from the brains of dead people. It's all documented. That last program must have been the one that sponsored Dr. Ramsey's research after he legitimately came into possession of Einstein's brain. The people who gave it to him must have figured he'd study it under a microscope and come up with some acceptable and predictable findings. But it would have been only possible with the backing of something like the Agency to do what he really wanted to, and develop his work to the fullest extent. It all fits together, and now I understand why George Henderson—who said he was from the FBI rather than the Agency—wanted to question you three after the bombing of Nathan's car in New York. As far as Nathan and Amanda's connection, once the Agency realized they were on the trail of the truth, all Henderson wanted was to shut them up . . . permanently. I'm sure that accounts for the bombing—which was carefully made to look like the work of an Arab terrorist group—and probably the dog attack in Greenacre Park. As for you, Paul, I suspect their motives were a little more confused. They certainly wanted to avoid having you discover the secret of your own brain, at all costs. That kind of revelation would be incredibly damaging in light of what has already come out about ARTI-CHOKE. It might compromise public perception of the Agency to a fatal degree. But apparently, they also realized you were on to an incredible scientific potentiality, which they wanted to see through, but under their own control."

"But how do we stop them?" asked Amanda. "Is there anything we can do?"

"I'm a strong believer in the effectiveness of shock value. I think it might be time to give them a simple and direct message."

New York

On mornings when he was scheduled for surgery, Norbert Ramsey went directly to his small, private locker room instead of stopping first at his office. The few minutes he sat there, thinking about the procedure ahead before changing into his greens, were often the only moments of solitude he could achieve during the day. Because he knew that as soon as he left the cubicle and headed down the hall for the elevator to the surgical suite, patients, fellow doctors, interns, residents, medical students, administrators, fundraisers, worried family members, and plain curiosity-seekers would all begin tearing at him, clamoring for a small, uncontested parcel of attention. And it would not stop until he left the hospital for the day, fourteen hours later.

And so it never occurred to him to expect a visitor in his metal-cabinet-lined sanctum, waiting to see him. It wasn't until he had removed his tie and bent over with his foot up on the bench to take off his shoe that he noticed the figure. He jumped backward with a gasp of surprise and stammered, "What the . . . What are you doing here?" His eyes finally focused on the intruder and he recognized Paul Garrett.

"Paul! What the hell are you trying to pull off? How did you get in here?"

"That's not really relevant at the moment, Dr. Ramsey. We have some other issues to discuss which are."

"Look, I don't know what's going on, but I don't think you do, either. Get out of here. Believe me, you should."

"You can forget about all that," Paul said calmly. "I know the whole story now."

"I haven't any idea what you're talking about. I've got to get to the operating room. If you want to talk to me after I finish up, go tell my secretary to make you an appointment for this afternoon." He went demonstratively back to untieing his shoes, but Paul slid over on the bench to block his reach.

"This won't take long . . . but it can't wait."

"Paul, you must realize by now there are people after you. Go away while you still have the chance. Trust me on that. That's all I can tell you."

"You don't have to tell me any more. I know the rest."

"I'm still not following you. Why did you break in here like this?" It was the same tone of intimidation Paul had seen him use on nurses and interns and, when necessary, patients. But now, finally, Paul was beyond its effect.

"Why am I here?" he repeated. "Primarily to tell you to tell your Agency buddies to lay off Amanda and me if they don't want their secret screaming across the front page of the *New York Times* and about ten or twenty other leading newspapers and magazines around the world."

"What in the name of God . . . ?"

"Dr. Ramsey, let's stop wasting each other's time with this senseless parrying. We know about the transplant, we know about ARTICHOKE, we know about George Henderson, we know about the whole thing."

Ramsey had turned ashen. His eyes were wide with amazement. He opened his mouth to speak, but said nothing.

"We figured that through you would be the best way to get the word back to the powers that be. Just tell them we know everything, and so do other people who are ready to tell it all if we're harmed or harrassed further in any way. That's it. I won't take up any more of your time."

He slid back away from Ramsey, then stood up and headed for the door. He put his hand on the knob, then paused, turned back around and said, "Just one more thing. This wasn't on my original agenda this morning, but I doubt I'll ever get the opportunity to ask again." Deep down, Paul had to admit to himself this final flourish was purely sadistic on his part. He relished the thought of seeing Norbert Ramsey, the cold, efficient, arrogant perfectionist, backed against the ropes, confronted by the hideous truth of what he'd done, trembling, perhaps wailing and begging for absolution of his sins. He had to know the destruction of his professional reputation was as simple as the twitch of an eyelash. Yes, Paul said to himself, for once I can take pleasure at twisting the knife.

His eyes were just as accusing as his voice as he shouted out, "How could you do this?"

"How could I *not* do it?" Ramsey shot back, and Paul blinked in stunned surprise, totally unprepared for the aggressiveness and lack of contrition. "I was in an incredible position, a position other people don't dare dream of. I had the greatest brain of the last three hundred years, and through my animal experiments, I'd discovered a way to keep it alive! Other researchers had done it with other organ tissue, but never with a brain, at least not for more than a few hours. I kept it alive for four years while I worked out my experiment! Four years! I had that brain and a chance to preserve it and keep it functioning, at least for a while."

He paused and breathed in slowly and fully, as if he would take all the air in the room. "I had that brain," he repeated. "And now you have it!"

"But this is the work of a Frankenstein," Paul countered. "How could you be so cavalier about playing with our very souls?"

"There was nothing cavalier about it. You were a dead man, Paul. You must have realized that. How many people back then recovered from a grade four oligodendroglioma, or a medullo blastoma, or glioblastoma multiforme? Even the celebrated Norbert Ramsey didn't save them. But I saved you, and I saved Amanda, and I saved Kagan. It was a long shot, but I knew there was a chance my theory of 'invasive tissue dominance' would work, and in your three cases, it did. No other surgeon could have pulled it off."

"Are you claiming you stuck a piece of Einstein's brain in our skulls on the off chance it would turn our cancers around?" Paul said derisively.

"Of course not," Ramsey admitted without hesitation. "This was a unique opportunity in the history of science. For the first time we could begin to uncover the secrets of the mind; to map the physical correlatives of thought; to see what is anchored to the tissue itself. Any scientist would have attempted it if he could. It was too important not to try. And it had to be done on living human beings—that was the only way. It was I who insisted it be done on patients who were going to die anyway. And that's what all the accumulated wisdom of medicine said was going to happen to you. Your only beef with me, sir, is that you lived."

Paul's eyes narrowed with rage.

"It's easy to be high and mighty now, outraged at how your body was tampered with," Ramsey said. "I wonder what you or Miss West or any other imminently dying person would say if they were offered a chance to stay alive by taking on a part of another person's brain. And in your case, you were led nearer to the greatest discovery in physics since relativity in the bargain. I'm not surprised your sensibilities were offended by the way you were kept in the dark. I'm sorry it had to be that way. There was no alternative. I just wish you could bring yourself to see the total picture."

"I could destroy your career in a minute with this revelation."

Ramsey nodded seriously. "I suppose you could. I hope you won't; not only for my sake but for the sakes of all the people who might have a second chance at life if I get to operate on them. I know you think I'm arrogant, but I'm just objective enough to know that it took a lot of resources to create the competence I now have within my own brain and hands. And there aren't that many people in the world who possess that particular competence."

Paul twisted around and slammed his fist into the metal locker. "For the sake of your work!" he shouted. "Did you stop to consider the consequences of your work? Or was it all a detached, intellectual exercise for you?"

"What makes your work any different from mine, sir? I know what you're doing; what you're trying to do. We're both the same as far as what we might cause to happen to unsuspecting people. Your work just affects more people in the long run, that's all. Maybe Dr. Einstein didn't stop to foresee Hiroshima when he figured out how to transform small bits of matter into enormous quantities of energy. But that mistake's been made once already. And you have even less excuse for making it again than I do."

"Is that the party line your Agency friends gave you? Maybe they even brainwashed you along with all their other ARTICHOKE victims."

"Don't kid yourself, Paul. You're as tied to them as I am. Who do you think endowed your professorial chair at MIT? The Agency! Who do you think's been following your progress more closely than anyone else? The Agency!"

Paul listened to him aghast, thunderstruck, unable to comprehend what he was hearing. He felt his body going limp, then completely numb. Amanda had used the right word; he had been totally violated. From the time he went into the hospital in his early twenties, his whole life had been one giant manipulation. And the most incredible part was that it all could have happened for so long without an ounce of awareness on his part. He felt a raw, burning pain traveling up from his gut to the top of his throat, a wave of nausea came violently over him and he fought with himself against being sick. Everyone had worked hard and diligently for their own venal ends, and no one—not one single person—had stopped to consider . . .

"I would kill you right here with my bare hands if I thought it could change anything, or give me an ounce of peace," he erupted. "Amanda and Nat may have acquired Einstein's pacifism, but in my case, it was lost in the shuffle." He grabbed Ramsey by the shirt front to emphasize his point and shook him viciously. "Everything's all right with you people as long as it suits your purposes . . . regardless of the consequences." He slammed the surgeon back against the locker. "What's the difference between you and the Nazi doctors who did the experiments in the concentration camps?"

"I won't even dignify that with a response," Ramsey stated, wiping away a thin trickle of blood from his chin. "Though I do deeply regret all the suffering you've evidently gone through since I operated on you. Maybe you're right. Maybe I should have just let you die." His tone had finally changed and Paul struggled to maintain his own sense of outrage.

"What makes you any different from the Agency people?" he demanded. "They must have killed my wife. And you must have known about it!"

"I did know . . . after it happened. Believe me, Paul, had I known what they were going to do, or if there was anything I could have . . . They said she was collaborating with an international espionage organization called the Foundation. They said she was giving away your secrets."

Ramsey shook his head back and forth despairingly. He walked over to where Paul was standing and tried to put a hand on his shoulder, but Paul pulled away resentfully. "God, I wish this was a different type of world. But it isn't, and we have to take it the way it is. You try to learn the unlearnable; I try to cure the incurable, and we both know our efforts are weak and insignificant against any objective standard. People get sick and die and other people are used and betrayed and the vast majority of people everywhere are nothing but innocent, stupid victims. And through it all, in our sublime and tantalizing ignorance, we stumble around looking for ways to make it better, or less painful, or even just more intelligible. The things I've said to you are all true, at least I believe them. And given the opportunity, I might even do it all again, even to the extent of taking the support of the Agency. But whatever torment I've caused you, or Amanda, or Nathaniel Kagan, I apologize for with all my heart. It may not mean much to you at this stage, and I know you can say it of Dr. Frankenstein just as easily as of Alexander Fleming and Jonas Salk, but my instincts were good and right. Whatever I can do to make amends, I certainly will do. Though at this late date, I don't suppose there's much."

"No," Paul answered. "I don't suppose there is." He walked back to the door, opened it, and left.

Ramsey stared for a moment at the space where Paul had just been standing, shook his head sadly once again, and tried to ward off that hollow sensation from the pit of his stomach all the way up to his heart. The eventuality he had thought about and dreaded for more than twenty years had just taken place and nothing, of course, could ever be the same again.

David and Wendell Fuller were both waiting in Wendell's apartment when Paul and Moshe Baruch returned.

"The message has been delivered," the Israeli announced.

"How'd he take it?" Wendell asked Paul.

"I'm not sure. It was almost as if he'd been waiting for me for years to confront him. Everything he said to me, it was as if he'd spent a long time trying to say it to himself first."

"As a scientist, you've got to have some compassion for the guy. The most incredible achievement in the history of neurology, and he had to keep it to himself. That's quite a burden for a man of science to bear."

"There are bigger burdens," David pointed out.

"Of course," Wendell said regretfully.

"I'm sorry to have to cut this short," Moshe stated. "But we'd better be getting to the airport. It's important that we get out of the country as fast as we got in."

Paul nodded and rose, and he and David approached

each other solemnly, throwing their arms around each other in an emotional embrace.

"Take care of yourself," David said with a sigh. "We'll all be thinking of you and praying for you both."

"Thanks. Thanks for everything. You're a true friend; perhaps my only one. We'll be back as soon as we can."

"I know."

Then they shook hands firmly and Paul turned to Moshe. "All right, time to get back to work and pursue the talents that God—and Norbert Ramsey—gave us."

Chapter Nineteen

Rehovot

They had all read about stroke or accident victims who, struggling slowly toward recovery, have to refashion all of the basic, everyday responses from scratch, learning as if for the first time the names of familiar people and objects, and reacquainting themselves with such abstract concepts as courage, fear, and happiness. In the wake of their concussive realization of their cerebral legacy, Paul, Amanda and Nat felt a need to relearn, or at least rescrutinize, all of their own basic responses. But as they saw it, the difficulty of their task was intensified by the emotional detritus they still carried with them. They lived with the burden of too much awareness, rather than too little.

Zvi Netzer met with the small group of psychologists and neurologists screened by the Mossad and entrusted with the secret, and presented his own observations made during this early "post-realization" phase. The tendency, he explained, was for them to mistrust all of their normal and traditional reactions, feeling they were tainted by the influence of the foreign brain section acting on their own brains. This often led them to act against their instincts, which had the potential to produce unpredictable and possibly irrational behavior. Accepted psychiatric theory suggested that these were understandable emotional responses. But since this case involved the unprecedented phenomenon of the physical *combining* of two sets of apparently emotion-producing neural tissue, there was no way to say for sure just what the long-term outcome would be. As another member of the group pointed out, it was really more a matter for philosophical than psychiatric speculation at this point.

But there were some definitive healthy signs. Instead of closing themselves off from further insights into Einstein's character, they seemed driven to even greater knowledge.

"I'm the only one of the three of us who is Jewish," Nat said to Netzer. "Why would I have been the one to pick up on Einstein's Zionism? Paul and Amanda feel it now, but I was the only one who carried it with me right from the time of the operation."

"The brain is an incredibly elastic mechanism," Netzer commented. "And it is quite possible that even a transplanted section adapts to dominant and pre-existing influences. A 'Jewish mind' would be more likely, I would think, to pick up on the Zionist tendencies of the new section, whereas someone like Paul, already interested in medicine, picked up on the science. And you and Amanda both picked up on the *attitude* toward science."

Then there were other indications Netzer noticed. The work with Perlman in the laboratory grew even more intense and the old man prodded them continually.

"Time is short," he said. "I have little energy left in me, I can feel it, and you will be leaving for London in a few days. We have much work yet to do."

"Yes," Paul agreed. This immersion in the intellectual abstraction of work had become a welcome deliverance from the lurking anxieties that continued to hover near the surface of his consciousness. "Ever since the explosion in my lab at MIT, I've been trying to figure out why the destruction all took place from a height of two feet up, and everything below that, including us, was undamaged."

"Well," Perlman said in the manner of the old teacher he was, "what are the possibilities?" He had come to think of Paul as his beloved pupil—certainly with his age and infirmities, his last pupil—but one who had so far transcended the teacher that it was a constant mental effort to keep up.

"I had a ring of ferro-silico alloy magnets set up six feet out from the center of the experiment, two feet off the ground to create a secondary field. And I had them supercooled with a liquid nitrogen core, trying to create the magnetic equivalent of the Josephson Effect of superconductivity."

"Yes, well there is your answer, then."

"But it couldn't be," Paul protested. "The secondary magnetic field was controlled by a different set of capacitors, which weren't even turned on at the time! And yet all of my calculations since then indicate that the field must have been activated, but so much stronger than I could have predicted it even if the power was on."

"Keep in mind what you're working on—the unity of energy fields. The explosion itself provided the energy, which the magnetic field absorbed to enhance itself, and therefore actually directed the explosion's energy release away from itself; that is, above the two-foot level."

"Yes! I'm such an idiot!" Paul shouted. Amanda looked at him with amusement. "Of course! The power came from the energy release itself and therefore created a superstrong magnetic field. It only lasted for the split second of the explosion itself, but it was tremendously more powerful than the one I'd arranged, powered by the capacitors. Why didn't I see that myself?"

"Reasoning is a dialectical process. At Princeton, I often saw Dr. Einstein elicit the most brilliant responses from other physicists simply by asking the obvious questions. That is all a good teacher can hope to do."

"If that magnetic field could withstand that much force, it seems to me that's got to represent a practical application," Nat said.

"Yes, it does," Paul triumphantly agreed. "Think of a garden hose. The water just runs out the end wherever it wants to go. But with a nozzle, you can direct the spray. That's what this field could do for us. If we can duplicate and control the field we created with those magnets and that explosion, we can direct that much force wherever we want it, such as under a car that doesn't need wheels or gasoline to move, or under a house, for that matter. We're talking about so much potential power, the size of the object is practically irrelevant! It's like a magnetic valve that controls and directs the repellant force just where and when we want it."

"That's just what we need to go to London with," Amanda said. "You not only set forth the theory, but can document the practical workability of a key component."

"Exactly. Even though we haven't yet defined the specific nature of the unity of fields, we've at least pointed to its existence and brought out the first practical demonstration." He grabbed her around the waist and lifted her off the floor. "Honey, this is history! This is what every scientist dreams of!" She giggled like a little girl on a merry-go-round as he boosted her euphorically up toward the ceiling. "You'll have to get a new dress for Stockholm!"

"Put me down!" she said playfully. "We're going to London. When would we go to Stockholm?"

He let her touch the floor again. "When they give out the Nobel Prize in Physics!"

"Well, well. Aren't we getting a swelled head," she came back, tapping him on the nose with her fingertip.

"It's understandable," he retorted. "That head contains more than the average amount of brains."

She looked at him quizzically for a second as the conversation appeared to miss a beat. She started to say something, bit her lower lip, then she and Nat and Paul all burst out laughing, a laugh that built of its own momentum. Through his twisted, quivering mouth, Yakov Perlman began to laugh as well. It wasn't much of a joke, but it was the first time they had been able to react with any humor to their situation, and he was gratified. This laughter represented an exultation, a release, he thought, from the demons of their own minds and their own pasts. Now, please God, they might be able to go forward with their lives with a sense of renewal. He had been hoping for a moment like this.

"Now you must spend the rest of the day working out the equations that support your super field," he said, trying to shift into the role of the stern teacher.

"Right away," Paul said. "Yakov—how can I ever repay you for everything? How can I possibly express my gratitude?"

And now Perlman could say what he had wanted to say all along, but did not dare until the milestone of the previous moment. "It is I who am being allowed to repay, my friend. What I have tried to do for you since you came here is little compared to what Dr. Einstein did for me. I thank God for this opportunity to give some of it back to him."

Paul's eyes glistened and Amanda let the sentiment hang in the air for a time before speaking.

"You three may be stuck here working all afternoon," she said. "But Ariel and I are going to the beach this afternoon to soak up the glorious Mediterranean sun."

He thought back to the last time he had seen her in a bikini. It had been just three small dark blue triangles, and she looked sensational. "You be careful, now," he warned.

"Don't worry. Ariel is very handy with a Beretta, and there'll be other people with us, anyway."

"That's not what I meant," he smiled. "Ariel's very dark and you're very fair. Make sure you don't get sunburned."

She lowered her chin, clasped her hands together backward and stood with her knees knocking—all very little-girl-like. "I'll try to remember," she promised with mock seriousness. He nodded sagely and planted a kiss on her forehead and slapped her behind. Perlman watched the scene with continued satisfaction. A few days before, such lightness and frivolity would have been unthinkable. Yes, he believed, they were adapting to awareness. Perhaps the psychologists were correct. Perhaps the human mind is resilient enough even to accept an altered perception of itself.

And so the only cloud that shadowed the mood was what he was about to tell them. But now, he knew, it had better not wait any longer.

"Nat, in the bottom drawer of the filing cabinet you will find a bottle of schnapps and some glasses. It's awkward proposing a toast and not being able to manage the pouring, but you'll have to do it for me."

Nat went over to the cabinet, took out the bottle and poured four glasses. He handed one to Amanda and another to Paul and held another ready near Perlman's mouth.

"Very soon you will be going to London. I am afraid that before you could return to Israel, I will no longer be living. It is a very short time that remains to me, I know. At my age, in my condition, I have no regrets about dying except one: that I will not see the culmination of your inspired work."

Amanda tried to interrupt and redirect his solemn words, but he lifted his one somewhat usable hand far enough to keep her quiet.

"My consolation, though, is these days I have been able to spend with you three, and you have become for me old friends, just like Professor Einstein was my friend. And like him, I also believe that I am so much a part of all life that my individual passing will mean little in this unending stream. I just wanted to say this to you all while I still had the chance, and to share with you what will likely be our final drink together."

He motioned Nat to bring the glass up to his lips and to raise his own glass.

"*L'chaim!*" he shouted.

New York

He had directed so much of his effort over the years toward challenging the inevitable that Norbert Ramsey had failed to recognize it in his own life. Once the decision had been made to actually *use* the brain in a living, vital way instead of just carving it up and sticking it under the microscopes of a dozen leading neuropathologists, everything that happened afterward had been preordained, out of control.

His confrontation with Paul Garrett had been reverberating through his mind since that morning, never completely leaving. How simple and clear-cut the whole thing had seemed when he had first met Garrett —a twenty-two-year-old med student without a snowball's chance in hell of recovery. Events had made him both a victim and a beneficiary. Events, Ramsey kept telling himself, not just his own decision. Everything had come together, as if fate had willed it. Einstein had died, directing that his brain be removed and studied just at the point when Ramsey had had his breakthrough keeping alive whole gorilla and chimp brains. Serious research was just getting started on the physical location and mechanisms of mind, and the Agency was well underway with their own mind function experiments. How could a dedicated scientist have all those conditions come together and not take advantage of them?

And in retrospect, at least on a scientific level, he had been successful. Not only had he been able to avert three medical death sentences, he'd also come up with critical evidence on the mind-brain dichotomy. He hadn't been able to publish it, for obvious reasons, but someday it would come out. Someday, after all the individual participants in the program were gone, his research would emerge, and the next generation of surgeons and neurologists would be able to take off from a new plateau of understanding. And nothing could be more important. The brain is, after all, the *sine qua non* of human existence. Without it, there is nothing else. Besides it, nothing else matters.

But his human culpability was just as clear, Ramsey had to admit to himself. Had his theory of invasive tissue dominance not worked and the three subjects simply died after a matter of weeks or months, the moral issue, while not resolved, would have been moot. But his theory had worked, everything had worked out far better than he could have possibly hoped. And so he had to face the consequences of his own success.

It was 3:30 AM and he had been behind the locked door of his office since 8:00 the night before. His wife was out of town as it turned out, but that would not have been a problem anyway. Like many of the top surgeons he knew, they had an "arrangement." He had gone through his locked file cabinet, organizing all of the important material, some of which he hadn't even looked at in fifteen years. Now he had to put it in a logical, rational order that would be comprehensible to someone reading it cold.

Once he finished the organization, he set up his Dictaphone machine and began recording his recollections, articulating as carefully as he could the motivations that led him to risk transcending the established frontiers of ethics. He finished by saying, "It is my hope that someday the liberties I have taken in the cause of science can be, if not forgiven, then at least understood, and the contributions I have tried to make to the field of neurological research can be of benefit and . . ."

High-sounding and eloquent phrases came into his mind, but he dismissed them. Neither philosophy nor lofty rhetoric had ever been his forte, and he saw no reason to start with either one at this point. Instead, he played back the last several paragraphs and, convinced that he had said what he wanted to, switched off the machine.

He then tied a rubber tourniquet around his right arm above the elbow, made a fist, and picked up from his desk a syringe filled with a potassium-cyanide solution he had prepared earlier in the evening.

Chicago

J. Tyler Kendrick held in his hand the program for the World Congress of Physics convention and waited for John Christopher to read the appropriate entry.

"And if you read between the lines or listen to any of the gossip that's been filtering out, he's not only going to explain how the first half of his Unified Field Theory fits together but also describe a way to repulse matter through electromagnetism."

"Just what your demonstration in Zurich showed," Christopher said.

"The beginning of it, at least. But the point is, once this gets out, who knows how many people are going to take hold of it. It might be only a few years before we start seeing the first products and inventions coming out of it."

"If I were Garrett, I think I'd keep the whole thing to myself until I was finished instead of cutting anyone else in on it, much less the whole scientific establishment."

"Evidently, Dr. Garrett is not motivated by the same forces that govern the behavior and judgment of normal people," Kendrick noted derisively. "But be that as it may, once Garrett gives his dog and pony show in London, we might as well forget about it. It'll be out of our hands and we'll just have to sit back and wait for the other shoe to drop. I don't like being in that position."

"Yes, I know," said Christopher with a faint smile. "But I don't understand what went wrong with the Agency. I thought that after you met with George Henderson, they were supposed to keep their hand in and keep Garrett under wraps."

"I thought so, too. But perhaps they discovered that we weren't exactly living up to the letter of the agreement, either. They must have tied the kidnapping attempt at MIT back to us." He shook his head with disgust. "I never have trusted those Arab commando teams. I don't know why I decided to use them. At any rate, for some reason now the Agency's spooked, if you'll pardon the pun, and I can't figure out why. Garrett's got some kind of leverage over them and they've essentially dropped out of the case. I have that on very good authority."

"So do we follow suit?"

"Not yet. Not while there's still a chance. Until Garrett actually gives his speech and publishes his results, we've still got a chance to neutralize him. Which is just what we're going to try to do."

"But how?" Christopher asked, wondering if Kendrick was now so obsessed with the project and had so much of his ego on the line that he'd finally lost touch with his own limitations.

"I'm not taking a chance on Arab commandos or anyone else this time. I'm taking personal charge of this operation myself."

"What do you mean?"

"I'm flying out to London tonight."

New York

George Henderson was still at home in McLean, Virginia, when he got the news, but Cooper had been visiting the Manhattan office, so he sent him to Goddard to maintain the situation until he could get there himself.

He arrived at the hospital about mid-morning and by then the administrative areas of the Neurological Research Unit had been cordoned off. Henderson would have preferred to carry through the procedure outside of normal business hours, but the exposure in waiting until the end of the day was too great. And besides, when a body is removed, people start talking anyway. Thankfully, the cops had had the presence of mind not to let anyone near it until the hospital's own coroner arrived. With any luck and a bit of leverage, they could probably push through heart attack as cause of death, and that would simplify everything.

When Henderson got there, Cooper and his men already had a handcart waiting, stacked with locking canvas bags.

"All right," the Chief announced, "we have to go through every page of every file. Here's a list of key words and names. Anything bearing them goes into the bags. Anything that's ambiguous or you're not sure about, bring it to me. I want to get out of here as soon as possible, but I'm more concerned with thoroughness than speed."

He walked slowly and observantly around the room, went over to the desk, opened the Dictaphone and put the belt in his coat pocket. "I also want you to check the hospital mail room," he said to one of the agents. "Make sure there's nothing going out with Ramsey's name on it. If there is, bring it back here."

"Do you think he was telling the truth about Garrett

coming to see him with the message to get off his back?" Cooper asked.

"It doesn't matter whether he was or he wasn't," Henderson replied. "Either way, *he* was giving us a message. And either way, if we want to keep this thing under wraps, we've got to go along with it. We can take care of everything here, but between Ramsey and Garrett, who knows who else has the information by now."

He gazed down at the empty syringe on the desk, its needle now bent at an odd angle. "If everyone else would be as considerate as the late Norbert Ramsey, we wouldn't have a problem."

Chapter Twenty

London

Nigel Dunninger was met in the lobby of the Dorchester Hotel by a man he had never seen who seemed to recognize him instantly. The man said nothing to him until he was no more than six inches away, then in a clipped accent as properly British as Dunninger's, he asked, "Mr. Dunninger?"

"That's right."

"Come with me, please."

They walked across the green and gold lobby, its patterned marble floors partially covered with venerable oriental rugs, and headed down the elegant, bay-windowed arcade to an unmarked door. On the other side Dunninger was frisked, his umbrella was examined, and then they proceeded up a service stairwell three flights and out into a blue and white Regency-period hallway meticulously decorated like fine Wedgwood.

The man knocked at the door at the end of the hall, which was opened by a similarly dressed man with a virtually identical accent. Dunninger could tell at once that both speaking styles were acquired rather than natural, but they were so carefully practiced that it was impossible to tell where the two men came from originally. Obviously, this was the intended effect.

The man who had met Dunninger in the lobby stayed in the sitting room of the comfortable pastel suite, while the other one showed him through another door to a second sitting room. In contrast to the hallway, these rooms were furnished in the delicate, gently curving Queen Anne style. Dunninger had always enjoyed that aspect of the Dorchester. So many pleasing styles were combined in such a tasteful, harmonious fashion, just as the diversity of the interesting, influential guests combined into a recognizable, yet distinctive single entity. Just before he sat down he handed his umbrella and bowler to the gentleman attending him, then waited patiently on the deeply upholstered lounge.

Less than a minute later Paul Garrett and Nathaniel Kagan came through the far set of carved double doors to greet him.

"Dr. Dunninger, it's a pleasure to finally meet you," Paul said. "I've read about your work for years."

"The pleasure is mine, I assure you. I've been looking forward to this honor for quite some time. Though I confess, I almost despaired of ever reaching you here. When I contacted the convention headquarters they told me to call a Mr. Moses, for whom I had to leave a message and be rung back. He then had me go to . . . well, I won't bore you with the details. Had I known you were staying at the Dorchester, it might have made the whole thing a bit easier from the beginning."

"I'm sorry for the confusion. We're not actually staying here," Paul explained. "For security reasons, they're having us move around."

" 'They' being the World Congress of Physics?"

"Ah, no. 'They' being our, uh, current sponsors."

"I see," said Dunninger soberly. He knit his eyebrows, pursed his lips and displayed that hesitant expression typical of refined Britishers uncomfortable about bringing up an awkward subject. He placed his hands on his knees and rocked slightly forward, his back still rigidly straight. "Well, then. I suppose there's no profit in beating about the bush."

"The Foundation?" Paul asked quietly.

Dunninger looked slightly stunned. "You know of us?"

"Not much," Paul confessed. "It was mentioned by

one of my adversaries . . . in connection with the death of my wife."

"A horrible tragedy," the Englishman confessed.

"But there is also something in the back of my mind . . . something I can't put my finger on. Well, whatever it is, please go on with your explanation."

Dunninger rose to his feet, as if he could command greater attention that way. "The Foundation was formed in 1946 by the great German chemist, Heinrich Luddendorff, who as you may remember came up with a number of tremendously important industrial formulas during the nineteen twenties and thirties, which earned him a sizable fortune in royalties. Though highly nationalistic and dedicated to his country, he was sickened and appalled by the Nazi rise to power, and though Hitler honored him repeatedly, he had nothing but contempt and loathing for the man he always referred to as "the Austrian housepainter.' But like so many other top German scientists, he was forced to place his skills and talents at the disposal of the Third Reich, and came to regret his discoveries that benefitted the despotic regime.

"So thoroughly shaken was he by the Nazi years that after the war he set up a secret society to which he invited many of the other great scientists of the world, regardless of their nationality. The only criterion was that they share his views on the role of science in the world order, which he said were best expressed in a letter Albert Einstein wrote to his colleague Paul Ehrenfest in 1915: 'A small group of scholars and intellectuals must form the only fatherland which is worthy of serious concern to people like ourselves.' "

At the mention of Einstein's name, Paul and Nat jolted to attention.

"Luddendorff called this society simply, the Foundation. And it has sought to do in an organized fashion what scientists have independently attempted for centuries—to keep important breakthroughs out of politics and venal nationalistic considerations and to allow scientists, rather than politicians, to control their own works and destinies. This was the concept. On a practical level, the Foundation sought to stay in the forefront of scientific research for its own sake, to encourage and nurture that work, and to *control* and *release* that research whenever and in whatever country it felt was most beneficial and least threatening. For example, a new and highly efficient water desalination system has been placed in the hands of scientists in the Central African nations and will be publicly revealed in the near future.

"Dr. Garrett, we've followed your work for many years. We want you to join us. All of your expenses and financial needs will be taken care of in any manner you wish. Money will not be one of your concerns. You may live wherever you want, and do whatever you wish."

"And what do I have to do in return?"

"Withdraw your presentation from the convention. Reveal your further progress to no one until the Unified Field Theory is completed, then meet with the Foundation's board to discuss the best channels for this most important of all modern breakthroughs."

"And then who benefits from the outcome, assuming it's successful?" Nat asked.

"The world benefits!"

"According to your interpretation."

"According to the proper interpretation of scientists, not politicians."

"Dr. Dunninger, we've been used, betrayed and threatened by people we never knew existed in these last few months," Paul said. "Why should we trust you or believe in what you tell us?"

"Because people *you* trusted believed in us and cooperated with us."

"Who are you talking about?"

"Harry Gillette for one. And your wife, for another."

"Please go on," Paul said tensely, his lips tight across his teeth.

"Dr. Gillette had been working with us for several years. He told us about every one of your break throughs. That is how we were able to evaluate your work so carefully. And we know he was someone whose beliefs you trusted implicitly."

"And my wife Julia."

"The same."

"Why did you go to her instead of me directly if you weren't merely trying to spy on me and steal my work?"

"We knew your reputation, Dr. Garrett. We knew the realm of things that concerned you and the realm that did not. We felt Julia would be more receptive to us than you would. We knew at that point you wouldn't even consider the effects or applications of your work. But Julia would."

All the arguments, all the discussions he'd had with Amanda about the responsibility of the scientist, the need to destroy the notion of scientific detachment, came flooding back through Paul's mind. He knew it was the two sides of Einstein's outlook warring with each other, and he could feel a cold sweat begin to bead along his hairline, but he said nothing as Dunninger continued.

"The last time our representative talked to your wife, she said she would consider what we'd said and think about cooperating. She was approached again a weekend you were out of town, at the Eastern Shore of Maryland, I believe. They had a long conversation and she agreed with our goals and said she would try to get you to 'see the light.' She died within a matter of days after that."

"She was killed by the Central Intelligence Agency, who thought she was divulging my 'secrets' to foreign spies."

"I'm appalled, but not surprised. This is exactly the mentality the Foundation is struggling against. Dr. Garrett, the Foundation sets great store in your work, as does just about everyone else by now. But that, in a sense, is just the danger. What you are letting loose on the scientific community has the potential for tremendously expanding the horizons of our knowledge and easing many of our burdens. But at the same time, it is also potentially a Pandora's Box. I implore you to join us, to maintain *your own control* over your work rather than letting events take their own course."

"You mean, letting the Foundation maintain control," Nat said.

"We are not at cross purposes," the Englishman replied.

"What would withholding the information at this point accomplish?"

Dunninger seemed taken aback by the rabbi's question, as if this point was an article of faith amongst them and required no explanation. "Well, to avoid a repeat of the atomic tragedy, for example."

"I'm not sure I follow."

"Once Einstein, Hahn, Meitner and the others had published their theories and let the rest of the world in on their thinking, the applications were out of their hands. Can you imagine how different and better the world might be today if only one thing had happened differently—if only atomic energy had first been developed for peaceful purposes instead of for bombs? If we knew nuclear power as a beneficial, constructive force rather than as the symbol of ultimate destruction?"

"I suspect it would have ended up being used for bombs just the same," Paul commented.

"I doubt it," Dunninger said. "Once they saw and understood its benefits, the people of the world would not have stood for it! And now, you have the same opportunity, if only you'll take advantage of it."

"I appreciate your faith in me and admire your faith in the good feelings of the human race in general. But I question your line of reasoning. The only way a scientist can be certain his work will not be corrupted is not to do it in the first place. And that is only if no one else comes up with a similar concept."

"But we can help. We've been helping all along. By protecting you, by protecting your friend Amanda West in the department store in New York . . ." He told them of the secret connection between the Foundation and the Scientific League, taking pains to assure Paul that they were not out to trick or betray either him or Amanda. Their best interests were always part of the Foundation's thinking.

"I don't disagree with the stated aims and goals of the Foundation. You know that. But I also believe I've learned one lesson, though it's taken me this long to learn it. If I'm going to presume to carry through this research, I must also presume to accept the responsibility myself for what I'm doing, not shift it to the Foundation or anyone else. My purpose here at the convention is to describe my findings about the relationship between gravity and electromagnetism. If there are those who are sufficiently inspired and interested to further what I've already done, they are welcome. Actually, the more who do—in as many ways and in as many places as possible—the safer for all of us."

Dunninger was silent for several moments, then stood and walked over to a hall stand that held his hat and umbrella. "You've taken a tremendous burden upon yourself," he said. "I pray to God you are up to it."

"So do I," said Paul.

The Englishman extended his hand to both of them. "I shall be looking forward to your presentation at the convention, then. Though I still hold out the hope you will reconsider."

"One more thing, if you don't mind," Nat asked. "Has anyone else who's been approached for membership in the Foundation ever turned it down?"

"Only one."

"And who was that?"

"Albert Einstein."

"It's coming back to me," Nat said after Dunninger had left. "The whole Foundation 'memory.' It's true that after Hiroshima and Nagasaki, Einstein felt deeply betrayed. He had been told the bomb would be dropped in some remote area where its deterrent power could be demonstrated without killing innocent victims. And on the heels of this he was approached by Heinrich Luddendorff and the Foundation. But even though he shared their views, he was just as fearful of a massive concentration of power in the hands of brilliant scientists as he was in the hands of ruthless, but basically stupid politicians. He told this to Luddendorff. It was the last time they ever spoke."

Moshe Baruch came through the door and without stopping said, "Let's get back to the house. I don't want you out here any longer than necessary. I didn't even want you to meet with this man."

"I'm not surprised," Paul responded, glancing at his wristwatch. "But I'd like to attend the opening sessions of the convention. We've already missed some of them."

"No," Baruch said flatly. "We agreed it was too much of a risk. There still might be people trying to stop you."

"Isn't it a little late for that?"

"Not if they're desperate enough. You can't appear at the convention until the last afternoon. It would be too easy to spot you there. That's why we're letting Amanda and Nat go in your place. They can certainly tell you everything that happens."

"It's not the same. They're still not scientists."

"I'm sorry, Paul. I'm not even comfortable about letting them go, but I finally agreed because you said you couldn't give your presentation without knowing what the other scientists had said. That's the best I can do."

"Don't worry," Nat consoled. "We won't let you down."

"Just remember," Baruch warned him. "I don't want you going off with any of your anti-nuclear friends. I want you both accounted for at all times."

"See you later!" Nat said, clapping Paul on the shoulder.

"Stay close to your bodyguard," Moshe called after him, then turned back to Paul, who was watching Na leave like a little boy who couldn't follow his playmates to the swimming pool because of the mumps. "Come on," he said, trying to counteract the sulking. "I'll take you to Bloom's. It's a terrific kosher restaurant in the East End. They have wonderful corned beef and even better blintzes. I wish we could get food like that in Israel. You'll love it. . . ."

As much as the science and industrial museums that form its backdrop, The Royal Albert Hall captures the unswerving sense of purpose and faith in self that characterized the Victorian era. Looming hugely across Kensington Gardens and flanked on one side by the Royal College of Art and by the Royal Geographic Society on the other, the round, colonnaded, glass-domed amphitheatre owes its design to ancient Roman forms. But the message it conveyed to nineteenth-century Britishers was one of progress and optimism and pride in technology. As imposing now as it must have been when completed as a memorial to the Queen's late and much-lamented consort in 1871, the hall was a perfect setting for the World Congress of Physics convention. Because more than any other major group, this one continued to conform to the Victorian ideal that life was infinitely perfectable if only the powers of the mind were properly developed.

"Well, did you learn anything?" Ariel asked as she and Amanda made their way through the clutch of humanity disgorging from the building onto Kensington Gore.

"Not much," Amanda admitted. "It all seemed pretty dry to me. I hope it gets better as they go along, or we're in for a long couple of days before Paul gives his presentation."

"You'll have to let me know if it gets better," Ariel said. "I'm sure I won't know for myself."

"I'm not sure I will, either." Amanda smiled. "We're meeting Nat for lunch at a place up on Bayswater Road. Here, we can cut through the park."

They passed by the exhibition hall's companion piece

—thematically, though not architecturally—the Albert Memorial, Giles Gilbert Scott's intricate, spired Gothic vision that houses at its center a fifteen-foot bronze statue of the Prince.

"These people certainly take themselves seriously," Ariel commented.

They continued down Lancaster Walk, the promenade that cuts across the serene and lovely Kensington Gardens. For Amanda, leaving the convention, even for an hour, was welcome relief. She felt as if she'd been set free. She hadn't been to London since the summer after her junior year at Barnard, when she spent two months studying theater and moral philosophy at Trinity College, Oxford. She had to laugh to herself reminiscing about it, gearing up every morning at breakfast to be witty and dramatic for the flamboyant theater instructor, then trying to bring herself down to a serious, introspective level at lunch to face the afternoon of intellectual truth-seeking. She didn't know in retrospect whether she'd found much of that truth she sought, but she had become enchanted with the British Isles that summer, and dreamed of coming back. Somehow, she'd never made it back until now. And London was still the inexhaustible city she remembered.

The Peter Pan statue in the Gardens was one of the most delightful memories of all. Set off in the midst of a seemingly impenetrable glade, near the Long Water where swans floated casually by, the figure of the little boy blowing on his pipes atop a magically landscaped pedestal of rabbits and mice and fairy creatures brought back a special time for her. It was the time before she was nine years old; before the tumor began silently invading her head; before all the light and innocence of her blissful childhood evaporated instantly into the adult world of doctors and hospitals and pain. She wanted to convey all of that to Ariel, whom she had come to love so deeply; with whom, despite the differences in their cultures and intellects, she felt it so easy to share. But when she saw the beautiful, dark-haired young Sabra gazing up at the little boy's twinkling eyes with her own look of wonder and childish delight, she realized it would be wrong to impose her memories. Ariel would conjure up her own.

They finally left the statue and walked along the Long Water toward the Fountains and Marlborough Gate. The Gardens had put Amanda in a wistful mood and she said to Ariel, "I feel I know you so well, but I realize I don't know one of the most important things. What made you decide to join the Mossad?"

"I don't know that I ever really decided to join. It just sort of happened after I got out of the army."

"Well . . . what is it that you like about it?"

She shrugged. "I guess the same things you like about your job. It's interesting, I get to travel, I've met a lot of fascinating people, and I always feel as if I'm alive."

"Doesn't the danger frighten you?"

"Of course. But that's part of what makes me feel alive. I guess the Israelis have a different attitude about it than the Americans or Europeans do. I can't explain it exactly, I'm not that good with words, especially in English. But our existence has always been so tenuous, we don't really think about danger the same way you do." Her tone lightened and she grinned mischievously. "And there's another reason, I guess. I'm very good at what I do."

Amanda wondered what else her job entailed, but thought better of asking her outright.

The weather was so perfect that Amanda was tempted to forget about lunch and remain in the park all afternoon. That would definitely be more stimulating than another round of dry physics discussions. But she'd promised Paul she'd be there, so she had to go back.

"There's the place, the Hawk and Dove," she said when they reached Bayswater Road. Nat and his Mossad guard, Mordechai Bar-Levah, were waiting for them on the corner. Amanda smiled when she saw them.

"How were the presentations you heard?" he asked her.

"Boring. How about yours?"

"I missed most of them because of that meeting with Dunninger," Nat said. "I'll tell you about it at lunch. You'll be interested. They paid your salary."

"How do you mean?"

"They're the secret backers of the Scientific League."

"Hmm. The plot thickens."

"So does the air at the Royal Albert Hall." They both laughed.

A blue Rover 2000 zipped up the street and then slowed down when it reached them. Instinctively, Ariel and Mordechai turned to each other.

"Let's go this way," she said.

"But the restaurant is that way."

"Never mind. Do as she says," Mordechai ordered.

But by then another Rover had come down the road from the opposite direction, slammed on its brakes and two men jumped out and bolted over the parked cars to the sidewalk. Ariel spun around and saw two more men coming from the first car.

"Run!" she yelled to the startled Amanda, and yelled it again to Nat. "You take them," she barked to the other agent. "I'll take these here."

She pulled the Beretta from her handbag and fired off two shots squarely in the faces of the first two men.

Both screamed in agony as the bullets tore directly through their eye sockets and lodged in their brains. Ariel seldom missed her target, especially at close range. The eruption of blood momentarily halted the other two attackers as they saw their companions crumple to the ground.

"Stop," they screamed to Amanda and Nat, who were already running back into the park. They were running mindlessly, merely reacting, their senses numb and their hearts pounding wildly. One of the two men aimed his gun at Nat but Mordechai drew aim on his forehead before he could steady his arm. As he toppled, his own Smith and Wesson .38 flew from his spastic hand.

But as Mordechai jumped around to face the next rank of attackers from a third car, spreading his legs and bracing the gun against his belly, the second man already had his barrel pointed at his chest. He fired three times and the force of the impact knocked the Mossad agent back several yards onto the grass.

Ariel whipped around in the direction of the blast and was able to take out another attacker before the man's companion got her. She doubled over before her knees gave out and as Amanda looked back through the corner of her eye she saw the red stain spreading across the chest of her friend and protectress, now sprawled on the sidewalk.

"Ariel!" she wailed, the horror welling up in her throat. She and Nat both raced back, oblivious to the remaining gunmen.

Amanda bent over her. Ariel's chest was heaving relentlessly. Her eyes were glazed, her pupils dilated, and her tongue hung crookedly at the side of her mouth.

"Oh God!" Amanda screamed. "No!" She tore open Ariel's blouse and pressed her ear against the naked chest. Nothing. Frantically, she picked up a wrist and felt for a pulse. Still nothing. Blood continued to gurgle out of the three small holes above her breasts.

"Amanda! Run!" It was Nat. He was standing above her, with Ariel's Beretta trained on the three hovering attackers. "Get out of here! Back into the park."

She staggered to her feet, unwilling to leave.

"Run! Now!"

She took one step and heard another crack fill the air. She turned. They'd gotten Nat! She rushed back to him.

"Help!" she yelled, scanning the street to see if anyone was there. She had Nat's head cradled in her hands. He had been shot right below the throat. Oh

God, she screamed to herself. Where was the gun? She would get them; get them all. They would kill her, she knew that. But she would get them first.

And then she felt a hand clap over her mouth from behind. Her eyes bulged, she gasped for breath, and then saw a handkerchief slip in between the hand and her nose and mouth. She tried to yell for help again as the fumes from the soft cotton cloth penetrated her nostrils. A few seconds later and everything disappeared.

Chapter Twenty-One

"I can't believe it!" Paul cried, still as paralyzed with anguish as when they came to him with the news more than an hour before. "How could you let this happen?"

"I don't know," Moshe Baruch answered, dazed and grim-faced himself. "You insisted they both go to the convention. I don't even know why they were together. I gave them strict orders . . ."

"How could I do this? How could I be so senseless? You stopped me from going. Why didn't you stop them?"

"You know I tried."

"Why did I need to be there? I knew what I was going to say. How could I do that to them? Nat dead . . . and Amanda . . ."

"I thought the less conspicuous their guard, the better. Evidently I was wrong."

"Yes!" Paul screamed, turning on him. "Evidently you were! What about all your crack Israeli commandos who rush in and save any situation?"

"You know that's meaningless. Any time we let someone outside we run a risk. No matter what we'd done short of surrounding each of them with a small army, something like this could have happened. We just didn't think it would. We thought you would be the only target at this point."

From facing Baruch, Paul turned to look out the window onto the protected inner courtyard. "So what are you going to do now?" he demanded.

"I'm not sure. I have everyone out looking for her,

looking for clues, anything. More agents are already on the way from Israel."

"Oh God!" Paul roared. "Do something! I can't stand this!"

"How do you think I feel?" Baruch snapped back at him. "You're not the only one grieving for a loss!"

Paul bit his lip and the tears welled up in his eyes. "Forgive me, Moshe. Please, please, try to forgive me. For that, and for whatever else I'm bound to say."

Baruch nodded silently.

"What's going to happen now?"

"Well, whoever mounted the attack obviously wanted Amanda alive. And speaking strategically, there's no reason to have her alive except as a means of getting to you. The whole thing is obviously to gain some sort of leverage. We'll just have to wait and see."

"Isn't there anything we can do in the meantime?"

"Nothing that we aren't doing already. Why don't you lie down for a while? Try to get some rest."

"How can I rest now? I'm so keyed up I could walk on the ceiling. The one thing I can't do is sleep."

"I'll have the doctor give you a shot."

"No. I have to be in on every step of this. After all, you said it's me they really want, and you're obviously right."

"Still, Paul, there's nothing you can do. Let me get you the shot."

"I refuse!" he stated. They both remained silent for several minutes. Baruch sat in the lounge chair next to the red telephone and Paul paced around the drawing room of the elegant Belgravia mansion that served as the Mossad's London safe house. After several more minutes Paul asked quietly, "Did you see them . . . after they brought them back?"

Baruch nodded affirmatively, gripped the arms of the chair and tried to choke back his own tears. "Three bullets, right around the heart. I think she must have died right away. Very little suffering. At least I can be thankful for that. And thankful also for the way she died. Like a soldier. Nathan had one bullet, right below the neck. He died quickly, too, I think. Those people were good shots. And Nathan, too, turned out to be a soldier after all. We all hope we can go that way when our time comes, whenever it comes." He repeated, "Whenever it comes."

"I'm so sorry. I'm so horribly sorry. If the first ones had killed me up in Boston, none of this would have happened."

"That's a ridiculous exercise. If Israel had lost the 1948 war, our boys wouldn't have died in the next three wars. But then they also might not have been alive to have a chance to die, if you see what I mean. You know, I often thought about this happening. With the kind of work she and I were both in, you couldn't help thinking about it. But somehow, I could never imagine her actually dying. Maybe she seemed so much full of life, more than anyone else I ever knew. Maybe that's why I loved her." He shook his head sadly.

The door opened and a Mossad agent entered, carrying a buff-colored envelope that looked like a telegram.

"This just arrived for Paul in care of 'Mr. Moses' at the convention," he announced, handing the envelope to Baruch.

"Has it been screened for plastic explosives?" he asked.

"Yes."

Baruch tore it open and scanned grimly down the page.

"What is it?" Paul asked, his heart leaping up into his throat.

The Israeli read:

WE HAVE AMANDA WEST. WE CAN KILL HER AT ANY TIME. IF YOU WISH TO SEE HER ALIVE, WITHDRAW YOUR WORK FROM THE CONVENTION, DESTROY IT, AND SHOW UP ALONE IN THE PARK BEHIND SHELL-MEX HOUSE ON THE STRAND. IF IT EVEN LOOKS AS IF ANYONE HAS ACCOMPANIED

YOU, AMANDA WEST WILL DIE INSTANTLY AND SO
WILL YOU. YOU CAN BE SURE OF THAT. YOU
CANNOT ESCAPE US FOR LONG. THERE IS NO SENSE
RESISTING. IT WILL BE TERRIBLY PAINFUL FOR
BOTH OF YOU IF YOU DO. MAKE SURE YOU
COOPERATE.

Amanda awoke in a bare room, wood paneled to the
chair rail, faded, chipping plaster above. She was tied
to a chair, padded on the seat and back but still
uncomfortable. And judging from the numbness in her
limbs and the deep red lines on her skin under the
ropes, she guessed she'd been there for several hours at
least.

As soon as she regained consciousness she was aware
of pounding pain throughout her head—from the temples to the top of her spine. She was still dizzy and
ached in places she didn't even remember injuring. It
all must have happened after they drugged her and
carried her away.

Nat and Ariel. God, she couldn't believe it. She
couldn't let it sink in. Those lifeless eyes and that
bloody chest as she lay on the ground. Him toppling
over as the bullet hit him, all the while urging her to
run. It was all riveted in her mind as if it were actually
branded on the tissue of her brain. Two more lives on
her conscience. Plus Mordechai. That was three. And
Jesus, other than Paul, who in the world had meant
more to her than Nat and Ariel? In such a short time,
Ariel had become so special to her, almost like a sister.
Nat . . . she couldn't even articulate her feelings for
him. He was part of her. That was the plain truth of it,
wasn't it? And now, like so much else, both of them
had been taken from her. She had watched them die
violently, viciously, and most certainly, painfully. Both
trying to protect her. How much more could a person
withstand?

A jolt of fear shot through her and made her heart
forget a beat. How much more would she have to

withstand? What was she doing here? Who had brought her? And why? Was it the Agency? It couldn't be the Foundation. What was happening? Her body went limp with fear, she had no control over it, and she was afraid she might wet her pants. When she thought about it, it seemed an insignificant consideration at a time like this.

She decided to try screaming for help. But then, anyone who had gone to this much effort to get her would not have left her in a place where her screams could be heard. She gradually faced the realization that she was absolutely helpless.

An hour, maybe two, passed in that conscious agony. She couldn't tell for sure since her watch hand was tied behind her back. The door finally opened and a man came in, almost totally devoid of expression, who looked cut from the same mold as the agents who had detained and grilled her in Washington. It wasn't the same man, she knew, but it might as well have been.

"Good evening, Miss West. Sorry for all the inconvenience."

Why do they always have to begin with a sarcastic remark? Maybe it accentuates their power or something.

"What do you want?" she demanded.

"I'm pleased to see you're so prepared to cooperate. That will make this much less tiresome for all of us. We have to get in touch with Dr. Garrett. So far he has not responded to any of our entreaties."

"Call the World Congress of Physics convention. They can reach him," Amanda said.

"We've tried that. But it involves going through several intermediaries. Our business with him is too delicate for that; which is why we've asked you here to help us."

"Asked me here? And killed my friends in the process?"

"You might have observed that they killed four of our people and were prepared to kill the rest."

"Protecting me from them!" What was the point in

even going through this? It was all obvious. "What do you want from me?" she repeated.

"We want you to tell us where Dr. Garrett is so we can go talk to him."

"No."

"I'm sure you'll reconsider once you think about it."

"Absolutely not."

"Miss West, I might as well tell you up front, this matter is of utmost importance to us. We're prepared to do whatever we have to to arrange this meeting."

"Why do you want to see him?"

"That aspect doesn't really concern you."

"Of course it does!"

The man put his hands on his hips, paced away from her, then turned around. "You seem to forget the situation. You're not really in much of a position to make demands." His voice was rising steadily in volume and irritation level. "Now just do as I say and you won't be hurt any further!"

Any further? What did he mean? What were they going to do to her if she didn't cooperate with them? Even in her dazed condition, it didn't take much insight to realize these people, whoever they were, were playing for keeps. Would it hurt to tell them where Paul was? After all, he had protection. But if she did tell them, there was still no assurance they would let her go. Why should they? What would they have to gain? And what did they want from him? She needed time to think this out.

"Where is he?" the man demanded again.

"I don't know."

"Of course you do. You share his goddamned bed with him, don't you?"

"No, not now. Not since we got to London. He's too busy. We haven't been together. It hasn't worked out." She didn't know what she was saying. Something, anything that might sound plausible and keep him off the track. Her mind was racing, trying to figure out some strategy while her mind was still rational.

"I'll ask you again. Where is he?"

"I told you. I don't know."

"And I told you, I know you do know. And I assure you, soon you'll be begging to tell us. We can wait this out longer than you can."

"I've got to go to the Strand and meet these people," Paul insisted vehemently.

"No!" Moshe Baruch insisted, just as vehemently. "It won't do any good."

"They'll kill her if I don't."

"There's no assurance they won't even if you do. And they'll kill you in the bargain. We've already lost three!"

"It's worth a chance!"

"Not that kind of chance. Your life is critical to the progress of this work."

"I don't care about the work anymore!" Paul shouted. "That's been my problem all along. That's all I ever cared about. But now I'm beginning to see how empty it is by itself."

"You're just tired and upset . . . and understandably so. But I can't let you throw your life away. Remember, your responsibilities go beyond Amanda now."

"But I don't care about anything beyond Amanda, I keep trying to tell you!"

Baruch poured himself another glass of Jack Daniels and frowned sadly.

"What do you think they want from me?"

"Obviously, they want to keep you from revealing or progressing with your work. And Amanda's life is supposed to be the bargaining chip."

"If it's a question of withdrawing my presentation from the convention, I'm willing to do it if it means getting her back."

"What makes you think they'll give her back alive even if you cooperate with them?" Baruch pressed him.

"Because if they don't, I'll just reveal it at the next conference. In fact, once I have her back, what leverage do they have then? I can still go ahead."

"I think you're being naive."

"How?"

"First of all, they want to shake you up. They've already done that, quite clearly. Even if they returned Amanda, which I'm not saying they would, for the rest of your life you'd be looking over your shoulder that they would harm her again. The chances are you'd never go forward with your work. Even if you wanted to then, your mind would be so clouded by fear and worry it might be hopeless. And, number two, you know how these things work. If you withdraw your presentation less than two days before you're supposed to give it, that would completely discredit you in the scientific community. Even if you completed the entire Unified Field Theory later on, no one would take you seriously."

"That's not true!"

Baruch shrugged. "Maybe it's true, maybe it's not. What's the point of arguing?"

Paul stood up, walked over to where Baruch was standing and stuck his face into Moshe's. "You know something? I almost think you want Amanda to die. That way, there'll be nothing to distract me from what you consider the only really important thing in my life. And if she is killed, and you bring her bloody body back to me, you figure I'll be so consumed with righteous rage that I'll do everything I can to defeat them; that I'll pursue the theory all the more ruthlessly."

Baruch remained silent.

"But there's something you seem to be forgetting, Moshe. Sure what I've come up with so far is important. But it's not the end product. There's still a lot more work to be done. And keep in your mind, it isn't just me alone. Amanda and I both got our inspiration from the same place. We're both part of the same entity. I don't even know if I can pull it off now that Nat Kagan's dead. Without Amanda, there's no chance!"

"I'm not sure that's true," the Israeli said quietly, "but again, I won't argue with you."

"So you're just writing her off? Is that it?"

"No! Of course not! We're doing everything we can. We have agents combing this entire city. But you know what the chances are of finding her before your presentation. I'm just trying to prepare you for . . . for what might happen."

Paul pounded his left fist nervously into his right hand, pacing around and trying to think of a line of reasoning that would get through to Baruch. "Look, let's be honest, Moshe. You and the Mossad haven't been helping us all this time just for the fun and intrigue of it all. You want something from me. You want the applications of my work to benefit Israel—in defense, or energy sources, or whatever."

Baruch nodded his head in agreement. "All right."

"So it isn't the physics per se that matters to you, and it shouldn't matter to you whether or not I give my presentation, as long as I continue working for you. So listen, if I get Amanda back alive, whether I give the presentation and publish the data or not, I promise to continue working for you and go back to the Weizmann. Okay?"

"Paul, you don't seem to understand. If it was just a question of not making your presentation at the convention, it wouldn't be a problem. But that's not going to get Amanda back. What they want is you dead. And then there's no reason to let her live, either. And they want you dead before you have a chance to tell the rest of the scientific community about your work. I'm sure they're working on Amanda right now trying to find out where you are and whether there are any duplicate copies of your notes. You can't figure this rationally, Paul. This is a desperation play all the way around."

J. Tyler Kendrick looked at the gold Patek Philippe on his wrist. "No response from Garrett, I take it?" he said to the man in the gray suit who had just walked into the room.

"None. And I haven't been able to get anything out of the woman, either."

Kendrick sighed wearily and tried to rub some of the

fatigue from his eyes. "Well . . . time is running out. I'm going to have to take things into my own hands, I'm afraid." He rose, and instinctively smoothed out the wrinkles at the elbows of his navy-blue pinstripe suit.

"Shall I go in with you?" the man asked.

"No. I've always found that one-on-one negotiation works the best." He extracted from his breast pocket a pair of mirror-finish sunglasses, the type that totally obscure the eyes of the wearer. He sighed again and walked through the door.

The figure entering the room had an altogether different aura from the others, Amanda sensed immediately. There was something sharper, more intelligent about him. It was clear right away that this was the man in charge. All the other interrogation sessions had been mere preludes. This would be the confrontation that counted.

"Let's dispense with formalities, Miss West," J. Tyler Kendrick announced as soon as he came in. "We have to know where Paul Garrett is right away. We haven't any time to lose. Of course, this is a disadvantage for us, but it is also a disadvantage for you in that we can't afford to indulge in any niceties of back and forth discussion. I'm certain I've made myself clear."

Here was a man who was obviously used to getting everything out on the table to begin with, acknowledging both sides' positions and relative exposures from the outset. A man who prided himself on his toughness and his bluntness.

"I have nothing to say," Amanda stated.

"Then let me point out something else to you. We have nothing personal against you, please believe that. But this is a business concern that potentially affects millions of people. The life of one individual more or less is insignificant. You have to tell us where he is."

"It won't do you any good. He's under heavy guard and you'd never be able to reach him."

"Let us be the judge of that. You just tell us where he is."

"I have nothing to say," she repeated.

Without warning, Kendrick brought his arm back and slapped her across the face with such force it strained the muscles in her neck. She looked up at him with shock and terror and felt the blood begin to trickle out of one side of her nose.

"My patience is not unlimited," he said calmly.

"You're insane!" she gasped.

He struck her just as brutally from the other side and again her head snapped around like it was being pulled on a chain.

"I am perfectly rational. I know exactly what I'm doing, and what I intend to do if you continue to refuse to cooperate." With that, he slapped her again repeatedly, making her whole head ring and opening up the lip that had just recently healed.

"Oh God! Stop!" she yelled.

"All I need is information," he said.

"I don't have it! I don't know where Paul is."

"Come now, Miss West. We've already made more progress than that. Now I am rational, but I'm also losing my patience. Now talk!" He grabbed a bunch of her hair and jerked it straight up, forcing her to look directly at him. Her eyes were wide with fear as she saw him hit her face again and again. The ridges around her eyes felt like they had already begun to swell, and her left eye was beginning to close.

"I'll give you a few minutes to think about this," the man in the elegant suit informed her. "Then I'll be back."

A second letter had arrived, similar in content to the first, but with a reminder that time was running out. As Moshe Baruch anticipated, it sent Paul into a new wave of demands that he go to the park behind the Strand to negotiate for his lover's life. Baruch, morally and intellectually in accord with the absolute Israeli prohibition against negotiating with terrorists, stood solid. He remained in the sitting room of the late Georgian house in Belgrave Square, overseeing the growing team of agents who continued to scour the city.

"We're pretty sure it's the work of the Partners for Progress," he said. "As I told you in Israel, information about them is sketchy because the people who run it—unlike the politicians who run countries—are highly intelligent and don't make mistakes."

"Is there any chance you'll find where they're keeping her?" Paul asked.

"There's always a chance. I've got agents out around the clock. And they're using all the contacts—informants, Interpol, MI-six, even some subtle inquiries through the CIA. But even if she's still in London, which we have to assume she is, this is a city of close to ten million people and God knows how many thousands of buildings. There's no way we can get to even a tiny fraction of them before your presentation tomorrow afternoon."

"Even if you did find out where she was, you probably couldn't get her out alive," Paul said dejectedly.

Baruch's ears pricked up. It was as if, after all that had happened in the past many hours, Paul had now wounded his pride. "Don't forget, we're the ones who engineered Entebbe. If we could find her, we could get her out."

"If . . ." Paul repeated, his sigh acknowledging that it was the most formidable word in the language.

"That's right," Baruch said. "If . . ."

When her tormentor returned, he was carrying a metal police truncheon in one gloved hand and a black leather riding crop in the other. Beneath his jacket an oblong shape bulged out at the beltline and when the coat fell open it was revealed as a thin, pointed knife similar to the one Ariel had carried in her purse.

"I hope you're not going to make me use these," he said, "but you leave me with few options."

Options. That was a typical business word, sh

thought, trying desperately to force her mind off the upcoming terror through concentration. He must be with the Partners for Progress they'd been told about in Israel. She fought to maintain control of her senses. If it's the business cartel that wants Paul, she desperately pushed her brain, it can only be to stop his work from progressing. And the only way to stop his work from progressing is to kill him. There's no middle ground. I can't tell them where he is, she resolved. No matter what he does to me, I can't tell them where he is.

She wanted to say something to him, to fight back in some way. But there was nothing she could do.

"You can't get away with this," she panted, trying to catch her breath through her fear. "A whole team of people is looking for me right now. When they find me, they'll kill you. They'll kill all of you!" Whether it was true or not, it gave her some small satisfaction to say it. If only she believed herself it was true. If only . . .

"That's most impressive," he responded. "Only you're in the center of a soundproof, fortified, and well-disguised block of flats, which we exclusively control. It is on Marsham Street, right beyond Horseferry Road—an extremely unlikely place for them to come looking for you in the first place. They'll check every warehouse in the dock districts before they'll come down a strictly residential street. The odds of them finding you in the next several hours—which is all we have, I'm afraid—are overwhelmingly small. We'd have to send out printed directions to 'the second building down, left side of the street.' So to ease your mind, you can eliminate the rescue scenario from your thoughts and we can get down to business. Because as I say, Miss West, time is of the essence. Now talk!"

She gritted her teeth and then gasped for breath as the searing, burning pain felt like it was ripping her in half.

He had lost almost everything else of meaning to him—his wife, his security, his peaceful academic way of life, his own distinct mental identity. Now Paul had to prepare himself to lose Amanda, too, who meant more to him than anything.

If it came down to a simple question of stopping his work cold and even destroying everything he'd accomplished so far if only they would send her back to him, he knew he would be happy to do it. Regardless of what Moshe Baruch or any of the others said, that would have been an easy decision. One thing Amanda had done for him was get his priorities in order. And having her alive was all that really mattered.

But he knew Moshe was correct in his evaluation of the situation. He was dealing with desperate, irrational people whose only hope for success was that he would react just as desperately and irrationally as they did. They didn't merely want to meet with him and negotiate, they wanted to kill him. That was the only possibility. And even if it came down to trading his life for Amanda's, he would do it in a second. That would have been easy. But regardless of what he did, they couldn't afford to let Amanda live. Moshe said they might have killed her already—as soon as they drove away from the kidnapping site. But maybe he didn't really believe that. Maybe he'd only said it to prepare him for the inevitable.

This was the time to begin the mental adjustment, he knew. The time to begin thinking Einsteinian thoughts about the ongoing stream of life and the insignificance of individual termination and how he and Amanda would always be together on one level, even after they both were gone.

But it wasn't working. No amount of mental abstraction could turn him away from his anguish. The *reality* might be that they were both little more than random collections of molecules that inevitably disintegrate over time; that thinking was certainly part of his intellectual legacy. But regardless of the reality, the *truth* was that they were the most important entities in the universe, capable of caring and loving each other and grieving over loss. That was his emotional legacy.

And perhaps the mark of a first-rate mind is the ability to distinguish truth from reality when they aren't totally overlapping.

If only he could see her once more, only for a moment, and tell her how much he loved her. How nothing else was important to him but her love. How the months since the party on the Eastern Shore, while they were in some ways the worst and most horrifying of his life, were also, because of her, the best.

He thought once more of defying Baruch and going over to the park behind the Shell-Mex building for the meeting. He had no doubt they would kill him, but then, in a sense, he and Amanda could die together. After this, what was the point of living anyway?

The only thing that kept him from doing it was the realization that if he did, Amanda's killers would have won their complete victory, and she would have died totally in vain. As it was, they still might have won. Without her, Paul didn't know if he could ever work again.

"She's hanging tough," J. Tyler Kendrick reported to the small contingent waiting for him on the other side of the door. He glanced at his watch. "I'll make one more attempt at breaking her, but she seems willing to die rather than tell us where to find Garrett. Unfortunately, we will have to kill her one way or the other now. And I want that to be painless. She'll have been hurt enough by then."

"No problem. But what if she still won't talk to you when you go back in and 'escalate'?"

"We'll just have to do what we can," Kendrick replied. "And I still believe Garrett will show up at the meeting point. He'll do everything he can to save the woman's life. Everything in his psychological profile points to it."

Her clothes ripped, her body covered with cuts, bruises, and caked-on blood, Amanda could do little more than curl up on the wooden floor into a fetal position, trying to blunt her senses to how much she hurt. She reminded herself of a pitiful kitten licking its wounds, knowing full well it is to be tormented further and more severely.

She had already endured more punishment than she imagined possible and knew that when he came back, she would die.

Well, she tried to reason with herself, what else could she do? Either way they were going to kill her—that was unalterable. But if she didn't talk, Paul would live. Once she had resigned herself to death, the rest of the pain would be easier to bear, especially since she had a purpose for suffering it.

She wouldn't think about that anymore. At least she'd try not to. She would die better than she possibly could have lived—for something and someone—and that was that. Now she'd force herself to stop thinking about the terror and the agony and the cruelty and whatever else might face her in her final ordeal. Until then she would only think of Paul, and the time they had had together, and what a unique, extraordinary pair they were together, and how they had given meaning to each other's lives. Even the revelation of the brain implant, which by all rights should have killed her with shock right there at the Weizmann Institute, even that was possible to bear because of him. A warm glow came over her and concentrated in her loins as she thought about him lying in bed next to her, the first time, in that dreadfully furnished apartment in the Watergate. Never before had lovemaking been so breathlessly thrilling. Never before had another person been so thrilling. She closed her eyes tightly and for the first time since she had been captured, she smiled.

If only she could see him and let him know of the sacrifice she was making happily for him. If only she could tell him how much she loved him. Of course he knew, but it still wasn't the same as being told. If she was sure he knew, it would be easier to die in peace. If only she could tell him where she was so he could come and see it in her face. She smiled again at her own simple-mindedness. If she could tell him where she was, he could come and rescue her. She wouldn't have to die at all. In her stupor of pain, it seemed almost funny.

But did he know what was going through her mind right now? Could she be sure he understood? Why not? Hadn't he always known what was in her mind? Hadn't they both known what was in each other's minds, right from that first night, from the bridge game at Shore-cliffe? That was part of the Einsteinian legacy—the same brain, even in pieces, is on its own wavelength. They'd certainly proved that often enough.

Her mind jolted to lucidity.

They *had* been able to communicate before when they'd been together. What about when they weren't together? The man in the pinstripe suit had told her they were in a block of flats on Marsham Street, just beyond Horseferry Road. Paul would be at the Mossad house in Belgravia. That really wasn't far. But was it too far? Einstein believed thought projection was possible, but that its wave energy decreased with the square of the distance. But they had been able to know what each other was thinking before—that meant the two brains were harmonically in phase. And being in phase, they might reinforce each other and generate enough energy to make the transmission possible. It was a question of the same brain communicating with itself. That was much more likely than two brains trying to talk to each other.

It was the only chance, but it was a chance. There wasn't much time—that's what they kept telling her. She didn't know when her torturer might return.

She uncurled on the floor and lay completely flat, using what she remembered from her Yoga class to totally relax her body. Every joint was still and every square inch of skin still hurt terribly from the beating, but she willed herself to put that all out of her mind. She had to be completely, totally relaxed.

Then she drew up all the energy in her body into her brain, and concentrated on the area right on top and in the front—the cerebral cortex of the frontal and temporal lobes—the sections she shared with Paul. She focused that energy exclusively on the description and location of the building. Nothing but that. There was space for nothing else in her mind.

Over and over she stated the information, visualizing just where she thought Paul was. Everything else disappeared—the floor, the walls, the light, the rest of her body. There was nothing to her now except this one concentrated thought. And she dedicated everything she had to it.

Moshe Baruch was sitting not ten feet away from him, but Paul was not even registering his presence in the room. He was thinking about Amanda, or rather replaying in his mind each of their moments together. He was recollecting every inch of her golden body and what it had been like the first time he'd experienced it.

That was the only thing that gave him the slightest peace right now. He thought of the dark blonde hair cascading down to her shoulders, the exquisite face, made all the more poignant by the long scar line down her temple. The firm, perfect breasts, the long, trim, muscular legs. The tawny, auburn-colored pubic hair and the gently curving buttocks and the first time he pulled down her panties to reveal them. It seemed almost disrespectful to be thinking of her sexually now; almost sacrilegious. But he couldn't bring himself to think of her as dead. He had to picture her as she was most alive.

He had almost totally lost himself in the dream of her when the bright image began to fade. He was irritated and annoyed with himself for letting any other thoughts intrude while he was cherishing the memory of his love. But he couldn't get it out of his mind. It was dull, methodical, persistent, and it wouldn't leave him. It was like one of those Einsteinian thoughts that kept imposing themselves on his consciousness, that still felt like having someone else thinking for him.

What was it? What was coming into his head? A repeating rhythm, not even an idea. It was growing stronger and more persistent and he shook his head repeatedly trying to get rid of it.

"Block of flats, Marsham Street just beyond Horseferry Road. Two buildings down, left side of the street."

That was crazy, it didn't mean anything. He didn't even know where Marsham Street was.

"Block of flats, Marsham Street just beyond Horseferry Road. Two buildings down, left side of the street."

Come to think of it, he'd never even heard of Marsham Street.

Wait a minute! How could he think of a name he'd never heard of? He roused himself into full attention and the message played over and over again in his head.

"Moshe! Do you have a London map?"

"Of course," the Israeli replied, surprised by the sudden burst of energy. He signaled his assistant, Eliezer Yadin to get it.

"See if there's a Marsham Street on it," Paul directed.

"Yes. Over in Westminster, not far from Lambeth Bridge. It's not far from here."

"See if you find a Horseferry Road!" His tone was even more breathless, more urgent.

"Yes. They intersect."

"Moshe! I know where Amanda is!"

"What?"

"I know where she is!" he insisted.

"How? Did it come to you in a dream just now?"

"No. She's telling me."

"I didn't hear the phone ring."

"I'm perfectly serious! She's sending me the message. Our brains are in sync. You know that."

"Yes. I also know you are tired, terribly upset, and not fully in command of your senses."

"I am so, goddamn it! Listen to me! We haven't got any time to lose. You said if you knew where she was, you could get her."

"I did say that," Baruch agreed.

"Well, now you know where she is! Go get her!"

"Paul, be reasonable. We don't know where she is. I can't take thirty men and break into a private building and start shooting up the place because you had a sudden inspiration. That would cause an incredible incident. Lives would be lost. I might even lose some of my own men. If it was a false alarm, as it most assuredly would be, England would cut off its diplomatic ties with Israel. It would be sheer madness."

The message was still coming in strong. "Moshe, I'm sure of it. You have to do it!"

"No, Paul. It's out of the question."

"Everything's been out of the question ever since she was captured. Now listen to me and listen carefully. From now on, I'm running my own show. I'm calling my own shots."

"And just what does that mean?"

"If you don't go rescue her in that building, I'll go myself, or with the police if I can get them. And I swear to you, either way—whether the rescue works or not—I will never lift another finger to help you or your country. I'll do whatever I have to to make you pay for your stupidity; go to the Arabs or whatever. And if you don't like that you might as well shoot me now. Because before I go, I'm going to call the World Congress of Physics and withdraw my work, tell them it was all erroneous, and tell them to burn it."

"You're crazy. You don't know what you're saying."

"Try me."

Baruch studied him for several moments while Paul returned his gaze intensively. He took a deep breath, looked to Yadin, and for perhaps the first time in his adult life, didn't know what to do. "You are absolutely sure, understanding all the consequences I just outlined for you?"

"Absolutely."

"All right. Let's move. Eliezer, call everyone in. I want them all together in ten minutes downstairs." He turned back to Paul. "God forgive me. I know I'm a fool."

"No you're not."

Baruch just shook his head ominously.

"One more thing, Moshe."

"What's that?"

"Give me a gun. I'm coming with you."

Within eight minutes, eighteen men had changed into flak jackets and assault uniforms and assembled in the basement weapons room. The only ones not similarly attired were the four agents dressed as London policemen, whose responsibility it would be to keep bystanders out of the way.

They departed immediately in two unmarked delivery vans and two phony police Rovers, and as they drove down Eccleston Street to Belgrave Road, they tested the communication system each man had plugged in his ear. Paul sat next to Moshe Baruch, whom he assured he knew how to handle a gun.

The two police cars pulled up first and blocked off the short stretch of Marsham Street at both ends. They would only be able to hold it for a few minutes, but one way or the other, that was all they would need. Mossad actions were predicated on surprise, speed, and perfection of execution.

The sidewalks were narrow and the delivery vans pulled up close enough so that it was impossible from the buildings to get a visual angle on the agents disgorging from the vehicles. The general strategy had been determined on the ride over, and when Baruch saw the actual building, he quickly ordered men to specific places.

The building in which Paul insisted Amanda was

being held was a gray, marble-faced apartment block that wrapped around a courtyard. Access to the center was through an arch large enough to drive an automobile through, since the courtyard served as a parking lot for tenants. Baruch took up his own position under the arch and dispatched several men up to the roofs of the adjoining buildings. From where he was standing, he could peer around the corner and see the entrance to the building, which was in a corner of the courtyard. But when he pulled his head back, he knew that he could not be seen. Other agents pressed themselves against the walls of the building and inched along toward windows that would give them access.

One by one the men radioed in that they were in place.

"All right," Baruch said in Hebrew, "put on the gas masks."

A moment later he took a long, deep breath and ordered, "Move!"

Simultaneously, six tear-gas grenades shattered windows at all points on the building and everybody moved at once. The men on the roof swung in through top-story windows on ropes attached to grappling hooks, their extended boots knocking out the glass ahead of them. The raiders in front of Moshe and Paul charged the entrance. They had been given instructions only to shoot at people with weapons, which called for split-second judgment while moving at top speed.

But there was no problem evaluating the situation. As soon as they piled through the double glass doors two men behind the concierge counter immediately drew their guns. They were both mowed down by the spray of Uzi submachine guns before their arms stopped moving. These two taken out, the raiders swarmed up the stairs that wrapped around the open-cage elevator.

Paul and Moshe were right behind them in the second assault wave. As they got to the second-floor landing, three more men jumped out from behind closed apartment doors and opened fire. Paul instinctively threw himself against the corridor wall and fired back in the direction of the shots. One man crumpled. The other two ducked back in as the first raider team blasted out both doors. Paul could hear the screams of death coming from behind them.

As the first team climbed up another flight of stairs, a third group came up and forced open every remaining closed door. They did not move on until they were satisfied the entire floor was empty.

Paul and Moshe reached the fifth floor only moments after the shooting began there. Three bodies already littered the hallway, none of them Mossad. The mental vibrations were growing increasingly more intense, and Paul pushed his way past the three gun-wielding agents in front of him and raced ahead to the last door on the corridor. Moshe Baruch tried to catch his arm to stop him, but Paul forced his way out of his grasp.

As he grabbed the handle and ripped the door open a burst of automatic weapons fire tore past his head. He dove for the floor as the three Israelis behind him converged their aim on the man holding the machine gun. For an instant he flattened out against nothing but midair, his arms outstretched like a scarecrow's. Then he collapsed in a clattering heap.

There was one other man in the room and Paul caught his first glimpse of him as he steadied himself on the floor. He was tall and deeply tanned and wore a navy-blue pinstripe suit. As Paul propped himself up on his left hand the man reached for his own belt. But it was not the man's hand Paul focused on. It was his eyes. There was a mixture of terror, hatred and awe in them. He had never seen anything exactly like it before. And immediately he knew. It wasn't all those other men lying dead in the hall outside and on the floors below who mattered. They were merely preliminary. This was the enemy. This was the man he had to get through. This was the man he loathed.

The man had the gun barrel nearly down to the

proper level when Paul sprang to his knees, slapped his left hand over the other side of the pistol butt and pulled the trigger three times in rapid succession. The man in the suit snapped backward, a faint gasp wrenching from his body. He staggered a step or two and fell to the floor.

Moshe Baruch rushed past Paul into the room, went over to the body, picked up the wrist for a sign of pulse and then dropped it again. As he did so, the gold Patek Philippe watch smashed with the impact. Moshe Baruch checked the frozen time against his own Rolex. The entire operation had taken less than three minutes.

A door at the other end of the room opened and the leader of the roof assault team, who must have come in through the window, called over to Paul, "This way! In here!"

Paul stood up, walked over, and through the door opening saw his beloved Amanda lying on the floor. A Mossad agent was just fitting a gas mask on her head, obscuring her battered and swollen face. He rushed over, cradled her in his arms, and lifted the mask just long enough to cover her bleeding lips with his own.

"Oh, Paul," she whispered, straining even to make herself speak. "You heard me."

"Don't try to talk, honey. Don't try to talk."

She closed her eyes and lapsed into unconsciousness as the assault team's medic made his way into the room. He rolled up her torn sleeve and jabbed a needle into her arm, then signaled for the other agents to carry her out.

Paul watched them leave the room, then turned to Baruch, trying to figure out what he was going to say.

But the Israeli removed the problem, stating proudly, "A perfect mission! Objective accomplished without one single casualty."

"How can I ever thank you?" Paul sighed.

"You've already thanked me . . . by being right

And let me tell you, I've never been so happy to be wrong." He clapped his arm across Paul's shoulder and led him out of the room. "Come on. You have a presentation to prepare for. And after that, maybe you ought to think about intelligence work! You've obviously got a talent for it."

Chapter Twenty-Two

When he saw her propped up in her bed at the London Clinic, Amanda already looked much better. The swelling around her eyes had gone down, and although her lips were still blue, her face had returned to its normal lovely contours. Every time she shifted her position she winced with pain, but that was all part of the healing process.

As soon as he came through the door she smiled at him, and her eyes brightened with delight when he produced an enormous bunch of flowers from behind his back.

"Oh, Paul, they're beautiful," she purred.

"And so are you." He sat down on the edge of the bed and looked lovingly at her.

"So how did the presentation go?" she asked.

"Magnificently," he replied.

"I'm so sorry I couldn't be there to see it. I begged the doctors to let me out just for the afternoon."

"And I ordered them not to."

"Were you a big hit?"

"A very big hit." He grinned. "You should have heard the comments. 'Major breakthrough,' 'Logical successor to Einstein,' stuff like that."

"I'm so proud."

"Well, you have a right to be. None of this is mine alone. You shared in it all the way down the line. So did Nat. And you'll continue to share in it as we solve the whole Unified Field Theory!"

She seemed suddenly to grow sad as he said this. "That's what I want to talk to you about, honey."

"What's that?" he said with the anxiety showing through his voice.

"First of all let me say that no matter what, I love you more than anything else in the world, anything I could have possibly imagined."

"But what?" he prodded nervously.

"Maybe now that this is all over, especially since Nat is gone, we should each try it alone, at least for a while. Try going our separate ways."

"Amanda! What are you talking about? We belong together. We've known that right from the start. That's why we were able to save you yesterday."

"That's just the point, Paul. We're so close because of what happened to us that we're practically the same person. In some ways, we are the same person. And I don't know if we can survive together as independent beings. I keep remembering how shattered I was when I found out about the brain and how I thought I could never be me again. Well . . . maybe the only way I can even try to be me again is by being on my own. Try to de-emphasize Einstein's influence on me rather than amplify it, as we've both been doing together. That's the only way I might be able to realize my own new identity."

Paul's face had drained of color. "But what about our work together? Think of that. This presentation today was just the beginning. Now other people will get involved. We'll be the focal point of a massive scientific effort. That's enough right there to give meaning to our lives."

She smiled at him indulgently. "You know it's not. If nothing else, that's the one thing you've learned from me. While I was lying here this afternoon, thinking about you and the scientific visions you were conjuring up for the physicists at the convention, something came to me. I realized it was another thought of Einstein's, and I wrote it down." She picked up an index card from the top of her nightstand and read:

"I do not believe that a moral philosophy can ever be

founded on a scientific base. You could not, for instance, teach men to face death tomorrow in defense of scientific truth. Science has no power of that type over the human spirit. The evaluation of life and all its nobler expressions can only come out of the soul's yearning toward its own destiny."

She replaced the card next to the telephone and said, "That's what I have to do, Paul. That's what we both have to do. We both have to find our own soul's destiny. Science is important. It's the legacy we'll both leave after we're gone. But it isn't in itself what we are. It's only what we do."

"That all may be true," he said, the tears brimming around the corners of his eyes. "But there are other things that are just as true. I love you, more than anything else I've ever known, and you said the same about me. Yesterday, and the day before, when I thought you were dead, or soon would be, I felt as if my whole life was over. Nothing had any meaning without you, even the convention and the scientific achievement and all the rest. I couldn't come to grips with losing you then, and I can't now. We can't do anything about what was done to us twenty years ago. And in those twenty years we've both been pawns in a giant game of manipulation, everyone trying to second guess everyone else. Well . . . that's got to be over now. We can't even second guess ourselves. Neither one of us can be happy without the other one. You know that and can't deny it. Now we're finally in the position to enjoy some happiness, and I think we deserve it."

"Maybe you're right," she said, reaching her hands up around his neck and pulling his head down to hers. "We'll try it out and see what comes of it. I guess the most important thing is that we remember that with Einstein's brain and our own, we can create something new, and continue to grow."

"That's right, my darling. That's all I'm saying."

"I don't know what will come of it, but I know I am

happy now. And if we work together, and through each other, maybe we can also find some of the peace we've both been looking for, too."

He bent down further and they hugged fervently. They didn't say anything further to each other.

They didn't have to.

Epilogue

Cambridge, Massachusetts

"You're a tantalizing challenge for a psychiatrist," David Sherman said, taking another sip of the Scotch Paul had poured for him. "You're the one case I'll ever come across that could give me immortality in the field, and yet I can't say anything."

"Are you complaining?"

"No, not really," he smiled. "I'm just happy you're both back in one piece."

"That's what's yet to be worked out," Amanda said. "Whether we're to consider ourselves as one piece or two." She was sitting cross-legged on the sofa, her feet bare, wearing her traditional jeans and "Aurora Illuminates!" T-shirt. "And with your help, we will work that out," she added.

"As you know, my door is always open to both of you."

"And I'm sure we'll be going through it a lot," Paul said. "We're still feeling our way around a lot of things."

"At least you can do it comfortably. What are you going to do with all your royalty money?"

"Well, the first three hundred thousand is going to endow the Nathaniel Kagan Fellowship at the Weizmann Institute. The next three hundred thousand goes for a memorial fellowship in Yakov Perlman's name. And we'll buy Margie the new car we promised. Beyond that . . ." He held out his arms in a gesture of indecision. "Beyond that, I don't know. Our two salaries pretty much take care of our needs. We were thinking of buying you a new house."

"That's overwhelmingly kind, but unnecessary."

"There's no way we can repay you, and so many other people, for what they've done for us. Money is the least of our problems right now. We're counting on you to help us with the serious matters."

"By the by," Amanda asked, "how is your sister getting along, David? How is she taking Charles' . . . absence?"

"Not terribly well," he replied. "But about as well as can be expected, I guess."

"Does she know anything?"

"No. I decided there was no point in telling her. In her case, it wouldn't be any kindness." He took another swallow and asked her, "So do you enjoy being back at the magazine?"

"I love it. It gets a bit hectic commuting back and forth between here and New York, but I'm getting him to come there almost as much as I get up here. Maybe all that time apart will keep the relationship going, give us the room I think we need to be ourselves. I should actually be in New York today. But I'm playing hooky so I could stay over and see you."

"Well," Paul announced, "I hate to break up this gathering, but it's time for me to go teach. I'll see you both at dinner."

"What subject?" David wondered.

"Introductory Physics."

"The world-famous Paul Garrett is teaching Introductory Physics?"

"Why not? I'm a good teacher."

"No reason." David grinned. "I think it's terrific. So let me ask you one more question before you go out."

"What's that?"

"Have you thought about marriage at all?"

"What a question!" Paul exclaimed.

"Why do you ask?" said Amanda.

"Well, I just think it'd be a shame for you both not to have children. They'd certainly have an excellent shot at being brilliant with such intelligent parents."

NEW YORK, Feb. 23 (AP)—When famed physicist Albert Einstein died in Princeton, New Jersey, in 1955, his body was cremated. But his brain was first removed for scientific study, in accordance with his wishes, it has recently come out. The brain was entrusted to Dr. Norbert Ramsey, the celebrated neurosurgeon at the Goddard Institute in Manhattan. Ramsey died of a heart attack at age 64 and his research on the most accomplished brain of the twentieth century has now been published. The results are sadly inconclusive.

In more than twenty years of study, Ramsey and his associates were able to discern no physical differences between Einstein's brain and any other cadaver brain they had observed. "Our knowledge of the actual intellectual workings of the human brain is so primitive," Ramsey wrote, "that it would have been much more surprising than not had we been able to learn anything substantive from this distinguished mass of gray matter. Hopefully, future research will begin to unlock the secrets of this most complex of all mechanisms. But from all our work over the years, it seems that Einstein's brain has no tale to tell."

Other than a number of thin sections preserved under glass microscope slides and a portion of the cerebellum maintained in a laboratory jar of formaldehyde, the whereabouts of Einstein's brain is unknown. It is believed to have been destroyed at the Goddard Institute more than ten years ago.